The Culture of Joyce's *Ulysses*

NEW DIRECTIONS IN IRISH AND IRISH AMERICAN LITERATURE

Claire A. Culleton, Kent State University
Series Editor

The Culture of Joyce's Ulysses

R. Brandon Kershner

First published in 2010 by
PALGRAVE MACMILLAN®
in the United States—a division of St. Martin's Press LLC,
175 Fifth Avenue, New York, NY 10010.

Where this book is distributed in the UK, Europe and the rest of the world,
this is by Palgrave Macmillan, a division of Macmillan Publishers Limited,
registered in England, company number 785998, of Houndmills,
Basingstoke, Hampshire RG21 6XS.

Palgrave Macmillan is the global academic imprint of the above companies
and has companies and representatives throughout the world.

Palgrave® and Macmillan® are registered trademarks in the United States,
the United Kingdom, Europe and other countries.

ISBN: 978–0–230–10868–4

Library of Congress Cataloging-in-Publication Data

Kershner, R. B., 1944–
    The culture of Joyce's Ulysses / R. Brandon Kershner.
      p. cm.—(New directions in Irish and Irish American literature)
    Includes bibliographical references.
    ISBN 978–0–230–10868–4 (alk. paper)
     1. Joyce, James, 1882–1941. Ulysses. 2. Popular culture in literature.
3. Newspapers in literature. 4. Dublin (Ireland)—In literature. 5. Authors
and readers—History—20th century. 6. Modernism (Literature) I. Title.

PR6019.O9U67235 2010
823'.912—dc22
                                           2010017937

A catalogue record of the book is available from the British Library.

Design by Newgen Imaging Systems (P) Ltd., Chennai, India.

First edition: December 2010

10 9 8 7 6 5 4 3 2 1

Printed in the United States of America.

For Christina Carlton

Contents

Acknowledgments

Portions of this book have been previously published in very different forms: a part of chapter two in "The Culture of Ulysses," Vincent Cheng, Margot Norris, and Kimberly Devlin, eds., *Joycean Cultures/Culturing Joyces* (Newark, NJ: University of Delaware Press, 1998), 149–62; parts of chapter three in "Joyce and Popular Literature: The Case of Corelli," Diana A. Ben-Merre and Maureen Murphy, eds. *James Joyce and His Contemporaries* (New York: Greenwood Press, 1989), 51–58, and "Joyce and Stephen Phillips' *Ulysses*," *James Joyce Quarterly* 13 (Winter 1976), 194–201. About half of chapter seven appeared in a different form as "The Strongest Man in the World: Joyce or Sandow?" *James Joyce Quarterly* vol. 30, no. 4 (Summer/Fall 1993), 667–94 (special issue on "Joyce and Advertising," eds. Garry Leonard and Jennifer Wicke). A substantial portion of chapter eight first appeared as "*Ulysses* and the Orient," *James Joyce Quarterly* vol. 35, no. 2/3 (Winter/Spring 1998), 273–96, and about half of chapter nine as "Framing Rudy and Photography," *Journal of Modern Literature*, vol. 22, no. 2 (Winter 1998/99), 265–92, © Indiana University Press, 1998. In all cases I am grateful for permission to reprint.

Some of my early research into Irish and British newspapers and magazines was accomplished with the aid of National Endowment for the Humanities grants in the early 1970s, and several University of Florida Division of Sponsored Research grants after that. I am grateful to these institutions for this support, however long it has taken for it to bear tangible fruit. During a teaching exchange at University College Dublin in 1984, I was helped in many ways by the remarkable faculty there, especially Seamus Deane, Declan Kiberd, J. C. C. Mays, Mary Daly, and Augustine Martin. I will always be grateful for their kindness, and for the opportunity to teach Joyce on his home ground. Other Dubliners were also generous with their help, especially Professor Louis Cullen of Trinity, John Ryan, Gerry O'Flaherty, who loaned me the only copy of Sandow's book I had ever seen, and Hugh Oram, who shared with me his encyclopedic knowledge of Irish newspapers.

The community of Joyceans has been so helpful and supportive to me over the years that it is difficult to single out individuals, but certainly I would have to mention Cheryl Herr, a good friend who from the beginning shared the idea of the importance of popular culture to Joyce's works; Morris Beja, who appreciated my work, however different it was from his own; and Robert Spoo, for many kindnesses. I want to acknowledge two former students and current colleagues in whose work I take an unearned pride: Garry Leonard and Keith Booker. Vince Cheng has supported my work from the start, and his own work has been a model of scholarship to which I've aspired. I would like to thank Carol Shloss, Fritz Senn, Walton Litz, Sean Latham, Richard Brown, Mark Osteen, Christine O'Neill, Judith Harrington, Mary Lowe Evans, Joe Valente, Sebastian Knowles, John McCourt, Vicki Mahaffey, Jean-Michel Rabaté, Richard Pierce, Austin Briggs, Bonnie Kime Scott, Mike O'Shea, Anne Fogarty, Christine van Boheemen-Saaf, Michael Groden, John Gordon, and the late Zack Bowen, all for various favors, discussions, and friendship over the years. I owe thanks to Philip Wegner, William Cliett, and Claire Culleton. Finally, I want to acknowledge the debt I owe to the late Bernard Benstock, Ian Watt, and Leslie Fiedler, each of whom offered inspirational work and support for my own first efforts.

Joyce Citations

Joyce criticism traditionally uses (among others) the following parenthetical references to standard editions of Joycean work:

CW   Joyce, James. *The Critical Writings of James Joyce*, ed. Ellsworth Mason and Richard Ellmann. New York: Viking Press, 1959.

D   Joyce, James.*Dubliners*, ed. Robert Scholes and Richard Ellmann. New York: Viking Press, 1967.

FW   Joyce, James. *Finnegans Wake*. New York: Viking Press, 1939.

JJI   Ellmann, Richard. *James Joyce*. New York: Oxford University Press, 1959.

JJII   Ellmann, Richard. *James Joyce*. New York: Oxford University Press, 1982.

Letters I,   Joyce, James. *Letters of James Joyce*. Vol. 1, ed. Stuart Gilbert. New York: Viking Press, 1957. Reissued with corrections, 1966.

Letters II, III Joyce, James. *Letters of James Joyce*. Vols. II and III ed. Richard Ellmann. New York: Viking Press, 1966.

P   Joyce, James. *A Portrait of the Artist as a Young Man*. The definitive text corrected from Dublin holograph by Chester G. Anderson and edited by Richard Ellmann. New York: Viking Press, 1964.

SH   Joyce, James. *Stephen Hero*, ed. John J. Slocum and Herbert Cahoon. New York: New Directions, 1944, 1963.

U   +episode and line number. Joyce, James. *Ulysses*, ed. Hans Walter Gabler et al. New York and London: Garland publishing, 1984, 1986. In paperback by Garland, Random House, and Bodley Head and by Penguin between 1986 and 1992.

Chapter One

Introduction: Dialogics and Popular Culture in Joyce's Novel

I hope *The Culture of Joyce's "Ulysses"* will evoke a variety of possible interpretations for the reader. In the first place, I mean it to suggest the culture, both "high" and "popular," that surrounded Joyce's novel at its publication in 1922 and formed the inescapable context for its reception. As a historical exercise in what has become known as "cultural studies," this book claims that field as its purview. A second obvious meaning is the culture of Dublin in 1904, the date of the book's setting—a material culture painstakingly documented, celebrated, and contested by Joyce, often in ways we no longer recognize. But a third interpretation, the broadest, would be to the culture of the figure Ulysses or Odysseus—which is to say, not so much the culture of Homeric times, but the pseudo-Enlightenment culture that Adorno and Horkheimer portray as the legacy of the Ulysses figure and whose contemporary forms they critique rigorously (see chapter two). In this sense, at least, the culture of both Ulysses and *Ulysses* is our culture, the culture of modernity. And one of my themes will be the forgotten aspects of that culture from the turn of the last century, figures and phenomena whose absence from popular memory is an effect of our contemporary mechanisms for disseminating cultural amnesia. Modernism, I believe, both resists and is complicit with this act of literary/historical forgetting. In several ways, then, I hope this project will be a contribution to the recent wave of historical work on modernism that is intended to refigure that concept (Rainey, Lewis, Mao, Matz, North, Latham, and Walkowitz; see also articles in *Modernism/Modernity*).

Ulysses is a historical novel in at least two senses: written mostly in the 'teens and early twenties of the twentieth century, it addresses 1904 and does so with a curious combination of scrupulous historical exactitude and minor anachronisms. But it is also a novel whose subject is history, specifically the history of the twentieth century, and here the gap between the book's setting and the time of its composition gives Joyce some leverage. If he is able to see where, for

example, journalistic trends will take the relatively innocent publications for young ladies of 1904, he is also, remarkably, able to
deduce that anti-Semitism would be a major theme of the century.
Joyce has been critiqued for creating a rather nostalgic portrait of
Dublin that concentrates on the moribund city center rather than
the more vital, expanding suburbs (Mays), but in fact his unbal-
anced emphasis on the commercially hollow city center accurately
portrays an economy that continued to decline until at least the
1930s.

Ulysses is clearly a novel that addresses the impact of modernity upon an urban backwater that had been unsystematically but
effectively denuded of a productive economy and was suffering the
vicissitudes of emphatically uneven development under modernism.
Mary Daly comments, "The lack of dynamism from the rural Irish
economy and the failure of Dublin businesses to manufacture and,
in some cases, even to distribute the manufactured goods which
rural Ireland needed, plus the apparent stagnation of the port in
the third quarter of the nineteenth century[1] all meant that Dublin
failed to provide adequate employment, either for the indigenous
Dublin population or for even a small proportion of the surplus
population of rural Ireland" (15). The only exceptions to the pattern of industrial decline were in "the comparative success of printing and metal and engineering, and the sharp increase in numbers
employed in food and drink which was mainly attributable to the
success of the brewing industry" (20). If the newspaper business
seems to figure largely in *Ulysses* and if barrels of porter are a major
contribution to Joyce's evocation of urban circulation in "Aeolus,"
those, after all, are the two healthy industries colonial occupation
has left to the deposed capital. The Dublin of *Ulysses* simply does
not have the atmosphere of a modern industrial city. Declan Kiberd
points out that "Dublin in 1904...was already a rapidly expanding conurbation dominated by persons and values imported from
the countryside. Sheep and cows were still commonly herded to the
docks through the major thoroughfares of a city which Joyce liked
to dub 'the centre of paralysis'" (269). The artificially retarded
industrialization combined with the city's still noticeably rural culture produced a populace unusually susceptible to the attractions of
the British popular culture industry.

Luke Gibbons, surveying the social and economic conditions
of post-famine Ireland, notes that in addition to the Irish handi-
cap of a crippled economy, Dubliners suffered from the failure of
the Catholic Church in Ireland to inspire or support any agenda

of social reform, either for dealing with the massive poverty of the working class or the susceptibility of women and children to domestic violence (168). But in so doing, it should be noted, it was following the English laissez-faire approach to colonial territories. Joseph Lee explains,

> the fact that England industrialized primarily on the basis of private enterprise decisively influenced English concepts of the proper role of the state in economic development. If the state maintained the sanctity of contracts and the rights of property, it could safely leave individuals to their own enterprise, secure in the conviction that the invisible hand would maximise economic growth. (20–21)

The English reluctance to intervene in progressive or even pragmatic ways, rather than in blindly legalistic ones, was exemplified most lethally in government's halting and inadequate response to the famine of the 1840s. Joyce's famous diagnosis of paralysis, which critics have long approached as if it were a mysterious spiritual failing of his countrymen, had a solid economic basis.

The culture Joyce's writing reflected and in which he matured was, of course, Irish, with all the internal divisions that implies, but it was hardly Irish in the cultural-nationalist sense of the word. At all cultural levels, as F. S. L. Lyons insists, we must bear in mind

> the extent to which nineteenth-century Ireland existed within the English cultural context. When we come to review the different cultures that collided within Irish society, we shall have to bear in mind always that these cultures are principally to be defined not so much by their relations with each other, critical as these were, but by their relations with the English culture under whose shadow they existed and to which they had always to respond. Indeed, it is hardly too much to say that for most of the nineteenth century English culture was the most effective unifying force in Ireland. (6–7)

That this cultural hegemony came to be imposed most thoroughly in the nineteenth and early twentieth centuries was, of course, no coincidence: the rapid industrialization of England in production and transportation allowed for the dissemination of English material culture throughout the smaller island. And the effect of this shared culture in enforcing a sense of shared nationhood with England, despite the obvious injustices of colonization, should not be underestimated: "nationalism and patriotism had become almost the new religion of modern industrial society, as mass education carried the heady brew of patriotic idealism onto the meanest slum classroom or the remotest village school. Modern mass communications, railways, delivery vans, the telegraph, wireless and the newspapers also fostered a greater sense of nationhood" (Stevenson, 48). The nationalist fever that possessed much of Europe in the years leading up to the Great War was shared by many in Ireland who valued their identity as members of the British Empire, and this included not only members of the Protestant Ascendancy. Redmond's National Volunteers, founded to support the war effort, decimated the ranks of the republican Irish Volunteers (Lee, 153).

Because of our distance from the ephemeral writings that Joyce cites, we often have no idea how pervasive such imperial cultural pressure could be. When the boys in "An Encounter" rebel against their assigned Roman history by reading *The Apache Chief*, we might imagine they have found access to a vision of anarchic freedom in these "chronicles of disorder" (D 21; see Kershner 1989, 31–45). In fact, *The Apache Chief* has only a small part for Cochise, who is not particularly rebellious in this tale; the hero is an upper-class British gentleman who visits the American West and demonstrates his natural superiority in riding, shooting, and such skills (Winston). Like most of Harmsworth's publications for boys, it bore no trace of Harmsworth's Chapelizod origins, but demonstrated his complete identification with the British Empire and its values. In his lecture on "The Necessity for de-Anglicising Ireland" in 1892, Douglas Hyde saw the greatest danger to a culturally Irish identity—whatever that might consist of—as coming from the popularity of English publications aimed at the masses. He insisted on "the necessity for encouraging the use of Anglo-Irish literature instead of English books, especially English periodicals. We must set our face sternly against penny dreadfuls, shilling shockers, and still more the garbage of vulgar English weeklies like *Bow Bells* and the *Police Intelligence*" (Lee, 138).

By 1904 it was clear that in most respects Hyde was fighting a losing battle. Where Hyde imagined that the "natural" fare of Irish men and women would be an elevated, spiritual kind of writing and blamed the English for the obvious fact that this was not so, English critics tended to blame the Education Act of 1870 for extending literacy to a class and gender that might not make the best use of it. By 1900 the literacy rate in England was over 90 percent for both sexes and was even higher in London (Bloom, 32). In Ireland about 41 percent of the populace was literate in 1861; in 1901, the figure was 79 percent and, of course, was higher in the cities. The Irish Education Act of 1892 provided for compulsory school attendance for children between the ages of six and fourteen, if they lived in cities, towns, or townships, and allowed for a full or partial abolishment of fees (*Thom's*, 633). Matthew Arnold in 1869 had warned against people who, seeing a new group of consumers and assuming that they would never ask for "the best that has been thought and said," "will try to give the masses…an intellectual food prepared and adapted in the way they think proper for the actual condition of the masses. The ordinary popular literature is an example of this way of working on the masses" (Arnold, 1150).

Arnold's objection here was based on his sanguine assumption that the masses needed no special fare. Culture, by which he meant "high culture," would automatically recommend itself to everyone, regardless of social class, through a force that, like gravity, was invisible and pervasive. H. G. Wells, on the other hand, writing in 1896, suggested that a natural degradation in taste followed the Education Act: "And while the male of the species has chiefly exerted its influence in the degradation of journalism, the debasing influence of the female, reinforced by the free libraries, has been chiefly felt in the character of fiction. 'Arry reads *Ally Sloper* and *Tit-Bits*, 'Arriet reads *Trilby* and *The Sorrows of Satan*" (74).[2] It is no coincidence that Ally Sloper appears at *U* 9.607 and *U* 15.2152, *Tit-Bits* makes its first appearance at *U* 4.467 and recurs regularly, *Trilby* is alluded to at *U* 15.2721 and *U* 18.1041, Corelli's *Sorrows of Satan* at *U* 9.19. In popular novels, as in newspapers, magazines, plays, and music hall entertainment, Joyce's characters read and see what everyone read and saw at the time, throughout the British Isles and, to some extent, throughout the substantial area of Anglophone cultural hegemony.

Popular Reading and Popular Fiction; Dialogism and Genre

In the mid-nineteenth century popular fiction was for the most part viewed askance by the upper and upper-middle classes. It was attacked on many familiar grounds, but also on the rather surprising one that it was a distraction from the proper concern with empire. An 1874 review in *Temple Bar* argues,

> indeed we have been, since the Romans, the only truly imperial people. We have embraced the globe with the arms of our ambition; we have scoured every sea; we have colonized every sphere. But the insularity with which we were once unfairly rebuked is at last becoming…our

characteristic and opprobrium.... We are determinedly insular, and we find even the island too big... 'our neighborhood' is the most delightful and absorbing thing in life.... It is this quality of narrow curiosity which is the paralysis of all wide and noble interest, which the novel stimulated and feeds.... these are the concerns of a once imperial people. (cited in Gilbert, 72)

Here the concerns Mr. Deasy announces as proper to a great people in "Nestor," and which Stephen epitomizes as "those big words... which make us so unhappy" (*U* 2.264), are diametrically opposed to the private concerns of the popular novel. And yet by late in the century the popular novel had become "almost respectable." William Gladstone, one of the more intellectual and scholarly Prime Ministers, late in the century was observed at a political club engrossed in reading not the *Iliad*—which he was at the time engaged in translating—but Rhoda Broughton's 1870 best seller *Red as a Rose is She* (Bloom, 1). The anecdote not only illuminates the greater degree of acceptance gained by popular novels, but helps explain why in "Eumaeus" the sailor Murphy, professing himself to have been a great reader at one time, claims Broughton's book along with *Arabian Nights* as his favorites (*U* 16.1680).

The expansion of the popular readership in the late nineteenth century was evidenced in a huge increase in publication of both books and serial publications, such as newspapers and magazines. While in the first half of the nineteenth century roughly 600 books appeared annually, in the latter half the number grew to 2,600; by 1901 it was over 6,000 and by 1913 over 12,000 (Orel, 14). John Gross's examination of census figures for Great Britain finds the number of people claiming the professions of author, editor, or journalist to have grown from 3,400 in 1881 to around 6,000 in 1891, 11,000 in 1901, and 14,000 in 1911 (199–200). Most observers experienced the burgeoning of popular fiction around the turn of the century as somewhat chaotic, and books were not marketed by category as they are in major bookstores today. Clive Bloom argues that it was only shortly before the 1920s that the popular novelistic genres began to sort themselves out into categories such as detective fiction, romance, adventures of empire, family sagas, and Christian morality tales (86–87). But he also asserts that "at the end of the twentieth century the two leading popular genres were the same as at its beginning and still commanded the greatest sales: detective fiction and women's romance"; these two categories, broadly construed, represented at least 50 percent of genre fiction sales (13, 85).

If we take detective fiction to include the "masculine" genres of thriller, espionage, and certain types of action and adventure novels, in addition to the hugely popular works of Conan Doyle, and the romance to include the varieties of "feminine" domestic narratives that could range from the salacious to the insistently Christian, then we can see how these meta-genres dominated popular writing. We can also recognize how Joyce used these two as the basis for his pair of major parodic narratives, the matched chapters "Cyclops" and "Nausicaa." While "Cyclops" mimics the oral delivery of an anonymous barfly, it also has characteristics of "hard-boiled" American-style mystery fiction and of several of the paranoid conspiracy subgenres of the time, such as those about the invasion of England or a Jewish plot to discredit Christ and thus wreck Western civilization. Of course the "mystery" sedulously investigated in the "Cyclops" episode concerns who is responsible for the fallen state of the Irish, and the answer—foreigners and Jews—is a foregone conclusion. The chapter is no more satisfying when seen as an adventure story, climaxing as it does with an escape by horse-drawn cart and a flung biscuit tin, but Joyce's final parodic touches make it clear that he would view the overblown action climaxes typical of the genre with an equally jaundiced eye. Aside from the "Cyclops" parody, *Ulysses* as a whole shares much with the detective story. It demands of both its characters and its readers scrupulous attention to detail and active interpretation ("Signatures of all things I am here to read"; *U* 3.31). As Hugh Kenner pointed out, it presents a kind of civilian allegory of Conan Doyle's creation, juxtaposing "the insolent amorality of the clue-reader with the trepident admiration of the decent but muddled citizen: Holmes, Watson; Stephen, Bloom" (161).

It is certainly no news that Joyce parodies the sentimental women's domestic romance novel in "Nausicaa," and at least since Suzette Henke's essay "Gerty MacDowell: Joyce's Sentimental Heroine," it has been generally recognized that a major target of the parody was Maria Cummins's *The Lamplighter*, which Gerty has read, and which features her namesake. But *The Lamplighter* is rather muted in its Christianity, while what Joyce termed "mariolatry" is a vivid thread in the tapestry of "Nausicaa." Because the modern inheritors of this genre—the Mills and Boone publications in England or the Harlequin romances in America—tend to avoid overt religiosity, it is easy to forget that around the turn of the century a rather strenuous Christianity was often interwoven with the mild eroticism of the genre. Robert Hichens' work is an example, and so, in a somewhat skewed fashion, is Marie Corelli's. Another, published not long after

Bloomsday, was Florence L. Barclay's *The Rosary* (1909). The book
ends with a transport of wedded bliss such as Gerty imagines for herself, deeply infused with an aura of religiosity. The blinded husband
seduces his wife thus:

> Come in, beloved, and I, who see as clearly in the dark as in the light,
> will sit and play *The Rosary* for you; and then, *Veni Creator Spiritus*;
> and I will sing you the verse which has been the secret source of peace,
> and the sustaining power of my whole inner life, through the long,
> hard years, apart.
>   "Now," whispered Jane. "Now, as we go."
>   So Garth drew her hand through his arm; and as they walked, sang
> softly:
>   Enable with perpetual light,
>   The dullness of our blinded sight;
>   Anoint and cheer our soiled face.... (cited in Bloom, 88–89)

By 1924 this had sold over a million copies, with numerous transla-
tions. The message of spiritual consolation rather confusedly com-
mingled with the erotic union of husband and wife certainly resonates
with the major themes of Gerty's inner monologue, so that, whatever may have been the specific generic target of Joyce's satire in
"Nausicaa," it clearly combines the erotic and the spiritual in a style
that Joyce's modernist sensibility found comic.

If for purposes of the present argument we accept the idea of
opposing "male" and "female" meta-genres of the popular novel,
then we should recognize that, on the one hand, the distinction
between popular and serious novels is similarly generic, and that, on
the other, popular novels in the mid- to late nineteenth century fell
into numerous subgenres, some publicly acknowledged, some apparent only in retrospect.[3] There were "scare" stories warning of the
imminent invasion of Great Britain by Germany or Japan, or playing on the pervasive fear of racial degeneration around the turn of
the century. There were several varieties of religious or mystical novels, notably including Corelli's religiously themed romances, perhaps
reaching their popular apotheosis in Lew Wallace's *Ben Hur*. There
were the remnants of the spate of "silver fork" novels of high society
that Bulwer-Lytton inaugurated. One of the best-known genres of the
nineteenth century, generally termed the "novel of sensation" (and
which today has been absorbed by more specialized forms, such as
the "thriller"), was produced by well-known figures such as Dickens
and Wilkie Collins, as well as by its most famous genre practitioner

at the time, M. E. Braddon. The novel Molly quizzes Bloom about in "Calypso," *Ruby: The Pride of the Ring* (*U* 4.346), belongs to a tiny splinter genre, termed "circus novels," that both exploited and protested the putative immorality of the conditions in which girls drafted to work in the circus were forced to live.

In discussing popular literary genres of the nineteenth century, there is simply no consensus as to a list of mutually exclusive types. Genres overlap; they rise and fall in popularity and often look very different in historical perspective than they did to contemporaries. Once we realize that, for instance, science fiction will become an important genre in the twentieth century, it no longer suffices to term some of the works of Conan Doyle or Wells "romances." The very concept of novelistic genre includes the novel itself, which was a synthetic genre among the inherited classical ones, and which Bakhtin chooses to regard as a meta-genre, potentially incorporating all the others. At the opposite extreme, we could regard the works of a single distinctive author as a genre. This is, of course, a grouping we do not usually treat as generic, but is a logical extension of the term. Indeed, Bakhtin pushes the idea of genre even further, to embrace splintered fragments of individual novelistic texts, through his concept of "speech genres." While "any utterance...is individual and therefore can reflect the individuality of the speaker (or writer): that is, it possesses individual style," Bakhtin points out that this kind of style is mostly possible in artistic writing, whereas a stylization that is more directly socially determined may "obtain in speech forms that require a standard form" (Bakhtin, 1986, 63). So genre represents a cross section of linguistic and social usage that can be taken at virtually any level of generalization or particularity.

It is equally difficult to decide on the category occupied by genre itself. Following Bakhtin and others, Pamela Gilbert critiques formalist notions of genre as an egregious example of ahistoricizing texts, and instead offers a social and dialogical understanding of it:

> Genre acts both as a topographical feature of the terrain of the marketplace and as a set of reading instructions anterior to the text itself. It is produced discursively as a social category and is aligned with other social categories such as gender and class....Thus, once an author/text is established within a certain generic domain, that is, coming from a certain "location" within the marketplace and appealing to a certain consumership, critics, publishers, authors, and readers will enforce, through master-readings (reviews), packaging, textual references, and reading assumptions, a reading of that text which is congruent with its assigned generic pedigree. (Gilbert, 59)

By invoking something like Fish's reading protocols here, Gilbert use-fully stresses the involvement of the popular genres with the market-place and the implied dialogical interchange with readers that was a characteristic feature of popular publishing in the late nineteenth and early twentieth centuries. Her definition of genre here does flirt with tautology, in the implication that a genre is anything the market-place (wherever that may be) decides to call a genre. Instead, I would suggest that, as Todorov puts it in a summary of Bakhtin's thought, "genre is a sociohistorical as well as a formal entity" (Todorov, 80). According to Todorov, Bakhtin finds genre more important than indi-vidual stylistics or groupings, such as literary schools, because it is quasi-independent of individual decisions, and "the privileged posi-tion of genre is linked to this mediating function" (81). Still, Gilbert is correct in suggesting that there is nothing either inevitable or intrinsic about genre, and popular texts can in fact be read "against the grain," so as to bring out features that would be obscured when the same text is approached with generic expectations. Indeed, much of the branch of cultural studies concerned with popular literature is the result of reading generic works in some non-generic perspective. In the present study, popular works will sometimes be interrogated from a generic perspective, sometimes against the grain of their apparent genre: for example, I will both consider the turn-of-the-century newspaper as a genre and also examine the newspaper's novelistic qualities.

Problems of Allusion

Joyce is a notoriously allusive writer, and the current study, like many others, relies on this aspect of his writing. More traditional studies, and most of the work from the early, "heroic" phase of Joyce stud-ies, focused on the relationship of his writing to the "greats" whose names, works, or lives cropped up in *Dubliners*, *Portrait*, *Ulysses*, or the *Wake*—Shakespeare, the Bible, Dante, Bruno, Vico, and of course, preeminently in the case of *Ulysses,* Homer's *Odyssey*. The first serious, extended critical work on Joyce, Stuart Gilbert's *James Joyce's "Ulysses,"* is in great part an explanation of the ways in which the book alludes continuously to Homer's *Odyssey*. Simply because he discusses the book's episodes by their Homeric names as he runs through the novel, Gilbert implies that this allusion constitutes a fun-damental level of meaning, and this assumption has been maintained in much of the later criticism. Of course Gilbert, who was something of a spiritualist, probably saw the motif of "metempsychosis" in more literal terms than Joyce may have intended, and this would lend the Homeric allusions an added significance. Joyce himself apparently laid great stress on the Homeric allusions while working with Gilbert, who seldom questioned whether Joyce was always being either sincere or accurate with him. But Gilbert's stress on the Homeric parallels was also motivated by the Anglo-American literary-cultural situation. During the early years of Joyce criticism, from the 1930s up through the 1960s, at least part of the trajectory of literary criticism was determined by the New Critical campaign to lend legitimacy to High Modernist works by exploring their references to (and thus, it is implied, continuity with) great literature of the past.

Eliot's well-known essay "*Ulysses*, Order, and Myth" made this argument explicit in his claim that Joyce's work, by invoking classical myth, provides a structuring principle for the chaos of modern life: "Instead of narrative method, we may now use the mythic method. It is, I seriously believe, a step toward making the modern world possible for art" (681). Eliot's formulation here rather strangely implied that certain of the allusions in Joyce were the most important reason his novel had artistic significance. A similar assumption lies behind Gilbert Highet's discussion of Joyce and Eliot in *The Classical Tradition* (1949). The "tradition" Highet invoked was essentially that of Eliot's essay "Tradition and the Individual Talent," an ideal array of the best works of the past, which was always open to—and could be slightly modified by—the addition of modern works of sufficient genius. F. R. Leavis's *The Great Tradition* (1948) relied upon a similar concept, although Leavis chose to put greater emphasis on moral seriousness (and chose Lawrence rather than Joyce as his modern exemplar). Such concepts, by restricting the canon to a limited number of aesthetically "serious" works and by implying that each member of the group is somehow in dialogue with all the rest, puts a formal premium on what would later come to be called "intertextuality."

Throughout the first phase of Joyce criticism, Joyce benefitted from the New Critical revaluation of complexity, especially the sort of textual difficulty and density that the frequent use of allusion made possible. He also, perhaps wrongly, benefitted from a basically conservative valuation of classical sources, so that the association of his writing with that of Homer was taken to suggest that the effect of Joyce's work should be similar to that of his classical model. But this of course is not necessarily the case. In a thoughtful essay on Joyce's relationship to Homer, Fritz Senn suggests that while "utramodernist Joyce always turned back to the classics, Aristotle, Homer, Ovid; to medieval figures like Augustine, Aquinas, Dante; and later to Giordano Bruno, Nicolas of Cusa, Pico della Mirandola, or Shakespeare..., history, Vico, and *Finnegans Wake* all say that each impulse of new life is a *revival*" (71; Senn's emphasis). In other words, with each new invocation of a classical or medieval source everything starts afresh. As Keith Booker observes, commenting on this essay, "For Senn, Joyce does not use *The Odyssey* as a structural model for *Ulysses*. Instead, Joyce sets up the relatively pure and homogeneous style and language of Homer's epic as a starting point against which he can define his radically heterogeneous text as the antithesis" (22).

There are several questions bearing on this issue, most fundamentally (a) how significant is Joyce's use of a series of allusions to Homer's *Odyssey* in *Ulysses*; and (b) if it is significant, in what way is it so? If we assume that the *Odyssey* bears importantly on *Ulysses*, it is possible, even likely, that it does so ironically. After all, Molly, Joyce's version of Penelope, is emphatically *not* faithful to her wandering husband; Bloom, in confronting his "Cyclops" in a bar, is more tongue-tied than verbally clever, and instead of slaying even one suitor he appears to be a relatively complaisant cuckold. Thus we would have a Joyce who, like the traditional Eliot, shows the destruction of traditional values in our debased modern world. If we invert this same reading, we might argue that Joyce's novel implicitly critiques the conservative, masculinist, classist, militarist values of Homer, instead offering for our admiration Bloom's pacifism and androgyny.

Of course most readings of Joyce find him located at neither extreme, but instead partially affirmative, partially oppositional in his relationship to his classical precursors. But an even more skeptical and pragmatic reading might emphasize that readers unaware of Joyce's sheets of correspondences and their elaboration by generations of critics might well miss virtually all the "parallels" cited there, just as the initial readers of *Ulysses* did. As A. Walton Litz has pointed out, a good number of the Homeric parallels Joyce listed were never actually used in his novel, while many others were added very late in composition, as finishing touches in the book's elaborate embroidery: certainly they were not "structural" in any meaningful way (21). And even if they are taken to be structural, that does not necessarily imply that they are important to the *reader's* experience. More than one critic has insisted that the Homeric references are precisely a scaffolding that allowed Joyce, as author, to create his masterpiece, lending it a form other than that dictated by simple narrative; but once the book was written, we readers could just as easily dispense with these references.[4]

The question of the role of the *Odyssey* vis-à-vis Joyce's novel epitomizes the ambiguous nature and function of allusion in his writing.

Like Stephen's idea of an author, Homer is both omnipresent and invisible in *Ulysses:* the title directly alludes to his protagonist, although rather oddly in the Roman rather than the Greek form, and yet Joyce specifically refused to allow the "schema" he had given Gilbert to be printed as part of *Ulysses*, despite the pleadings of Bennett Cerf. So the Homeric allusion is both present and absent in the book itself: it exists most fully in a document that was generated by Joyce and publicized by him, but was scrupulously withheld from publication *as part of the novel*. As many critics have pointed out, this parallels the situation of Eliot's footnotes to *The Waste Land*, although only roughly. I believe Joyce's idea here—one that will surface in many forms in the present study—was to actively involve the reader in the production of the text. If the schema had been somehow included within the novel, and/ or if Homeric chapter titles had been used in it, then that much of the interpreting would have been generally regarded as a closed question. As things stand, though, these allusions are in some degree *occult*: they both do and do not bear the signature of the author, and readers must take their own positions regarding their significance.

So we can distinguish between direct allusions, in which a writer or work is specifically named or quoted in the text, and occult allusions, in which there is extratextual evidence that a writer or work is to be invoked. The most frequent sort of direct (or semi-direct) allusion in *Ulysses* is not the one in which a cultural figure is named, but the one in which he or she is invoked stylistically, as in the "Oxen of the Sun" passages mimicking the history of English prose, or as in the "Nausicaa" chapter, whose style suggests a sentimental-domestic "women's novel" (such as the one actually named, *The Lamplighter*). A far more common problem is the indirect allusion, in which Joyce appears to be invoking a given passage or cultural phenomenon, but in an indirect, and thus usually a debatable, way. Robert Boyle, S.J., in *James Joyce's Pauline Vision: A Catholic Exposition*, recognizes at one point in his argument that he is hanging a complex reading of a passage in the *Wake* on a debatable Biblical citation, and faces the problem directly:

> My own conviction—that the Pauline text shines out from *FW* 482: "What can't be coded can be decoded if an ear aye seize what no eye ere grieved for"[5]—may seem at first glance to require some relatively esoteric circumstances:...a Catholic alertness to the religious profundities of the text; a philosopher's sensitivity to its metaphysical implications; a consideration of Joyce's constantly deeper use, and his decreasingly acrimonious toleration, of religious and specifically Catholic doctrines and attitudes to express his own literary theory and

practice; and other elements. Maybe so. My own judgment is that what
I see is actually present in Joyce's text, and not merely in my own reading of it. But even if it is not,...I consider that the evidence I intend
to bring to bear upon my perception of the text will, in illuminating
Joyce's total product, justify my procedure. (x-xi)

This issue comes up quite frequently, in different forms. Critics eager
to find echoes of Dante, or Shaw, or William Stead in Joyce will be
far more likely to detect their presence in Joycean passages, images, or
dramatic situations than will others. The same is true when hunting
for allusions to popular literature. Many titles are popular phrases,
so when Bloom thinks about a man attempting to back out of a
secret society and being anonymously stabbed in the back, his phrase
"Hidden hand" (*U* 8.459) may refer to E. D. E. N. Southworth's 1888
novel by that title, or to Tom Taylor's 1864 melodrama by the same
title, or simply to the cliché phrase. Probably the best way to determine the truth of the situation would be to investigate both anterior
texts to see if a case can be made for a dialogical interchange with
the passage from *Ulysses*, or whether on the contrary the two texts
remain stubbornly independent of one another.

An excellent example of the indirect allusion about whose presence
each reader must make his or her own decision is furnished by a man
named Joseph Pujol, known by the sobriquet "Le Petomane," which
we might translate as the "flatulist." Between about 1892 and 1900
he was the toast of Paris, and in a time when the immensely popular
actress Sarah Bernhardt might make at best 8,000F in a evening, Le
Petomane brought in 20,000F in a single Sunday at the Moulin Rouge.
He was undoubtedly one of the most famous low-comedy performers
of Paris, the city in which Joyce spent most of his adult life. According
to a memoir written by his son, Pugnol discovered the abilities that
his somewhat unusual anatomy allowed him to exercise when, as a
young man doing military service, he was bathing with other soldiers. He found he was able to suck in an enormous amount of water
through his rectum and then eject it forcefully, to the delight of his
companions. More than this, he discovered that having cleansed his
pipes in this way, he was able to make musical sounds of a variety
of pitches and, with practice, was even able to do imitations of different musical instruments, not to mention artillery and the voice of
an opera singer. As his son observed, "The word 'fart' is somewhat
vulgar. But my father had transformed this action into an art since
having taken in air that way he used it to make music or, if you prefer

it, to modulate sound from the smallest and almost inaudible to the sharpest and most prolonged, simply according to the contraction of his muscles. He could do what he liked with his stomach—and there was no smell" (Nohain and Caradec, 22–23).

Unfortunately the details of Le Petomane's act are now unrecapturable—gone, we might say, with the wind—but it seems he comported himself at all times quite seriously, as an artist, which of course added to the general astonished hilarity. A contemporary observes, "I can truthfully say that I have never seen houses laugh, shout, and scream as they did when this little man with his William II moustache, crew cut hair and deadpan face pretended to be unaware of his incongruities....People were literally writhing about. Women, stuffed in their corsets, were being carried out by nurses which the cunning manager...had stationed in the hall, well displayed in their white uniforms" (12–13). I might add that Le Petomane went to great lengths to demonstrate that there was no trickery involved in his performances. He gave private audiences for men only in which he performed in a bathing costume with the critical part cut away, and on one occasion was tipped a 20 franc gold piece by the King of Belgium.

Bloom, of course, is no Petomane, and unlike him will not make theatrical history; he is an amateur who merely adds his own musical coda to the performance of the bar habitués in "Sirens." It is most unlikely that he has ever heard of Le Petomane; but, on the other hand, it is quite likely that Joyce had when he crafted this episode to feature Bloom as the final performer of the Ormond Bar concert. Throughout the chapter, Bloom, a non-singer, must listen to heartrending ballads of love, loss, and betrayal, and must somehow defend himself against them and against the despair that must accompany them. He does so, triumphantly, at the end of the chapter, as he walks out, still digesting his lunch of burgundy wine and a Gorgonzola sandwich. He sees a picture of Robert Emmet in a shop window and thinks of his famous last words, words Irish schoolchildren still sometimes learn by heart. Following his conviction of treason for his leadership of a nationalist rebellion, Emmet was asked if he had anything to say before the death sentence was pronounced, and gave the famous reply, "Let no man write my epitaph....When my country takes her place among the nations of the earth, then, and not until then, let my epitaph be written. I have done." Words like these, Bloom realizes, with their heroic resignation, are a trap for him, and he must empty them of their pathos by a musical modulation into the key of farce. He also has the practical problem that while walking down the sidewalk he needs to pass gas and is hoping for some loud noise to cover up the process, such as a passing tram:

> Seabloom, greasabloom viewed last words. Softly. *When my country takes her place among.*
> Prrprr.
> Must be the bur.
> Fff! Oo. Rrpr.
> *Nations of the earth.* No-one behind. She's passed. Then and not till then. Tram kran kran kran. Good oppor. Coming. Krandlkrankran. I'm sure it's the burgund. Yes. One, two. *Let my epitaph be.* Kraaaaa. *Written. I have.*
> Pprrpffrrppffff.
> *Done.* (U 11.1284)

If we admit the allusion to Le Petomane, it should probably be classed as a contextual allusion, since no specific verbal echo is involved, either directly or indirectly. Although it would seem impossible to establish whether there is an allusion to Le Petomane inherent in this passage, it is impossible to read "Sirens" the same way once we are aware of that possibility. Insofar as Le Petomane's history constitutes a text, there is, undeniably, space here for dialogical interplay with the conclusion of "Sirens."

A closely related kind of allusion is the formal one, in which no specific verbal sequence, but instead the form of the Joycean passage, implicitly offers an allusion. The best-known example here is the form of "Ithaca," in which complex, remote, often abstract questions are posed by an unknown interlocutor, to be answered sometimes with epigrammatic brevity, sometimes with inhuman loquaciousness. In the Gilbert schema, Joyce terms the chapter's "technic" "catechism (old)," emphasizing the ritual, depersonalized character of the recitation and implicitly offering it for comparison with the "catechism (young)" of "Nestor," where Stephen quizzes his students and is quizzed by Mr. Deasy. Other critics have pointed out the chapter's similarity to a police report and a school *viva voce* examination. Critics soon identified as a model *Richmal Mangnall's Questions*, which is mentioned as one of Stephen's textbooks in *Portrait* (P 53). The book exists in editions as early as 1800, and in a mid-nineteenth-century version even has a section devoted to astronomy:

> Mention some of the most noted astronomers of ancient and modern times.
> —Ptolemy, Pythagoras and Hipparchus among the ancients; and Galilei, generally called Galileo, Copernicus, Tycho Brahe, Kepler, Sir

Isaac Newton, and Sir William Herschel in modern times. (Mangnall, 284)

However, the same format was used for many nineteenth-century school texts in Ireland, especially for teaching history. William O'Neill Daunt's *A Catechism of the History of Ireland Ancient and Modern* (Dublin: James Duffy, 1844) engages several issues that Joyce also raises:

> *Q.* Whence did the whole Irish nation receive its Christianity?
> *A.* From Rome.
> *Q.* Who states these facts?
> *A.* They are stated by many ancient historians of the highest credit; namely by Saint Prosper of Acquitain, in the year 434; by Saint Columbanus, an Irish prelate, A.D. 701; by Probus, an Irish writer of the ninth century... [etc.]. (Daunt, 4)

The point here is that Joyce was most probably deploying a verbal pastiche or satire of a common Victorian formal mode of writing for instruction, rather than a single source. In some ways it might come closer to constituting a discourse than it does a single text, and thus we should be alert for ways in which "Ithaca" puts into question the value of catechistic learning as an epistemological mode—something he more directly does in "Nestor" through Stephen's unanswerable riddle and his surreal definitions (of God as "a shout in the street," for instance).

Despite all the difficulties involved, the history of Joyce criticism is greatly occupied with attempts to trace allusions in his writings (see Kershner 2001). In the New Critical campaign to confer literary respectability on modern writing, stressing the classical and medieval allusions in Joyce's writing conferred a kind of respectable seriousness by association upon modernist works whose value was not yet apparent to all. These, then, were the allusions most thoroughly explored by early Joyce critics. Although "low," "mass," or "popular" cultural allusions in Joyce's work were sporadically identified by critics from the start of Joyce scholarship, more or less in the assumption that anything in Joyce, no matter how obviously trivial, was worth at least identifying, it is probably fair to say that very few critics, with the notable exception of those looking at the role of popular song in Joyce's writing, took the subject at all seriously until the 1980s. Before then, as Michael North observes, "antipathy to popular culture [became], over the years, an indispensible part of accepted definitions of modernism," at first because "the line was drawn as a cordon sanitaire around the great works of aesthetic modernism by their critical advocates" (North, 141).

Popular Culture and High Modernism

The paradigm shift within the critical profession that allowed for a change in the way popular culture was evaluated with respect to high culture took place originally in the 1960s with the influx of European cultural theory, especially via the work of Roland Barthes and Umberto Eco. The avowed antihumanism of the structuralist enterprise allowed for analytic methods through which Barthes could discuss professional wrestling, or Eco could meditate on Superman, as readily and with the same complexity and subtlety as could be seen in Barthes's treatment of Racine, or Eco's of medieval texts. To a considerable extent, structuralism was not evaluative, or at least not in the immediate, insistently moralizing way that was true of Cambridge English under Leavis, or even the Agrarian branch of the American New Criticism. Meanwhile, beginning in the 1960s, in both England and the U.S., influential public intellectuals began to contest the consensus position that had regarded popular culture as a social pathology (see Brantlinger). The founding of the Birmingham Center for Contemporary Cultural Studies in 1964 lent support to the kind of pioneering work done by Raymond Williams and Richard Hoggart, whose critical writing explicitly took into consideration factors of class and historical situation in evaluating texts, as opposed to the putative "timelessness" that Leavis and the New Critics had found in "great works." Stuart Hall, who was significantly influenced by European theory, eventually encouraged the Birmingham Center to deploy a criticism sensitive to gender and to race. In the U.S., where the dominant critical formalism and aestheticism in academia reflected the general political quietism of the postwar period, Leslie Fiedler and the Canadian Marshall McLuhan were the most influential voices protesting the academic abjection of popular culture. Fiedler, championing an antiacademic and somewhat anti-intellectual cultural movement beginning with the "Beat" movement, and McLuhan, with his technological millenialism that attributed unprecedented significance to the new broadcast media, were representative of a changing cultural focus. Not coincidentally, both of them were Joyceans who found support for their minority positions in Joyce's writing.

In Europe, the most influential social commentators were probably those associated with the Frankfurt Institute for Social Research, which notably included Theodor Adorno, Max Horkheimer, and Leo Löwenthal; the Institute's collective attitude toward what they termed mass culture or the "culture industry" was severe. Adorno stated:

> The total effect of the culture industry is one of anti-enlightenment, in which…enlightenment, that is the progressive technical domination of nature, becomes mass deception and is turned into a means for fettering consciousness. It impedes the development of autonomous, independent individuals who judge and decide consciously for themselves.…If the masses have been injustly reviled from above as masses, the culture industry is not among the least responsible for making them into masses and then despising them, while obstructing the emancipation for which human beings are as ripe as the productive forces of the epoch permit. (Adorno, 18–19)

Adorno's apparent scorn for most forms of popular culture, including jazz music, which he saw as agents of domination, was potentially countered by the more ambivalent work of Walter Benjamin, despite his peripheral status with respect to the Institute. As members of the Anglo-American critical establishment during the 1970s and 1980s began to move increasingly toward the analysis of social and political issues in their evaluation of writing practice, the basic concerns of the Frankfurt School were widely adopted, even as their conclusions were questioned and sometimes reversed. Benjamin became a more important posthumous figure than any of the other Western Marxists, and his ideas were taken up and elaborated during the critical refiguration of both modernism and modernity that has occupied the last twenty years.

By the 1980s it was generally agreed that popular culture could not simply be dismissed as the functional equivalent of ideology, a form of *panem et circenses*. Andreas Huyssen's influential formulation argued that popular culture had been abjected by modernist high art, removed from aesthetic consideration in large part because it had been coded as feminine. On the other hand, what Huyssen in his book's second edition termed postmodernism was presented as a concept of art that eschewed hierarchy and produced works that indifferently mixed elite and popular, high and low forms, in part by embracing characteristics (such as melodrama or sentimentality) that had previously been rejected as feminine. Alternatively, in *The Political Unconscious* (1981) Fredric Jameson finds the romance genre in the modernist text *Lord Jim* to be "the prototype of the various 'degraded' subgenres into which mass culture will be articulated (adventure story, gothic, science fiction, bestseller, detective story, and the like)." Thus, from the structural breakdown of the older realisms in the late nineteenth century there emerges "not modernism alone, but rather two literary and cultural structures, dialectically interrelated and necessarily presupposing each other for any adequate analysis: these now find themselves positioned in the distinct and generally incompatible spaces of the institutions of high literature and what the Frankfurt School conveniently called the 'culture industry,' that is, the apparatuses for the production of 'popular' or mass culture" (Jameson 1981, 207).

Jameson's formulation here, unlike Huyssen's, opens the way for a refiguration of modernism. It is arguable that the notion that modernism always and everywhere rejected the popular is more a function of the New Critical and Leavisite schools, than it is a characteristic of modernist art in itself. In retrospect, it is clear that Joyce, and even Eliot, welcomed several forms of "low" art, and indeed that during the modernist heyday many consumers were simultaneously interested in Joyce, Stein, Faulkner, jazz music, Chaplin, and other especially inventive forms of popular culture. As early as 1923, the American critic Gilbert Seldes published *The Seven Lively Arts*, whose title was meant as a contrast and a tribute to the classical seven arts and to the (recently defunct) eponymous journal. The book is an appreciation of a variety of types of American popular culture, including jazz and ragtime music, the extravaganzas of Florenz Ziegfeld, the circus, the burlesque and vaudeville, the Krazy Kat cartoon, mass-market movies—preeminently those of Chaplin—and even "popular" writers like Ring Lardner. Near the book's conclusion, Seldes sets forth a group of "propositions" that he holds self-evident:

> That there is no opposition between the great and the lively arts.
> That both are opposed in the spirit [*sic*] to the middle or bogus arts.
> That the bogus arts are easier to appreciate, appeal to low and mixed emotions, and jeopardize the purity of both the great and the minor arts.
> ...
> That there exists a "genteel tradition" about the arts which has prevented any just appreciation of the popular arts, and that these have therefore missed the corrective criticism given to the serious arts, receiving only abuse. (Seldes 1962, 294–95)

But whether popular culture was to be viewed as an aspect of postmodernism, which was seen as antielitist and thus politically progressive, or whether it is seen as imbricated with modernism—sometimes conjoined with it in an odd alliance against the middlebrow—it had become plain that it could not simply and universally be dismissed or castigated for its psychological and social effects. Nor, in a critical climate that had brought into serious question the aestheticism of the New Criticism, was it sufficient (or even meaningful) to dismiss the popular as "bad art." Instead, there was a growing realization "that all cultural production must be seen as a set of power relations that produce particular forms of subjectivity, but that the nature, function, and uses of mass culture can no longer be conceived in a monolithic manner" (Collins, 16).

This has been the posture of the majority of work addressing Joyce and popular culture over the past two decades, beginning with Cheryl Herr's *Joyce's Anatomy of Culture* (1986) and continuing with my own *Joyce, Bakhtin, and Popular Literature* (1989).[6] If there has been a universal object of condemnation for cultural critics in the twentieth century, it is probably the advertising industry, and so the most unusual aspect of Jennifer Wicke's *Advertising Fictions: Literature, Advertisement, and Social Reading* (1988) and of Garry Leonard's *Advertising and Commodity Culture in Joyce* is that neither of these books assumes that either advertising or the consumer society are obvious evils. Leonard in fact suggests that advertising provides Gerty MacDowell with a kind of "owner's manual" for her commodified body, and thus paradoxically empowers her. All such critical work, of course, has to address the complication that in speaking of popular culture in Ireland in 1904, we are often speaking of the effect of the cultural product of a colonizing power upon the colonized, who do not always or entirely regard themselves as separate from the colonizers. This is one dimension of the difficult situation addressed by Derek Attridge and Marjorie Howes's edited collection *Semicolonial Joyce*. Joyce's position resonates with that of both the colonized and the colonizer, and, to some extent, that describes the Irish cultural producers (such as those responsible for newspapers and magazines) who would identify themselves as Irish, but turn out a product generically dependent upon the Empire. Recently, of course, a great deal of critical work has examined the Irish and British Imperial dimensions of Joyce and his work (Duffy, Lloyd, Nolan, Gibson), a discussion whose political implications might be seen as framing my work here. Be that as it may, with the exception of newspapers, and to some extent Orientalism, most of the texts, institutions, and figures I treat here originated in Britain, while my focus is on their reception in Ireland, as mediated by their appearance in *Ulysses*, where Joyce could be said to impersonate the Irish cultural consumer, as well as portraying his characters as such.

Topics and Arguments

The present work does not aim to survey Joycean examples of popular culture from *Ulysses*, because the potential field is too large: there are literally hundreds of allusions of this kind that could be tracked down and investigated. Instead, I have chosen to investigate a scattering of texts, figures, and institutions that I think have considerable (if often surprising) significance for the act of reading *Ulysses*. The present, introductory chapter offers a few examples of popular cultural figures that arise in that book. It deals with some fundamental issues emerging from the issue of modernism's relationship to popular culture, such as allusion and genre. I have tried to present a brief history of the development of approaches to the relationship between modernism and works of popular culture, with particular attention to popular literature. A few concrete examples are invoked in order to explore some of the complexities of this field of study. I argue that a formal approach to popular literary genres is inadequate, and that social and political dimensions are necessary as well. Here I also briefly reprise the history of Joycean popular culture criticism, tracing the gradual superseding of a uniformly dismissive approach to popular culture by a more nuanced analysis that assumes each individual artifact must be evaluated within its cultural context.

Chapter two starts from the problem of the massive quantity of material detail of the book, which many critics have interpreted as satiric. I establish an overview of *Ulysses* as a political and social critique of modernity by reading it against Horkheimer and Adorno's *Dialectic of Enlightenment*, a book that I argue indirectly alludes almost continually to Joyce's. Two areas of interest for Horkheimer and Adorno are of special interest here, the chapter on the *Odyssey* as an allegorical anticipation of bourgeois hegemony and the one on de Sade as an inevitable outcome of domination. I suggest that Joyce anticipated the Frankfurt School critique of enlightenment as a disguise for domination. I also point out that Joyce's use of anti-Semitism as a major theme in the treatment of the twentieth century that he offers in *Ulysses* is almost prophetic in 1922. The chapter as a whole establishes a political context for my reading of Joyce's deployment of popular cultural references in *Ulysses*. Then my examination moves to specific examples of popular culture. The third chapter examines two writers at different cultural "levels," Stephen Phillips and Marie Corelli. Both of these are noncanonical figures who had a substantial literary presence at one time, although by the time Joyce wrote them into *Ulysses* they had both faded considerably from cultural memory. I argue that Phillips's verse drama *Ulysses* and Corelli's work as a whole, but especially *The Sorrows of Satan*, the best-selling novel up to its time, establish dialogical presences in Joyce's book. Since Phillips was considered a "serious" author by many of his contemporaries, the section discussing him is closer to a traditional influence study, exploring what Joyce might have gleaned from the verse drama *Ulysses*, which Joyce is known to have read. The concluding section on Corelli introduces perhaps the best-known popular novelist of her time, and argues that her aesthetic and writing furnish a continuous commentary on literary modernism, not entirely from the outside. After all, Corelli's rather experimental play with the novel genre in many ways could qualify as a (paradoxical) "melodramatic modernism." She shared enough with Stephen Dedalus that his friends jokingly accuse him of writing one of her books, and enough with Joyce to provide him—and his modernist contemporaries—with a distorting mirror.

Chapter four further establishes one of the main themes of this study, which is that *Ulysses* works to disestablish the traditional writer/reader dichotomy established through the professionalization of fiction writing during the nineteenth century. Informally, we might say that the book is designed to engage the reader in its own writing, much as the newspapers and light weeklies of the "new journalism" established, engaged, and became dependent on the contributions of readers for their composition. Here I rely on Walter Benjamin's more hopeful comments on the new variety of journalism that was emerging in the early years of the century. I suggest that the reading of *Ulysses* confronts the reader with a series of puzzles, riddles, and lacunae that (s)he is encouraged to fill in, becoming in a sense *Ulysses*'s coauthor in a way that had not been the case before modernist writing and the institutionalization of popular literature arose as an interlinked cultural complex and the contemporary institutionalization of popular literature. My overall argument here is that early twentieth-century mass publications, especially newspapers and the "light weeklies," in a dialogical perspective can be seen to pioneer some of the same ground that Joyce does in his notorious collection of puzzles and conundrums. The fifth chapter expands specifically on the history of Irish newspapers and discusses their role in *Ulysses*, both as consumer items and as formal models for many of the novel's innovations. My historical discussion of Irish newspapers relies on archival research done at the National Library and at Colindale in the 1970s, when I held an NEH grant, and again in 1984, when I taught at University College Dublin. I offer the fullest discussion to date of Joyce's use of newspapers in his novel, and argue that understanding the historical context of the *Freeman's Journal* in 1904 is necessary to an understanding of "Aeolus." Similarly, chapter six concentrates on *Tit-Bits* and *Answers*, the "light weeklies" that far outsold the daily papers and that established a new mode of relationship to the reader through contests, promotions, and the extensive printing of readers' letters and attempts at writing (e.g., the "prize Tit-Bit story" that Mr. Bloom fantasizes about writing to win a guinea per column). The chapter ends with a discussion of a genuine Phillip Beaufoy story in *Tit-Bits* that I have discovered, a story that stands in for the imaginary "Matcham's Masterstroke." I argue that the story functions as a particularly obscure but fascinating intertext in *Ulysses*—by no means the only one.

The last three chapters concentrate less on specific texts, and more on popular cultural phenomena that, I argue, give unusual insights into modernity within the United Kingdom and Ireland. Chapter seven discusses the bodybuilder Eugen Sandow as a cultural phenomenon whose self-promotion and indeed self-creation stands as a model for the rise of what we might call "personal institutions" under modernity. The remarkable ubiquity of the Sandow commercial empire, through its distribution in books, magazines, strength-building commodities, the arts, science, spas, and even into participation in government bureaucracies, is, I argue, a unique possibility of modernity in this period, and presents a bizarre parallel to the modernist "branding" and marketing of famous figures such as Joyce (Rainey). Here my argument moves well beyond the immediate implications of Sandow's several casual appearances in *Ulysses,* to larger cultural considerations. A different kind of institution is explored in the chapter on Orientalism, which touches on a variety of texts alluded to in *Ulysses*, but most centrally argues that *Arabian Nights* is a fundamental intertext for Joyce's novel—in some ways, more so than the *Odyssey*. I present Joyce as to some degree complicit with Orientalism, but to an important degree critical of its pernicious stereotypes, simply by virtue of the blatant way in which he highlights their manipulation of Bloom (and, less emphatically, Stephen). A good part of the chapter explores the fact that the Irish were themselves seen as Oriental by the British, and partially internalized this judgment even as (like Bloom, who thinks of Molly as excitingly Moorish) they indulged in the orientalizing of others.

The ninth and final chapter as a whole turns around the appearance of Rudy at the end of "Circe" and attempts to decode his appearance in terms of the significance of children's clothing in the United Kingdom in 1916. The last part of the chapter is a meditation on three forgotten forms of photography invoked by Rudy's materialization on a wall: spirit photography, fairy photography, and memorial photography. My argument is that our reading of the ending of "Circe" depends directly upon the conceptual models we have available to frame the hallucinatory, "impossible" appearance of Rudy, and that once we are sensitized to the imaginative possibilities of those photographic genres (which are no longer part of our cultural currency) our reading of this critical passage is forever altered. While some of my analysis here is semiotic, some of it is historical, and relies on an expansion of Bakhtin's work on genres. Indeed, the main thrust of my discussion here is social, and I am indebted to many of the critics who since the 1980s have explored Bakhtin's implications for history and the social sciences.[7]

Chapter Two

Odyssean Culture and Its Discontents

> Mr. Leopold Bloom was awakened by the buzzer in his digital clock radio. He was lying in a king-sized bed in the master bedroom of his house. He lay beneath a designer sheet and a comforter, which he tossed aside, and slid out of bed. The broadloom carpet in the bedroom felt soft and comfortable. He put on his slippers and went to the closet, where he took out his jogging outfit and got into it. He went for a jog around the neighborhood, returned, got undressed, put on a bathrobe, and ambled over to the bathroom. (Berger 39)

This passage introduces Arthur Asa Berger's student guide to the cultural analysis of everyday life; subsequent chapters explore the semiotics of the clock radio, king-sized beds, comforters, and so forth, suggesting the complexities that underlie the most quotidian of details in our life. Berger's gesture in assigning the central role in this drama to a person named Leopold Bloom pays homage to the fact that Joyce's Bloom is, at least materially, the most fully developed and thoroughly furnished of fictional existences. It is arguable that the quantity of represented physical detail that accompanies his actions—including, for example, eight different versions of the cat's cry and a unique representation of the protagonist's experience in the jakes—is less an indication of Bloom's particular character or of the novel's diegesis than it is of the general experience of everyday life in Dublin, June 16, 1904—the experiential dimension of "Joyce world." For many critics, in fact, the presentation of Bloom is the best available illustration of the quality of bourgeois "dailiness" under modernity. The opening pages of Henri Lefebvre's *Everyday Life in the Modern World*, the seminal work in this area, are an extended meditation on Joyce's writing, especially what Lefebvre calls the "profound triviality" of Bloom's presentation in *Ulysses*. I would like to use this critical crux as an introduction to the larger question of how we are to take Joyce's presentation of modernity, especially focusing on the example of commodity culture he deploys in evoking 1904 Dublin. The remainder of the present study will be devoted almost exclusively to specific examples of that culture; this chapter attempts to survey the issue globally, in critical perspective.

Historically, the analysis of the daily has led ineluctably to evaluative judgments, and the sheer quantity of *Ulysses'* quotidian detail, which was virtually unprecedented in the novel, is often assumed by readers to imply a commentary in itself. If Bloom seems adrift in trivialities—a term in itself laden with value judgment—then the reaction of many early readers of *Ulysses* was to interpret that fact as an indictment of Jews, Dubliners, or modern man. If the culture in which he exists is awash in advertisement and machinery, and his consciousness is continually drawn to the newspapers, popular reading, snatches of popular song, or figures from the entertainment industry, then, from an idealist point of view, it is tempting to read *Ulysses* as an indictment of twentieth-century European mass culture insofar as that culture is a distraction from more important political or aesthetic considerations. The sheer mass of detailed environment Joyce presents has often been seen as deadening; at least within the context of classical modernism, it is usually approached as a distraction from the genuine stuff of organic life and human authenticity. One of the few rejoinders to this assumption was offered by Fredric Jameson. In a frequently cited article, he argues that the verbal technique of "Ithaca," which apparently reduces all experience to material details, actually works against the naturalizing tendency of classical physical description and the problem of human alienation in the face of modern reality:

> [Joyce's response] is to be found in that great movement of dereification I have already invoked, in which the whole dead grid of the object world of greater Dublin is, in the catechism chapter, finally, disalienated and by the most subterranean detours traced back…less to its origins in Nature, than to the transformation of Nature by human and collective praxis deconcealed. (Jameson 1982, 140)

In order to investigate some of these concerns, especially the relationship between (popular) material culture and modernity, I would like to consider the parallels between *Dialectic of Enlightenment* by Max Horkheimer and Theodor Adorno, and *Ulysses*. There are a surprising number of parallels between these two books. Having first been brought out by an obscure publisher, both were originally underground classics, circulating in pirated editions until their growing fame led to their official reissue by a major publisher. Both books aspire to address the general situation of Western culture in the first half of the twentieth century, but I want to draw particular attention to some of the unusual strategies through which they approach the problem of portraying modern culture. Perhaps the most unusual such procedure is the way in which both books set up a running comparison between daily life in the twentieth century and selected episodes from the *Odyssey*—"Wandering Rocks," "Sirens," "Oxen of the Sun," and so forth—not so much in order to highlight our distance or difference from heroic, mythic times as to demonstrate unexpected and usually unexamined continuities with them.

A second unusual strategy is the books' continual concern—one might almost say obsession—with popular culture. Throughout, popular art is set against "high" or "elite" art, and the social implications of both are examined. The books touch on numerous aspects of what we now often term "mass culture" (—best sellers, newspapers, the literature of self-improvement, the stage, and so forth) —but concentrate especially on popular music—both Joyce and Adorno were trained musicians: Joyce a singer of ballads and light operas, Adorno an avant-garde follower of Schoenberg. After popular music, the text's most prominent concern is probably with sadomasochistic pornography; indeed, one entire chapter of each book takes as its point of departure an infamous nineteenth-century work of pornography—by de Sade in the case of *Dialectic* and Sacher-Masoch in the case of *Ulysses*. The last strategy toward which I want to point is the fact that both *Dialectic of Enlightenment* and *Ulysses* are strongly concerned with anti-Semitism, a phenomenon which is seen not as a cultural aberration, but as intimately involved with issues of domination and mass psychology in the modern world.

Admittedly, I have phrased the characterization of *Ulysses* here to highlight its social concerns; but after all, Joyce called himself a socialist in his youth. Like Adorno he was attacked by Georg Lukács, accused of decadence and avant-gardism, and criticized by more directly activist Marxists as a politically passive aesthete. Still, as many recent critics have argued, Joyce's works offer a powerful argument that socially responsible and responsive art first calls for a revolution in aesthetic form.[1] Unlike many earlier leftist critics, Adorno greatly respected Joyce's art and defended his technical innovations on grounds that were ultimately sociopolitical. Serious modern fiction, like Joyce's, fragments the narrative and avoids conventional narration, according to Adorno, because in the modern world, "the identity of experience in the form of a life that is articulated and that possesses internal continuity—and that life was the only thing that made the narrator's stance possible—has disintegrated." Similarly, the novelist can no longer simply be a storyteller, "for telling a story

means having something *special* to say, and this is what is prevented
in the administered world, by standardization and eternal sameness"
(Adorno, 3). Merely to use the conventional form of the psychological
or social novel, Adorno asserts, is itself a reactionary political statement, because "the narrator's implicit claim that the course of the
world is still essentially one of individuation, that the individual with
his impulses and his feelings is still the equal of fate, that the inner
person is still directly capable of something, is ideological in itself"
(Adorno, 31). There is obviously a great deal to be said about the relationship between Adorno and Joyce as high-cultural figures. Here,
though, I only intend to briefly survey *Dialectic of Enlightenment* in
the perspective of *Ulysses*, and vice versa, concentrating first upon
Adorno and Horkheimer's use of the *Odyssey* in their effort at epic
social triangulation, and second upon the role of popular or mass
culture in Joyce's novel and in the Frankfurt School work.

Enlightenment, Myth, and Domination

Dialectic opens with a chapter on "The Concept of Enlightenment,"
in which the authors argue that the potentially liberating intellectual
movement termed the enlightenment has, in fact, been put into the
service of increasingly totalitarian forms of social control or, to use
their favorite term, *domination*. Positivistic thought, which Adorno
and Horkheimer see as the logical extension of enlightenment rationalism, thus contributes to contemporary alienation and to the passivity of the human subject in the face of the administered world. As
Martin Jay puts it, "the new conception of the natural world as a field
for human manipulation and control...corresponded to a similar idea
of man himself as an object of domination" (Jay, 237). There follow
two chapters, each concentrating on a literary work used allegorically.
"Excursus I" is on "Odysseus or Myth and Enlightenment," while the
second "Excursus" explores de Sade's "*Juliette*, or Enlightenment and
Morality." (The parallel episode in *Ulysses*, "Circe," is of course based
broadly upon Sacher-Masoch's *Venus im Pelz* [*Venus in Furs*.])[2] The
next and most famous chapter is the one devoted to mass culture and is
entitled, "The Culture Industry: Enlightenment as Mass Deception";
and the final chapter is called "Elements of Anti-Semitism: Limits of
Enlightenment" (see here Davison, Reizbaum).

The presentation of myth in *Dialectic of Enlightenment* appears at
first paradoxical: myth is not opposed to enlightenment thought but,
in its later stages, is continuous with it. Once myth becomes codified

into epic—once it is transmuted into organized narrative and a mode of representation—the original immediacy and identity of god with attribute is shattered. "Myth intended report, naming, the narration of the Beginning; but also presentation, confirmation, explanation: a tendency that grew stronger with the recording and collection of myths. Narrative became didactic at an early stage" (Horkheimer and Adorno, 8). Indeed, Horkheimer and Adorno argue that the epic is already novelistic (Horkheimer and Adorno, 43–44). But in this process, unmediated meaning disappears. "On the road to modern science, men renounce any claim to meaning. They substitute formula for concept, rule and probability for cause and motive.... Myth turns into enlightenment, and nature into mere objectivity. Men pay for the increase of their power with alienation from that over which they exercise their power" (Horkheimer and Adorno, 5, 9). Mythic fate and the ineluctable will of the gods is replaced by the inevitability of deterministic and logical processes in whose grip individuals are identically helpless. Endlessly reductive rationalism leads to a sort of bottomless relativism "in which ever and again, with the inevitability of necessity, every specific theoretic view succumbs to the criticism that it is only a belief—until even the very notions of spirit, of truth and, indeed, enlightenment itself, have become animistic magic" (Horkheimer and Adorno, 11). There are some serious problems with Adorno and Horkheimer's idea of enlightenment, which seems at some times historically defined and at others to include almost any kind of rationality. But the rationalism run amok of which they speak here, I would suggest, is that of the insanely literalist interrogator of "Ithaca," or perhaps that of the mechanically inquisitional "Arranger" that becomes so obtrusive in the last half of *Ulysses*. That voice's ceaselessly mocking interpolations, it can be argued, actually drive the reluctant reader to embrace Bloom's naive humane affirmations.[3]

For Horkheimer and Adorno, the end of early mythic thinking and the beginning of enlightenment corresponds with the end of nomadic life and the establishment of property and, with it, of economic subordination. Odysseus, in fact, is "a prototype of the bourgeois individual" (Horkheimer and Adorno, 43). "A proprietor like Odysseus manages from a distance a numerous, carefully gradated staff of cowherds, shepherds, swineherds and servants" (Horkheimer and Adorno, 14). Horkheimer and Adorno's interpretation of the "Sirens" episode is particularly revealing. For them, the Sirens represent both the allurement of the past and a threat to the patriarchal order: they call to the laborers to cease laboring, to lose their identities. By threatening to destroy the socially constructed selfhood of their victims, they play the same role as the Lotus in that episode. They offer what art offers, although "the Sirens' song has not yet been rendered powerless by reduction to the condition of art." The ordinary laborers, who must "doggedly sublimate in additional effort the drive that impels to diversion," stop their ears, while Odysseus, the seigneur, adopts the other alternative, by binding himself to the mast of "practice" (Horkheimer and Adorno, 32–33). Thus he is enslaved by labor just as effectively as the laborers, even though he himself need not work. Unlike them, he can hear the Siren song of nostalgia, diversion, and self-indulgence, but his hands are tied.

Throughout, Horkheimer and Adorno stress that Odyssean cunning is the instrumental rationalism of one who sacrifices, who cuts his losses, who pays the price of "his own dream," who wins only

> by demystifying himself as well as the powers without. He can never have everything; he has always to wait, to be patient, to do without; he may not taste the lotus or eat the cattle of the Sun-god Hyperion, and when he steers between the rocks he must count on the loss of the men whom Scylla plucks from the boat.... The title of hero is only gained at the price of the abasement and mortification of the instinct for complete, universal, and undivided happiness. (Horkheimer and Adorno, 57)

With the rise of the Odyssean hero comes the fall from innocence of language, which had originally been one with fate, or *fatum*, and with identity. Where language had possessed immediate power in mythic times, now it degenerates into nominalism (which Horkheimer and Adorno call "the prototype of bourgeois thinking"). Language lapses into mere representation, and word separates itself from object. This is the significance of his encounter with the Cyclops: Odysseus learns "that the same word can mean different things. Because both the hero and Nobody are possible connotations of the name Udeis, the former is able to break the anathema of the name" (Horkheimer and Adorno, 60). And in this episode Odysseus is even more clearly separated from his fellows. "Hence universal socialization...from the start included the absolute solitude which emerged so clearly at the end of the bourgeois era" (Horkheimer and Adorno, 62).

Ulysses and the Modern World

Clearly Horkheimer and Adorno's allegory is itself susceptible to critique, or at least interrogation, on a number of grounds. Is their argument about enlightenment predicated on particular historical events and contexts, or are they arguing that rationalism broadly construed and domination are *necessarily* interconnected? What evidence, mythic or otherwise, can be brought to the debate? Can we accept their implied utopian vision of a world—either in the remote past or the anticipated future—in which the individual would *not* have to wait, be patient, or do without? But different sorts of questions arise when we take the Frankfurt school reading of the *Odyssey* and superimpose it upon Joyce's *Ulysses*—a book that, after all, Horkheimer and Adorno drew upon in formulating their reading of Homer. Their work offers, by implication, an alternative interpretation of *Ulysses*'s mythic structure that coincides with the standard modernist interpretation in some ways, and diverges in others. The modern world sketched in *Dialectic of Enlightenment* is one of mechanism triumphant, in which rationalism has run amok, vitiating the lived experience of individuals, and surrounding them with the dead products of a mindlessly consumer society. Oddly enough, this vision nearly coincides with that of Wyndham Lewis in *Time and Western Man*, a social critique we would now see as coming from the far right. Lewis saw *Ulysses* as symptomatic of the modern condition, and characterized it as "an immense *nature-morte*," an "Aladdin's cave of incredible bric-à-brac in which a dense mass of dead stuff is collected" (Lewis, 91). The implication of what he takes to be Joyce's "time-philosophy" is "the doctrine of a mechanistic universe" that is worked out in *Ulysses* (Lewis, 93). The characters in the book, consequently, are "walking clichés"—Bloom a stage Jew, Mulligan a stage Irishman, Haines a stage Anglo-Saxon—since they are all examples of the effect of mechanism upon the concept of human character (Lewis, 96).

Hugh Kenner, in his famous rereading of Lewis and Joyce, argues that Lewis is right about what he detects in *Ulysses*, but misses the fact that it is parody, a conscious critique of the "mechanical mind" behind much of twentieth-century culture rather than a symptom of it. Bloom is "a parody of the Enlightenment" (Kenner 1956, 217), the book "a huge and intricate machine clanking and whirring for eighteen hours." Are the characters walking clichés? "Of course they are," Kenner asserts:

> Bloom is in fact a low-powered variant of that mode of consciousness that imparts substantial form to the book. It is by the insane mechanical meticulousness of that mode of consciousness, the mode of consciousness proper to industrial man, that in *Ulysses* industrial man is

judged. *That* is, in a way, the 'meaning' of the book, the form in which
it remains as a whole in the memory. (Kenner 1956, 166–67)

Although Kenner eschews the vocabulary of the left and in other
respects holds views far removed from those of the Frankfurt school,
his argument here is very similar to Adorno's view of what Joyce is
doing. Speaking broadly of serious modern fiction, but with obvious
application to Joyce, Adorno writes:

> The contemporary novels that count, those in which an unleashed
> subjectivity turns into its opposite through its own momentum, are
> negative epics. They are testimonials to a state of affairs in which the
> individual liquidates himself.... These epics, along with all contempo-
> rary art, are ambiguous; it is not up to them to determine whether the
> goal of the historical tendency they register is a regression to barba-
> rism or the realization of humanity, and many are all too comfortable
> with the barbaric.... But by uncompromisingly embodying the horror
> and putting all the pleasure of contemplation into the purity of this
> expression, such works of art serve freedom—something the average
> production betrays, simply because it does not bear witness to what
> has befallen the individual in the age of liberalism. (Adorno, 35)

A more recent turn on this argument is offered by Fredric Jameson
in his essay, "*Ulysses* in History." Previously, especially in his book
on Wyndham Lewis, *Fables of Aggression* (1979), Jameson had deni-
grated Joyce for his impressionist aesthetic, for the subjectivism that
Jameson saw him sharing with Eliot. Joyce's use of myth to unify a
modern experience that had lost any human unity, Jameson implied,
was a politically deplorable alternative to Lewis's fragmenting objec-
tivism. Canonical modernism's "strategies of inwardness, which set
out to reappropriate an alienated universe by transforming it into
personal styles and private languages," were for Jameson politically
regressive (Jameson 1979, 2). In this later essay, however, he seems to
be rethinking his position and in the process creating a new, counter-
modernist *Ulysses*—or at least a *Ulysses* that is not modernist in the
way that movement has generally been conceived.

Against the unifying reading that stresses mythic parallels, he
argues, there is "a rather different form of reading which resists that
one in all kinds of ways, and ends up subverting it." This is the nonlinear reading necessary to follow references backward and forward
across the text, in the process fragmenting it beyond repair and resisting the text's tendency to settle into a fixed symbolic order (Jameson

1982, 132). In order to avoid saddling Joyce's work with the "bankruptcy of the ideology of the mythic," he suggests that we

> displace the act or the operation of interpretation itself. The Odyssey parallel can then be seen as one of the organizational frameworks of the narrative text: but it is not itself the interpretation of that narrative, as the ideologues of myth have thought. Rather it is itself—qua organizational framework—what remains to be interpreted. (Jameson 1982, 128)

He then proposes that we see the Odyssean scaffolding as just that—an ordering mechanism of strictly pragmatic value to the author, one that rather arbitrarily substitutes for the traditional ordering devices of plot, character, and so forth, which have lost their force in the twentieth century. Jameson privileges the later episodes, especially "Eumaeus" and "Ithaca," for their relative refusal of subjectivism. For Jameson, the latter parts of *Ulysses* withhold or destroy all traces of the authorial subjectivity, even the possibility of an implied author. In an echo of Horkheimer and Adorno, Jameson argues that capitalism produces an increasing separation "between the private and the public, between the personal and the political, between leisure and work, psychology and science, poetry and prose, or...between the subject and the object." In "Eumaeus" and "Ithaca" Joyce means "to force us to work through in detail everything that is intolerable about this opposition" (Jameson 1982, 139). Although it is not the same as Jameson's argument, my thesis that *Ulysses* uniquely impels us to become complicit in its own writing (see chapter four) is, I believe, similar. Both interpretations depend not upon the book's formal structuration, but upon its reading *as process*.

Jameson's move opens the door to a postmodern interpretation of *Ulysses*, one that avoids what some critics now see as the ideological pitfalls of modernist ideology; whether those pitfalls are, in fact, problems with the ideology of modernism, or with the ideology of the New Criticism that grew out of one strand of modernism, is still another question, and too large to be addressed here. What I do mean to stress are the political and aesthetic vicissitudes of the Odyssean parallel in *Ulysses*, set against the sheer mass of fact and furniture in the book. For T. S. Eliot, in his essay "*Ulysses*, Order and Myth" (1923), the former redeemed the latter, while for Wyndham Lewis the latter outweighed and vitiated the former. Kenner, while retaining the valuation Eliot had put on the formal ordering of *Ulysses*, recast Joyce's mechanisms in a parodic light.

In a way, Jameson continues and extends Kenner's reading, but where Kenner suggests that Joyce is launching an Eliotic critique of modern culture from the right, showing how we have lost our original bucolic sense of wholeness, harmony, and independent, individual selfhood, Jameson's Joyce is satirizing capitalism from the left, implying that we have lost any genuine sense of community or of human involvement in production.[4] Eliot's Joyce might be nostalgic for feudalism, or at any rate for life before the seventeenth-century "dissociation of sensibility," while Jameson's Joyce could only hope for a coming radical transformation of society. For Adorno, the import of Joyce's "negative epic" is its unsparing portrayal of a society alienated almost beyond redemption. But, in addition, Adorno and Horkheimer demonstrate how the *Odyssey* parallel may embody a social critique in itself; in other words, they show that we need not read that epic poem the way Eliot did. Where Jameson suggests that we see Joyce's use of the Odyssean references as an arbitrary ordering device, Adorno and Horkheimer open the further possibility of rereading the myth itself—not as if it were the alternative to contemporary culture, but as itself an interpretation of it that is, in fact, continuous with it.

Ideas of Mass Culture

But is the culture Joyce portrayed in *Ulysses* actually one of "barbarism"? There is little doubt that that is the way Adorno read Joyce, and little doubt that a significant element in his indictment was the popular culture that makes up so much of the daily furniture of *Ulysses*. For Adorno, Bloom would have been a man without meaningful culture, easy prey to the commodities surrounding him. Indeed, as an advertising canvasser, Bloom would have appeared to Adorno to be complicit with the forces destroying his subjectivity. James F. Knapp, one of the few critics to have remarked on the issue, admits that, to many readers, "Joyce's retelling of the myth of Odysseus has offered little more promise of cultural renewal than this dark German version, written in the shadows of fascism." But, he argues, "when the two are read together, the Irish fiction seems to draw an Odysseus who is not so inexorably caught in the history that defines him" (Knapp, 143). In our eyes, Bloom is a far more sympathetic figure than he could have been to a European cultural mandarin such as Adorno; and as for the barbarism surrounding him, it has a certain saving ambiguity of its own. We are now more attuned to the observation of Adorno's friend Walter Benjamin that "there is no document of civilization which is not at the same time a document of barbarism" (Benjamin, 256)—an observation that cuts both ways.

For Horkheimer and Adorno, however, there was still a sharp distinction between experimental "high" culture, with its saving negative potential, and the sort of twentieth-century culture that they thought was falsely labeled *popular*. As Martin Jay explains, "The notion of 'popular' culture, they argued, was ideological; the culture industry administered a nonspontaneous, reified, phony culture rather than the real thing. The old distinction between high and low culture had all but vanished in the 'stylized barbarism' of mass culture" (Jay, 216). Adorno's concept of the "culture industry," like Gramsci's notion of "hegemony," Althusser's "state ideological apparatuses," or even Lefebvre's "everyday life," thus crystallized a shared perception among the Western Marxists that culture is not merely the inert superstructure of an economic base that determines everything of importance, but instead that it functions actively to perpetuate the status quo. Patrick Brantlinger has demonstrated, in *Bread and Circuses: Theories of Mass Culture as Social Decay*, that the kind of social analysis that views mass culture pejoratively, as another opiate of the populace allowing the ruling class to maintain its dominance, has its roots in classical antiquity, and exists in both conservative and radical forms. But the term "mass culture" specifically gained currency in the 1930s "as a primarily political and apocalyptic term, used to refer to a symptom of social morbidity, the cancer or one of the cancers in a failing body politic" (Brantlinger, 31).

Horkheimer and Adorno's characterization of the culture industry is familiar in its outlines to most cultural critics. Up until the last fifteen or twenty years, some variant of it was the intellectual consensus in the American academy. Mass culture is described as monolithic, reflecting the monolithic nature of monopoly capitalism. It is seen as a pseudo-culture of endless repetition and a high degree of stylization (and thus the antithesis of true style) that appropriates everything, including real art, for the purposes of mechanical reproduction (Horkheimer and Adorno, 127). So sweeping is their condemnation that it includes all film—which "forces its victims to equate it directly with reality" (Horkheimer and Adorno 1986, 126)—and all popular music, even music such as jazz, which is associated with marginalized social groups and is often conceived by other critics and artists as potentially oppositional.

Perhaps surprisingly, Adorno and Horkheimer do not attack mass culture as licentious, but as fundamentally antierotic. Leo Löwenthal, writing to Horkheimer, spoke for most of the Frankfurt School in asserting that "Mass culture is a conspiracy against love as well as against sex. I think that you have hit the nail on the head by your observation that the spectators are continuously betrayed and robbed of real pleasure by sadistic tricks."[5] Similarly, Horkheimer and Adorno claim that humor, and even farce, in the popular arts, which might be seen as politically liberating (and which today is often framed that way in the light of Bakhtin's idea of carnivalization), is actually deadening and mechanical. It elicits a laughter that "overcomes fear by capitulating to the forces which are to be feared." "Fun is a medicinal bath," they observe. "The pleasure industry never fails to prescribe it" (Horkheimer and Adorno, 140).

A point of their analysis in which Horkheimer and Adorno might claim a degree of prescience—and which corresponds in many ways to Joyce's portrayal of twentieth-century culture—is their linkage of the processes and products of the entertainment and advertising industries. "If the need for amusement was in large measure the creation of industry, which used the subject as a means of recommending the work to the masses—the oleograph by the dainty morsel it depicted, or the cake mix by a picture of cake—amusement always reveals the influence of business, the sales talk, the quack's spiel" (Horkheimer and Adorno, 144). "The highest-paid stars," they observe, "resemble pictures advertising unspecified proprietary articles." In a radical turn on Marx's idea of the fetishizing of commodities, they assert that "the commodity function of art disappears only to be wholly realized when art becomes a species of commodity instead, marketable and interchangeable like an industrial product" (Horkheimer and Adorno, 156, 158). Further, "Culture is a paradoxical commodity. So completely is it subject to the law of exchange that it is no longer exchanged; it is so blindly consumed in use that it can no longer be used. Therefore it amalgamates with advertising" (Horkheimer and Adorno, 161). Shortly before this, they referred to the "fusion of culture and entertainment that is taking place today" (Horkheimer and Adorno, 143). In a discussion of this chapter within his book on Adorno, Jameson notes that the authors are not here discussing culture as the concept has come down through anthropology, through Benjamin, or through Raymond Williams, for that matter. Their argument "does not include a concept of culture as a specific zone of the social. This is why it is a mistake to suppose that Adorno's 'elitist' critiques of the 'Culture Industry' in any way define his attitude or position towards 'mass culture,' grasped now not as a group of commercial products but as a realm of social life...." The actual subject of

"The Culture Industry" chapter, Jameson suggests, is not culture, but business, and this is why Adorno's argument has been misconstrued (Jameson 1990, 107).

Clearly, Joyce puts these issues into play in *Ulysses*, but his attitude toward them has been a source of critical controversy from the beginning. Leopold Bloom is well aware of the interdependency of commodity production and advertising, although he would be baffled at the tone of apocalyptic protest that pervades Horkheimer and Adorno's discussion. Bloom knows that his art of advertisement is in some way now the mother (or the devourer) of the other arts. His own ventures at the production of art—the abortive libretto for a Dublin pantomime, projected Prize *Titbits* stories such as "My Adventures in a Cabman's Shelter" or "The Mystery Man on the Beach" (*U* 13.1060), the recitals he imagines organizing for Stephen and Molly—are all unashamedly commercial. Indeed, he is used to analyzing most cultural phenomena in terms of advertising strategies: the best-known example is his appreciation of the techniques of the Church, in "Lotus-Eaters":

> Good idea the Latin. Stupefies them first....Now I bet it makes them feel happy. Lollipop. It does. Yes, bread of angels it's called....Then all feel like one family party, same in the theatre, all in the same swim....Blind faith. Safe in the arms of kingdom come. Lulls all pain. Wake this time next year. (*U* 5.350)

"Squareheaded chaps those must be in Rome: they work the whole show," Bloom marvels. "And don't they rake in the money too?" (*U* 5.433). Later, overhearing the service in "Nausicaa," he makes the parallel even more explicit: "Could hear them all at it. Pray for us. And pray for us. And pray for us. Good idea the repetition. Same thing with ads. Buy from us. And buy from us" (*U* 13.1122).

There can be no doubt that in the world of *Ulysses*, as in *Dialectic of Enlightenment*, art, popular culture, and advertising all intermix and interpenetrate; whether this necessarily implies a universal cheapening, a destruction of "true" culture, however, is another matter. Joyce was well aware of the critique of consumer society that had been launched from both right and left, and played off that issue in his novel, but I would argue that he ultimately failed to endorse it. We can see an emblem of that critique when the *Photo Bits* nymph, Bloom's talisman of the erotic, and an excellent example of high art overtaken by mass culture, accuses Bloom in "Circe":

Mortal! You found me in evil company, highkickers, coster picnic mak-
ers...La Aurora and Karini, musical act, the hit of the century. I was
hidden in cheap pink paper that smelt of rock oil. I was surrounded
by...stories to disturb callow youth, ads for transparencies, truedup dice
and bustpads, proprietary articles and why wear a truss with testimony
from ruptured gentleman. Useful hints to the married. (*U* 15.324)

She sees herself as an avatar of Beauty hidden among commercial
garbage, and as a pearl of great price cast before the swinish Bloom.
This situation appalls the nymph, who claims, as an immortal, to
be "stonecold and pure" and to "eat electric light" (*U* 15.3392). It
also elicits abject apologies from Bloom, who has been trained in the
high school to give lip service to exactly the sorts of distinctions his
culture actually obviates. But the democracy of affect is, after all, our
condition, and Joyce suggests that the nymph protests far too much
against it: she finally strikes at Bloom's loins with a poniard and then
flees, "her plaster cast cracking, a cloud of stench escaping from the
cracks" (*U* 15.3469). Bloom is no plaster saint (or nun), and he correctly identifies her game as the "fox and the grapes": she exists only
to tantalize, always just out of reach (*U* 15.3464). As goddess and as
objet d'art the nymph may claim a status based on exclusiveness and,
ultimately, on a denial of the physical and the erotic. But that denial is
itself compromised, and indeed is revealed as a form of sadism more
perverse than any indulgence of Bloom's.

The crumbling, stinking nymph does not represent Joyce's jab at
Photo Bits, as many readers have assumed, or evidence of Bloomian
or Joycean misogyny either. Instead, it represents his attack upon the
very image of aesthetic transcendence, the myth of a classical art so
elevated that it pretends to have cast off any sexual suggestiveness even
in its portrayal of a naked woman. After the joyous, carnivalesque
leveling that takes place in *Ulysses*, Joyce leaves few aesthetic hierar-
chies standing. Like Horkheimer and Adorno, he suggests that there
is an unsuspected continuity between Odyssean myth and the peram-
bulations of a 1904 ad canvasser, a common denominator of struggle
and exploitation, and even a common subjugation to ideology. But
though he is tempted by its Siren song, Joyce finally rejects cultural
nostalgia. Finally, it is Joyce, rather than his critics, who is practic-
ing what we have come to call cultural studies. The significance of
Joyce's imposition of a classical matrix upon the vulgar, naturalistic
texture of the twentieth century, his scattering of high-cultural references throughout a novel packed with daily commodities, is simply an
assertion that never again will we be able to unmix the two.

Chapter Three

Authorial Interchanges

Shakespeare is the happy huntingground of all minds that have lost their balance. (*U* 10.1061)

Joyce is unique in the depth and resonance of allusions to other writers, both implicit and explicit, that surface in his work; he is a near-perfect example of what Harold Bloom would call a "strong" writer, unafraid of invoking literary models such as Shakespeare, Dante, the Bible, or Flaubert. The two writers I consider in this chapter cannot claim the sort of obvious presence that Shakespeare does in *Ulysses*, and neither can be considered a canonical literary figure. Stephen Phillips is nearly forgotten, although around the turn of the century he was widely celebrated as a major dramatic poet. Marie Corelli on the other hand was considered to have little literary merit by critical consensus during her life—although there were significant exceptions to this opinion—and now even her vast popularity has been forgotten. She is directly alluded to in the "Scylla and Charybdis" chapter and, I would argue, plays a significant role in it largely through the mediation of Shakespeare, who was an important figure to her, just as he was to Joyce. By contrast, Phillips might be termed an implicit rather than an explicit allusion, an allusion by inference, although I would argue that since Joyce demonstrably read Phillips's verse play *Ulysses* when he was an impressionable adolescent, the dramatic poet has an undeniable textual presence imbricated within Joyce's treatment of the Ulysses theme. This theme was already echoing with the efforts of a long list of writers who approached it before either Phillips or Joyce, so that to fully explore the Ulysses theme in Joyce's book from a Bakhtinian perspective would be a nearly endless occupation. But Corelli is a more interesting and complex dialogical presence within Joyce's novel than seems likely at first. In her own (not entirely separate) sphere, she was as much a phenomenon as was Joyce, and her astonishing success was as much a result of the social tendencies that enabled the modernist revolution as was Joyce's. Clearly I do not mean to investigate the dialogical resonance of Corelli and Phillips as in any way typical or representative of writers with whom Joyce establishes an intertextual relationship; on the contrary, I hope these are surprising figures, unexpected by comparison to Homer, Shakespeare, and Wilde, but also by comparison with George Moore or Thomas Lyster. My contention here is that dialogism in *Ulysses* is a postmodern effect, resistant to being reduced to a neat hierarchy of influences. Once we have become sensitized to, for instance, the melodramatic worship of art that Corelli promulgates, or the lyrically eroticized version of Homer's story for which Phillips is responsible, both can come to seem pervasive and surprisingly significant in Joyce's text.

As I suggested in *Joyce, Bakhtin, and Popular Literature*, Bakhtin establishes three broad applications of dialogism in a literary text: (1) between authorial language and protagonist's language; (2) between protagonist's language and the languages of other characters in a text; and (3) between the language of a text or a protagonist taken as a whole and the languages of other relevant texts to which explicit or implicit allusion is made. This third area of dialogism immediately suggests the notion of *intertextuality*, as developed by various contemporary critics, notably Julia Kristeva, Michael Riffaterre, and Jonathan Culler. Bakhtin's dialogism does not wholly coincide with structuralist and poststructuralist intertextuality, because, for Bakhtin, the model of language is spoken, rather than written, a distinction to which Derrida lends great force; "but in practice, because Bakhtin avoids all implication of origin, 'presence,' and authority in his characterization of voice, the play of voices in his work resembles the play of text in Derrida's. [Bakhtin's] interest is clearly in 'double-voiced' discourse, that is, discourse oriented toward the discourse of another" (Kershner 1989, 18–19). Of course, "language," for Bakhtin, has little to do with the literal, formalist conception of a writer's language that would only be detectable in the work of another through verbal echoes. Language is also ideological, redolent of its original social and political context. It is pregnant with the writer's characteristic themes and, through Bakhtin's powerful notion of *intonation*, with his or her attitudes as well. When I speak of Phillips's "influence" below, I mean to refer to this textual effect, rather than to any psychological presence or gesture.

Joyce and Stephen Phillips

In preparing for his own epochal treatment of the Ulysses theme, Joyce assiduously read most of his important predecessors, assimilating into his own conception whatever he found useful. In the verse play *Ulysses*, published in 1902 by Stephen Phillips, he found a new emphasis which was to be central in his own work—the motivation of lyrical, slightly fin-de-siècle sensuality—and a number of secondary themes and techniques he could comfortably adapt. It is far less surprising than it would appear that a writer whom we would think of as obscure should have significantly influenced Joyce. Although by the 1930s his name had ceased to crop up in literary conversation, Phillips was one of the brightest stars around the turn of the century in England. His reputation as a dramatic poet, according to the *DNB*, was "stupendous." Phillips first attracted attention with his long poem *Christ in Hades*, which won the Academy prize for poetry in 1896. Even William Ernest Henley, who took second place, uncharacteristically heaped praise upon his new rival (Cruse, 81). Phillips's volume of *Poems* (1898) appeared to justify the acclaim of both critics and the reading public, as did his immensely popular verse plays *Paolo and Francesca* (1900), *Herod* (1901), and *Ulysses* (1902). The plays were even more successful in performance than in publication, undoubtedly aided by Beerbohm Tree's lavish production of the latter two. According to a contemporary source, Phillips was mentioned as a likely successor to Tennyson in the office of Poet Laureate (Escott, 275).

Just when Joyce first became acquainted with Phillips's work cannot be established with any certainty. Constantine Curran remembers that during his own initial First Arts class in English Literature, Professor Darlington asked Joyce whether he had read Phillips's *Paolo and Francesca*, to which Joyce replied indifferently, "Yes" (Curran, 3–4). This would have been in 1899, during the writer's second year at University College Dublin. Although the verse drama's official date of publication was 1900, according to the *DNB* John Lane actually brought it out in 1899. In any case, Joyce must have read the book very soon after it became available. Then, in 1901, when Phillips's reputation was at its highest, Joyce's interest in the lesser writer would have been revived by a correspondence he had begun with William Archer (*Letters*, II 7–11). Archer had written Joyce in April, to inform him of Ibsen's response to his *Fortnightly Review* article, and four months later Joyce ambitiously presumed upon his correspondent by sending him his early play *A Brilliant Career*. Archer's response, in September, was kindly but lukewarm. Changing the direction of his attack, Joyce then apparently sent the critic a group of lyrics in the late summer of 1901; unfortunately, neither Joyce's letter nor the poems themselves have survived, but Ellmann (*Letters*, II 9, n. 2) suggests that the group included the villanelle "Are You Not Weary of Ardent Ways."

Archer's evaluation, sent in September 1901, was again lukewarm, mingling general encouragement with what Archer himself termed "pedantries" regarding Joyce's prosody. Joyce apparently defended his slightly irregular variety of meter and rhyme, possibly with reference to the French Symbolists; again, his letter has been lost. Archer patiently replied in late September, directing Joyce to his forthcoming book of criticism, *Poets of the Younger Generation*, and in particular to the section on Stephen Phillips.

Even if Joyce had not been familiar with Phillips's work up to this point, it is highly likely that he would have sought it out soon after Archer's letter. He must have consulted Archer's book when it became available in Dublin, if only because some of their correspondence revolved around it: Joyce had evidently urged Archer to include in it a section on a young disciple of George Russell named Paul Gregan. He would have found praise mingled with pedantries regarding Phillips's lyrics, but almost unqualified praise for Phillips as poetic dramatist: "He is a totally new phenomenon in English drama of the past two centuries—at once an inventor of situations and a master of language" (Archer, 338). Of Phillips's style, Archer writes, in a phrase which must have intrigued Joyce, "it is essentially epic, yet it is full of lyrical modulations which render it vividly dramatic" (Archer, 339). Nor was Archer's praise of Phillips at all unusual at the time; among the reviews printed at the rear of the Bodley Head edition of *Ulysses* are raves by Max Beerbohm and Richard Le Gallienne. The *Times*'s reviewer felt that Phillips's writings "contain the indefinable quality which makes for permanence," and Churchton Collins, in the *Saturday Review*, suggested Phillips's close kinship with Sophocles and Dante. In an outburst of enthusiasm both he and Phillips may later have regretted, Archer, writing for the *World*, characterized the poet as "the elder Dumas speaking with the voice of Milton."

Granted that Joyce read Archer's book, he would have had a multitude of reasons for reading Phillips's poetry. It is moot whether he would have been attracted more by Archer's praise or by his criticism. Phillips was as self-conscious a prosodist as Joyce, and Joyce would have seen him as engaged in a battle like his own to subvert the regular iamb, similarly chastised by stodgy old men of letters. And Phillips actually did write some first-rate poetry, of a variety that might well have appealed to the young Joyce. A late lyric, "Beautiful Lie the Dead," shows Phillips in his most successful manner:

> Beautiful lie the dead;
> Clear comes each feature;

Satisfied not to be,
Strangely contented.
Like ships, the anchor dropped,
Furled every sail is;
Mirrored with all their masts
In a deep water.

Phillips's verse in general is most reminiscent of Tennyson, but also combines echoes of Milton and, in the shorter and later pieces, an apparent, if unlikely, suggestion of Emily Dickinson. His lyrics are, like Joyce's, intensely personal, and yet are given a dignity and scope through control of tone. In most of Phillips's verse dramas the tone is less personal, closer to "high sentence." As J. C. Squire put it in a negative evaluation written after the poet's rapid decline and death, "Phillips tended to make all his characters minor poets, who were willing at any moment to hang up the play with unrevealing irrelevancies, faintly reminiscent of the great passages in great poets" (quoted in Untermeyer, "British Poetry," 342). But while Squire's assessment may be painfully accurate for most of Phillips's dramatic work after 1902, it does not do justice to his *Ulysses*. Phillips's writing in general now seems spotty in its successes, but at least in *Ulysses* he surpassed himself; certainly most of the play is as good as anything else which was then being written in the genre. Around 1902, when the play was published, Joyce was at work on his own verse play, a drama with songs entitled *Dream Stuff* (*JJII* 80). Judging from the surviving examples of Joyce's late adolescent verse, it seems likely his verse play would have combined the mauve sensibility of the 1890s with Miltonic elevation, very much as Phillips did.

Be that as it may, we have Stanislaus's testimony that Joyce did indeed read Phillips's *Ulysses* sometime before he began his own effort. In response to a query by W. B. Stanford, he submitted the following list of writers on Ulysses whom his brother had studied: Virgil, Ovid, Dante, Shakespeare, Racine, Fénelon, Tennyson, Phillips, d'Annunzio, and Hauptmann (Stanford, 276 n.6). And then, soon after his reading of Phillips's *Ulysses*, coincidence intervened. Richard Ellmann (1972, xv–xvi) claims that the incident which was the germ of the novel *Ulysses* took place on June 22, 1904, when Joyce, after being beaten in a drunken brawl, was dusted off and taken home by one Alfred Hunter, rumored to be Jewish and to have an unfaithful wife. Phillips's book, where Ulysses is given the epithet "a hunter" (an epithet not included in the Homeric version), would still have been fresh in Joyce's mind.

As W. B. Stanford has amply demonstrated, the primary source of Joyce's interest in the Ulysses theme was his schoolboy text, Charles Lamb's *Adventures of Ulysses*, an adaptation of Chapman's version (Stanford, 1951). Each of the other versions Joyce read contributed to the cacophony of voices resounding in his own far more original treatment of the theme. But, as is always the case with Joyce, the magnitude of the source is not necessarily commensurate with the magnitude of its effect on his work. Given how Joyce was probably first brought to read Phillips's *Ulysses*, briefly examining that work could suggest which of its aspects might have contributed to the work that was brewing in Joyce's mind during the succeeding decade.

Phillips explains in an Author's Note to the play that in converting from epic to dramatic form he was forced to sacrifice five-sixths of the Homeric episodes, and cites as precedents Ronsard's and Bridges's dramatic adaptations, both of which treat only actions after the hero's return to Ithaca. Phillips also included two earlier episodes: the sojourn with Calypso and the descent to Hades, "for telling dramatic presentment and dramatic contrast." Among the other major alterations Phillips enumerates, two in particular were also adopted by Joyce: "the stay with Calypso made to precede the descent among the dead instead of following it" and "Calypso herself endowed with some of the attributes of Circe" (Phillips, 147).

Phillips's *Ulysses*

The structure of the verse play is relatively simple. A "Prologue on Olympus" establishes that Zeus is torn between Athene's plea to return Ulysses home and Poseidon's hatred of him. He grants Athene's wish, but allows Poseidon to "work him mischief on the way" and stipulates that first "he must go / From dalliance to the dolorous realm below" (Phillips, 16, 17). In the first act we are shown the suitors reveling, Penelope prevaricating, and Telemachus—having been berated by Athene—weakly resolved to do something. We then switch to Ulysses on Calypso's isle as he is freed from his spell. The substance of this excellent scene is Calypso's inquisition of Ulysses. She is unable to understand why he might choose Penelope over her, an experienced goddess. "The love that shall not weary, must be art," insists Calypso, asking whether Penelope can compete with her. "She hath no skill in loving—but to love," he answers. Joyce's Calypso is a paradoxical amalgam of Molly herself and Martha Clifford, along with elements of the *Photo-Bits* Nymph hanging on the wall; but insofar as his main parallel is Martha, he is drawing the same opposition between a debased "art" of managed, commodified sexual attraction and one of apparently natural, spontaneous life. Bloom's courtship of Martha is purely literary; he uses a pseudonym and consciously crafts his letters to arouse her. And just as Ulysses must reject Calypso's more directly erotic art for his earthly Penelope, Bloom must resist the phantasmic Martha to have a hope of returning to the actual woman in his bed. In both cases, it is a triumph of the human over the divine or the imaginary, a victory of "reality" over "play." As Phillips's Ulysses puts it,

> We two have played and tossed each other words;
> Goddess and mortal we have met and kissed.
> Now I am mad for silence and for tears,
> For the earthly voice that breaks at earthly ills... (Phillips, 57)

The second, and weakest, act takes place in Hades, where Hermes guides Ulysses. Phillips's Hell is Virgilian rather than Homeric. There, the hero meets and talks with Spirits of Newborn Children, Furies, Suicides, and Lovers who still love. Each encounter gives rise to philosophical and emotional conversations about life and love, but at least in its substance, the act holds relatively little that would have interested Joyce. Perhaps Phillips's interruption of the dramatic movement in order to present a series of encounters between Ulysses and various typological figures may have encouraged Joyce to do likewise in the "Wandering Rocks" episode; indeed, Joyce does the same thing more subtly in "Hades" itself, where Bloom's carriage passes numerous characteristic Dublin figures, like Reuben J. Dodd, whose idiosyncrasies spur conversation. Phillips's Ulysses meets Eurydice, Charon, Tantalus, Sisyphus, Tiresias (who will not tell him whether his wife is faithful), Agamemnon (who claims she will murder him), and finally his mother (who reassures him). Throughout, Phillips's emphasis is on Ulysses' fear of sexual betrayal, certainly more so than in Homer's version, and this, of course, is one of Joyce's most unremitting themes. The last act of Phillips's play generally follows the classical outline. Ulysses, returned to Ithaca, takes shelter with Eumaeus, arranges his ploy with Telemachus, and overthrows the suitors. The play closes on his wordless reunion with Penelope.

Perhaps what most clearly distinguishes Phillips's version from previous versions, both in theme and in tone, is its eroticism. The poet is equally at home in a Tennysonian and a Swinburnian vein, and is not above injecting a little Yellow Book eroticism where he feels it appropriate. The suitors in the second scene are shown pouring wine over themselves and some willing handmaidens; they in turn cover the suitors with figs, apples, pears, grapes, pomegranates, and white and purple flowers. The suitors, like Blazes Boylan, pose the threat of riotous, mindless sensual indulgence, as opposed to Ulysses' and Bloom's tenderness. Sex in the play runs the gamut from the bawdy to the mystical, as it does in Joyce's work. In the Prologue, after Poseidon has accused Athene of unworthy motives in her defense of Ulysses—"Thy marble front of maidenhood conceals / Such wandering passion as a wanton feels" (Phillips, 15)—the gods begin a sly discourse of their weakness for the allures of humankind. Zeus himself admits "That Danaë, Leda, Leto, all had place / In my most broad beneficent embrace" (Phillips, 18). And Calypso waxes almost clinical as she berates Ulysses: "I have shown you amorous craft, tricks of delay, / Tears that can fire men's blood ..." (Phillips, 53)

In the last act, Phillips modulates the eroticism into a minor key. In a very effective scene, the suitors are discovered reveling with their women at the banquet table while the minstrel Phemius sings. Just before the entrance of Ulysses, disguised, the minstrel breaks off the song and stares in horror at the company, seeing a black mist and blood dabbled over everyone; as if in a dream, the suitors repeatedly "laugh together softly and sweetly" (Phillips, 119). Phemius's vision of horror as the sensuality approaches a climax shows Phillips's mastery of the entwined strands of fate, death, and the erotic. It shows, too, the "mysticism" that Joyce found so attractive in Lamb's post-Enlightenment version of Homer. Thematically, love and sexuality are central for Phillips's *Ulysses*, as they are for Leopold Bloom, and as they generally are *not* for earlier versions of the myth. Phillips, in fact, has sketched something like an amorous quadrangle, as he explores the different sorts of love for Ulysses felt by Calypso, Athene, and Penelope. And just as Bloom, throughout his wanderings, is continually beset by memories of Molly, Ulysses in this play seldom speaks or acts without reference to his Penelope. When Ulysses in Hades encounters the spirits of lovers who still love, he learns that death has not quieted their ardor, and realizes that he himself shares their punishment: "Do I not burn for a breast unreachable?" From this romantic and erotic version, Joyce's Ulysses is the next stop on the way to Robert Graves's self-consciously hedonistic Ulysses—"All lands to him were Ithaca: love-tossed / He loathed the fraud, yet would not bed alone."

A classical trait of Ulysses that Phillips, like Joyce, underlines, is his cunning suspiciousness. When Calypso tells him that he is free to depart, Ulysses asks for details. Half apologizing, he explains,

> I have learned to dread what cometh suddenly,
> And sniff about a sweet thing like a hound:
> And most I dread the sudden gift of gods. (Phillips, 50)

Learning that the directive came from Zeus, he mutters, "Zeus himself I trust not over-far," though he immediately adds, "Hurler of bolts! I speak it reverently" (Phillips, 51). The character's evasiveness and hesitancy, his suspicious submission to the inevitable, and particularly the hint of a sense of humor in him, all suggest Joyce's protagonist.

Finally, a few less tangible parallels suggest themselves. Phillips's world, like Joyce's, is Manichaean. Twin, opposing attributes of Zeus, the positive and negative attributes of Athene and Poseidon, rule Ulysses' voyage. Ulysses has Joyce's and Bloom's sense of life as the tension of balanced opposites. Arguing with Calypso, he makes a point Bloom might have made in a less poetic way: "I would not take life but on terms of death, / That sting in the wine of being, salt of its feast" (Phillips, 58). Bloom, a son and friend of suicides and a man acquainted with pain, is aware of the opposing urges toward life and death. His voyage must be a difficult middle course between Scyllae and Charybdi. Having overcome the drugged lassitude of the Lotus-Eaters episode, he must also avoid losing himself to the Circean bacchanal in Bella Cohen's brothel. In the end, only his naked will can bring him home again. So, Phillips's Ulysses is neither a mere plaything of the gods nor a man with an inevitable destiny. Entering Hell, he asks, "Is it sworn I shall return / Upward and homeward?" and Athene answers, "In thy will it lies. Thou, thou alone canst issue out of hell" (Phillips, 71). As Ulysses' questions make clear, the hell is, as much as anything, a subjective one of doubt over his wife. Phillips's drama, like Joyce's novel, is internalized; the important conquests to be made are within the character's mind, and this is, of course, an aspect of the two works' modernity. Both *Ulysses* are more soliloquy than adventure. In the climax of the drama, Ulysses' routing of the suitors is, like Bloom's, mainly symbolic: he kills only Antinous and a fawning servant, while the others are driven out by timely thunder and lightning provided by Athene. Perhaps, like Joyce, Phillips felt that wholesale slaughter was "unUlyssean."

Joyce and Marie Corelli

Soon after his arrival in Pola, Joyce began to immerse himself in current popular English novels, perhaps as an attempt to fight linguistic homesickness. On February 28, 1905, he wrote to his brother,

> I have read the Sorrows of Satan [by Marie Corelli], A Difficult Matter (Mrs. Lovett Cameron) The Sea Wolves (Max Pemberton) Resurrection and Tales (Tolstoy) Good Mrs. Hypocrite (Rita) Tragedy of Koroshko (Conan Doyle) Visits of Elizabeth (Elinor Glyn) and Ziska [also by Corelli]. I feel that I should be a man of letters but damn it I haven't had the occasion yet [....] If I had a phonograph or a clever stenographist I could *certainly* write any of the novels I have read lately in seven or eight hours. (*Letters*, II 82–83)

Frustrated by his long, slow work on *Portrait of the Artist*, Joyce here, like Bloom later, is fantasizing a popular literary success. In fact, Corelli's *Sorrows of Satan* had, at the time of its publication, higher initial sales than any previously published novel (Bigland, 156). Clearly, the book had a dubious fascination for Joyce, who, from the way he mentions it casually, seems to have assumed that everyone had read it. Years later, he described Marcel Proust arriving at a party in Paris in heavy fur coat, "like the hero of *The Sorrows of Satan*" (Colum, 151). By the time he was drafting the Scylla and Charybdis section of *Ulysses*, Joyce had John Eglinton refer to a project of Stephen's: "Have you found those six brave medicals, John Eglinton asked with elder's gall, to write *Paradise Lost* at your dictation? *The Sorrows of Satan*, he calls it" (*U* 9.19). Stephen, after smiling "Cranly's smile," merely recites mentally a bawdy Mulliganesque rhyme about a "jolly old medical" who "passed the female catheter."

Whether the six medical students are a variant of the infinite number of monkeys with typewriters, upon whom Stephen will rely to duplicate Milton's effort, or whether they are to be the amanuenses for a wholly new *Paradise Lost*, directed toward a modern sensibility—and seen from the point of view of Satan—is unclear. But we do have Corelli's work—a book with a contemporary turn-of-the-century setting that reinterprets the fall of Satan. Rather than a *Paradise Lost*, *The Sorrows of Satan* is a Faust variant; it involves the experience of one Geoffrey Tempest, an aspiring author, with his close friend Lucio Rimanez, a thinly disguised Lucifer. The novel has dated for a contemporary reader; it resembles the work of a somewhat awkward and very British d'Annunzio. Nevertheless, it still retains a curious sort of obsessive power. More surprisingly, I would argue that it has a number of elements that Joyce adapts to the form and substance of *Ulysses* (see Magalaner).

As with Joyce's works, the author's life looms behind *The Sorrows of Satan*. Corelli was a fascinating figure, notorious in the popular press at the time Joyce read her work, although she is almost completely forgotten today.[1] The oblivion into which Corelli has been cast is itself an important cultural effect, in part the result of the modernist movement with which she was contemporary. Suzanne Clark asserts that "[t]he modernist exclusion of everything but the forms of high art acted like a machine for cultural loss of memory" (6), and for numerous reasons Corelli should have been especially hard to forget. On its publication in 1895, *The Sorrows of Satan* achieved its astonishing sales record despite the fact that she had steadfastly refused to allow any review copies to be sent to the press. Everyone from Victoria and Gladstone to working-class women avidly read it. Because of her half-innocent taste for making inflammatory accusations, she had earned the mocking title, "The Life-Boat of Journalism." Corelli's first book, *A Romance of Two Worlds*, struck a chord with the public; her personal mysticism, which she dubbed "Electric Christianity," was at base a conventional enough Protestantism laced with elements of the popular Eastern religions, Theosophy, reincarnation, vague talk about "science," and a highly spiritual emphasis. A character in her novel *Ziska* defines art as the idealization and transfiguration of nature, and there is no reason to think Corelli would disagree with this idea. Although Joyce himself avoids this sort of language, it is well to remember that Virginia Woolf in her early essay, "Modern Fiction," praises Joyce by identifying him as a spiritual writer instead of a materialist like Wells, Galsworthy, and Bennett.

From childhood, Corelli dramatized herself; by her death in 1924, she had so confused the biographical issue that it only gradually emerged that she had been born out of wedlock to Charles Mackay, a failed man of letters and a journalist. After his wife's death, he married the woman who had borne the child and adopted his own daughter, Minnie (Bigland; Masters). Minnie Mackay, in Rebecca West's rather snobbish words, "had a mind like any milliner's apprentice; but she was something much more than a milliner's apprentice" (cited in Bigland, 39). After a failed attempt at a career as a piano *improvisatrice* and singer, Corelli took to writing to support her indigent and neurotic father and half brother, Eric, both of whom she worshiped, and both of whom specialized in treacly sentimental domestic verse, which generally failed to capture the public's fancy. The peculiar late

Victorian romanticism of Corelli's home coupled with its insistence on middle-class propriety contributed to a strange, hybrid sensibility in the young writer. More pragmatically, so did the combination of enormous aesthetic ambition with the pressing demand for an appropriately large income. The result in Corelli's writing—and in her life—was an especially extreme embodiment of many of the ideological contradictions of the late Victorian period. Notable among these were the contested terrains of "high" and popular art, of science and religion, and of materialism and spiritualism. Politically, Corelli articulated both the enthusiasm for democracy and the reverence for aristocracy, and in her figuration of womanhood she managed both to launch a radical protest against the secondary status of her sex and to affirm the image of Woman as the virginal Angel of the House. She would alternate between asserting that the highest art, such as her own, was not to be confused with popular novels churned out for a mass public and, when attacked by critics, claiming that the mass readership were the only fit judges. Although her explicit concerns shifted during her career—for instance, her attacks on Catholicism became more vicious after the turn of the century—most of her themes are sounded in her first published book, *A Romance of Two Worlds* (1886).

Corelli's *Romance* capitalized upon spiritualism, a major social movement that by 1886 had already established some respectability, but could still be presented as a radical challenge to bourgeois norms—a movement that simultaneously hinted at dark mysteries and comfortable Anglicanism. The *Romance* both stakes Corelli's claim to her own original variety of spiritualism and provides a running commentary on aspects of the movement that preceded her. Even minor details of the book, such as the sympathetic American couple who seem to serve no function in the plot, are illuminated when we remember that the spiritualist craze was originally an American import, and the more important spiritualist practitioners were often American up through the turn of the century.

But as her later work demonstrated, Corelli did not need to rely on the trappings of spiritualism for her popularity, although her image as a public figure retained the atmosphere of cultism and social transgression that had been established in *Romance*. Her second and third books, *Vendetta* (1886) and *Thelma* (1887), leaned heavily on spirituality but made no use of spiritualism or the supernatural. Corelli blended dialogically several of the novel form's subgenres, including the "silver fork" romance of high society, perfected by Bulwer-Lytton and Disraeli and practiced in a "feminine" mode by an immediate precursor whom she admired, "Ouida" (Marie-Louise de la Ramée,

1839–1908). With this she crossed the popular Christian romance suggested by Lew Wallace's *Ben-Hur: A Tale of the Christ* (1880), a genre whose best-known practitioner was her contemporary rival Hall Caine, and which was later brought to an erotic fever pitch by Robert Hichens. The mingling of eroticism and Christian spirituality may now seem unpromising material for bestselling novels, but it should be noted that the same perverse combination informs some of the work of Corelli's contemporaries the Decadents, notably Wilde, John Gray, and Lionel Johnson. It can be found in a playful form in Swinburne's "Laus Verneris" or "Anastoria," or in profoundly serious form in Hopkins. The same ideological conflicts that were being exercised in the work of these "high culture" writers found another field of play in the popular literary arena.

According to Brian Masters (6), before the First World War about 100,000 copies of her novels sold yearly, as compared to 45,000 for her nearest rival, Hall Caine, 35,600 for Mrs. Humphrey Ward, and 15,000 for H. G. Wells. By her death she had published some 34 volumes, mostly in her own distinctive subgenre of mystical romance, but also including poetry and topical essays, as well as scores of articles in newspapers and journals. Indeed, her novels came increasingly to include dialogical responses to issues of the day as presented in the newspapers, and especially to be aggressive rejoinders to critical attacks upon her. Much of the narration of her later novels could be characterized by Bakhtin's term, "the word with a sideward glance." And yet this did not much bother Corelli's audience. In her early survey of popular writing, Q. D. Leavis cited Corelli among "the great names of popular fiction," including Gene Stratton Porter and Hall Caine (62). Interestingly, Corelli is her marker not only of popularity, but also of artistic failure: "Dickens and George Eliot were near neighbors," she asserts, "but there is an unbridgeable and impassable gap between Marie Corelli and Henry James" (169).

In part, Corelli's success was due to the sincerity she was able to project. Rimanez, in *The Sorrows of Satan*, observes, "Not one author in many centuries writes from his own heart or as he truly feels—when he does, he becomes well-nigh immortal." Not only did Corelli claim to write from the heart, she publicly admitted that she considered herself the handmaiden of God, writing the outline of the true religion from inspiration. Indeed, *The Sorrows of Satan* was hailed on its publication by a number of influential churchmen. This, and the public adulation lavished on her, Corelli enjoyed as her due. She was shocked by the malicious press insinuations that she was working on a sequel, to be entitled *The Sins of Christ*, and by the rumors—probably unfounded—that she was engaging in Byronic incest with her beloved half brother. On the one hand, her books were hailed by readers like Gladstone as contributions to the spiritual salvation of England; on the other, they were frequently banned from libraries for fear of their pernicious influence.

But what first wounded then frustrated and finally enraged her were the damning press notices she received in nearly all the literary journals. Her revealed religion was labeled "pure bosh." One anonymous wit claimed that the secret of her popularity was that she wrote in "impeccably bad taste." In Reading Gaol, Oscar Wilde was asked by a friendly jailer whether he considered Corelli a great writer, and replied, "Now don't think I've anything against her *moral* character, but from the way she writes—*she ought to be here*" (Bigland, 164). Honestly baffled as to why so many reviewers she had never injured could fail to see her genius, Corelli launched a counterattack on the press. The press, willingly or not, were in league with Satan, she decided, and the fashionable "new" novels in the wake of Ibsen and Zola, her two *bêtes noirs*, were in fact responsible for the moral decay of England. Joyce, in his epistolary and poetic diatribes, could muster no more bitterness against the publishing establishment than did Corelli. This complaint against the critical establishment is the burden of *The Sorrows of Satan*. Where Corelli felt that the mass readership was corrupted by realism in literature, especially the popular novels of high society that exploited the loose morals of the rich for popular titillation, she treats in exactly the same way Grant Allen's *The Woman Who Did*—a serious, indeed "spiritual," exploration of love without marriage—and Ibsen's social dramas. Had she read it, *Dubliners* would no doubt have equally appalled her. Joyce, as *Ulysses* makes clear, saw the problem differently. When Lenehan spots Bloom pawing through used books and suggests he is purchasing *Leopoldo* or *The Bloom is on the Rye* (U 10.524), he is making Joyce's point—that we buy ourselves from the huckster's cart.

The Sorrows of Satan

Despite her huge female readership, Corelli's book does not really belong to the genre of sentimental domestic romance; and, in fact, rather than enlightening Gerty or Molly for us, it bears particular ironic significance for Stephen. The book is light on plot, but what there is concerns an aspiring author, Geoffrey Tempest, whose spiritually sensitive writings have been blasted in the press. Like Stephen,

Tempest enjoys fantasizing about literary revenge: "I smiled as I thought of the vengeance I would take on all those who had scorned and slighted me in my labour—how they should cower before me—how they should fawn at my feet like whipt curs and whine their fulsome adulation" (18); Stephen invokes exactly the same image in "Circe," when he exclaims, "Break my spirit, all of you, if you can! I'll bring you all to heel!" (*U* 15.4236). Suddenly, Tempest is rescued by an inheritance of several millions from a mysterious relative. Just as he learns of this bequest, the enigmatic Prince Lucio Rimanez, an infinitely wealthy and well-traveled exile, who offers to conduct Tempest into society and show him the uses of his money, visits him. As Tempest agrees with a handshake, thunder booms and the lights go out. In the remainder of the book, Tempest is guided through gambling hells and horse races by the dark prince, then attracts and marries the noble-born Lady Sibyl, who reveals herself as irrevocably corrupted by reading fashionable novels. She attempts to seduce Rimanez, who sadistically rejects her as Tempest looks on, and ultimately she dies horribly by her own hand. The heavy-handed morality play offers no real suspense or surprise of its own, and serves mainly as a scaffold on which Corelli loosely hangs a running commentary on contemporary mores, the corrupting influence of wealth, and, of course, the degeneracy of the popular and literary presses.

Ostensibly, the book's suspense should come from our awaiting the identification of the mysterious Rimanez, but in fact it is clear from the first pages that Rimanez is Ahrimanes, which is supposed to be a Zoroastrian name for Satan. Nevertheless, Corelli plays out the melodramatic mechanisms of suspense, including the death of one of Satan's victims just as he is about to reveal Rimanez's real nature. For Corelli, literary gesture overrides context and content. The novel is really a series of tableaux interspersed with abundant social commentary by the narrator, Tempest, or the principal speaker, Rimanez. Indeed, *tableaux vivants*, arranged by Rimanez, figure heavily in the novel. A related metaphor for the book's unnovelistic structure would be grand opera: at crucial points Rimanez bursts into song. We are constantly submerged in the melodramatic tradition of moral and sentimental tableaux of the sort, which Joyce parodies in "The Dead" as he shows Gabriel fatuously entitling his wife's pose "Distant Music."

But Corelli's didacticism is responsible for a series of technical ironies which, although the result of incompetence, must have intrigued Joyce. First, Tempest, having been established as a noble artist, one of the saved, is completely corrupted by his money and then saved again when, at the book's end, he sees the error of his ways. The narration is retrospective. Thus he fluctuates between his role as satirical butt and his earlier—and later—roles as Corelli's spokesman. Further, Rimanez, the diabolic figure, is made immensely attractive— handsome, dark, powerful, a brilliant raconteur, scientist, pianist, and singer; he is also, Corelli explains, very much a fallen angel, play- ing out a diabolic role. Although he must tempt Tempest, his deepest desire is that Tempest should turn away from him—indeed, on several occasions he tries to tell this to the obtuse Tempest—because he can reascend to heaven only when all mankind can turn toward God. "Pray for me then," he begs, "as one who has fallen from his higher and better self,—who strives, but who may not attain—who labours under heavy punishment,—who would fain reach Heaven, but who by the cursed will of man, and man alone, is kept in Hell" (339).

Thus Rimanez, no less than Tempest, alternates between devil's advocate and Corelli's advocate, until we have an overlapping series of ironies reminiscent of Stephen Dedalus's alternating identification with Christ and with Satan in *Portrait* and *Ulysses*. It is as if Corelli, through what appears to be a lack of technical mastery, winds up producing an effect of sophisticated modernist irony. For Stephen plays out his own diabolic role, from casual blasphemy to his ulti- mate *non serviam*, at one minute destroying the universe and defying all comers, at another cowering at the crack of thunder. A performer throughout, Stephen disavows even his most complete work of art in the book, his Shakespeare soliloquy in Scylla and Charybdis, claim- ing not to believe in his own theory. As Rimanez observes when ques- tioned about whether he believes what he has just said, "I think I was born to be an actor...I speak to suit the humour of the hour, and without meaning a single word I say" (64).

Passionate and violent, dégagé and sophisticated, he shares super- ficial qualities with both Heathcliff and Wilde, though without the former's emotional intensity or the latter's actual brilliance. Like Stephen, he is the relentless enemy of materialism; like Stephen, he suffers the Agenbite of Inwit, or as he puts it, "A very strange ill- ness...Remorse." Like Stephen, he fears and scorns women—all women, that is, except the angelic Mavis Clare, a popular author of surpassing spirituality, adored by millions of readers, but attacked, out of sheer jealousy, by the critics. Clare, who, like Corelli, lives in a cottage with her two cute dogs, surrounded by framed quotations from Shelley and Byron, plays no part in the novel's plot; she is simply there, charming, graceful, eternally youthful and surpassingly lovely, the confidante of princes and men of real genius, for Rimanez and, eventually Tempest also, to worship.

Corelli, Modernism, Feminism

Fredric Jameson, discussing the breakdown of the "older realisms" at the end of the nineteenth century, argues that out of it emerged "not modernism alone, but rather two literary and cultural structures, dialectically interrelated and necessarily presupposing each other for any adequate analysis," i.e., "high" literature and "popular" or "mass" literature (Jameson 1981, 207). Thus, it is no coincidence that the beginning of popular literature as a "mass" phenomenon, which most analysts date around the end of the nineteenth century, should coincide with the flowering of an oppositional literary ideology, later formalized as a tenet of the professional teaching of modern literature that stressed the enormous distance between popular and high art. Trinh Minh-ha is one of several recent critics who have argued that the "myth" of such a distinction serves political purposes:

> The elite-versus-masses opposition [must remain intact], basically unchallenged, if it is to serve a conservative political and ideological purpose—in other words, if (what is defined as) "art" is to exist at all. One of the functions of this "art for the masses" is, naturally, to contrast with the other higher art for the "elite," and thereby to enforce its elitist values. The wider the distance between the two, the firmer the stand of conservative art. (Minh-ha, 13)

Further, as Andreas Huyssens has argued most fully, (male) Modernism projected popular art as its feminine Other, the repressed second term of an aesthetic binary opposition. And since Corelli's public image was a hypertrophy of the "feminine," her public pronouncements were, within a limited arena, overtly feminist, and her work relied on a traditionally feminine aesthetic of sentiment and melodrama, she was the perfect victim of the Modernist work of cultural forgetting.

Yet it was far from obvious at the start that Corelli could be dismissed. George Meredith and Oscar Wilde, Gladstone and Henry Irving were early admirers, as were Ellen Terry and Ella Wheeler Wilcox. She was the only writer to be invited to Edward VII's coronation, at the King's express wish. Her fellow spiritualist, Yeats, called upon her in Stratford, though he refused the offer of her gondola out of a reluctance to be "paragraphed." Even writers who never took her seriously sometimes found themselves perversely fascinated by her work. I believe Joyce was one of these. It is possible that Bloom's mysterious erotic correspondent, "Martha Clifford," is a disguised allusion to Corelli, who was accused by the journalist W. T. Stead of portraying herself as Mavis Clare ("whose initials it may be remarked are the same as the authoress") in that novel (cited in Bigland, 163). After all, Joyce presents the question as a conundrum in "Ithaca": "Let H. F. be L. B.... find M. C." (*U* 17.1841). Still later, in *Finnegans Wake*, the artist-figure Glugg is searching for "the best and schortest way of blacking out a caughtalock of all the sorrors of Sexton" *(FW* 230).

Joyce's insistent return to Corelli may be more significant than it appears at first glance; indeed, the similarities between Joyce and Corelli are at least as striking as their differences. Both began writing with an ambitious pseudonym, used thinly disguised versions of themselves in their novels, and were convinced of their own genius from the beginning of their careers, a conviction that took the form of a near-obsession with Shakespeare. Both bitterly protested the sort of books boosted by major reviewers, and used the medium of literature to enact elaborate revenge for personal slights. Both acutely felt their own marginalization by the cultural elites, Joyce because of his Irish Catholic background and his family's fall into poverty, Corelli because of her gender and her family's fall into poverty; both Joyce and Corelli indulged in fantasies of aristocratic family backgrounds. Both were utterly convinced of the ultimate importance of their art. If Corelli asserted, "I believe the Power of the Pen to be the greatest power for good or evil in the world" (Corelli 1905, 304), that is no different from Joyce insisting to Grant Richards that in his writing of *Dubliners*, "in composing my chapter of moral history in exactly the way I have composed it I have taken the first step towards the spiritual liberation of my country" (*Letters*, I 62–63).

This conviction of the significance of their enterprise was one tenet Modernists as diverse as Mallarmé, Eliot, and Lawrence shared with the Romantics, and one way this significance was manifested was through the inward sense of election. But setting aside the author's self-image, Modernists also looked to negative critical reaction for the outward sign of their inner grace. At least since Flaubert, serious artists have invoked the enmity of philistines as the guarantor of their own quality. As Flaubert put it in a letter to Louise Colet, "You can calculate the worth of a man by the number of his enemies and the importance of a work of art by the amount that it is attacked."[2] Joyce, Pound, and Lawrence in different ways frequently endorsed this sentiment, and so did Corelli—although, unlike the others, she was able to add an appeal to the instinctive taste of the public, as opposed to the reviewers. And, at least from one angle, the objections of bourgeois reviewers to Corelli's work—that it was indecorous and unrestrained, plotless and without distinct characters, sexually provocative, almost blasphemous, that it offended against standards of decorum, that it was "too much"—echo, in another key, their objections to Modernist works.

I have already argued that Corelli's distinctive blend of sensuality and a somewhat offbeat Christianity was paralleled in the work of the Decadents who were her contemporaries, and the same argument can be extended to the foregrounding of the sexual and sensual within a "spiritual" context that we find in Joyce, Lawrence, and late Yeats. The characteristic Modernist use of myth through scattered allusions operating within a present-day narrative is equally characteristic of Corelli, especially in novels such as *A Romance of Two Worlds* or *Ziska*, and just as Joyce creates a modern Odysseus in the corrupt contemporary world of *Ulysses*, Corelli in *The Master-Christian* imagines Christ returned as a child to the corruption of modern Europe (and especially that of the modern Roman Catholic Church). If Lawrence's characters lose a kind of individuality because they inevitably embody larger principles of his own cultural myth, so clearly, do Corelli's. Critics see Yeats's spiritual cosmology as Modernist, the working of his own "individual myth"; Corelli's idiosyncratic and eclectic Electric Christianity is less elaborate, but it is no more zany. Even on a formal level it could be argued that Corelli structures her narratives musically, with frequent thematic references to music, just as Modernists from Mallarmé through Forster are said to do. Her use of melodramatic *tableaux* to punctuate and culminate the action has a curiously Modernist effect in disrupting the novel's diegesis. But perhaps the most provocative coincidence between Corelli's works and those of the Modernists is that both are inescapably *internal* narratives, whatever novelistic gestures the authors make. Corelli's best works, such as *The Sorrows of Satan*, resemble *Heart of Darkness*, *The Waves*, or *Women in Love*, in that each has the obsessive internal coherence and conviction of a powerful dream.

How, then, is Corelli unlike the Modernists? Or, to put it another way, to what are we responding when we immediately classify her work as Not Serious Art? One element is no doubt verbal style: Corelli never strays too far from cliché, although she seldom lapses into it entirely. Allowing for historical differences in what a reader would find to be interesting discourse, we would have to call her style immensely readable. In part this is because it is primarily oral in character—repetitive, self-interrupting, pleonastic, paratactic. Corelli's later success as a lecturer, even before intellectual audiences, shows that her rhetoric was naturally adaptable to the lectern. Another, related, element, is the lack of *difficulty* of her work; where Modernists often erected barriers to the immediate assimilation of their narratives through allusions, narrative disruptions, or stylistic complexity, Corelli seldom does this. Although she does scatter arcane allusions throughout her work (for instance, to ancient Chaldean wisdom), the reader soon gathers that he or she is not expected to be knowledgeable in such areas. Where Modernists appealed to an elite of intelligence and cultural fluency, Corelli appealed to an elite of the spirit—one that was much easier for a young or little-educated reader to imagine herself joining.

But undoubtedly the major reason we would exclude Corelli from the ranks of serious artists is her use of the related modes of sentimentality and melodrama within the framework of novelistic romance. Yet even this move is ambiguous, for, as Peter Brooks has argued, we must "recognize the melodramatic mode as a central fact of the modern sensibility" (Brooks, 21). Brooks's characterization of melodrama certainly describes Corelli's work, with its "indulgence of strong emotionalism; moral polarization and schematization; extreme states of being; situations, actions; overt villainy, persecution of the good, and final reward of virtue; inflated and extravagant expression; dark plottings, suspense, breathtaking peripety" (Brooks, 11–12). But then, to a degree, this also describes the novels of D. H. Lawrence. One difference between her work and that of the canonical writers Brooks discusses is that Corelli's is a *literalized* melodrama. Where Brooks finds in Balzac a charge of more intense significance behind the surfaces of things, a pull toward the spiritual reality, which is the true scene of the novel's drama, in Corelli this spiritual dimension is quite explicit. Rimanez *is* Satan, just as the nameless boy in *The Master Christian* is Christ returned. Still, if James and Conrad—to name only two early Modernist writers—make frequent use of the melodramatic mode, then it is difficult to say why they are *essentially* different from Corelli. A parallel argument can be made for the closely related mode of the sentimental. Suzanne Clark in *Sentimental Modernism*, extending the arguments of Jane Tompkins, Nina Baym, and Janet Todd, proposes that the Modernist excision of the sentimental is related to the exclusion of women writers such as Millay from the canon. The modern woman writer is thus stymied, because "the past exists as an unwarranted discourse, tied to the sentimental domestic configurations which wrote the modern woman into social existence" (Clark, 37).

As a cultural figure, Corelli combined the attractions of a controversial popular novelist like Alexandre Dumas *fils* with the somewhat dubious moral authority of a Mary Baker Eddy. She was always difficult to *place*, despite her talent for exposing to public scrutiny her own contradictions and hypocrisies. However strenuously she insisted on her European origins and her self-bestowed title of Contessa (an affectation that greatly annoyed Ouida, who had genuine aristocratic connections), she was just as emphatically British and—aside from her idiosyncratic brand of feminism—insular in her politics. "Speaking personally as a woman, I have no politics, and want none," she asserted. "I only want the British Empire to be first and foremost in everything" (Corelli 1905, 156). She would lambaste the press for its toadying reports of "high society" events, and then complain to a newspaper because it neglected to mention her among the Prince of Wales's guests at a function. The newspaper, of course, gleefully pounced on this contradiction. But however readily she offered herself to mockery, there were undoubtedly also elements of envy and misogyny in the relentless attacks she sustained during her life and—in her biographies—up to the present day. She was, after all, the classic "old maid," without husband or children, and her enormous success must have seemed a variety of witchcraft to critics and to bitter rivals such as Hall Caine. Mark Twain, who visited her in Stratford, described her in his diary as "fat and shapeless; she has a gross animal face; she dresses for sixteen, and awkwardly and pathetically imitates the innocent graces and witcheries of that dearest and sweetest of all ages." In sum, "she is the most offensive sham, inside and out, that misrepresents and satirizes the human race today" (cited in Masters, 4). Admittedly, Twain was unwell during his visit and had been somewhat manipulated by Corelli; but still, the violence of his reaction to her elaborately lionizing him suggests that she had struck unconscious chords in him.

Corelli's feminism, however limited in its scope, was very strongly expressed in one area: she felt that women artists were not taken seriously because of their gender. As for the authoress attempting to make a career:

> She must fight like the rest, unless she prefers to lie down and be walked over. If she elects to try for a first place, it will take her all her time to win it, and, when won, to hold it; and, in the event of her securing success, she must not expect any chivalrous consideration from the opposite sex, or any special kindness or sympathy from her own. For the men will consider her "out of her sphere" if she writes books instead of producing babies, and the women will, in nine cases out of ten, begrudge her the freedom and independence she enjoys. (Corelli 1905, 334)

Frequently, she argues, men have either slighted women artists or have attempted to claim credit for their work. "Of how many books, bearing a woman's name on the title-page it is said—'Her husband helped her,'—or 'She got Mr. So-and-So to write the descriptive part!'" (Corelli 1905, 157). Here Corelli was speaking from painful experience, as her half brother, Eric, for many years secretly insinuated that he was responsible for her works. In *The Master Christian*, when the fiancé of the painter Angela Sovrani, himself a minor artist, is confronted with her masterpiece, he first speculates as to how he might claim credit for it, then belittles it with polite criticism, and finally in a jealous rage literally stabs her in the back.

Everywhere Joyce looked in Corelli, he would have found a curiously distorting mirror. If Dedalus is a triumph of ambiguous self-portrayal, Mavis Clare is a horrible warning against the novelist's autobiographical impulse. By the time she wrote *The Sorrows of Satan* Corelli was already a victim of authorial megalomania, an obsession Joyce was able to distance and, at times, to mock in himself. Corelli felt no such ambivalence. In later life Corelli's fascinated identification with Shakespeare led her to move to Stratford-on-Avon, keep an Italian gondolier on her permanent staff, and hint mysteriously at literary reincarnation. Lady Asquith's driver once observed to Shaw, "I believe it was an attribute of great artists that their own immortality was apparent to them during their lifetime," to which Shaw returned, "What about Marie Corelli gliding down the Avon in a gondola with her parasol?" (O'Connor, 224). Whatever sense of identification Joyce may have felt with the great dramatist, it gave way to Stephen's brilliant attempt to prove by algebra that Shakespeare was really Stephen Dedalus.

Corelli and Joyce stand at the start of our century, both convinced from youth of their own genius; both busy writing and acting out the myth of themselves. Each was bitter against the publishing establishment, and sought literary revenge for slights; each was obsessed by betrayal; each was fascinated by the Byronic pose. Both authors, irresistibly drawn to self-portrayal, were convinced of the ultimate, religious importance of art, and the crucial significance of its cheapening for a mass readership. And yet, the judgement of cultural elites through the first half of the twentieth century first constructed them as polar opposites within the literary spectrum and then, with the same gesture that hailed Joyce as the ultimate modern figure of the artist-hero, cast Corelli into outer darkness.

Chapter Four

Riddling the Reader to Write Back

—Wait, said Cissy, I'll run ask my uncle Peter over there what's the time by his conundrum. (*U* 13.535)

The Reader's Challenge

My thesis here is that some modernist writers, and, preeminently, Joyce in *Ulysses*, create a new relationship to the reader by not only inviting the reader's participation in the literary act (which is itself a dialogical interchange created by the interanimation of the acts of writing and reading), but also by soliciting the reader's engagement in actively creating the text that the reader then goes on to read. In part, this is a quality of writing that Barthes claimed characterizes the *writerly* text as opposed to the *readerly*, the modern as opposed to the classic literary text, but I mean something entirely less metaphoric than this when I speak of the reader's active engagement. That reading *Ulysses* is an unusual experience, one with rules and conventions of its own, is a familiar idea in the history of Joyce criticism; indeed, it seems to have hit nearly everyone who has had the experience of teaching the book or participating in a reading group devoted to it. At the beginning of *Reading Joyce's "Ulysses,"* Daniel Schwarz comments that "*Ulysses* teaches us how to read itself," and adds that "the ventriloquy of its various styles establishes an unusually complex relationship between text and reader" (Schwarz, 2). Declan Kiberd makes a similar point when he states that *Ulysses* "is offered as a book that is co-authored rather than simply read" (Kiberd, 473). It is full of moments in which readers are invited—I would say *required*—to take an active hand in the book's composition. As a trivial example, in the opening chapter, Mulligan begins to recite a bawdy rhyme:

> —*For old Mary Ann*
> *She doesn't care a damn.*
> *But, hising up her petticoats…(U 1.382)*

And then continues inaudibly, cramming his mouth with fry. It is left to the reader to continue the rhyme with a line such as

>   *She's pissing like a man.*

I do not mean to refer here to the fact that Mabel Worthington located an Irish song whose chorus concluded with a line like this, presumably making it the "correct" choice for the reader (Gifford, 21). It is perfectly possible to come up with a similar line in total ignorance of the canon of Irish bawdry. My point is that the reader's activity in looking for a line that would fulfill the formal requirements of a recognized verse form while also fulfilling the narrative requirements of the crude anecdote—a line that would also be appropriate to the interpersonal situation between Mulligan and Haines, his main audience—models the activities in which the reader will tacitly be asked to engage throughout the book. Bakhtin does not discuss this sort of reader/author relationship, but it might be argued that it constitutes a kind of literalization of the dialogical relationship itself, wherein the reader's language (no longer merely a reaction to the novel's narration), once it is offered as a response to the puzzle, itself then becomes part of the novel to which the reader must respond.

A complete taxonomy of such instances is not really possible, because the activities of the reader become so complex and the demands upon her so various and ambiguous as the text progresses. But Patrick McCarthy has made a start, suggesting that "true riddles," like the one asked by the Sphinx, are "descriptions of objects in terms intended to suggest something entirely different" (McCarthy, 18). He continues:

> Closely related to the "true riddle" are other types of difficult questions. Classified according to the relationship between question and answer, the most important of these varieties of riddles may be grouped in the following categories: conundrums and other witty questions [often based on puns]; genealogical and arithmetical puzzles; and questions that are not meant to be answered, either because the questions make no sense or because they deal with the private experience of the riddler or require other arcane knowledge. (McCarthy, 18)

The conundrum could be exemplified by Athy's question in *Portrait* ("Why is the county Kildare like the leg of a fellow's breeches?"; *P* 25), by Lenehan's question ("What opera is like a railwayline?") and its answer ("The Rose of Castile," punning on "rows of cast steel"; *U* 7.588, 591);

and by the question Bloom has intermittently worried at for thirty years ("Where was Moses when the candle went out?"; *U* 17.2070) and only on the evening of June 16, 1904, has managed to solve. Here, the answer ("in the dark") depends on how the word "where" is construed.[1]

The genealogical riddle, McCarthy points out, is exemplified by Bloom's mildly enigmatic self-description, "Brothers and sisters had he none, / Yet that man's father was his grandfather's son" (*U* 17.1352). Stephen's riddle in "Nestor" may belong to the last category. We are given "the answer" to it ("the fox burying his grandmother under a holly bush"; *U* 2.115), and then we are confronted with the puzzle of what Stephen's "solution" itself means. At that point, we may embrace the various anagogical solutions offered by the New Critical tradition allied with Freudian interpretation (the grandmother stands in for Stephen's buried mother, the fox is Christ, who is also Stephen), or we may ask whether in fact it "means" anything at all, or rather whether it stands in for a "nonsense" solution, a kind of Zen *koan*— which itself is a kind of solution, however dismaying to those (like his students) who are attempting to play the game.

When Joyce told Benoît-Méchin, "I've put in so many enigmas and puzzles that it will keep the professors busy for centuries arguing over what I meant, and that's the only way of insuring one's immortality" (*JJII* 521), the professors naturally enough thought in terms of significant motifs, major themes, and greater meanings; but I suspect that Joyce was thinking, as he wrote, on the local level. Throughout *Ulysses* we are presented with riddles, puzzles, and conundrums, all reminiscent of the offerings of the "light weekly" magazines, notably *Answers* and *Tit-Bits*, that formed a staple of popular reading around the turn of the century, and about which I will have a great deal more to say in chapter six. Some puzzles hardly seem to merit the name, although even Stephen's witty definition of a pier as "a disappointed bridge" (*U* 2.39) proves too riddling for some of his students. Some are incomplete, such as the rhyme Stephen thinks of just before delivering his own to the students: "*Riddle me, riddle me, randy ro. / My father gave me seeds to sow*" (*U* 2.88). As Thornton explains, one variant of this continues, "The seed was black and the ground was white. / Riddle me that and I'll give you a pipe," the traditional solution being "writing a letter" (Thornton, 30). We might think of the more semiotic writing image that occurs to Stephen in the next episode, "signs on a white field" (*U* 3.415).

But puzzles need not be thematically explicit or identified as such in *Ulysses*. Initial readers of the book, including some online reading/ discussion groups, inevitably tend to push the discussion toward a group of interpretive puzzles, most of them familiar to Joyceans, a few of which are the result of an initial naive reading. Some of this happens because Joyce writes in the peculiar way he does; some of it happens because, in the twentieth century, we read in the peculiar way we do, with an odd gusto for puzzles included. A particular sort of puzzle is offered by Joyce's use of stream-of-consciousness narration and its attendant narrative shortcuts. These create problems for the reader that are exacerbated by Stephen's allusive habits of thought. One such allusive and puzzling passage occurs as Stephen is walking on Sandymount Strand. He imagines the drowned corpse reported in the papers being eaten by fish, and thinks, "God becomes man becomes fish becomes barnacle goose becomes featherbed mountain" (*U* 3.477). Here the reader's ingenuity is tested as Stephen imagines a chain, each link of which is composed of different kinds of substitution or metamorphosis: God becomes man in the incarnation; man becomes fish either when the fish eats the man (as he has just envisioned happening to the drowned man) or when Christ becomes identified with the sign of the fish; the fish becomes barnacle goose either because Stephen imagines the goose eating the fish, or because, as Gifford informs us, the medieval Irish once imagined geese were born from barnacles, which might in turn be imagined to be a form of fish; much of the goose becomes a featherbed when plucked; and Featherbed Mountain is in the vicinity of Dublin. There are, of course, other possibilities to explain the loosely conceived transformations here; but my point is that the reader must supply them.

In this exercise, we are trying to follow Stephen's train of thought as he consciously creates a poetic train of images and we supply the unstated rationale for each transformation. A similar "reader quiz" is offered by any of the numerous passages in which Bloom's stream of consciousness leads from one item to the next in a way dictated by his experience, but with the actual logic of the links suppressed. One such occurs as Bloom sits in the Ormond, writing to Martha Clifford, but pretending to Richie Goulding that he is answering an ad for a commercial traveller.

> Blot over the other so he can't read. There. Right. Idea prize titbit. Something detective read off blottingpad. Payment at the rate of guinea per col. Matcham often thinks the laughing witch. Poor Mrs Purefoy. U. P.: up. (*U* 11.901)

Nothing terribly subtle is going on here, and most readers will have no trouble following the associations, but they must keep in mind the particulars that have occupied Bloom during the first part of his day. Bloom is probably reminding himself to use the blottingpaper several times so as to confuse the reversed image, in case Goulding later tries to read what Bloom has been writing. Bloom realizes this might be an idea for a *Prize Titbits* story, although the detective reading a message by holding the blotter to the mirror was a hoary chestnut even in 1904. Thinking of the remuneration for a *Prize Titbits* story, he naturally thinks of the opening sentence of Beaufoy's, which he read in the jakes, and since he once already has confused the names Beaufoy and Purefoy in talking with Josie Breen (*U* 8.276), he thinks again of his friend Mina Purefoy. But he also thinks of the former Josie Powell (from whom he learned about Mrs. Purefoy's confinement), now saddled with an addled husband who is trying to sue over the anonymous postcard reading "U. P.: up."

None of this is particularly difficult. Further, we should note that none of the readerly skills called upon by this passage are strictly literary or poetic. It demands of the reader a good memory, concentration, and an eye for significant plot details—the same sort of qualities called upon by the puzzles in the light weeklies. Hugh Kenner describes the "aesthetic of delay" in *Ulysses* and presents many examples in which various subtleties depend upon our noticing trivial details and keeping them in mind, since, as he says, "Joyce is all trivia" (Kenner 1987, 76). Indeed, Kenner's famous dispute with Wyndham Lewis, where he argues that Lewis is right about the book being like the grinding of a huge machine, but fails to notice that Joyce's purpose in building it that way is parodic, could be stripped of its ideological wrappings to suggest that *Ulysses* instead has important links to the conceptual and formal universe of *Tit-Bits* and *Answers*. Indeed, Kenner early on spotted Joyce's reliance on the popular culture of his time—the "thrillers, patent medicine tracts, and comic books" which he perused "in search of their metaphoric assumptions as social images." These assumptions Kenner identifies as, "that mind is mechanism, that the Body Politic is wired together, that human relationships, domestic or civic, are reducible to problems in engineering" (Kenner 1956, 162). We might try imagining the import of such a statement shorn of its reflexive New Critical humanism and its eagerness to find mechanistic reductiveness anywhere outside canonical literature. Kiberd articulates that sort of transmutation in attitude when he argues, "if Leopold Bloom's mind is a tissue of quotations from editorials, articles and jingles, Joyce does not mock him for that....Unlike Nietzsche or Lawrence, who feared and fled mass man, Joyce showed how lovable and reassuring such a creature could be" (Kiberd, 468).

Riddles in *Ulysses*

Ulysses is seeded with puzzles and games, and some of the puzzles have kept Joyceans happily occupied for generations: Who is M'Intosh, who narrates "Cyclops," what is the meaning of "U. P.: up," who is Martha Clifford—a puzzle that appears in "Ithaca," in good *Answers* format, as "let H. F. be L. B...find M. C." (*U* 17.1842). Just as Mulligan claims that Stephen "proves by algebra that Hamlet's grandson is Shakespeare's grandfather" (*U* 1.555), here we are invited to prove by algebra the identity of Bloom's correspondent. Similarly, in "Ithaca," the question "Who was M'Intosh" is presented as a "self-involved enigma" that Bloom did not comprehend as he prepared for bed (*U* 17.2063). Although much of "Ithaca" presents requests for information (for example, as to Bloom's thoughts and actions), fairly frequently the questions take on the aura of a quiz, puzzle, or riddle, calling not upon special knowledge, but logical, verbal, or mathematical manipulation. The question, "What relation existed between their ages?" yields a long paragraph of rather arbitrary numerical manipulations ("In 1936 when Bloom would be 70 and Stephen 54 their ages initially in the ratio of 16 to 0 would be as 17 ½ to 13 ½"; *U* 17.446).

Certainly there is an element of parody in this, especially in the outrageous extremes to which the numerical comparison is forced, but there is no doubt that we are also invited to join in the calculations. And a puzzle to cap this one is suggested by the fact that the calculation is mined with rather obvious errors throughout, leaving us to wonder whether Joyce was bad at arithmetic, or whether Bloom was, or whether whatever intervening paraliterary entity, such as an "Arranger," we may conjure up is to be held responsible instead. Bloom's keeping of Martha Clifford's "transliterated name and address...in reversed alphabetic boustrophedonic punctated quadrilinear cryptogram (vowels suppressed) N.IGS./WI.UU.OX/W.OKS. MH/Y.IM" (*U* 17.1799) has, as John Gordon comments, "the feel of stage-managed make-believe." Why not, he asks, keep the secret name and address between the pages of *Thoughts from Spinoza*, where Molly would never find them; in fact, why write them down, since he knows them by heart? "There is a juvenile secret-handshake-and-code-ring quality about all of this that has more to do with fantasy than with the serious management of a serious affair" (Gordon, 83–84). Gordon goes on to cite the discovery of Richard Hemminge that the boustrophedonic code in fact breaks down in the last line, to read not B.RN for the "BARN" part of "DOLPHIN'S BARN" but "NR.B"—suggesting Nora Barnacle? (Gordon, 87). Or perhaps simply suggesting that Joyce, or Bloom, is no master at puzzles, however fond he was of them. A far simpler puzzle—one that is patently insoluble, although no reader can resist trying—is the completion of the sentence that Bloom begins to write on the beach, "I...AM. A." (*U* 13.1258). Man? Jew? Naughty boy? Stick in the mud? Cuckold? Anonymous? The possibilities are endless.

Here, as often elsewhere, Joyce's point seems to be that even the remarkable access to Bloom's consciousness that we are afforded in this book will not necessarily give us the answers to fundamental questions: How does Bloom see himself, in a word? What is the extent of his complicity in Molly's infidelity? Who was responsible for the interruption of their marital relations? Such, for Joyce, are the mysteries of the thinking mind. Ellmann records that he asked Budgen one evening, "Why all this fuss and bother about the mystery of the unconscious? What about the mystery of the conscious? What do they know about that? (*JJII* 436). Like Bakhtin, Joyce believes that the consciousness is as complex and unknowable as any posited, but unobservable, id could ever be. I have always felt that it is possible that neither Bloom nor his wife knows which of them is responsible for the cessation in their marital relations—each seems tacitly to blame the other, and our access to the consciousness of each, amazingly enough, does not resolve the question. This is the sort of mystery we usually relegate to the unconsciousness, but that, as Joyce was almost uniquely aware, also pervades the consciousness—and which he modeled in Bloom's unremitting, but unsuccessful, efforts to banish Boylan from his awareness.

Riddles, problems, puzzles, and quizzes such as these may be said to exist on the surface level of the text, but Joyce's narrative technique is responsible for another, submerged set of problems that closely mimic those at the immediate textual level. These are questions or issues we may feel we need to resolve in order to have a satisfactory reading experience, but which Joyce does not directly pose as problems. Because so much of the novel is filtered through the subjectivity of one or another character, we are not informed of items that do not strike the consciousness of the protagonists; and because Joyce's narration here, as in *Portrait*, is fragmentary rather than continuous, much occurs that is never narrated. Thus another set of questions: Do the Blooms have an indoor toilet in addition to the outdoor one, and if so, where is it? Who paid the rent at the tower? Were Molly's parents married, and in any case, just who is Lunita Laredo? Who moved the furniture in the Blooms' house, and why? How did Stephen get to Sandymount Strand from school? Indeed, there are a group of minor uncertainties regarding the exact paths the characters take during the day—uncertainties that in an ordinary novel would not even arise, but that, in this novel, we are almost compelled to consider (see Gunn and Hart, passim). The questions arising from untold events are even larger in implication: What happened during Bloom's goodbye to Molly in the morning, and what did he tell her? How did Stephen injure his hand? Kenner's thesis, that he hurt it in a fight with Mulligan at Westland Row station, is wonderfully imaginative, if unlikely (Kenner 1987, 116). But it demonstrates the lengths of collaborative involvement to which readers are enticed—or driven.

Another "silent" issue in the novel arises from the problem of setting. Aside from some ambiguities about the details of his apartment, we are relatively well acquainted with Bloom's house, perhaps because it is a conventional setting for an urban novel. But, as Fritz Senn was among the first to point out, the opening of the book at the tower, assuming we knew nothing whatever about the book before beginning it, would be baffling in the extreme, almost as if Joyce were playing a joke on the reader's expectations. What location has a "gunrest," a "stairhead" (whatever that may be), a parapet, surrounding mountains, and Dublin bay? A tower is mentioned, but since Mulligan blesses it, we would probably assume it is visible to him, not that he is inhabiting it. But once we have deduced or been informed of that fact, we are still not told reliably of its location (Sandycove) until much later in the book. And what is going on? Mulligan is conducting a mock mass, but the import of this is rather muffled by the fact that we are never informed of a very fundamental fact—whether he is protestant or catholic. This is, perhaps, even more puzzling since at least during most of the first page it appears that he is the book's protagonist. And he is responsible for one of the book's first minor puzzles, in that the "long slow whistle of call" (*U* 1.24) he gives is mysteriously answered by "two strong shrill whistles" (*U* 1.26) from someone or something: From Haines, down below? From Stephen, despite his displeasure? From a passing mailboat, whose plume of steam Mulligan sees at a distance and anticipates with his own whistle, like the tawdry magician he is impersonating?

A final sort of puzzle, problem, or challenge, is the one posed by Joyce's use of stylistic "filters," beyond which we can often dimly discern the virtual existence of realistic passages in something like the book's initial style. Roughly from "Aeolus" on, we also have passages of fantasy, satire, ironic commentary—recuperate them how we will, they are clearly something other than narration in the book's initial realistic style. And increasingly, as we approach the "Circe" chapter, we must decide whether there is a way in which a presumption of ordinary realism can be maintained, or whether it breaks down completely. Perhaps those critics (like Stuart Gilbert) who believe in telepathy, metempsychosis, séances, and other psychic phenomena (or who, like John Gordon, simply believe that Joyce, to some degree, believed in them) negotiated a kind of compromise. This goes some way to explaining the places where, for example, Bloom in "Circe" seems to hallucinate (if that is what the character is meant to be doing) words that only Stephen has heard, earlier in the day. But Gordon's devotion to the empirical world leads him into the recognition (or invention) of some wonderful puzzles where others fail to see any: for instance, during Bloom's trial in "Circe," where J. J. O'Molloy testifies in the persona of Seymour Bushe and begins to quote from him in the words Stephen has heard in the newsroom, Gordon demonstrates that Bloom might well have failed to replace the receiver after speaking with MacHugh, and thus would have heard at least a garbled version of the speech (Gordon, 172–73). Here, it is only because Gordon is looking for a pragmatic explanation for Bloom's knowledge—or what we interpret as Bloom's knowledge—that he is driven to find such a clever explanation for it.

As the book progresses, there are many instances where the reader must invent or resurrect passages that a conventionally realistic novel, or even the novel implied in the book's initial style, would have made explicit. As Joyce introduces increasingly dense and distorting narrative and stylistic filters, it becomes increasingly difficult for the reader to do this. Still, for the most part the text holds plenty of clues. To take a simple example, in "Nausicaa," where a romance novelist is narrating the spiritual union of Gerty and the handsome stranger on the beach, when we come to the line, "His hands and his face were working" (*U* 13.694), we are quick to "translate" what in a romance novel would be a conventional signifier of overpowering emotion into a statement that in reality, Bloom is feverishly masturbating. This process involves a sort of double reading, in which we first assimilate the situation described through the extreme stylization and then reexamine the narration for clues to a sort of parallel reality that we regard as the book's literal level. Of course, our assumption that the "true" series of events is the more naturalistic, the less dignified, of the alternatives is itself an ideological choice; but it is of a kind we make daily. The problem of translation becomes most acute in "Oxen of the Sun," in which Joyce overlays the minimal action with dense stylistic filters reprising the canon of literary styles in English. Because the kind of ideology and life-world these passages are normally used to portray are very distant from Joycean naturalism, we are left with stylizations requiring considerable leaps in translation. When a passage in the style of Malory states that Bloom has been smitten by a dragon, we must consult other less- or differently distorted passages in the book to realize that in conventional novelistic terms (or in the consensus life-world that is implied beyond the stylistic filters) he was stung by a bee.

The Secret Passage

I would like here to consider at greater length one of the most entertaining and baffling passages in "Oxen." The Purefoy birth has just been announced and is followed by an animated discussion of misbirths, climaxed by the medical and ethical problem of Siamese twins, one of them born dead. Stephen, who is appealed to by Bloom, invokes "the ecclesiastic ordinance forbidding man to put asunder what God has joined." The text continues:

> But Malachias' tale began to freeze them with horror. He conjured up the scene before them. The secret panel beside the chimney slid back and in the recess appeared...Haines! Which of us did not feel his flesh creep? He had a portfolio full of Celtic literature in one hand, in the other a phial marked *Poison*. Surprise, horror, loathing were depicted on all faces while he eyed them with a ghastly grin. I anticipated some such reception, he began with an eldritch laugh, for which, it seems, history is to blame. (*U* 14.1010)

Haines continues, melodramatically claiming responsibility for the Childs murder, and then lapses into mock-Synge, claiming he has been "tramping Dublin this while back with my share of songs and himself after me the like of a soulth or a bullawurrus." He claims that this images both his and Ireland's hell.

> It is what I tried to obliterate my crime. Distractions, rookshooting, the Erse language (he recited some), laudanum (he raised the phial to his lips), camping out. In vain! His spectre stalks me. Dope is my only hope...Ah! Destruction! The black panther! With a cry he suddenly vanished and the panel slid back. An instant later his head appeared in the door opposite and said: Meet me at Westland row station at ten past eleven. (*U* 14.1022)

As Haines vanishes, our narrator evokes the tears of the "dissipated host" and the pronouncement of the "seer," who cries, "the vendetta of Mananaun," and of the "sage," who announces, "*Lex talionis*." Without attributing the statement to anyone in particular, the narrator gives us Stephen's telegram to Mulligan about sentimentalism (*U* 14.1028). An increasingly nonsensical cascade of sentences ("The lonely house by the graveyard is uninhabited....It is haunted. Murderer's ground") concludes the passage (*U* 14.1034).

Who, or what, we might ask, is speaking in this passage? In one way of looking at it, from an "external" perspective, Joyce, the "Arranger," or the narrator(s) of "Oxen" is parodying gothic novelists such as Horace Walpole, and perhaps Sheridan LeFanu (author of *The House by the Churchyard*), a parody established both by the incongruity of the subject to the style and by a certain stylistic exaggeration.[2] Indeed, as the passage progresses, the stylistic target broadens, taking a detour via Synge, and in the final lines, with their abrupt tying up of all loose ends (including some totally unrelated ones), the entire genre of the "novel of sensation" popularized by Wilkie Collins and Charles Reade, is mocked, as well as its gothic precursors: "The mystery was unveiled. Haines was the third brother. His real name was Childs. The black panther was himself the ghost of his own father. He drank drugs to obliterate. For this relief much thanks" (*U* 14.1032). Indeed, Joyce is probably taking an anachronistic leap ahead to the full-blown, over-formalized mystery story of the 1920s, with its drive toward resolution at all costs. But this is all an analysis from the point of view of the literary influences dialogically interacting in the passage, focusing especially on the stylistic aspect of genre. From another perspective, what is important is that somewhere beneath the intervening rhetoric, Mulligan is speaking, entertaining the company by recounting Haines's visit to the literary soiree at George Moore's home earlier in the evening.

Although the texture of this speech has been suppressed, or, rather, overlaid, we know enough about Mulligan to make an attempt at reconstructing it. Indeed, the logic of the chapter and our experience of Mulligan in the book's initial style more or less require that we do so. We may guess that Mulligan has a variety of motivations in speaking. He is giving an amusing character sketch of the Englishman as buffoon; at the same time, he is reminding Stephen that even the despised Haines has attended the party to which Stephen was not invited. Additionally, perhaps to pique Stephen's jealousy, Mulligan is informing Stephen that he himself has an appointment to meet Haines later that night. Even Mulligan's early-morning performance for Haines, in which he "explains" Stephen's Shakespeare hypothesis by a mock-algebraic nonsense formula (*U* 1.555), is echoed in the text. So, in many ways, Haines is central to this passage.

But how does the subject of Haines arise in the first place? This is not at all clear from the explicit text of the passage. Stephen has just delivered one of his better *mots*, the line about Siamese twins. I would like to suggest that the passage above—if it were written in the initial style of *Ulysses*, in what I would like to call the "implicit" narrative— might look something like the following:

> —Ah, Kinch, lovely!—sell that one to our local Sassenach. Gentlemen, you must meet this jewel of the crown, Mr. Haines. I was by Moore's earlier, and in he popped for his daily dose of Celtic culture—God knows who invited him. I believe he's addicted to us Irish. Your man was in a confessional mood, explaining his perverse passion for the Gael, how his folk have mistreated our folk for centuries and how the fact troubles his sleep. Begob, he near told us his bad dreams. Another *mauvais quart d'heure* with us and the bloody man would have confessed to the Childs murder. Anyway, he finally bids us adieu and then pops in again cool as you please just to tell me to meet him at Westland row station at ten past eleven. Moore was totally pissed, of course, laughed till he wept. Our prophetic Mr. Russell began quoting himself about the revenge of Mananaun and such, and Magee said something beautiful about the Lex talionis. But talk of your sentimentalists, Dedalus, that bollocks Haines takes the biscuit: he makes a profession of penance. Gurgling his mirth, Mulligan subsided.

If I suggest that a "realistic" dialogue in the book's initial style, barely detectable beneath a palimpsest of other discourses, would run something like this passage, I do not mean to imply that the text of "Oxen of the Sun" is always translatable from some naturalistic base. It often is, but the last sentences of the paragraph, for instance ("The mystery was unveiled. Haines was the third brother. His real name was Childs," etc.), are not. They are simply delivered by the narrator, who is obligingly satisfying (and thus mocking) our readerly desire for closure. I refer to them as "authorial interpolations" mainly to stipulate that they are motivated by the narrative form more than by the naturalistic situation.

There are, obviously, dangers involved in attempting to recapture a theoretical anterior text stating more plainly what the narration might have stated if it were not involved in a stylistic *tour de force* such as "Oxen" at the same time. Hugh Kenner has warned that "decoding a paragraph from 'Oxen' may not be the most rewarding way to read it" because we will be left with "a short flat paragraph worded by ourselves" (Kenner 1987, 122). But my point is that our paragraph, if sensitively decoded, will be as much Mulligan's speech as our own, and that Joyce has ensured this with his previous models in the initial style and with the clues embedded in the "paraphrase" we find in "Oxen." This need not be any flatter or more disappointing than Kenner's own exegeses, which gather such energy and brilliance from Joyce's sentences. After all, a master is instructing us here.

In Joyce's passage we have, in Bakhtin's terms, one of the most multiply voiced, multi-directed discourses in literature. Perhaps we can distinguish between two *levels of voicing*, one of them at the *textual level*, best described in terms of intertextuality and reader-relations, and one at the *character level* of representational dialogics. On the level of character, Mulligan's speech to the medical students and hangers-on is being described, as he uses Stephen's joke to force an entry for his own narration of the party. The paraphrase retains his constant mockery—in this case directed against Haines—and his desire to entertain his auditors with broad comedy and to impress them with some literary name-dropping. At the same time, he wants to annoy Stephen without ever quite directly expressing or eliciting the real, barely suppressed hostility between the two.

On the textual level, the Arranger's narration engages in dialogic relations with the level "below"—i.e., with Mulligan and the audience of characters—by travestying their desire for a "good story" at all costs and highlighting Mulligan's dramatizing, self-mocking mode of speech. Still on this textual level, the Arranger's narration relates "vertically" to the authorial voice as well, which is represented by the total narrative of *Ulysses*. We can describe the narrative at this point, seen globally, as a dialogical interaction between the author and a momentarily gothic narrator. If we were arbitrarily to distinguish between these two voices—or functions—we might say that while the gothic narrator supplies the rhetoric and much of the furniture of the passage—the secret panel, the phial of poison—the author supplies details like the portfolio of Celtic literature and "distractions," such as rookshooting and camping out. If we read responsibly, we as reader-writers are being asked to mediate between the two.

Let me sketch some of the motivations behind the wording in my translation of the text. I think that the gothic narrator's contribution is to suggest that the monomaniacal devotion to Celtic literature is both a trivial amusement and a drug (this applies not only to Haines, but to any Irish enthusiasts of the time, and accurately reflects Joyce's attitude toward the movement). Similarly, while the gothic narrator, predictably, has Haines announce that his hell is in this life—that is, he is a suitably damned protagonist for a gothic tale—an authorial interpolation adds that the same is true of Ireland, a country obsessed by its own past and condemned to tell its own story to whoever will listen. As the crowning touch, the interpolator even suggests that the painful spectacle of Haines wandering about, working out his atonement, is part of Ireland's punishment. All who are in range are punished, and this is their darkly romantic fate, says the passage, in a style whose excesses make the entire proposition hilarious.

On the other hand, at some point in the course of the passage we become aware that, however exaggerated and melodramatic Haines's portrayal may be, he *is* the representative of a country that has, like a gothic villain, forfeited its claims to ordinary humanity precisely by treating the colonized people as less than human. We may recall that the Irishman Bram Stoker epitomized the vampire mode of gothic fiction, and, as Joseph Valente has demonstrated, there is a clear homology between vampirism and colonization. So, in other words, while the authorial voice undermines the authority of the literary voice being adapted, the gothic voice makes its own reciprocal comment on the representational text it has engulfed.

Mulligan's line, "He near told us his bad dreams," in my passage of implicit narration refers to Haines's dream of the black panther, who makes a guest appearance in the explicit narration, while the Childs murder, another repeated motif in *Ulysses*, was a popular topic of the time, especially in the "light weeklies," to which Mulligan might well refer in parodic exaggeration. Mulligan also uses Stephen's insulting telegram to him at the Ship bar ("The sentimentalist is he who would enjoy without incurring the immense debtorship for a thing done"; *U* 14,1030) in a private aside to Stephen, meanwhile trying to rob the quotation of its sting by deflecting its target to Haines. The identification of "the sage," "the seer," and the host is clear enough to a reader of the "Scylla and Charybdis" section, of course; they are identified in this suggestive way in Joyce's passage in order to further the atmosphere of cut-rate mystery, and perhaps also to suggest that, at some level, they are interchangeable parts in a crude morality play.

The protean narrator, in the course of Joyce's passage, impersonates gothic and sensational narrators, briefly personalizes himself by taking a place at the table ("Which of us did not feel his flesh creep?"), and mocks our readerly expectations with a parody of novelistic closure. And, of course, the passage we are examining is itself far from a single voice: each of its components relates dialogically to the others. The line of naturalistic dialogue when Haines makes his appointment with Mulligan—which I suggest is a literal transcription of Haines's remark after he has left the soiree and then awkwardly reentered it—undercuts the high melodrama of his other pronouncements; the sudden intrusion of daily naturalistic dialogue ("Meet me at Westland row station") on gothically heightened dialogue ("the inferno has no terrors for me") has considerable comic effect. Meanwhile, the lines of Synge dialogue, juxtaposed against the high gothic mode of the surrounding passage, are exposed as somewhat artificial and folkishly gothic in their own right ("Tare and ages, what way would I be resting at all...."). Cross the gothic novel with a copy of P. W. Joyce's *English as We Speak It in Ireland*, Joyce suggests, and you get Synge.

But the details of these dialogical interactions are, of course, less important than the overall effect, which comes from the juxtaposition of all these wildly different discourses, each of them clearly inappropriate to the subject. Karen Lawrence observes that the point of "Oxen" is to display the limitations of all literary styles (Lawrence, 145). I would add that the major effect of that display is the comedy that results from the mad series of clashing linguistic contexts, a sort of joyous intertextual babble that embodies the carnivalized quality of complete dialogism. And Joyce's use of the implicit narrative, which must be generated by the reader, adds a strong participatory dimension to the dialogics. By the time we have translated the Gothic Passage, we are completely enmeshed in the writing of *Ulysses*, and Joyce—of all people—has succeeded in breaking down the capitalist dyad of author/literary consumer. In "Oxen" we do not in fact have the spectacle of a literary mandarin performing high above our heads; instead, we are invited to join a sort of literary tennis match in which the ball is just as frequently in our court as in Joyce's. The chapter is very funny, but the joke is not on us: thanks to the way Joyce trains his readers to be writers, the joke is ours as well.

Chapter Five

Newspapers and Periodicals:
Endless Dialogue

From individual examples of popular reading, such as were discussed in chapter three, we move to what has often been viewed as an even more commodified cultural object: the newspaper. And here we might recall that Benedict Anderson refers to the newspaper as "the first modern-style mass-produced industrial commodity," and that, in some respects, it is merely an " 'extreme form' of the book," its logical extension rather than, as some feel, its opposite (Anderson, 34). The very definition of dailiness (as opposed to the transcendent values of real literature), the newspaper is often seen as an anonymous farrago of unrelated items, either a major contributing factor to the interpretive vertigo that besets life under modernity or, at best, offering a middle-brow consensus evaluation that fails to take account of the significant contradictions of modernity under what Anderson terms print-capitalism. In *Ulysses*, "Aeolus" is usually interpreted as another center of the Dublin paralysis ("We'll paralyze Europe"; *U* 7 628), and the editor's offer to have Stephen join the "Pressgang" is seen as a ludicrous and insulting temptation to the young poet. But Joyce was far more deeply and consistently involved with newspapers than we usually realize, and the "great divide" of traditionally conceived modernism has made this difficult to see clearly. Furthermore, generalizing about newspapers under modernity is of limited value; it is important to understand the political and historical context of Dublin newspapers of Joyce's time in order to understand their function in *Ulysses*. An important part of this understanding, in fact, is an implication of their formal structure as a genre, which helps clarify their social function, both in 1904 Dublin and in *Ulysses*. Finally, a consideration of the structure and content of *Ulysses* and of daily newspapers and magazines of 1904 will lead to the conclusion that newspapers are an important model for the structure and content of Joyce's novel. Declan Kiberd has made a point similar to this, though with a different emphasis: "James Joyce's *Ulysses* can be read as a slow-motion alternative to the daily newspaper of Dublin for June 16, 1904..., a reappropriation of newspaper methods by an exponent of the threatened novel form.... By calling himself a scissors-and-paste man, he was casting himself as editor-in-chief of the counter-newspaper that was *Ulysses*" (Kiberd, 463). My intent in this chapter is to explore *Ulysses*' appropriation of newspaper format and content, and in the next to examine specifically the "light weeklies" that are mostly forgotten today, but that model Joyce's realignment of the author-reader relationship. In addition, I would like to attribute to Joyce some of the reluctance to accept environmental causality (so crucial to the traditional novel) that Bakhtin attributes to Dostoevsky:

> "[H]is position as a journalist...required that everything be treated in the context of the present....Dostoevsky's passion for journalism and his love of the newspaper, his deep and subtle understanding of the newspaper page as a living reflection of the contradictions of contemporary society in the cross-section of a single day, where the most diverse and contradictory material is laid out, extensively, side by side and one side against the other—all this is explained precisely by the above characteristic of Dostoevsky's artistic vision." (Bakhtin 1984, 29–30)

Joyce and Newspapers

Joyce's relationship to newspapers is ambivalent, and a useful recent article by James A. Reppke summarizes Joyce's experience with newspapers, casting it in a more positive light than many earlier critics have done. Scornful of their idea of literature, and especially of the poetry they printed, yet eager to take advantage of them as an unparalleled publicity machine, Joyce early in his career tried to support himself by writing for the newspaper in all three modes available to him—as editorial writer, reviewer, and even as straight reporter. Patrick Collier, who has thoroughly investigated Joyce's relationship to the newspapers of his time, points out that Joyce exploited his father's connections with the *Irish Times* to get his article about the Gordon Bennett Cup race published (Collier, 114; *Letters*, II n.3).[1] Joyce had plenty of connections to the newspaper business through his father's friends; reporters Joe and Frank Gallaher were at one point his father's neighbors (Jackson and Costello, 126). John Stanislaus could introduce Joyce to Jimmy Touhy, the *Freeman*'s London stringer, and to T. P. O'Connor, who worked with the journal *M.A.P.* and began the popular literary magazine *T. P.'s Weekly* in 1901 (Jackson and Costello, 224). Joyce's father asked T. P. O'Connor about a job in journalism for his son, but was rejected because of his son's youth (*JJII* 77). John Stanislaus's acquaintance with the editor of the *Evening Telegraph* led to Joyce's father being briefly employed as an advertising canvasser for that and the sister publication, the *Freeman* (Jackson, 190). Even Joyce's father's in-laws had newspaper connections: John Murray worked at the *Freeman* in the accounts department (Jackson, 312). Joyce repeatedly asked Yeats to get him work with the Dublin *Daily Express* and the English *Speaker* and *Academy*.

Before he left for Paris, he believed that his father had arranged for him a position as a French correspondent for the *Irish Times* (Shloss, 325). Although this fell through, he wound up writing twenty book reviews for the *Express* between December 1902 and November 1903. Following his surprising initial success getting the essay on Ibsen published in the London *Fortnightly Review* in 1900, when he was only eighteen, he wrote several literary-philosophical pieces intended for U.C.D.'s magazine *St. Stephen's*, including "The Day of the Rabblement," which was rejected and subsequently self-published as a broadside. But starting in December 1902, almost immediately upon his arrival in Paris, he began publishing a series of book reviews for the Irish *Daily Express*, from which he hoped to eke out a living—six of them written in Paris, fourteen after his temporary return to Dublin. These were interspersed by a more extensive piece on Ibsen, published in London's *Speaker*, and by a piece of what we would consider ordinary journalism—an interview with a champion French auto racer published in the *Irish Times*. There was a plan for Joyce to collaborate with his friend Sheehy-Skeffington in editing a new Dublin newspaper on the continental model to be called *The Goblin*; they chose the editor of the *Irish Bee-Keeper* as their business manager, but again the plan came to nothing (Shloss, 325).

Like his father, whose profession he once described on his university entrance application as "going in for competitions" (Scholes and Kain, 175), Joyce sometimes dreamed of winning the "missing word" puzzle contest in *Ideas* (*Letters*, II 89). In 1905, he planned to send Stanislaus a sealed, registered envelope with his answers to ensure against trickery, but in the end mailed his solution too late to qualify for the prize (*JJII* 199). Like Conrad before him and Virginia Woolf, his contemporary, he entered the "*Tit-Bits* Prize" contest for a short work of fiction (Trotter, 63), with a tale about anarchists that, according to Stanislaus, he later burlesqued as "Matcham's Masterstroke" (*JJII* 50). In 1904, George Russell, editor of the *Irish Homestead* paper, suggested that Joyce could send him a story of about 1800 words and be paid a pound: "It is easily earned money if you can write fluently and don't mind playing to the common understanding and liking for once in a way" (*Letters*, II 43). After all, we should recall that, despite the young Stephen's scorn for the idea of lowering his aesthetic standards, newspaper and periodical publication was an accepted way of establishing intellectual currency (Reppke). Joyce's early Dublin renown as an aesthete and an intellectual, such as it was, depended upon his having managed to get a review of Ibsen published in the *Fortnightly Review*. His plans to support himself while studying in Paris by writing reviews and articles for the popular press (see, e.g., *Letters*, II 27) were inspired by his precocious success as a literary journalist. After his arrival in Trieste, he began publishing a series of more expansive articles on Irish subjects, written in Italian, in the *Piccolo della Sera*: three in 1907 on Fenianism, Home Rule, and "Ireland at the Bar"; two in 1909 on Wilde and Shaw; another on Home Rule in 1910; one on Parnell in 1912; and finally two essays entitled "City of the Tribes" and "The Mirage of the Fisherman of Aran" also in 1912 (CW). In 1912 Joyce also published a subeditorial in the *Freeman's Journal* on hoof-and-mouth disease; immediately following it, the newspaper announced an upcoming article in the *Piccolo della Sera* by "Mr. James Joyce, an Irish-Italian journalist." We might wonder for what audience this item was intended; but at the least it shows that the editor knew Joyce.

Journalism and, indeed, writing as a profession were unusual ways of earning a living at the turn of the century in that, unlike most professions dependent upon an industrial base, they could be practiced from anywhere. Dublin at this period had very little functioning industrial base; its colonial status meant that British manufacturing firms had little difficulty in driving their Dublin competitors into insolvency. By 1900, Dublin's main areas of economic productivity were printing and the production of alcoholic beverages. Aside from this, the former capital was in deep economic depression (Daly, O'Brien). The exodus that had started with the famine in the 1840s had continued in a more limited way through the remainder of the century and beyond, as young Irishmen discovered their prospects were better overseas.

Joyce, once he had moved to the more solvent and less expensive continental Europe, could support himself first by teaching English and second by writing—originally for papers and journals, eventually for the unique avant-garde market for literature that developed in the 'teens and 'twenties. In both cases, he was avoiding the crisis that colonialism's uneven development had caused in the manufacturing

base of Dublin and taking advantage of the unique st? duction and consumption of words. To put it another ·
a beneficiary of the communications revolution of
that was to more clearly shape social life later in the cei.ı.. ,
the subject matter of his writing, it is reasonable to say that Joyᴄᴄ
remained a virtual citizen of Dublin, although one who took advantage of the material advantages of European residency. Thanks to the
unique commodity status of words, Joyce could live anywhere, without abandoning Ireland's imagined community.

It is worth pointing out that when Myles Crawford tries to talk
Stephen into writing for the press, he believes he is offering member-
ship in a sort of knight-errantry, in which Stephen will be empow-
ered to strike a blow for truth. The notorious muckraking Irish editor
William Stead, editor of the *Pall Mall Gazette*, claimed that the newspaper "is the great court in which all grievances are heard and all
abuses brought to the light of open criticism," while James Gordon
Bennett, the founder of the popular *New York Herald*, announced
that "a newspaper can be made to take the lead...in the great movements of human thought, and human civilization. A newspaper
can send more souls to Heaven, and send more to Hell, than all the
churches or chapels in New York" (Smith, 143, 136). The mystic and
newspaper editor A.E., for all his belief in the deeper, hidden causes
of human events, allowed that "the journalists of Ireland have a great
power, greater than that of any public men, who, to a great extent,
rise and fall at their bidding" (A.E., 3). And indeed both the aspirations and the social status of reporters were quite different from what
they are today. Around 1907, Hugh Oram observes, "[M]any newspaper reporters wore morning coats and striped trousers. They doffed
their hats to ladies of their acquaintance when they passed them in
the street" (Oram 1983, 114). Clearly, like John Joyce, they regarded
themselves as gentlemen; and after all John Joyce worked intermittently for the *Freeman* as advertising canvasser (Delaney, 75), while
Joyce's uncle, "Red" Murray, worked for the same paper's accounts
department (*JJII* 19).

The group gathered in the *Evening Telegraph* newsroom in
"Aeolus" attests to the social pretensions of pressmen, underlined
by the presence of the expensively educated "professor" MacHugh
and the well-connected and gentlemanly O'Molloy. Rather unexpectedly, the newspaper office becomes the arena for performances, just
as the librarian's office will later. There is, in the scene, both a sense
of expectant nostalgia and a regret for great times past. That this is a
historical allusion is illustrated by a passage evoking the 1860s in the

ctially autobiographical novel *When We Were Boys* by William O'
Brien, who was later the editor of *United Ireland* and an MP:

> I have seen the dingy Reporters' Room of the *Freeman's Journal* flash-
> ing and flashing again with a war of wits that would have made the
> old rafters of the Mitre Tavern split for joy—wit kindlier and perhaps
> not much less keen, than if the tossing curls of the dear old Chief who
> presided had been the scratch wig of the grim Doctor himself. But who
> shall repeat this dainty aerial music of such hours? (397)

However, by having Lenehan as an active and intrusive presence,
Joyce makes it clear that this is also a place where spongers and ne'er-
do-wells congregate and are tolerated for their entertainment value.

We might also note that none of these people, except for Crawford,
actually work for the newspaper, and even Crawford is more concerned with getting a drink than with getting a story or an ad—when
Bloom, an actual newspaper employee, appears on business, he is
immediately dismissed. As Kenner pointed out, "Bloom as advertisement canvasser spends the day selling something that doesn't exist
(the ad with the design of the crossed keys) on behalf of someone who
isn't anxious to sell it (the Editor) to someone who doesn't want to
buy it; a deep-cutting epiphany of commerce" (Kenner 1956, 245).
Still, these are all people who value words. Although Stephen may
feel slightly out of place in "Aeolus," he is, in fact, more comfortable
in the newspaper office than he is in the library among the literary
folk. He is entertained by the verbal wit on display and moved by the
examples of oratory, and he chooses this audience to hear his "Pisgah
Sight of Palestine" story, however ironic his intention. Finally, we
should notice that this is the location where he and his father come
closest to each other and even play somewhat interchangeable roles.
Like it or not, Stephen is already a member of the "pressgang."

As an exile who was committed to using a great deal of naturalistic detail in his writing, and who was also committed to writing
exclusively about the Dublin he had left for good, Joyce was unusually dependent upon newspapers from home. Patrick Collier points
out that "in 1906, James Joyce was living in Rome and avidly reading
every Irish and English newspaper he could get his hands on" (107).
He kept track of a scandalous divorce case and complained when
he missed a day's coverage; he was thinking at the time of writing a
story about a well-known Dublin cuckold. Writing to Stanislaus, he
defended the *United Irishman* as "the only newspaper of any pretensions in Ireland," and claimed that, although it was "deaf to any

intellectual interest," its seriousness was preferable
of his old friend Sheehy-Skeffington's *Dialogues of*
II 157–58). Shortly afterwards, he complains that
does not send copies of *Sinn Fein* regularly enough (*Le,*
November 1906 he praises to Stanislaus the Edgar Wal.
the *Daily Mail* (*Letters*, II 188), but in December he tel ᴜᴛner
that he is giving up on the *Daily Mail* supplement because, whereas he
enjoyed the "mystery and money" part of the fiction, "now the love
interest has begun" (*Letters*, II 198). On January 10, 1907, he sends
Stanislaus a copy of *The Republic*, a nationalist weekly published in
Belfast during that year, and a month later sends him copies of the
Freeman's Journal containing coverage of the Abbey riots (*Letters*,
II 211).

In carefully following papers from home he was probably no different from many other Dubliners living abroad, but, as he conceived
the project of *Ulysses*, it must have soon became clear to him that he
would need access to all the newspapers he could get from the period
around June 16, 1904; indeed, several of those papers—notably the
Freeman's Journal and *Evening Telegraph* for June 16, 1904—would
be woven directly into the texture of the novel in a way no earlier
novel had ever attempted. Frustrated during the war by the difficulty
he had in getting access to Irish and English newspapers, Joyce frequently wrote to friends for copies of papers and magazines; some of
these letters have survived, but probably many more were written that
have not. And Joyce's use of the material he gleaned from newspapers
was idiosyncratic. As Shloss points out,

> Sometimes...he simply copied newspaper accounts verbatim; some-
> times he recomposed what he remembered from experience; sometimes
> he transposed what he found in widely disparate record books. Events
> from 1912, 1909, 1903 masquerade in the novel as current events.
> Events which Joyce insists happened on 16 June did not: the Lord
> Lieutenant did not ride through Dublin then, nor was Elijah the quack
> evangelist there. (Shloss, 331–32)

After the war, he was still dependent on friends to send him popular
books, papers, and magazines in English. On January 5, 1920, he
writes to Mrs. William Murray asking for "a bundle of other novel-
ettes and any penny hymnal you can find as I need them" (*Letters*,
I 135), while in September of that year he writes to thank Frank
Budgen for a bundle of letters and papers, "the latter very useful,
especially *Bits of Fun* of which send me any back numbers you can

(*Letters*, I 144).[2] Indeed, at times he seems interested in popular writing *as detritus*: he writes Budgen on February 21, 1921, to ask for a cheap handbook on Freemasonry "or any ragged, dirty, smudged, torn, defiled, effaced, dogeared, coverless, undated, anonymous mis-printed book on mathematics or algebra or trigonometry or Euclid from a cart" (*Letters*, I 160). From the tone of these descriptions, clearly he is not interested in the texts as sources of reliable informa-tion, but more as a kind of cultural *bricolage*, random remnants of the great Victorian age of information.

Newspapers in *Ulysses*

Newspapers also served this function for him, providing a grab bag of popular *topoi* that would surface in *Ulysses*. A survey of news-papers and magazines (and some of the material treated in them that is used in *Ulysses*) may help to illuminate their function in the novel. Of course, the main contents of the *Freeman's Journal* and *Evening Telegraph* for Bloomsday appear in *Ulysses,* but other mate-rial from those and other papers certainly suggested minor themes and motifs in Joyce's novel. For example, the *Evening Telegraph* for June 15 has a passage, headed "Personal Paragraphs," that asserts, "Dr. Dowie is the most successful of all the religious imposters that Chicago has produced. Zionism has been enormously profitable to its founder....His earlier years are shrouded in mystery...[Dowie] became a 'faith healer' and worked wondrous cures by the laying on of hands" (p. 2, col. 8). Although he was in Europe in June, which may have led to his being mentioned in the *Telegraph* at some point, he was not, in fact, in Dublin during 1904; as Shloss points out, his advent on Bloomsday is Joyce's invention. And in his research, Joyce certainly had other opportunities to be reminded of Dowie: Rose and O'Hanlon note that the *London Times* of June 13, from which Joyce apparently took notes, refers on page 12 to Dowie as "Elijah the Restorer" and "General Overseer of the Christian Catholic Church in Zion" (p. 16). Rose and O'Hanlon also claim that by February 1919 Joyce had in hand a copy of the June 17, 1904, issue of the *Irish Independent*, from which he copied much of the description of the bicycle race in "Wandering Rocks" (Note and erratum).

Robert Martin Adams did the fundamental research showing Joyce's reliance on a variety of Dublin newspapers for detailed infor-mation about many casual topics that arise in the course of *Ulysses*. He traces to their sources the description of the Dublin waterworks

(*Irish Independent*, June 15, 1904); the discussion of British flogging (*Freeman's Journal*, July 15, 1904); the English hangman vacationing in Ireland and trying to keep his hand in (*Weekly Freeman*, January 14, 1899); the Canada swindle case (*Freeman's Journal*, July 12, 1904); and Bello's reading matter from the evening paper as he sits on Bloom (*Evening Herald*, June 16, 1904; Adams 226–29). But other minor items in *Ulysses* may also have been inspired by newspaper contents. The June 16 issue of the *Evening Telegraph* has an article discussing the effect of electric light on the growth of flowers:

> Electricity in Horticulture
>
> Some of the queer things which happen to flowers when they are exposed to the electric light are described by the "Washington Post." Violets are doubled and trebled in size. A race of pansies has been raised up to measure two inches across their faces....In a modern plant experimental laboratory the electric light arc creates transformations that astonish the most hardened investigator. Reds are converted into purples, and blacks and whites into all the colors of the rainbow. But the flowers fade quickly. (p. 1 col. 8)[3]

While nobody in the novel acknowledges that the *Evening Telegraph* has treated the subject, Stephen and Bloom discuss the "influence of gaslight or the light of arc and glowlamps on the growth of adjoining paraheliotropic trees" (*U* 17.13) as they walk home. The same issue contains an advertisement for "Plumtree's Home-Potted Meats," and a classified ad in search of a young lady (R.C.) to serve as a photographer's assistant in Castlebar (an ad that also runs in the *Freeman's Journal* for the same day). It also has the story of a young man who falls into the Liffey at Sir John Rogersons' Quay, and is rescued by a passing stranger who holds him up in the water until a ferryboat man pulls them both in. "Skin-the-Goat," in "Eumaeus," mentions one Colonel Everard, in Cavan, successfully growing tobacco (*U* 16. 996), a story that Weldon Thornton has traced to the June 9, 1904, issue of the *Irish Homestead* (Thornton, 443). Gerty's former reliance on the Widow Welch's Female Pills may have been suggested by their being frequently advertised in a variety of papers: for instance, "Kearsley's Widow Welch's Female Pills" are advertised in the *General Advertiser*, no. 3526 (June 4, 1904) as "Awarded Certificate of Merit for the Cure of Irregularities, Anemia, and all Female Complaints. Approved by the Medical Profession." Paging through these newspapers, we find numerous items that may have set off a chain of associations for Joyce. Whatever led to the slapstick scene where a newsboy shouts in Bloom's face, "Terrible tragedy in Rathmines! A child bit by a bellows!" (*U* 7.969), in the *Evening Telegraph* for June 13 on page 3 we can find, "Child Drowned in a Bath at Rathmines," which may have struck Joyce as nearly as bathetic.[4]

We will never know with any assurance what newspapers Joyce chose to consult, or was able to consult, in preparing *Ulysses*. Carol Shloss has shown that, at some point, Joyce consulted the 1904 *Irish Times* and several other newspapers. Danis Rose and John O'Hanlon's reconstruction of "lost" notebook VI.D.7 relies on entries from the *London Times* between June 1 and 17, 1904, which Joyce probably made in 1917 (Rose and O'Hanlon). Joyce corresponded with Stanislaus in Dublin about an article in *T.P.'s Weekly*, which his brother apparently sent him (*Letters*, II 82, 86). And from references scattered throughout *Ulysses* it seems likely that he was acquainted with a wide variety of weeklies, both newspapers and magazines (a distinction it is very difficult to draw during this phase of periodical publication). Gerty recalls an advertisement for curing drunkenness with pills from *Pearson's Weekly* (*U* 13.291), and Gifford gives the text of one such (Gifford, 388), although these ads were common enough: the *Weekly Freeman*, for example, for June 11, 1904, carried an ad reading, "To Cure Drunkards with or without their knowledge, send stamp for free trial package... (p. 2, col. 7). In addition, the magazine entitled the *Princess Novelette* has an ad headed, "Drunkenness cured: On receipt of stamped envelope, a lady will gladly send free particulars of a simple remedy, which cured her husband (without his knowledge) of the craving for alcohol, to which he had been for many years a victim" (n.s., no. 1, August, 1904, p. 1). Clearly, this advertisement is lightly disguised as a personal offering to the community of readers, so that Gerty might be able to convince herself that in writing away for it she would be involved in something other than a commercial transaction. Much of the advertising in this periodical, as in many others, attempts to disguise itself as friendly advice. While answers to the questions of correspondents are featured in the magazine, so are ads like the following, which begins: "Don't ask your best friend to go with you to choose material for your new dress. If she is not prevented, by jealous motives, from telling you what suits you best, she will most likely, fearful of the shop attendant, refrain from expressing her candid opinion. ..." At the end of a long paragraph, suitable for the opening of a short story, the writer suggests sending to a particular address for a choice of sample fabrics and patterns, so as to inspect them at leisure (no. 946, vol. 37, p. 267).

Bloom's "Bath of the Nymph" is purportedly culled from the Easter number of *Photo Bits* (*U* 4.370), and the nymph plays as large a role in his consciousness during the day as does the story "Matcham's Masterstroke," from *Tit-Bits* magazine (*U* 4.502). I have been unable to check the source of the nymph (see Marsh). I am fairly certain that, while someone under the name of Philip Beaufoy actually wrote for that magazine, the Beaufoy story Bloom reads did not appear as such (see chapter six below). All the major newspapers that appear in *Ulysses*, on the other hand, are real. When Deasy asks for help publishing his letter, Stephen thinks immediately of the *Telegraph* and the *Irish Homestead*, since he knows both editors slightly (*U* 2.432). Joyce probably needed no help in naming a pornographic work in French, and when Stephen somewhat later thinks of the "rich booty" he brought back from Paris, *Pantalon Blanc et Culotte Rouge*, Thornton no doubt is correct in suggesting that this is Joyce's variant on the journal *La Vie en Culotte Rouge* (Thornton, 53). But Thornton does not seem to realize that Stephen need not have traveled to Paris to find it: this latter title is listed in the October 12, 1903, issue of the *Dublin Evening Mail*, in a story about the arrest of a Frenchwoman for displaying indecent publications.

Similarly, Stephen needs no special inspiration when he uses the phrase "Found drowned" (*U* 3.471) that categorizes one kind of death, but in the March 27, 1904, *Freeman*, under the head "Found Drowned in the Dodder," is a brief story of the discovery of the body of a young woman, Violet Davies, and the jury's verdict, "Found drowned" (p. 5, col. 5). Bloom thinks about Griffith's paper running articles complaining about the prevalence of venereal disease in the British army (*U* 5.71), which it indeed did. In the carriage to the cemetery, appropriately, Bloom scans the death announcements that were printed down the top left-hand column of page 1 of the *Freeman's Journal*, although neither the names he reads there nor the memorial poem, "It is now a month since dear Henry fled," appears in the actual *Freeman* of that date (*U* 6.158). There are plenty of models for the poem in other issues of the *Freeman*, though: the May 27, 1904, issue has a poem "In sad and loving memory of Dennis Kelly" which reads, "We deeply mourn the loss of one / We did our best to save: / Beloved in life, regretted gone, / Remembered in the grave" (p. 1). Somewhat less slick is the poem in the June 15 *Freeman*, "Five years today, and still we miss him; / Friends may think the wound is healed, / But they little know the sorrow / Lies within our hearts concealed" (p. 1).

As we page through *Ulysses,* we encounter a miscellany of popular papers and magazines. Bloom considers the graveyard as "an ideal spot to have a quiet smoke and read the *Church Times*" (*U* 6.945). Thinking about the features that really sell a paper, he associates the "personal note" with T. P. O'Connor's *M.A.P.*, which he ironically translates as "Mainly all pictures" instead of its true title, *Mainly About People* (U 7.97). He is also aware of which Dublin writers are associated with what newspapers: he recalls that J. J. O'Molloy has done "some literary work" for the *Daily Express* along with Gabriel Conroy (U 7.307) who was called a "West Briton" for doing so by Miss Ivors (D 190). Joyce himself, of course, also also published in the *Express*. Lenehan emerges from the inner office of the *Telegraph* carrying "tissues" of the sister publication *Sport*, which has a "dead cert" recommendation for the Gold Cup race, Sceptre (U 7.387). Annoyed by Crawford's attack on barristers, O'Molloy scornfully allows, "Ignatius Gallaher we all know and his Chapelizod boss, Harmsworth of the farthing press, and his American cousin of the Bowery gutter sheet not to mention *Paddy Kelly's Budget*, *Poe's Occurrences* and our watchful friend *The Skibbereen Eagle*... Sufficient unto the day is the newspaper thereof" (U 7.736). This is a treasure trove of newsman's in-house talk. Harmsworth was indeed born in Chapelizod, and his American friend was Joseph Pulitzer, another press magnate. The *Budget* and *Poe's* are both famous early newspapers, *The Skibbereen Eagle* a minor Irish one, famous for having warned the Prime Minister of England and the Czar of Russia that it had its eye on them.[5]

Pursuing Myles Crawford, Bloom passes by the offices of the *Irish Catholic* and the *Dublin Penny Journal*, and shortly afterwards he passes by the offices of the *Irish Times*, thinking of the personal advertisement he paid for that netted the response from Martha Clifford, and assuring himself that the *Times* is the best paper for a small ad, despite its fawning attitude toward the gentry ("All the toady news"; U 8.334). The *Irish Times* for June 16, 1904, is indeed striking for the number and variety of small ads, which are well categorized through the second and third pages. Bloom, however, might do well to read the note on the second page: "The Postmaster-General has given notice that letters addressed to initials or fictitious names at the Post Office will in all cases be returned to the writers. Advertisers are therefore requested not to use such addresses.... All advertisements must be authenticated by the name and address of the sender" (col. 1). But perhaps Bloom's specially printed card with the Henry Flower identity is sufficient authentication. He recalls that the *Times* director, James Carlyle, also bought the weekly *Irish Field* (U 8.339), an example of Joyce's understanding of the shifting commercial allegiances of the popular Irish press. In "Wandering Rocks," it is reported, in language appropriate to a newspaper legal report, that "an elderly female, no longer young, left the building of the courts of chancery…having heard…[t]he case in lunacy of Potterton" (*U* 10.625), while the *Freeman* for that date reports, under the heading "Law Intelligence," the subheading "Law Notices—This Day," and sub-subheading "High Court of Justice, Chancery Division" before the "Lord Chancellor": "In lunacy—before the Registrar—11:30 o'clock—Courtenay, of unsound mind, ex parte…Potterton, do., do." (p. 2, col. 4). The basic information about the three cases the lady observes was available in several of the daily newspapers. Robert M. Adams claims that the passage in *Ulysses* follows nearly word for word the reportage of the legal calendar on page 2 of the *Irish Independent* (Adams, 226), but the *Independent* and *Freeman* seem to me both to contain identical information in nearly identical format—not at all an unusual circumstance among Dublin papers of the period, which assiduously copied one another and foreign sources, as well—with the Potterton case far down on the list of lunacies, described only by a series of "dittos."

In the Ormond, listening to Ben Dollard sing, Bloom thinks he is a "decent soul," but a "bit addled now. Thinks he'll win in *Answers* poets' picture prize." He goes on to make it clear that the puzzle is extremely simple, making the winner a matter of a lottery (*U* 11.1023). The Citizen, reading from his pile of newspapers in Barney Kiernan's bar, speaks scornfully of the *Independent*, which, he says, was "founded by Parnell to be the workingman's friend" and taken over by William Murphy, "the Bantry Jobber." His friend Alf, somewhat later, is giggling over the *Police Gazette,* which the narrator characterizes as containing "secrets for enlarging your private parts. Misconduct of society belle. Norman W. Tupper, wealthy Chicago contractor, finds pretty but faithless wife in lap of Officer Taylor" (*U* 12.1165). Later, the bar crowd admires the picture of a butting match and the coverage of a lynching in the same publication, a clear American precursor of modern "yellow journalism" that contains material too spicy for Irish publications of the time.[6]

Gerty, of course, is a *bovariste* of the women's press, who reads and relies upon not only the *Princess Novelette* but also the *Lady's Pictorial* (*U* 13.110) and, doubtless, several others as well. Thinking of Wordsworth's poem "Grace Darling," Bloom also thinks of the journal where it was first published, in 1876, the *Royal Reader.* He is proud to be a reader as well as a correspondent of magazines, having contributed a letter on the need for a fingerpost at Stepaside to the *Irish Cyclist* (*U* 15.233). In "Circe," newspapers do not escape the general transmutation of people and things into a beastly register. Crawford answers his phone, "*Freeman's Urinal* and *Weekly Arsewiper.* Paralyse

Europe" (*U* 15.812), and a "Voice from the Gallery" continues the excremental theme and suggests Bloom's defacement of Beaufoy's story, chanting, "Moses, Moses, king of the jews, / Wiped his arse in the Daily News" (*U* 15.847). Davy Stephens, the "prince of Dublin newsvendors," appears selling the *Messenger of the Sacred Heart* and the *Evening Telegraph* with the St. Patrick's Day Supplement, "containing the new addresses of all the cuckolds in Dublin" (*U* 15.1124). The anonymous stage director of "Circe" describes a hobgoblin in the image of Punch Costello as having an "Ally Sloper nose," a sort of tribute to the familiarity of the cartoon character (*U* 15.2152). Bello, who turns into a comically exaggerated version of a John Bull figure, claims (s)he will smoke a cigar during breakfast, while reading the *Licensed Victualler's Gazette* and enjoying a slice or two of Bloom, who thus becomes the victuals (*U* 15.2898). We may recall that a note in Joyce's Trieste Notebook, no doubt referring to his father, asserts, "He read Modern Society and the Licensed Victualler's Gazette" (Scholes and Kain, 104). Certainly this kind of reading had strong emotional associations for Joyce.

Bloom recalls being present when Parnell and a band of supporters took over the "*Insuppressible* or was it the *United Ireland*" (*U* 16.1334). When the acting editor of the *United Ireland*, which had been formed as a Parnellite paper, wavered in his support during the crisis of December 1890, Parnell and his followers stormed the building and the anti-Parnell faction, defeated there, formed their own paper, the *Insuppressible*. Bloom also recalls having written a poem for a contest run by the weekly newspaper the *Shamrock* (*U* 17.395). He has apparently saved an article on corporal chastisement in girls' schools from the English weekly journal *Modern Society* (*U* 17.1802)—something that seems extremely unlikely, judging by the copies of the magazine I have been able to review. Meanwhile, Molly considers buying a special corset of the kind she has seen in the *Gentlewoman* (750). Perhaps this was the "corset of the century," described in a passage from the May 7, 1904, *Gentlewoman*:

"The Corset of the Century" is the name Madame Cooke, of Newark-on-Trent, has given to her special Regain and Retain Figure corset. Stout figures can easily obtain a straight front below the waist by wearing this ingenious corset, which Madame Cooke has patented, and which in white, black, and dove coutille costs 25s., post free, suspenders being 2s. 6d. extra. This corset may be had with a high or low bust. Its distinctive feature is that on each side below the waist a triangular piece is cut out of the corset, an elastic belt at the base of the triangle keeping the corset in position, preventing the busts from poking out, and at the same time giving a most comforting support. (no. 723, vol. 28, p. 704)

Her husband is so droll, Molly thinks, "somebody ought to put him in the budget" (*U* 18.579). Although a budget is a popular miscellany, the journal entitled the *Budget* was a popular British weekly devoted to light news and entertainment and published by Harmsworth's group. Apparently Molly, also, at one time, like many lower-class readers, followed the radical/libertarian *Lloyds Weekly News*, though this may have been more because of an attraction to its sensationalism than to its radical politics. She recalls having seen a picture of a "hardened criminal who murdered an old woman" (*U* 18.992).

Joyce was not simply an assiduous reader of newspapers; he also continued to correspond with them for special purposes. Joyce wrote a letter to *Sinn Fein* (the newspaper run by Arthur Griffith and whose predecessor, the *United Irishman*, he was known to praise; *Letters*, II 158), giving a synopsis of his attempts to get *Dubliners* published. In later life, he wrote to newspapers in support of his campaigns for the English Players stage company or the Irish tenor John Sullivan (*Letters*, II 461; *Letters*, III 199). Far more than is the case today, journalism in the late nineteenth and early twentieth century was the context in which literature originally appeared to the public. The editors of the *Waterloo Directory of Victorian Periodicals* remind us that

> the penny newspaper, the shilling magazine, the six-shilling quarterly, the ephemeral religious tract are obvious enough illustrations of Victorian journalism. Many of the novels and essays, and much of the bardic poetry of the period also appeared first in a journalistic medium, and the student of Victorian literature and ideas could usefully give attention not only to that original form but also to the broader context. *Sartor Resartus*...and *The Mayor of Casterbridge* shared an important world with...*The Morning Chronicle*, *The Echo*...and *Tit-Bits*. (Wolff et al., preface)

Most crucially, Joyce's stories "The Sisters," "Eveline," and "After the Race" first appeared in George Russell's weekly, *The Irish Homestead*, which Joyce disparagingly referred to as "the pigs' paper," especially after the editor asked him to submit no more stories, because there had been complaints about those that were printed. Uniquely, the publication combined Russell's interest in Theosophy and things spiritual with an ostensible expertise in matters agricultural. When Stephen offers Mr. Deasy's letter to Russell to pass along to Mr. Norman, the editor (*U* 9.316), he has probably found the ideal place for it. The juxtaposition of subjects was less surprising than it might seem to us; most of the leading figures of the Irish revival published in the newspapers and magazines of the time, and figures like Yeats and Russell both associated mystical knowledge with the Irish peasantry. The breadth of material covered in the *Irish Homestead* was not that surprising at the time, either; around the turn of the century newspapers still saw themselves as general interest publications, offering a wide variety of material to supplement what we would think of as "news." Still, it is both disconcerting and rather suggestive to read an early version of "The Sisters," as did its first readers, printed just above a large advertisement for a milking machine.

After 1907, Joyce published little in Anglophone newspapers, but did have nine significant essays published in *Il Piccolo della Sera* over several years. He also broke his newspaper silence in 1912 at the behest of a friend, Henry Blackwood Price, who had heard, in Austria, of a possible cure for hoof and mouth disease, which at the time was ravaging Irish cattle. Joyce forwarded Price's letter, which appeared in the *Evening Telegraph*, to the president of the Irish Cattle Traders' Society. Then, Ellmann states, "Joyce surprised himself in writing a sub editorial about the disease for the *Freeman's Journal*"—probably meaning that he surprised Ellmann, who was committed to the belief that Joyce's attitude toward newspapers was unproblematically contemptuous (*JJII* 326). This essay, which was printed in the September 10, 1912, *Freeman*, like his *Piccolo della Sera* articles, is reprinted in Joyce's *Critical Writings*. The letter whose fragments appear in *Ulysses* is even more surprising, considering the shame Stephen feels in associating himself with it (he fears he will be called the "bullockbefriending bard"; *U* 7.528), and also considering the fact that the letter must appear at least somewhat anachronistic, since hoof-and-mouth disease was not yet a serious problem in Ireland in 1904. Ellmann feels that Joyce, in the fragments of the letter that appear in *Ulysses*, "is parodying not only Blackwood Price but himself," (*JJII* 327n), and finds several phrases from the Deasy letter in Joyce's *Piccolo* articles. Joyce goes on to have a good deal of fun parodying the idea that "high literature" and Deasy's letter are essentially different sorts of writing, since Stephen has torn an unused end off the letter in order to write down bits of the poem he composes in "Proteus," and then Crawford, seeing the torn end, suggests that Deasy was "short taken" (*U* 7.521). It was not, of course, Deasy who used his own writing for toilet paper, as Bloom did Beaufoy's story, but Stephen who used it for a writing pad—but by now the different levels and purposes of writing and the idea of excretion are thoroughly entangled in the reader's mind. Price's letter, as Ellmann quotes it, is nowhere near as stuffed with pompous cliché as the one Deasy writes, even judging only from the fragments Stephen reads to himself.

In fact, my feeling is that in *Ulysses*, Joyce has distorted several newspaper articles for parodic reasons. For example, although I searched several newspapers for a model for "Doughy Dan" Dawson's overwrought speech on "Erin, Green Gem of the Silver Sea" (*U* 7.236), I found nothing of his but reasonable, more or less plainly written articles on European technical or social innovations that Dawson thought Ireland might benefit from imitating (in other words, Dawson made the same kind of suggestion that Price was making).[7] But Joyce could easily have found examples of overblown writing by other authors that were nearly as bad as the one he presents in "Aeolus." For example, a letter on "Irish Characteristics," by one Patrick J. Fallon of Galway, printed in the *Weekly Freeman* for June 11, 1904, reads in part,

> now let us turn to the country around, and what a sight greets us! Sparkling streams are visible everywhere, and verdant hillocks, blue mountains, and noble rivers come into view in rapid succession. It is here we can enjoy the scenic charms of lake and mountain, of valley and highland, of wooded slopes, broad, fertile plains of country, or equally extensive moorlands. From such a lovely land filled with natural and artistic characteristics, could freedom ever go?

Concluding his peroration, Fallon replies to his own question, somewhat bathetically, "No" (p. 11). There is another example of such writing that Joyce must have seen. Joyce had a brief, signed review of Lady Gregory's "Poets and Dreamers" in the March 26, 1903, issue of the *Daily Express*, and on the same page an anonymous reviewer approvingly quotes Seamus MacManus's *A Lad of the O'Friel's*:

> If here you see the ripples on the sunny waters, and hear the wavelets falling on the shingly shore of our out-of-the-world lives; and that, leaving, you carry away with you, in your heart, a little music of minor chords, I shall have achieved the utmost I attempted. (11)

So there was no lack of overwritten lyricism in the Dublin papers for a satirical target. Yet it was evidently important to Joyce that the putative author of his purple passage be a well-known politician and former Lord Mayor of Dublin, as well as a former baker (see Garvin, 66).

An even more egregious example of Joycean exaggeration is in the "Madame Vera Verity" pages of the *Princess Novelette*, where Gerty supposedly reads advice about the proper use of makeup, such as "eyebrowleine" (*U* 13.111). While such a suggestion might appear in magazines of 1922 aimed at working-class girls, such as *Peg's Paper* (which Joyce consulted in composing the *Wake*), the *Princess Novelette's* pages in 1904 suggest only exercise and a healthy diet for young women. In the August 1904 issue, "Violette" offers advice on household problems, "Sylvia" on dress. Under the heading "Health and Beauty," Violette suggests apples for the complexion and a diet of steaks and vegetables to prevent anemia (n.s. no. 1, p. 3). Again we have something like an anachronism produced by the urge to parody—or perhaps by the desire to broaden the chronotope of *Ulysses*. Once we read *Ulysses* with an awareness of the conventions of the periodical publishing industry of the time, we are aware of a double chronological focus (which to some extent probably characterizes every historical novel): some of the most bizarre details regarding newspapers are often startlingly accurate, even while others, which on the surface seem reasonable historical details of 1904, in fact point to the 1920s. It is in part this historical slippage in *Ulysses* that gives us the impression of an Edwardian life-world being dragged rapidly, if reluctantly, into full-scale modernity.

The Historical Context

Newspapers and magazines, including the weeklies that were a peculiar sort of crossbreed between these categories, crop up throughout *Ulysses*. Indeed, according to the Irish historian Louis Cullen, a list of popular reading taken from the pages of *Ulysses* turns out to be a fair guide to the best-selling newspapers and magazines of Ireland in 1904 (Cullen 1984).[8] Obviously, part of Joyce's rationale in alluding so substantially to this printed matter is to provide a historically accurate portrait of the material culture of Dublin in 1904—and in this case, an aspect of the material culture that contributed significantly to the structures of popular consciousness. But Joyce's invocation of the newspapers of the time has a broader and more complicated significance for our reading of *Ulysses*, in that the newspapers themselves existed, quite literally, in a dialogical relationship with one another and with their readership, as well as with Joyce's novel itself, in which they represent a mixed chorus of contending voices. Around the turn of the century, in Great Britain and Ireland, the idea that a newspaper should assume some putative sort of "objectivity" was not so persuasive as the idea that each paper inevitably represented certain interests, which, more often than not, were those of the single owner. Thus, from the perspective of cultural studies, newspapers of that time were less deceptive than our contemporary ones that claim to maintain a "journalistic objectivity" that thinly disguises their actual social and political commitments. But the opposing concepts of newspapers were influenced by culture as well as historical period. During the twentieth century, according to Anthony Smith, "a steady gulf has grown between American and European practice, the former dedicated to a journalism of neutral, 'factual' information, untainted by party, unblemished by influence, the latter still clinging, half-contradictorily, to the view that journalists should carry their party affiliations open to view" (Smith, 167–68).

Newspapers of the time had no choice but to stake out a position on most of the issues of the day—nationalism versus maintenance of the Union, further Catholic emancipation versus the status quo, support of tenant rights versus support of landlords, Home Rule versus the rule of Parliament, and, of course, the question of whether or not to support Parnell, which continued to be a divisive issue for years after the man's death. Indeed, since newspapers took a rather more active involvement in cultural issues than they do today, and since those cultural issues themselves usually had political ramifications, papers were organs for the arts not only through reviews of and publicity for books, concerts, and plays, but also through the poems and stories printed in them on a regular basis.[9] Newspapers took positions on all these issues and more, not only in response to one another but also in response to their own histories and shifting ideological positions.

The late nineteenth century was a heyday for newspapers and other periodicals, which had spread and mutated into a stunning variety of forms of print. During the nineteenth century,

> a much greater range of forms was developing than had ever been known before—Sundays, evenings, regional and local editions, financial papers, women's papers—aided by a proliferation of experiments with new techniques and new methods of organizing the flow of material through private telegraphs, news agencies, syndication, serialization of fiction. (Smith, 106)

Thom's Dublin Directory for 1906 lists, under the heading "Newspapers and periodicals" published in Ireland, some 48 issued weekly or daily, and an additional 36 issued monthly or biweekly.[10]

While today a major city in the United States will probably boast, at most, two or possibly three newspapers, Dublin at the turn of the century had a multitude. Hugh Oram lists the following major ones as being published in 1904:

Dublin Daily Express (1851–1927)
Dublin Evening Mail (1823–1962), published from the same building as the *Express*. Fiercely Unionist. Buff colored.
Evening Irish Times (1859–1921), a conservative, pro-British paper, but increasingly independent. The first penny newspaper in Ireland.
Evening Telegraph (1871–1924), the evening version of the *Freeman's Journal*.
Freeman's Journal (1763–1924), a daily which also had a weekly version.
General Advertiser (1837–1923)
Irish Daily Independent (1893–1960) Seen as more vulgarly national- ist than the *Freeman*. After its purchase by William Martin Murphy in 1905, the *Irish Independent* became the first halfpenny paper in Ireland. Along with the approach of the "new journalism," bolder "American style" type was used. Linked to the *Evening Herald*.
Lady's Herald (1895–1908)
Morning Mail (1870–1912), linked with the *Evening Mail*.
Rathmines News and Dublin Lantern (1895–1907)
Sport (1880–1931), associated with the *Freeman's Journal*.
Warder (1822–1919), a Protestant weekly newspaper eventually sub- sumed into the *Evening Mail*.
Weekly Freeman's Journal (1817–1924)
Weekly Irish Times (1875–1941)

This list, of course, does not include the major British newspapers. As Alf MacLochlainn points out, there was a very efficient boat train linking Ireland with England, and most of the major British serial publications were readily available in Dublin (MacLochlainn). The great majority of these were conservative on Irish issues, but some of them, such as those run by Irish-born editors William Stead and T. P. O'Connor, were sup- porters of Home Rule. Neither does the list include newspapers with national aspirations published elsewhere in Ireland; even *Sport* (known affectionately as *"The Pink"* or *"The Pink 'Un"*), for instance, had its rival *Ulster Saturday Night*, whose Dublin success led it to change its title to *Ireland's Saturday Night*. In addition, there were the "leading provincial papers," among which Thomas Lyster, enumerating the National Library's offerings in the "Scylla and Charybdis" episode, lists the *Northern Whig, Cork Examiner, Enniscorthy Guardian* as well as the *Kilkenny People* for which Bloom is searching[11] (*U* 9.598).

In the light of some historical perspective, such as was already available to Joyce writing in the 'teens and 'twenties, the *Freeman's Journal* could be seen to be on the verge of a precipitous decline after reaching remarkable heights of influence in the late nineteenth century. Founded in 1763, it was originally, like nearly all newspapers, subsidized by the government and anti-Catholic in orientation. MacHugh's joking mention of the "Sham Squire" Francis Higgins (*U* 7.348) alludes to a rather shameful period for the paper at the end of the eighteenth century. Higgins, an attorney's clerk in Dublin, married a young woman of good social standing under false pretenses. Having made his money with gambling houses, he used his ownership of the newspaper to libel Henry Grattan and other patriots. Indeed, he was a paid informer for the Castle (Brown, 20; Gifford, 135). But following this period, the *Journal* carved out a more impressive niche for itself, supporting the Catholic cause during the mid-1800s, but not so vehemently as, for instance, the *Weekly Telegraph* (1850–57) and its successor the *Catholic Telegraph* (1857–66). The paper was bought by Catholic interests in 1830. Described as "always moderate and cautious to a fault," it came nevertheless to support the pro-Catholic reformer O'Connell and repeal of the notorious Act of Union, which had dissolved the Irish parliament (Brown, 36). By 1810, there were only about a dozen newspapers in Dublin, all owned by Protestants, a majority of them subsidized by the government, only three of which were at all pro-Catholic (Brown, 32, 23). But while the *Freeman's Journal* offered a strong contrast to such upholders of the status quo, supporting a gradualist parliamentary program that later would fit neatly with Parnell's program, it was equally a contrast to the radical and successful paper known as the *Nation*, with its mixture of news, literary criticism, poetry, and social commentary. Founded in 1842 and succeeded by the *United Irishman*, *Irish Felon*, and the suppressed *Irish Tribune*, the *Nation* was more a "budget" than a newspaper in the modern sense, and was the only major organ to call for national independence (Brown, 29; Oram 1983, 58).

Having risen along with Parnell, the *Freeman's Journal* slowly began to fall with him, despite abandoning his support with alacrity. This did not please all its readers, of course. Stephen Brown recalls that "some Parnellite sympathisers...carried out a mock funeral procession. Copies of the *Freeman* were burned and solemnly buried in the burial vault of the Sham Squire at Kilbarrack churchyard" (Brown, 39). Even when the paper was at its best, Arthur Griffith, founder of the *United Irishman*, is supposed to have pointed out snidely that the headpiece over the *Freeman* leader showed "a homerule sun rising up in the northwest from the laneway behind the bank of Ireland" (*U* 4.101), a clear indication that he found the paper pseudo-nationalistic. By 1904, while still the dominant newspaper in Ireland, the paper had lost its bearings and *raison d'être*, a condition suggested in "Aeolus" by the tipsy incoherence, confusion, and inaccuracies of the fictitious editor, Myles Crawford, who cannot even correctly identify the year of the Phoenix Park Murders. The actual owner, Thomas Sexton, for political reasons maintained a kind of news boycott, in which the names of certain MPs were never to be mentioned in his paper; according to Hugh Oram, "He was the man…who did the most to run the *Freeman's Journal* into the ground" (Oram 1983, 100).

But the position of the *Freeman's Journal* shortly after the turn of the century can only be brought into full relief by the realization that its eventual successor, the *Irish Independent*, was founded by Parnell after his fall, and began to be published in 1891, shortly after the man's death. It was acquired by William Martin Murphy in 1900 and gradually moved toward an anti-Parnellite and increasingly conservative policy. Soon amalgamated with the *Daily Nation*, for four years the paper was run at a loss—it was the first Dublin paper sold for only a halfpenny—in order to smash the *Freeman's* near-monopoly. Both anti-Parnellite and resolutely modern in style, and employing superior production techniques, the paper consciously imitated the format and approach of London's *Daily Mail* and *Daily Express* (Brown, 40). While some newspapers in Ireland did not print photographs at all until 1898 (Oram 1983, 79), the *Independent* featured them from its inception in 1893. It was also the first newspaper in Ireland to organize an advertising sales department (Oram 1984). If Richard Ellmann were correct in seeing newspaper journalism as Joyce's "principal emblem of modern capitalism…wasting the spirit with its persistent attacks on the integrity of the word, narcotizing its readers with superficial facts, habituating them to secular and clerical authority" (Ellmann 77–78), then the *Independent* would probably be the most prominent local example of such a tribute to the hegemony of capital and the pressures of modernity. It became increasingly influential as the century wore on, and was generally regarded as the unofficial organ of the Free State by 1921. Murphy adopted a modern stance of pseudo-objectivity for his newspaper, claiming that "the extravagances of partisanship will be unknown in the *Irish Independent*" (Brown, 40). In practice, this meant that Murphy's political opinions would be tacitly assumed without acknowledgment or critical examination. The time of *Ulysses* is the time when Alfred Harmsworth, Lord Northcliffe's brand of sensational, energized journalism was triumphing in the London press, and its American equivalent was becoming increasingly influential in Anglophone countries. Murphy, in fact, was a good friend of Harmsworth, and his Irish paper's remarkable success greatly followed from his emulation of the techniques that had worked so well in the London press.

Joyce naturally was well aware of the changing fortunes of the Dublin newspapers and hints at them in *Ulysses*. The evolution of the "heads" or "captions" in the "Aeolus" episode, from the wordy, inappropriately elevated language of Victorian times ("WITH UNFEIGNED REGRET IT IS WE ANNOUNCE THE DISSOLUTION OF A RESPECTED DUBLIN BURGESS"; *U* 7.61) to the breezy, slangy sporting heads late in the chapter (such as "SOPHIST WALLOPS HAUGHTY HELEN SQUARE ON PROBOSCIS"; *U* 7.1032) alludes directly to the victory of the new American style in newspaper format, which, in 1904, was still to be realized. But there is no doubt that it is the "new journalism" to which Joyce directs our attention. Patrick Collier quotes an anonymous contributor to the *Nation and Atheneaum*, writing in 1922, just after Lord Northcliffe's death:

> So, about thirty years ago, the "New Journalism" was born. Headlines, scareheads, "snappy pars," and "stunts" took the place of literature, serious news, and discussion. The note of papers rose from modulated reason to the yawp of an American baseball match, calculated not to convince but to paralyze the opponent.[12] Pictures appeared, with adjectival commendations: "A Delightful Photo of a Charming Little Hostess."...The change has been so complete that one no longer notices anything about it. ("From Essay to Stunt," *Nation and Athenaeum* 31 [18 Aug. 1922] 677, cited in Collier, 12)

A more recent evaluation of the journalistic movement describes it in these terms:

> In an attempt to entertain the public, the New Journalism used interviews, photographs, and typographical features, such as bold headlines, to break up the page. It had a more personal tone, more of a thrust toward social concerns, and became synonymous with lower standards and cheap effects. The papers published abridgements of speeches rather than the traditional unbroken verbatim columns. The vacated space was filled, in part, by revenue producing advertisements....Without advertising in mass circulation newspapers, cheap daily newspapers would have been impossible. (Thompson, 4)

It was the *Independent* that pioneered such innovations as a separate women's section, which it introduced around 1909 (Oram, 1984), and the *Independent* was the first to hire its own motor-van to deliver the paper to other cities (Oram 1983, 117). By the time Joyce wrote *Ulysses*, the offices of the *Freeman's Journal* and its sister publications had been destroyed in the 1916 uprising, neatly exemplifying the twentieth century's displacement of political gradualism by violence and armed revolution. Although the paper hung on until 1924, it was no longer a strong journalistic presence. If anything, the *Freeman's* employees were less ambitious than Bloom, who has time for an extensive personal life during his supposed work hours on June 16, 1904. Hugh Oram quotes an ad canvasser working for the *Freeman* in 1920, known as "Funge," as saying that he could easily do a week's worth of work in a single energetic Monday morning (Oram 1984).

Seen in this light, it is apparent that, like "The Dead," "Aeolus" is permeated by a nostalgia that seems all the more inappropriate in that it takes place in a newspaper office, a locale ostensibly dedicated to the present moment. While this newsroom seems to have a single telephone, on which Bloom attempts to consult with the editor, the reporters' room in the *Independent* the following year was well known for being packed with telephones in heavy use, the essential communications instrument of modern urban life. Ironically enough, the characters in the *Freeman* offices seem assembled by Joyce as examples of a preliterate, oral culture, hypnotized by the sounds of their own voices and the voices of their ancestors. "We were always loyal to lost causes," says "Professor" MacHugh (*U* 7.551), referring to the Irish people, but equally accurately characterizing the group gathered around him. The gang in the pressroom is celebrating great orators who are decidedly of the past, and whose oratorical styles are emphatically dated; "Professor" MacHugh's frequent references to the classical past (he teaches Latin) underline this quality.

And Miles Crawford, even when attempting to draft Stephen for what O'Molloy wittily calls the "pressgang" (*U* 7.625)—as if the only way apprentice reporters could be brought on board were through impressments on the high seas—tries to do so with stories of the great reporters of the past, especially Ignatius Gallaher.[13] O'Molloy, for one, is scornful of Crawford's linking Gallaher's name with that of significant political figures of the nineteenth century. Attacked by O'Molloy, Crawford insists, "Grattan and Flood wrote for this very paper...Where are you now? Established 1763. Dr Lucas. Who have you now like John Philpot Curran?" (*U* 7.738). Crawford, eager to defend the honor of his profession, is continually sidetracked by his suspicion that he can only assert the greatness of the paper's past in contrast to its degenerate present. Essentially, he speaks with two conflicting voices, one of them asserting the greatness of newspapers, the other lamenting their present-day decline. This is hardly a recipe for rejuvenating the press. His pursuit of Stephen, of course, is a clear indication that he has no idea of who would be likely to have journalistic talent, and Stephen's story, which outdoes Zola in naturalistic dailiness, is a perfect example of the anti-newspaper story, a sort of Dublinesque "dog bites man."

But Crawford's invocation of the fictional Ignatius Gallaher's stunt is also richly ironic. Gallaher was apparently working as stringer for the *New York World*, then owned by Jay Gould, but in 1883 bought by Joseph Pulitzer, and known for sensational and muckraking journalism of the sort William Stead pioneered in the British Isles. The *World* covered the Invincibles trial with special attention because of its large percentage of Irish-American readers. Gallaher's coup was a product of the technical limitations of the early twentieth-century communications network. The telegraph cable linking the British Isles with New York was, of course, incapable of transmitting a map, which is what the Invincibles trial especially called for; Gallaher's solution was to send a message referring the New York editors to a particular advertisement in a St. Patrick's Day issue of the *Weekly Freeman*, which the *World* offices would have on file, and then assigning key positions of the assassins and victims to letters used in the Bransome's Coffee ad on page four. In fact, the history of journalism in Ireland is filled with such stories of reporters taking shortcuts to scoop one another. Andrew Dunlop, who worked for the *Daily News*, *Freeman's Journal* and *Irish Times*, in his memoir *Fifty Years of Irish Journalism* gives examples of special trains being hired to get a jump on a story for a particular newspaper,[14] as well as newspaper employees "blocking the wires" so that competing reporters could not file their stories (Dunlop 109–18). Dunlop tells of having dinner at Mansion House with the Lord Mayor, Charles "Dan" Dawson, and James Carey, then a member of the Dublin Corporation, who was revealed as a leader of the Invincibles. Dunlop crossed to Holyhead by the night steamer with the story for London publication (105).

The Gallaher anecdote in *Ulysses*, whether historically accurate or not,[15] is a neat allegory for the situation of journalism: here is history—or, from another perspective, a sensational murder—brought to you quite literally by Bransome's coffee, via the advertisements that, according to Bloom, are what really sell a weekly paper instead of the news reporting (*U* 7.98). Gallaher is alert to the technical and formal limitations of the communications network, and knows how to take advantage of its possibilities. Interestingly, Joyce has combined the name of the real reporter, Fred Gallaher, with the first name of the founder of the Jesuit order, Ignatius, suggesting that Crawford's secular saint of journalism was the same sort of model for his followers that Ignatius Loyola was for his. But we must remember that Gallaher's triumph is over twenty years in the past at the time Crawford celebrates it—roughly the time of the *Freeman's* greatest influence. A more recent example would be the first usage of wireless telegraphy, in July 1898, when Marconi transmitted the results of the Royal St. George Yacht Club Regatta, using over 700 separate reports in Morse code. Here again, we must be struck by the disproportion between the highly sophisticated technical means and the trivial goal achieved; and we should note that it was not the *Freeman* who pulled off this coup but the *Dublin Evening Mail* under the Tory Lord Ardilaun of the Unionist Guinness family (Oram, 92).

But on the whole, the story of Dublin newspapers in the early twentieth century would probably center on the *Irish Independent*, as the progressive representative of the new journalism. One of the first places this would have a serious impact would be the advertising department: according to Hugh Oram, the *Independent* was the first in Dublin to organize an entire advertising sales department, professionalizing the job Bloom approaches as an amateur. What the *Independent* did was something the leading British and American papers were already doing by 1904 (Oram, 1984). By contrast, for all Crawford's energetic rhetoric, the *Freeman's Journal* is mired in past practices and the memory of past glories. The editor, when sober, would be well aware of this: he originally worked for the *Independent* and only left it on the promise of advancement (*U* 7.307). It may even be that his curt dismissal of Bloom, the ad canvasser, is rooted in his discomfort with the realization that advertising income increasingly supported newspapers, and sales and subscriptions decreasingly. Much as he might wish to demand that advertisers like Keyes kiss his royal Irish arse (*U* 7.991), under modern economic pressures the reverse is more likely to happen. Be that as it may, by 1904 he must be aware that the historical and commercial momentum is now with his former employer, and this is one of the dialogic forces motivating his doomed, nostalgic appeal to the triumphs of the past. We might also note that Joyce paid his final visit to the offices of the *Evening Telegraph* and *Freeman's Journal* not in 1904, but in 1909, after Murphy's recasting of the *Independent,* by which time the odor of failure would have been that much more pervasive.

Unfortunately, when discussing the actual readership of newspapers in Ireland around the turn of the century, there is curiously little hard evidence. Many of the records have been destroyed, either in the

1916 rebellion or during the "troubles." Professor Louis Cullen T.C.D., researching the history of the stationers/booksellers Eason's, came across records for the Belfast house for the year 1904 which are illuminating.[16] Although it is likely that in Belfast a good many more British papers and magazines were sold than would be the case per capita in Dublin, because of the larger Loyalist population in Ulster, it is nonetheless likely that London periodicals had thoroughly penetrated the Dublin market as well. If this had not been the case, there would be no point to the frequent complaints in Irish organs such as the *United Irishman* about the degenerative influence of British examples of the New Journalism. The following table shows a day's sales of the newspapers carried at a Belfast Eason's in June 1904; the first group of twenty-one are United Kingdom newspapers, the second group of seven are Irish publications. All the papers cost a penny, with the exception of the halfpenny *Daily Express*.

Daily Graphic	8
Times	2
Morning Post	1
Daily News	14
Daily Telegraph	15
Standard	3
Chronicle	3
Leader	2
Sporting Life	1
Financial News	4
Financial Times	7
Westminster Gazette	—
Sporting Chronicle	8
Daily Mirror	11
Daily Mail	89
Daily Express	10
Morning Advertiser	1
Star	—
Scotsman	24
Glasgow Herald	26
Scottish Referee	1
Independent	7
Express	5
Irish Times	24
Freeman	83
Newsletter	24
Northern Whig	27
Irish News	6

the *Daily Mail* is the dominant paper in the list, with
of 89 copies, exceeding even that of the *Freeman*, whose
ne accounted for nearly half the total circulation of Irish
d in the last group). We should also remember that newspapers   ne time were typically consumed by far more people than
the single purchaser, including multiple readers in libraries and among
social groups in pubs and cafes; Joyce in fact shows several examples
of this in "Cyclops" and "Eumaeus," as well as showing Bloom passing off his *Freeman's Journal* to Bantam Lyons in an effort to get rid of
him (see "consuming Newspapers," below). Although Joyce does not
show this, newspapers could also be rented at an hourly fee for much
of the nineteenth century, further increasing their effective circulation. Finally, we can see that Eason's carried a number of newspapers
despite a bare minimum of daily purchasers; a minority clientele was
clearly not only tolerated but cultivated—one that would not survive
in today's periodical market. Indeed, the total circulation of all the
dailies is surprisingly small, considering the size of the market.

Newspapers and the Structuring of Experience

Newspapers enter immediately into dialogic relations with the reader
once they are taken up, and because of the broad social function the
reader grants them, they can be said to contribute to the structuring
of experience. The conscious efforts editors made, increasingly during the 1890s and the early years of the twentieth century, to form
readership communities in which the magazine or newspaper readers
would participate actively in the relationship created through periodical consumption—or at least were given the impression that this was
occurring—gave substance to the dialogical metaphor. A man reading a newspaper is thus engaged in a sort of conversation in which one
party is human, the other a material commodity. As Bloom observes,
"Everything speaks in its own way," including the newspaper presses:
"Sllt. Almost human the way it sllt to call attention. Doing its level
best to speak" (*U* 7.175). At a number of points in *Ulysses*, Joyce
shows an interest—which was shared by other modernist artists—in
the interface between human and mechanical speech (Rice).[17]

Newspapers have been stigmatized as the very force that reifies
the chaos of modern experience, as a series of apparently random
items united only by their dateline, and this is certainly one way to
interpret the overall ideology of newspaper form. Benjamin argued

that in contemporary experience, "contrasts which...used to fertilize one another have become insoluble antinomies. Thus, science and *belles lettres*, criticism and original production, culture and politics, now stand apart from one another without connection or order of any kind. The newspaper is the arena of this literary confusion." Yet the actions of editors in inviting the readership into participation in the periodical *as process* begin to erode the distinction between author and public, so that "the unselective assimilation of facts goes hand in hand with an equally unselective assimilation of readers, who see themselves elevated instantaneously to the rank of correspondents.... Literature gains in breadth what it loses in depth."

> The reader is always prepared to become a writer, in the sense of one who describes or prescribes.... Authority to write is no longer founded in a specialist training but in a polytechnic one and so becomes common property. In a word, the literarization of living conditions becomes a way of surmounting otherwise insoluble antinomies and the place where the word is most debased—that is to say, the newspaper— becomes the very place where a rescue operation can be mounted. (Benjamin, *Understanding Brecht*, 89–90)

This potentially utopian stance underlies the argument of Donald Theall, who claims that "the newspaper as a cultural phenomenon affecting all poetry and arts that shape language and communication, accomplished precisely the kind of rhetorical liberation which literary language and the visual arts required at the turn of the century" (Theall 1995, 78). Theall's celebratory approach to mass communications is really centered in his reading of both McLuhan and *Finnegans Wake*, a book in which many critics find that Joyce means to affirm and demonstrate the interchangeability of all levels of cultural expression. Whether this is also Joyce's position while writing *Portrait*, or even *Ulysses* is, of course, another question, but Theall is not particularly interested in the stages of Joyce's development as a social thinker.

But rather than arguing generalities about the ideological effect of newspapers at the turn of the century, it may be more useful to examine one in more detail. The *Freeman's Journal and National Press* for June 16, 1904, is an obvious choice, and, fortunately for Joyceans, has been reprinted by the Chelsea Press. The newspaper's physical appearance is surprising to a modern reader: at 23" by 25" it is only slightly larger than an average newspaper of today, but where today's newspapers are formatted so as to be read folded in two, the *Freeman* must be read partially opened, four square feet of paper effectively hiding the reader from his or her neighbors and emphasizing the solitary nature of the newspaper reading experience. If the newspaper were to be unfolded completely, it would in fact be twice this size. Public copies of the newspaper, such as the one Bloom peruses in the Ormond, were often equipped with wooden "batons" to aid in holding them open. Bloom takes advantage of his paper to hide the fact that he is writing incognito to Martha Clifford, while pretending to be answering an ad for a salesman: "Hope he's not looking, cute as a rat. He held unfurled his *Freeman*. Can't see now. Remember write Greek ees.... Bloom mur: dear sir. Dear Henry wrote: dear Mady" (*U* 11.859). As he sits in the Ormond, the newspaper colludes with Bloom in frustrating his "natural" bonding with his physical neighbor, Richie Goulding, and encouraging his virtual, epistolary relationship with a person who may not exist as such any more than does Henry Flower. But then, encouraging this new, print-mediated kind of relationship is precisely the newspaper's institutional interest.

Despite its size, the *Freeman* is far more compact than newspapers of today, in two senses: the typography is much smaller, averaging about eight words per 2 1/4" column, with ten columns on each page and an astonishing two hundred lines printed vertically down each of the ten columns. The paper also gives a far more compact impression than newspapers of today, because of the relative lack of special display ads or blank spaces. Each page holds some 16,000 words, while the newspaper is comprised of eight pages, meaning that each morning Dubliners were greeted by some 128,000 words, roughly twice as many as an average novel, and perhaps half as many as the gargantuan *Ulysses* contains. This does not mean, of course, that even the paper's faithful readers consumed this amount of verbiage daily; readers were selective, perfecting the arts of skimming and information retrieval with a minimum of actual reading. In fact, the act of newspaper consumption alters with each reader—a fact Joyce highlights in his many portraits of newspaper readers reading. This process would be most obvious in dealing with the first and last, or "outside" pages, which were almost entirely composed of "Prepaid Advertisements," or what we would call classified ads. Whether or not these were among the main features that sold a newspaper, as Bloom believes, they were certainly highlighted at the turn of the century, and it would be some years before the newer American style, which threw news headlines onto the front page, would become dominant.

Meanwhile, the *Freeman* was organized inside out, from our point of view, with regular news features like "Law Intelligence," "Commercial News," "Market News," and "Shipping News" on the second and third pages, and headlines for what we would consider important national and international breaking news, like the "Appalling American Disaster" of the "Excursion Steamer on Fire," or news of the Russo-Japanese war, buried on the fifth page. This was, in fact, the traditional layout of newspapers in Britain from the beginning, perhaps reflecting the commercial origin of newspapers as primarily advertising sheets. Obviously Myles Crawford, who is invested in a heroic mythology of newsmen, would rather ignore this aspect of the business, although Bloom sees things differently. The question is what effect the layout has on the reader's perception of importance, and while our contemporary newspapers tend to organize themselves front-to-back in what their editors would call an order of diminishing importance, with the classified ads segregated at the end, the *Freeman* in 1904 was more of a gallimaufry, an apparently unordered collection of an extremely broad spectrum of items. A newspaper reader in "Eumaeus" predicts that someday "you would open up the paper...and read: *Return of Parnell*" (*U* 16.1298), thus emphasizing that the headlines of a paper, rather than serving as an immediate advertisement, would be a daily surprise—at least so long as you hadn't heard the newsboys crying the main news.

Joyce's interest in headlines considerably predates *Ulysses*. In *Stephen Hero*, Cranly stands as if mesmerized, reading out the items from a "newsbill" on the roadway "in his flattest accent, beginning at the headline":

EVENING TELEGRAPH
[Meeting]
Nationalist Meeting at Ballinrobe.
Important Speeches.
Main Drainage Scheme.
Breezy Discussion.
Death of a Well-Known Solicitor
Mad Cow at Cabra,
Literature &.
(*SH* 221)

The irony here, from Stephen's point of view, is fairly obvious: here is a culture that sees "Literature and so forth" as of less significance or general interest than the mad cow or a drainage scheme. Cranly, with his limited interest in art, questions the irony—an irony that is somewhat diminished for us as well who may better realize the possible life-or-death consequences of either of these social issues. But the point is that the newspaper itself, in its physical presence, unlike the newsbill, advertises no such hierarchy; instead, it is a kind of seemingly random vaudeville of events, many of which we would not think of as "news."

Joyce, in adding the "headers" or "captions" (or in Michael Groden's term, "subheads") to "Aeolus" rather late in the composition of that chapter (Groden, 105), clearly intends to call their function into question, both in this chapter and in the newspaper itself. Stuart Gilbert, despite calling them "captions," seems to have seen them unambiguously as newspaper headlines: "It will be noticed that the style of the captions is gradually modified in the course of the episode; the first are comparatively dignified, or classically allusive, in the Victorian tradition; late captions reproduce, in all its vulgarity, the slickness of the modern press" (Gilbert, 179 n.1).

As I have argued above, taking the titles as headlines suggests a direct allusion to the furor over the "New Journalism." M. J. C. Hodgart, on the other hand, claims they are "rather captions under imaginary illustrations, probably photographs, added by an anonymous sub-editor," thus directing us away from a strictly textual context and toward the interplay of text and graphic illustration (Hart and Hayman, 129). Others have suggested that they resemble the captions shown in silent movies, either giving necessary dialogue or supplying whatever diegesis has not been implied by the moving images alone. Further abstracting them from their direct function, Archie Loss has suggested that, with their forceful graphic presence, the newspaper headlines work similarly to collage in Cubist art.

Probably the most sophisticated discussion of the headings is that of Wolfgang Iser, who argues that, from the reader's standpoint, the density and complexity of the text in the chapter produces a need for "macrostructure," which the headings purport to provide. "The heading is an instruction as to what to expect" in the segment that follows (Iser, 35). And yet the column below usually frustrates our expectations by going off in unforeseen directions or by "fragmenting facts and occurrences in such a way that to comprehend the commonplace becomes a real effort" (Iser, 36). Iser, I think, is correct in directing attention not to the heads themselves but to the intervening passages, which are far more confusing and chaotic than at first appears. Because the "story" part of the page is relatively naturalistic, and because there are really only two simple lines of plot being pursued during the episode (Bloom in search of approval for the Keyes ad and Stephen in search of placement for Deasy's letter), we lose track of

how devious and complex the narrative line has grown by co
with, say, the preceding chapter.

This is mostly a matter of focus: new characters appear ......
introduction. Subplots, such as Bloom's hinting at Hynes's debt,
interrupt other unrelated events, such as Hynes turning in a story,
perhaps the account of the Dignam funeral, to Nanetti while Bloom
is trying to get approval for his ad (*U* 7.113). The cinematic eye that
surveys scenes—such as the trams in front of Nelson's pillar and
the draymen rolling barrels of Guinness onto the brewery float—
contributes nothing direct to the diegesis; if anything, it distracts us
from the main action. In many ways, the chapter is a direct prepa-
ration for "Wandering Rocks," in its fragmentation of the action
and willingness to follow previously unknown, minor characters into
their own dubiously relevant subplots, and certainly in its suggestion
that the true subject of the chapter is neither Bloom nor Stephen,
but the city. This is the first chapter in which both Stephen and
Bloom come onstage, and thus the first in which an enveloping narration must somehow comfortably encompass both of these radically
different subjectivities, each of whom Joyce has previously chosen to
present with his own appropriate style of narration, emphasizing the
difficulty of finding common representational ground for the two
men. So it is appropriate that the chapter's form mimics a newspaper;
after all, the newspaper is designed to generate a kind of narration
that can include, in some form, all the citizenry, at least potentially.
And before the day is out the *Evening Telegraph*, however inaccu-
rately, will note the presence of both "Stephen Dedalus B.A.," and
"L. Boom" (*U* 16.1259). As Benedict Anderson observes, modern
nationalism was greatly enabled by the growth of print-capitalism,
"which made it possible for rapidly growing numbers of people to
think about themselves, and to relate themselves to others, in profoundly new ways" (Anderson, 36).

My argument here is that Joyce wants to make substantial allusion to the subject of "Aeolus," the newspaper, and that the allusion
is both formal and historical. Viewed in this way, much of the content of the chapter—the invocation of great rhetoricians of the past,
for instance—is beside the point, because the impact of newspapers
is not dependent on the rhetoric they employ, so much as it is on
their overall form and organization. I would argue that their formal
implications are so powerful in their effect upon social consciousness
that they outweigh the putative ideology of individual newspapers.
By this I mean that while the *Freeman*, for example, can be identified

with Parnell, and thus with his political approach of parliamentary gradualism in the pursuit of Home Rule, this surface ideology may be outweighed by the overwhelming emphasis that any newspaper puts upon valorizing the present day in its nonhistorical immediacy. Insofar as it values one sort of event over another, a newspaper especially valorizes the sudden, unexpected event; the fully expected one is not "news."

But a newspaper, by definition, implies that all of the items it chooses to include are important; and newspapers around the turn of the century, which generally did not clearly rank their stories by prominent placement or by size of headline type, suggest that all their items are *equally* important. In fact, it is often difficult to distinguish advertisements from "news," and the notorious "par" requested by Mr. Keyes, a paragraph calling attention to a product or business, is expressly designed to blur the distinction between the paid classified advertisement and news of general interest. The *Evening Telegraph* for June 16, 1904, on the second page, second column, has a story about "the American Doctors and their Good Work," complete with subheads in the same typeface that the news stories employ. This in no obvious way announces itself as an advertisement, rather than a general-interest story about a Dublin clinic. At the same time, what we would call an editorial, expressing the opinions of the editors, often looks indistinguishable from a news story—and the news story itself is much more likely than it would be today to include a particular slant or implied judgment. But while they may belong to a wide range of categories, what unites the items in a given newspaper is their common participation in, say, June 16, 1904; this fact yields an inevitable focus on the ephemeral present that is the first message conveyed to any reader. In this respect, of course, newspapers have something else in common with *Ulysses.*

Socially, a primary function of the newspaper is listing the names of citizens. Perhaps we can distinguish three kinds of listing: the first, a mark of distinction and social prominence, is the name that appears in sections labeled something like "Fashionable Intelligence," where the movements of the aristocracy and the elite are chronicled. It is this that the "old specimen in the corner" of the cabman's shelter is supposedly reading when he announces, "Sir Anthony MacDonnell had left Euston for the chief secretary's lodge" (*U* 16.1666). A second, similar function is served by the numerous stories in which members of the bourgeoisie have their presence at ceremonies, meetings, or other civic functions attested to. This is the function of the *Evening Telegraph* story in *Ulysses* enumerating the mourners at Paddy Dignam's funeral, a listing that bestows a certain respectability upon both the deceased and those who are thoughtful enough to attend or, like McCoy, ask to have their names given to the reporter (*U* 5.172).

A third function, some would say the primary one in the view of social authorities, is naming or listing transgressors of various sorts, from the bankrupts who are routinely named in the "legal notices" to citizens accused or convicted of crimes. If the crime is interesting enough and/or the people involved prominent enough—as in Katherine O'Shea's divorce trial—intimate details of a person's life may contribute to a dramatic narrative whose publication itself is a kind of ritual shaming.[18] The suit for breach of promise covered on the third page of the June 16, 1904, *Telegraph* quotes very substantial portions of the engaged couple's love letters—a subhead refers to the "Amusing Correspondence"—and the frequent laughter of those attending the trial is noted throughout (p. 3, cols. 3, 4, 5). This is the function Joyce reflects when he has the newsvendor in "Circe" announce that he has the "*Messenger of the Sacred Heart* and *Evening Telegraph* with Saint Patrick's Day supplement. Containing the new addresses of all the cuckolds in Dublin" (*U* 15.1125). Newspapers performing this function are agents of Foucauldian surveillance, a surveillance intensified by Dublin's colonial status, on the one hand, and by the active involvement of the Church as social monitor, on the other: thus Joyce's unholy linking of the Catholic monthly with the *Freeman*'s sister publication.[19] Joyce's interest in this phenomenon may have been inspired during childhood when his father's name was printed in a blacklist of debtors in *Stubbs' Gazette* and *Perry's Weekly* (Jackson and Costello, 173).

That Joyce was particularly interested in this kind of social shaming through the periodical press is apparent from his treatment of it, beginning with "A Painful Case" and continuing, through several examples in *Ulysses*, to the mysteriously publicized incident of the cad in the park in *Finnegans Wake*. The public display of the private life of women arrested for drunkenness was virtually a genre in Dublin papers of this period. One example of the sort that may have provided a model for the *Dubliners* story is found in the October 16, 1903, issue of the *Dublin Evening Mail* under the double heading "A Sad Case" and "A Drunken Mother and Her Family":

> In the southern Police court today, before Mr. E. G. Swifte, a woman named Elizabeth Ennis was charged on a warrant with neglecting her children. The prosecution was undertaken at the instance of Inspector Neely....Patrick Ennis swore that two years after his marriage with the defendant she took to drink, and for the past eight years had been drinking all the time, with the exception of three weeks, when she was

supposed to have the pledge; but even then she was drinking light ale (laughter). She pawned his clothes, the children's clothes, and the bed-clothes, in order to get the price of drink, and was drunk practically from Friday to Tuesday every week....(p. 3, col. 1)

The report continues, with remarkable specificity and a complete disregard for the woman's privacy or the seriousness of her sentence (three months' hard labor). Three similar cases follow. From the reactions of the audience and the richly detailed narratives offered by the press, such cases combined the attractions of melodrama with those of broad farce. The stories are presented with the tacit assumption that we are witnessing a character flaw that deserves mockery and then physical punishment, rather than a serious social problem sprung from the situation of lower-class women.

Whether in their function of surveillance and shaming, or in their more socially neutral functions, newspapers curiously combine two fundamental functions of language, narrating and listing. Both take place in modified forms: newspaper narration is generally presented in the notorious "inverted pyramid" order, in which a brief version of the entire narrative is given first, and elaborations of increasing scope and detail then follow. This convention was at least partly a result of early telegraphic reporting, where a failure in the lines could cut off a reporter's story at any point, leading editors to demand a very brief initial summary narration, to be followed by detail and local color as the connection permitted. Thus, one effect of modern news technology is a disruption and reordering of the traditional function of narration. And certainly the effect of this on readers is apparent: where a reader will usually suspend judgment until a traditionally structured narration concludes, a newspaper reader will be inclined to pass judgment almost immediately, on the basis of the headline and first paragraph, which therefore accrue far more significance. And since the headline writer is virtually never also the reporter, this emotionally crucial function is left to a specialist who had nothing to do with gathering the story. Joyce points to this separation of functions in the increasingly extreme divergence of tone between "heading" and "story" in "Aeolus."

Perhaps he also points to the crucial function of the first lines of the newspaper story in the *Ulysses* chapter devoted to this subject: the references to the trolley changes, the postal exchange, and the "dullthudding barrels" of drink being loaded onto the brewery float (*U* 7.1–25), which we would be naturally inclined to read as mere *mise-en-scène*, take on another coloration if we imagine the circulation of mail, alcohol, and public transportation to be the fundamental "story" here and the business about Stephen, Bloom, and the newspaper hangers-on to be mere detail. Once we are reading as if an abstracted, inhuman process were the primary subject, again the parallel with "Wandering Rocks" becomes obvious. This sort of change of focus from the intimately personal realm of Stephen's and Bloom's internal monologues to the public, objective realm of Dublin street furniture, the administered modern universe of city traffic and commercial flow and exchange, is parallel to the change of focus in "Ithaca," where the characters' interests are continually subsumed in the text's irresistible shifts to a cosmic perspective. It also seems a clear anticipation of the antihumanistic techniques of the French *nouveau roman* of some forty years later.

Like its use of narrative, the newspaper's deployment of lists is somewhat unusual by the "natural" standard of oral delivery, since the lists generally occur within a narrative context—during the account of a funeral, for instance, when the attendees are named—and yet, in the service of a mechanical comprehensiveness, are far more extensive than would be the case in conversation, where both the auditor's attention span and the speaker's memory are limiting factors. There has been a great deal of critical discussion of Joyce's use of lists in *Ulysses,* but few have noted that he has modeled them precisely on the newspaper's use of listing. The sudden eruption of an apparently endless series of names or items when it takes place within the narrative context of a novel has effects that are both disorienting and comic— and yet, thanks to journalism's traditional practices, oddly familiar as well. Hugh Kenner early drew our attention to Joyce's unusual and suggestive use of lists, emphasizing that they demand our imaginative analysis in much the same way the Victorians found they were forced to interpret the testimony of facts (Kenner 1987, 142–45).

Another striking characteristic of newspapers of the time is their use of borrowed material. This is no doubt inevitable given the enormous amount of verbiage in each newspaper issue; it would take a battalion of writers to produce this amount of original writing on a daily basis. Nearly all the international news is attributed to either the Press Association or Reuters, and the great majority of such stories are printed just as they were written at the source; and so we frequently have stories in competing Dublin newspapers that are word for word identical. This is also the case in some of the categorized news, such as financial news or reports from the law courts; each newspaper may decide on one or two cases of extraordinary interest and cover those cases in depth with its own reporter on the scene, but the majority will simply be noted in a kind of telegraphic "legalese." Aside from this, there is a great deal of apparently random cannibalizing of the British and American press, especially for "filler" items in each paper. And each paper, to a degree, cannibalizes itself, so that in the Bloomsday *Evening Telegraph,* for example, the "editorial" section mostly covers again the news of the day, such as the American steamship sinking, but with the addition of some commentary—in this case, the idea that the disaster is somehow a result of the American cult of size. At the end of the editorial section the "Essence of Every Day's News" has short paragraphs mostly summarizing stories printed elsewhere in the paper (June 16, 1904, p. 2, cols 3–5). *Ulysses,* of course, has no peer novels to cannibalize, but source hunting has made apparent how much material (especially in "Ithaca") Joyce borrowed wholesale from newspapers, *Thom's,* and other such sources.

Both *Freeman* and *Telegraph* are striking in their variety of offerings, with different kinds of advertisement, local, international, and financial news, editorials, reports on parliament, legal notices, and court cases that have been singled out for extensive coverage. There is extensive sports writing (both discussions of events still to come, such as the Ascot race in the *Freeman,* and coverage of events that recently concluded, like the Ascot story in the *Telegraph*). If we extend our survey to the weeklies, a great many even more specialized, indeed stylized, kinds of items are on display: women's columns, including health, fashion, and domestic advice; children's features; games, puzzles, riddles, and jokes; general essays; poems and stories; reviews and accounts of performances; captions for illustrations; letters from readers and editorial responses; and the sort of anecdotal ironic or bizarre mini-narrative that the French term *fait-divers.* These are the sorts of "side features" Bloom thinks really sell a paper: "Nature notes. Cartoons. Phil Blake's weekly Pat and Bull story. Uncle Toby's page for tiny tots. Country bumpkin's queries" (*U* 7.94). Each of these, at least to some extent, has its own style and its own language, and the reader perusing the paper will encounter in rapid succession a cacophony of voices sounding democratically on any given page, each to all appearances unaware of and unaffected by the others. Yet all these voices are contributing to whatever unity a newspaper can be said to possess and all are deployed under the aegis of a single date and title.

Obviously the parallel here is to Joyce's procedure in *Ulysses;* nearly all the kinds of newspaper items named above are at least alluded to in the book. I want to suggest that Joyce, sensitive to the disturbing political implications of modernist specialization, what we might call the hypertrophy of the author function, is borrowing what Benjamin saw as a potential "remedy" from the newspaper, wilfully fragmenting his own authorial voice into the multitude of forms and voices that, in *Ulysses*, demands the reader's active participation. It may be objected that the parallel collapses in regard to authorship, since newspapers have no single author, but only a relatively passive chief editor. I would observe that one effect of modernity upon the newspaper was the creation of a "virtual author" in the dominant, highly personalized figures associated with the New Journalism or its equivalent—figures like Alfred Harmsworth or William Stead in Great Britain and Joseph Pulitzer or William Randolph Hearst in the United States. Editor/publishers such as these impressed their papers with the stamp of their verbal and intellectual style without necessarily contributing a single word to a given newspaper issue. Admittedly, to call them "authors" of their papers is to imply a new configuration for the function we imagine as authorship; but that is surely what, in any case, takes place under the pressure of modernity. As it happens, these were also the figures most responsible for promulgating the notion of reader participation in their papers through the development of a virtual reader's community. And I would argue that these three factors—the fragmentation of the author's voice (and the consequent shattering of its authority), along with the use of borrowed material and citation, combined with the active participation of the reader within the context of modernity—together created a new space of social possibility.

Consuming Newspapers

The effective circulation of newspapers at the turn of the century was far greater than its official net circulation, because each newspaper had the potential to reach numerous readers. Indeed, as I mentioned earlier, newspapers were frequently rented for an hour or two by readers who could not afford to purchase their own on a regular basis. Given the astonishing quantity of wordage in typical newspapers of the period, it is safe to assume that nobody who was not involved in newspaper production ever read a single issue through completely; each reader, in a sense, created his or her own paper by choosing which parts to read carefully, which to skim, and which to ignore. In *Ulysses*, some readers wish to consult the *Freeman* simply to check on a single item, like Bantam Lyons checking Bloom's copy for the runners in the Ascot Gold Cup (*U* 5.520). Although he is originally interested in another horse entirely, his spotting the name of Throwaway in the paper just as Bloom says he was about to throw the newspaper away convinces Lyons momentarily to back the dark horse; here Lyons is using the *Freeman* almost for a species of *sortes Homericae*, relying on the stochastic coincidence of his conscious concerns, Bloom's comment, and the newspaper's words to guide his actions. But then, many readers, dependent on chance to determine which of the multitude of newspaper items they read, do something similar. Benedict Anderson directs our attention to the "mass ceremony" of newspaper reading in modern cities, pointing out that Hegel saw it as a substitute for prayer. "What more vivid figure for the secular, historically clocked, imagined community can be envisioned? At the same time, the newspaper reader, observing exact replicas of his own paper being consumed by his subway, barber, or residential neighbors, is continually reassured that the imagined world is visibly rooted in everyday life" (Anderson 35–36).

But Joyce particularly wants to direct our attention to newspaper consumers who are dependent on another reader to determine what information they are given. In this interchange, news-reading becomes social performance, and there is a complex dialogical interchange among reader (who supplies intonation, selection, and sometimes commentary), newspaper, and (sometimes commenting) listener. We see two main examples of this: one in "Cyclops," where the Citizen reads from several newspapers to his friends and other bar patrons; and another in "Eumaeus," where both an old fellow sitting in the corner of the cabman's shelter and the sailor Murphy read out items to their accidental audience. "Cyclops" is dominated by the truculent and vivid personalities of the Citizen and of the nameless narrator, and our first impression of the episode depends greatly on the energetic and aggressive speech both of them use. But I want to suggest that in a more fundamental way the chapter is about the printed word, especially the newspapers that are piled around the Citizen's seat. The interpolated, highly stylized passages are obviously written rather than spoken, and nearly all of them are further identifiable as mock-newspaper features, such as the society-page wedding interpolation (*U* 12.1266–96), or the sports-page account of the Keogh-Bennett fight (*U* 12.960–87). Here, as with the account of the *Princess Novelette* in "Nausicaa," it looks as if, in his parody, Joyce had exaggerated the "sportiness" of the narrative style toward that of 1920s American sports writing.[20]

Similarly, the "legalese" that presents the judgment against Gerachty for stealing tea from Herzog at the beginning of the chapter (*U* 12.33) is a slightly exaggerated version of one of the "legal notices" that appeared in all the major newspapers. The ground bass of the parody throughout the chapter, of course, is the mock-medieval narrative style in which Irish heroic tales were generally paraphrased in English by writers such as Lady Gregory, a style that sometimes slips into a more authentic imitation of Old Irish mythic cycles, as in the description of the Citizen as Irish demigod (*U* 12.151). On the surface, there could be few styles we would identify less readily with newspapers; and yet any journal with cultural pretensions published this sort of literary narrative regularly. Joyce, who famously lacked enthusiasm for Lady Gregory's work, is making a kind of Dubliner's inside joke when he demonstrates that from a naturalistic point of view, such as is suggested by the barroom talk, Irish Medievalese is little different from the equally stylized, equally "tumescent" styles of sports writing and society notes, and, in the world of Dublin periodicals, is equally inescapable.

The narration and transcript of the spiritualist society meeting in which Paddy Dignam is evoked follows the scientistic, mock-objective style of numerous psychic society journals of the period ("the apparition of the etheric double being particularly lifelike owing to the discharge of jivic rays from the crown of the head and face"; *U* 12.340), and is immediately followed by the mock-heroic medievalism of "He is gone from mortal haunts: O'Dignam, son of our morning" (*U* 12.374). The divagations of the barroom conversation thematically trigger special features—for instance, Bloom's explanation of hanged men's erections leads to a science feature on the testimony of "Herr Professor Luitpold Blumenduft" (*U* 12.468). Garryowen's growling leads to a literary performance review, while the narrator's comment about Bloom having a "soft hand under a hen" (*U* 12.845) brings on a bit of "Uncle Toby's page for tiny tots" (*U* 7.94): "Black Liz is our hen. She lays eggs for us. When she lays her egg she is so glad. Gara. Klook Klook Klook" (*U* 12.846). If the barfly narrator feels free to accuse Bloom of thievery, the meta-narrator (or Arranger, as Hayman termed this function) can immediately imply that such an accusation is childish.

The Citizen's decorated handkerchief is extensively and appreciatively reviewed as if it were an illuminated manuscript or rare tapestry (*U* 12.1438). The mention of St. Patrick, followed by Cunningham's blessing on all present, brings forth a stilted, elaborate "church news" account of a festival procession (*U* 12.1676). At times the default parodic style is combined bizarrely with another, as when a case under Sir Frederick Falconer is described in terms such as a newspaper would use in its legal notices, but filtered through an inflated Irish medieval-ism (*U* 12: 1111). Meanwhile, throughout the chapter, the entrance of any character into the bar immediately triggers the romantic elevation of Irish medievalism, as if everyone were a hero until they became better known. The succession of parodic styles is very much like the experience of a reader glancing through a newspaper's varied offer-ings with their incommensurable narratives, a similarity reinforced by the frequent use of unreasonably extended lists that, in this chapter as in newspapers, serve as land mines disrupting the diegetic function of narrative.

The "Cyclops" chapter invokes newspapers through its substance as well as its form. The main topics, such as brutality in the British navy, are inspired by newspaper features: as the Citizen says, "Read the revelations that's going on in the papers about flogging in the training ships at Portsmouth" (*U* 12.1330). Sitting there surrounded by his heaps of newspapers, the Citizen monopolizes the conversation by borrowing their authority, even as he critiques their limitations. When Bloom passes by, the Citizen reminds his audience that the ad canvasser works for "the old woman of Prince's street" (*U* 12.218), the *Freeman*. When he reads from the *Irish Independent*, "founded by Parnell to be the workingman's friend" (*U* 12.230), he suggests that, judging by the extremely English-sounding list of names in the "births and deaths," the "*Irish all for Ireland Independent*" has sold out to the oppressor (*U* 12.222). Of course, he is perfectly well aware that despite Parnell's founding of it, the paper was almost immediately taken over by the anti-Parnellite faction. Although he is supposedly "reading out" the births, deaths, and marriage announcements, in fact the Citizen is both censoring and rephrasing. Gifford points out where he skips Irish names to put emphasis on the English-sounding ones, and where he also occasionally skips English names (Gifford, 327–28). He also condenses and rephrases, as follows: "Vincent and Gillett to Rotha Marion daughter of Rosa and the late George Alfred Gillett, 179 Clapham road, Stockwell" (*U* 12.227) appears more expansively in the June 16, 1904, *Independent* as "Vincent and Gillett—June 9, 1904, at St. Margaret's, Westminster by the Rev. T. B. F. Campbell, Edward Vincent, Whinburgh, Norfolk, to Rotha Marion Gillett, younger daughter of Rosa and the late George Alfred Gillett, 179 Clapham road, Stockwell" (p. 1, col.1). Every alteration he makes in the literal text of the newspaper inevitably increases the proportion of his dialogic power and authority in the act of public reading, as opposed to that of his source.

Even discussions of events one of the bar crowd has witnessed, like Ned's tale of the outcome of the Canada swindle case, are often just those stories covered (with some factual differences) in that evening's *Telegraph* (p. 3, col. 2).[21] The newspaper throughout is held up as the medium through which politics takes place—a state of affairs possible because politics in 1904 Dublin, Joyce implies, is almost entirely a verbal affair. Even the otiose narrator expresses his anger about the Citizen's dog by saying, "Someone that has nothing better to do ought to write a letter *pro bono publico* to the papers about the muzzling order for a dog the likes of that" (*U* 12.707). Perhaps most intriguingly, J. J. O'Molloy, capping a series of questions as to Bloom's identity, asks, "Who is Junius?" (*U* 12.1633). The allusion, as Gifford informs us, is to the signature of a regular contributor to the London *Public Advertiser* between 1769 and 1772, author of a series of pseudonymous attacks on George III (Gifford, 367). Cunningham informs the bar that Bloom's original family name was Virag, and the Citizen refers to him as "Virag from Hungary" and adds, "Ahasuerus I call him. Cursed by God" (*U* 12.1666)—thus adopting two very different approaches to the problem of naming and selfhood. Given the context in which everyone is questioning Bloom's identity, we are reminded that, like the Internet today, the public discourse of newspapers allows everyone to assume a virtual identity that may not correspond with the name by which they are generally known. Ironically, the newspaper is both the organ of formal civic record, assumed to have the same sort of objective truth that reference books like *Thom's Dublin Directory* claim, and at the same time, as we learn in "Eumaeus," it is riddled with pretenses, errors, accidents, and even the mechanically generated nonsense of bitched type. Bloom, alias Virag, is also, according to the written record, "L. Boom" (*U* 16.1260) and Henry Flower, and can easily argue that he is either Jewish, Protestant, Catholic, or none of the above (*U* 17.540).

The peculiar valence of names in this chapter, from the traditional mythic perspective, has its roots in the Homeric episode, where Odysseus escapes the responsibility for blinding Polyphemus by giving a false name—or literally, a "no-name," *outis*. But from another perspective we should remain alert to the social functioning of names under modernity, especially as mediated by the popular press. We should recall that while the narrator is nameless, "the Citizen" is himself operating under a *nom de guerre*. Joyce attached that epithet to various people, including Gogarty, and it was used by the historical figure who was his putative model, the founder of the Gaelic Athletic

Association in 1884, Michael ("Citizen") Cusack (Gifford, 316). But it is probably no coincidence that *The Citizen: A Monthly Journal of Politics, Literature, and Art* was published in Dublin and London beginning in 1839 and assumed many of the same attitudes taken by Joyce's character. Addressing the country's hopes at the beginning of 1839, the journal writes, "Enough that, whatever they were, they have not been realized; that, physically beheld, Ireland is a disgrace to the civilization of the era; and that, while politically she is denied the privilege of self-rule, she is treated as 'alien in blood, language, and religion.'... Compromise should find no apologist now. The temper of concession has been stung to death ..." (vol. 1, 128).

Throughout, the newspaper's tone and concerns echo those of the man in "Cyclops." Speaking of the hostility and inaccuracy of the British press, the *Citizen* states, "We promise to make a day of rational reckoning with them, before they have time for many more garblings and prevarications" (130). Interestingly, in a review of a book entitled *Victories of the British Army*, the paper comments, "So sanguinary, so sickening a history it has never been our lot to read—not a redeeming trait throughout the whole of it—blood, blood, blood.... " (137). The revulsion at British violence here directly parallels the Citizen's disgust at the brutality on board ships of the British navy. In another review, the *Citizen* argues that while Ireland might look to the continent for institutions to imitate, it should never look to England, because "few nations can, in all the essentials of national character, be more directly opposed than the English and the Irish: they are, as it were, the opposite extremes, in modern European existence, of the material and spiritual developments ..." (219). On the other hand, the *Citizen* is frank about its policy of praising whatever is Irish: "In our humble efforts to render good service to the cause of this country, we have adopted the plan of... vindicating the national claims to a high and honourable position in the ranks of art, science, and literature" (318).

However justifiable some of these attitudes may be in historical reality, it is disturbing to see so many of them unchanged in substance or rhetoric between 1839 and 1906. Particularly, the revulsion against any aspect of British culture has the look of an automatic, unthinking reaction in a mind imprisoned by binary structures.[22] Yeats wrote in his Journal about "all those thoughts which were never really thought out in their current form in any individual mind, being the creation of impersonal mechanism—of schools, of textbooks, of newspapers, these above all." He argues that people who hold such opinions are usually completely confident of their correctness and righteousness, as the first thinker of an original thought never is (Yeats, 139). In this sense, perhaps it is fair to say that the Citizen is indeed a newspaper, with its simple public ideological commitment and its assumption of impersonal authority. But what Joyce puts on show in "Cyclops" is not only a talking newspaper, but a man who takes it upon himself to select, censor, and alter items offered by a paper to make his own rhetorical points. The Citizen dominates the barroom with his fame but also with his physical size and aggressive personality; what we are actually witnessing here is an interface between a print and an oral culture. That is, we might imagine that in a purely oral culture the Citizen would claim the privilege of speaking for everyone through his ability to dominate physically and psychologically, while in a pure print culture (if such a thing could exist) everyone would be absorbed in the reading of their own newspapers. It is often said that the freedom of the press belongs to the man who owns one; Joyce might add that, in 1904 Dublin. it is greatly at the service of the man who holds and reads the papers.

In "Eumaeus," we see something like a minor key, exhausted version of "Cyclops," in which a group of auditors are drinking undrinkable coffee and a number of less authoritarian men take the Citizen's place as newspaper reader. Once again we see Bloom hide behind a paper, this time the *Evening Telegraph*, this time to avoid being spotted by the prostitute from Ormond quay (*U* 16.708). In fact, in a burlesque of communal newspaper reading, at one point in the chapter Bloom and Stephen are reading the same paper (*U* 16. 1274), Stephen reading Deasy's letter on page 2 (fictitious, of course) while Bloom reads the account of the Ascot race on page 3 (factual, although the account Joyce gives differs in several respects from the actual *Telegraph* story). The moment is a wonderful metonym for the way Bloom's and Stephen's radically different consciousnesses nevertheless manage to run in rough parallel to one another for the duration of the chapter. One is reading about horses and the other about cows, though in contexts entirely alien to one another, and yet both stories coexist in the same newspaper—in a way, they are part of the same narrative.

The transition from an oral to a print culture again is highlighted here, as several readers try their hands at captivating the "decidedly miscellaneous collection of waifs and strays" in the shelter (*U* 16.327). But it is probably more significant that D. B. Murphy first tries to do so by means of his tales and picture, but fails because what he offers is, as Bloom immediately recognizes, so conventionalized. "She's my own true wife I haven't seen for seven years now, sailing about" (*U* 16.421), says Murphy, and Bloom mentally choruses,

"With a high ro! And a randy ro!" (*U* 16.438). But the discussion fairly soon takes a more general turn, to assassinations, a topic that quiets the room, since at least some of the audience suspect Skin-the-Goat's identity, and when Murphy notices a man "reading by fits and starts a stained by coffee evening journal" he asks for the return of the card and seaman's discharge he has passed around as (somewhat inadequate) evidence of his veracity (*U* 16.601). Then, in a final effort to capture the room's attention, Murphy shows off his ambiguous, if entertaining, tattoos. If with his stories, which combine romantic melodrama, grotesquerie, and the *fait-divers*, he was imitating the lighter weekly papers, now he is adding illustrations to his repertoire. But unfortunately for his performance, the sailor calls the Irish peasant "the backbone of our empire" (*U* 16.1022), and the violently nationalist keeper of the shelter expresses his contempt for the empire and anyone who serves it; this leads to an extended altercation, a less articulate, parodic version of Bloom's argument with the Citizen.

Bloom and Stephen's conversation peters out as the misunderstandings and riddles that Bloom so far has managed to ignore reach critical mass and he realizes that Stephen has delivered "a rebuke of some kind" (*U* 16.1174). Trying silence rather than risking offense again, he thinks about writing up "*My Experiences...in a Cabman's Shelter*" for *Tit-Bits*, in hopes of the guinea per column prize (*U* 16.1231). Although this thought was probably inspired by the *Evening Telegraph* ("tell a graphic lie") that has migrated to his table, it is only at this point that he consciously acknowledges its presence. In fact, he begins to process the preceding conversation as if it were a baffling paradox ("I suspect...that Ireland must be important because it belongs to me"; *U* 16.1164) or rebus ("the vessel came from Bridgwater and the postcard was addressed A. Boudin find the captain's age"; *U* 16.1234) of the sort he would find in any of the light weeklies—or, for that matter, in the *Telegraph*. He begins the ritual of running his eyes over the captions (i.e., headlines) of the "allembracing give us this day our daily press" (*U* 16.1237), a communion he soon shares with Stephen, and that seems to soothe the tension between the two.

For an instant, Bloom imagines that the heading for H. du Boyes, an agent for typewriters, is actually a reference to Boylan and his cuckolding of Bloom; ludicrous as this may be, we have seen that public shaming through naming is indeed one of the social functions of newspapers. The incident parallels his sighting of the "Elijah" handbill and momentarily mistaking "Blood" for his own name (*U* 8.8). Joyce has had to import from elsewhere the du Boyes advertisement, which is not in the actual *Telegraph* for June 16, but which does name an actual typewriter agent (Gifford, 551). The remainder of the items Bloom finds in the paper are actually there, with the exceptions of the letter from His Grace and the account of the Dignam funeral. Oddly enough, although Joyce seems to be giving a verbatim account of the newspaper story of the Ascot race, for example, there are numerous minor differences: "Secured the victory cleverly by a length" (*U* 16.1286), for example, reads in the original paper, "Throwaway, however, stayed on, and won cleverly at the finish by a length …" (p. 3, col. 8). I would suspect that Joyce took notes of key phrases from the original paper and then later reconstructed the story from those notes alone.

Bloom's reading of the Dignam funeral story shows his sophistication as a newspaper "insider": he knows who must have written the piece ("Hynes put it in of course"), recognizes by the plug for the undertakers that Kelleher at some point must have put pressure on ("certainly Hynes wrote it with a nudge from Corny"), and even deduces from seeing where the linotype machine malfunctioned that it must be at that point that Bloom called Monks about the Keyes ad, momentarily distracting him. He notes the humor of the absent Stephen's inclusion among the mourners because he is a B.A., McCoy's because he asked Bloom to give Hynes his name, his own misidentification as "L. Boom," and the virtual presence of McIntosh—a man who can stand as emblem for the chapter's overriding theme of false or ambiguous identity. He is perfectly aware of the hypocritical praise heaped upon a man who selfishly drank himself to death, leaving a family shackled by debt; he may not be aware of the irony involved in stating that "his demise after a brief illness came as a great shock to citizens of all classes by whom he is deeply regretted" (U 16.1251)—an image of solidarity negating class distinctions in a story whose very existence is determined by a desire to compliment the middle class. No such story would recount the funeral of a worker without bourgeois friends, especially in the *Freeman's Journal*, an organ virtually identified with the Catholic upper-middle class and the interests of the Castle. Much like "The Sisters," here is a case where everyone is anxious to assert that all is as it should be when the death suggests that something is very wrong indeed.

Someday, the cabman affirms, "you would open up the paper … and read: *Return of Parnell*" (*U* 16.1298). And why not, since several absent people are recorded as having attended Dignam's funeral? Perhaps more than any other comparable political figure of the late nineteenth century, Parnell was a creation of newspapers and, eventually, was destroyed by them. Joseph Lee points out that the land reform agitation that brought Parnell fame achieved the largest active mass participation of any movement in Irish history, mobilising sectors of the population and areas of the country just beginning to be politicised. It raised newspaper circulation to unprecedented levels, harnessing the mass popular support for the land campaign. *United Ireland*, founded by Parnell and edited by William O'Brien occasionally sold 100,000 copies, dwarfing the circulation of any previous Irish newspaper—the *Nation* sold 10,000 copies at the height of its fame forty years earlier. (Lee, 93)

The incident Bloom recalls when Parnell led a group of supporters to take back the *United Ireland* offices by physical force (*U* 16.1334) shows the significance both parties attached to his having his own newspaper. By contrast, the general coverage of the O'Shea divorce trial was more lurid and thus more destructive than had been the case for most earlier divorces involving public figures. Bloom recalls that the story of Parnell's relationship with Katherine O'Shea "had aroused extraordinary interest at the time when the facts, to make matters worse, were made public with the affectionate letters that passed between them" (*U* 16.1361). The most famous detail of the trial was an unsupported story that had Parnell climbing out of Katherine O'Shea's window with the aid of a ladder. As Katherine Mullin observes, "The fire escape theatricalized Parnell's sexuality, transforming him into the cad of Victorian melodrama" (87). Bloom appreciates the fact that the ladder episode was an image that "the weeklies, addicted to the lubric a little, simply coined shoals of money out of" (*U* 16.1379).

   Bloom and Stephen decide to depart, and the scene in the shelter ends with dueling readers, the cabby reading from his paper that earl Cadogan had presided at the cabdrivers' association dinner in London, while the old man in the corner reads that "sir Anthony MacDonnell had left Euston for the chief secretary's lodge" (*U* 16.1667). This incites the sailor to ask for the paper, and he proceeds to read, "Lord only knows what, found drowned or . . . Iremonger having made a hundred and something second wicket . . ." (*U* 16.1683). Here Joyce's intermittently godlike narrator both knows and doesn't know: there are no "found drowned" stories as such in the *Telegraph*, but there is indeed a story about the game involving the famous cricketer Iremonger. Whether this is more or less relevant to their lives than the old man's "fashionable intelligence" or the cabdriver's theoretically interesting news about a cabdriver's association in another country would be hard to judge. We are left with the impression that late-night television would have riveted this audience, but in its absence they are willing to be entertained by whatever makes it into the daily press.

Through the example of the modern press, writes Be₁

> we see that the vast melting-down process of which I spok₁
> destroys the conventional separation between genres, betwe₁
> and poet, scholar and popularizer, but that it questions ₁ ₁ the
> separation between author and reader. The press is the most decisive
> point of reference for this process, and that is why any consideration
> of the author as producer must extend to and include the press.
> (Benjamin 1998, 90)

Of course, Benjamin is well aware that the Western press is still a creature of capital; his utopian reading is addressed to its potential here, not its accomplishment. Still, it is curious that Benjamin's diagnosis coincides with Bakhtin's otherwise very different analysis of the liberating potential of the dialogical interchange within the novel genre and the press. For Bakhtin, the highest expression of the literary imagination comes in the intermixing of what he sees as, broadly speaking, the written genres, including the "oratorical, publicistic, newspaper and journalistic genres, the genres of low literature (penny dreadfuls, for example) or, finally, the various genres of high literature" (Bakhtin 1981, 288–89).

It has been my contention that the newspaper of 1904 shares many characteristics with *Ulysses*, and that Joyce was well aware of this fact; no doubt he rather enjoyed its irony, given his earlier scorn for the popular media. The very formal oddities of newspapers that I have attempted to analyze here are all the more estranging when we encounter them in what we expect to be a novel—the inversion of narrative, the exhaustive listing and ritual naming, the interpenetration of genres such as editorial, news story, and advertisement, the communal authorship and, sometimes, virtual authorship, the fragmentation of experience and the leveling of categories, all deployed within an overriding focus on the present that highlights the most trivial detail as long as it pertains to *now*—to June 16, 1904. All this cumulative strangeness is enacted within the history of the newspaper's development, on the one hand, and of Ireland's struggle toward nationhood, on the other. And as Joyce is at pains to demonstrate, the newspaper emerges into meaning only within the context of individual readers, with all the bizarre mechanisms of consumption that the newspaper demands—just as does *Ulysses*, which continues to teach us new ways to read.

Chapter Six

Tit-Bits, Answers, *and Beaufoy's Mysterious Postcard*

I should subscribe to the Verdant One [*Tit-Bits*, for its green cover].
(*Letters*, I 396)

I have tried to demonstrate that Joyce's *Ulysses* is intimately involved with the newspaper culture of 1904 Dublin: that newspapers make up a substantial part of its subject matter, especially in "Aeolus," "Cyclops," and "Eumaeus"; that we cannot appreciate the implications of Joyce's portrait of the press without an understanding of the social and political context of particular newspapers of the time; and that the newspaper contributes in unexpected ways to the very form of Joyce's novel. In other words, newspapers can usefully be seen as an intertext for *Ulysses*, in that both the popular cultural artifact and the avant-garde work of novelistic art are parallel products of modernity in Joyce's slowly decolonizing Ireland. Although the *Freeman's Journal* is, in most respects, an Irish product, it is obviously also the direct offspring of the British Empire's machinery for news promulgation and management. And as I have argued, its formal implications promote an ideology little different from that of the *London Times* (or for that matter the *New York Times*), whatever the political slant of its content or its professed orientation. But we should not imagine that the dailies provided the main reading material for Dubliners of 1904. A category of weekly magazine known as the "light weekly" had a much larger readership, and these were virtually all British publications, though some of the more important of them boasted Irish connections. I have already discussed (in chapter four above) the importance of the riddling interchange in the experience of reading *Ulysses*. I have also suggested that in this interchange the author/reader dyad of print-capitalism is brought into question, if not destroyed. Now I would like to go a step further and connect this basic mechanism of reading Joyce to the rise of an extremely influential genre of mass communication. Once again, I want to argue that a historical understanding of the genre is crucial to an appreciation of its contribution to our reading of Joyce's novel.

The Light Wecklies

The late nineteenth century was, in many respects, the golden age of popular light periodicals with numerous advertisements, just as the mid-nineteenth century had been the heyday of the "serious" ones— the responsible weeklies like the *Atheneum* and *Saturday Review*, the quarterlies and fortnightlies like the *Academy, Quarterly Review*, and *Edinburgh Review* (Nevett, 223). For women in particular, popular periodicals were usurping the place of the hardcover novel. A bewildering variety of journals flourished, with an amazing show of reserve strength in some areas. In 1904, according to *Willing's Press Guide*, a homemaker could choose from among *Home, Home Chat, Home Circle, Home Companion, Home Fashions, Home Friend, Home Life, Home Links, Home Messenger, Home Notes, Home Stories, and Home Words*; if her interests were less domestic, she might prefer the *Ladies' Review, Lady of the House, Lady's Companion, Lady's Home Herald, Lady's Home Magazine, Lady's Magazine, Lady's-Own Novelette, Lady's Realm, or Lady's World*. A different sort of audience might receive the *Woman at Home, Woman's World, Woman's Life, Woman's Work, or Womanhood*. Such magazines had a variety of biases and special audiences, but in general one could expect a sampling of news, stories, advice, essays, and a generally high moral tone, all accompanied by pervasive advertisement.

A far smaller group of magazines, dedicated to entertainment—or what our broadcast media now characterize as "infotainment"—were especially fashionable in the British Isles around 1904. These were what have been termed "conundrum" magazines, offering a potpourri of stories for gentlemen, quizzes, puzzles, games, jokes, anecdotes, surprising facts, oddities and curiosities, and, above all, contests. The first significant example of the genre was *Tit-Bits*, created by George Newnes; another was *Answers* ("a weekly journal of instruction and jokes"), founded by Alfred Harmsworth as *Answers to Correspondents* and the foundation of his publishing empire. The latter magazine crops up in *Ulysses* as Bloom sits listening to Ben Dollard singing and muses on how far he has fallen since his early success—"Number one Bass did that for him" (*U* 11.1015). Now he is reduced to going in for competitions in the conundrum magazines: "Decent soul. Bit addled now. Thinks he'll win in *Answers*, poets' picture puzzle. We hand you crisp five-pound note. Bird sitting hatching in a nest. Lay of the last minstrel he thought it was. See blank tee what domestic animal?" (*U* 11.1023).[1]

As Bloom implies here, the prizes offered by these magazines are a poor person's idea of wealth, as is appropriate for the lower-class and lower-middle-class readership—a "crisp five pound note," for example, or a pound a week for life in the most popular contest ever run by *Answers*. The puzzles themselves might be arbitrary, like the picture puzzle Bloom suggests, whose solution might or might not be "the lay of the last minstrel," or else they are disguised lotteries, such as the childishly simply "see blank tee." In actuality, few of the puzzles were as simple as Bloom's satirical example. Such magazines did have to be careful about conducting too obvious a lottery, because on several occasions the government prosecuted (Pound and Harmsworth, 144). It is difficult to appreciate how important these "light weekly" magazines, with their contests, insurance schemes, and miscellaneous money-raising events, were in the imaginative life of the lower-middle class. They took the places that later in the twentieth century would be filled by major lotteries, current movies, televised news summaries, soap operas, advice columnists, and therapists. In many ways, for a nostalgic, new urban readership, they took the place of local rural communities.

The weekly papers were in a circulation battle with one another as well as with the daily newspapers. There were the "serious" news weeklies—several of the Irish daily newspapers also had weekly editions, like the *Weekly Freeman*, while other papers were only issued in weekly format. But it was the light weeklies, which mixed news with a variety of entertaining features, that posed the more serious threat to newspaper circulation. Indeed, they claimed to serve as a digest of the huge number of other popular magazines available to the public, and in several respects the contemporary *Reader's Digest* is their lineal descendent. This was a way of turning into a virtue their reliance on rewriting and reprinting material taken from a variety of printed sources that they shared with the dailies, especially American papers and magazines. In Newnes's words, printed in the inaugural number of *Tit-Bits*,

> It is impossible for any man in the busy times of the present to even glance at any large number of the immense variety of books and papers which have gone on accumulating, until now their number is fabulous...It will be the business of the conductors of *Tit-Bits* to find out from this immense field of literature the best things that have been said or written, and weekly to place them before the public for one penny. (cited in Jackson and Costello, 202)

Although this was a laudable enough goal, in fact *Tit-Bits* soon discovered that the smaller its "Bits" of information or fiction were, the better the readers liked it. This obviously set a limit on the seriousness or complexity of the stories the journal could hope to digest.

In Belfast in 1904, the best-selling light weeklies included:

Christian Herald	5090
Answers	4069
Budget	2834
Pearson's Weekly	2470
Forget-Me-Not	2392
Tit-Bits	2197
Ireland's Own	1660
Sunday Companion	1599
People's Friend	1370
Home Chat	1339
Sunday Stories	1235
T.P.'s Weekly	1370
Chips	1066
M.A.P.	1053
Horner's Stories	1001

Several of these (aside from *Ireland's Own*) had Irish connections. Harmsworth himself had been born in Chapelizod, although he did not consider himself Irish. His magazine *Answers* was handled in Ireland exclusively by his old friend W. F. D. Carr in Dublin, who had originally put up part of the initial money for the publication. In gratitude, Harmsworth arranged for his publications to be made available a day earlier in Ireland than they were in London. Since the other publications included the popular *Boys Friend, Chips, Comic Cuts, Forget-Me-Not, Home Chat, Home Companion,* and *Home Sweet Home,* this was a significant advantage, and probably helped spur the growth of Harmsworth publications in Ireland (Cullen, 1985). Thomas Power O'Connor, an Irish journalist and politician who produced *M.A.P.* and the *Star,* owned *T.P.'s Weekly* (U 7.687). *Pearson's Weekly* had no special Irish association, but, despite its dignified-sounding title, was another conundrum magazine, started by Cyril Pearson, who had originally won a *Tit-Bits* contest in which the prize was a position working for the magazine. When he saw that Newnes had no intention of continuing to advance him, Pearson started his own quite successful magazine (Pound and Harmsworth, 141). The major "news weeklies," on the other hand, included *Thomson's Weekly News, Glasgow Weekly Mail,* and *Reynold's News,* the latter of which upheld a relatively old radical tradition and is bought weekly by Bob Doran as a nostalgic gesture toward his freethinking youth (*D* 66). All these had a circulation between one and two thousand copies.

For the sake of comparison, in an Eason's report dated June 20, 1904, on Monday, a total of 408 daily papers were sold; on the same day, Eason's sold 4069 copies of *Answers*, 1660 of *Ireland's Own*, 1339 of *Home Chat*, 1001 of *Horner's Stories* and 130 of the *Princess Novelette*. On Tuesday, 397 dailies were sold as against 5090 of the *Christian Herald*, 884 of *Sunday Circle*, 195 of the *Heartsease Library*, and 312 of *Snapshots*. Again, the total list shows a surprising variety; the major sellers are all general interest, entertainment-oriented publications, but Eason's also offered plenty of specialist publications which might only sell one or two copies, such as the *Hairdresser's Journal, Timber Trades Journal, Scottish Farmer, Mechanical Engineer, Trotting World, Shorthand Weekly*, and so forth.

Shortly after breakfast on June 16, 1904, Bloom performs the most notorious act of literary criticism of the century upon the story "Matcham's Masterstroke." "Quietly he read, restraining himself, the first column and, yielding but resisting, began the second....Life might be so. It did not move or touch him but it was something quick and neat" (*U* 4.506), he thinks, in a passage packed with ambivalent references: "yielding but resisting" is precisely the language we might attach to the "laughing witch" won by Matcham, though here it first refers to Bloom's bowel movement. "Something quick and neat" undoubtedly sums up Beaufoy's story, but is equally appropriate to Bloom's production, which he notes is "not too big" but "just right" (*U* 4.509). As a *coda*, Bloom then tears away half the story and wipes himself with it. Unlike most authors, Mr. Philip Beaufoy has the opportunity to respond when, in Bloom's trial in "Circe," he proffers as evidence "A specimen of my maturer work disfigured by the hallmark of the beast" (*U* 15.844).

But it is not only Bloom's disrespectful act that has prompted Beaufoy's anger: when challenged by the Watch, Bloom has unwisely impersonated Beaufoy, claiming to "follow a literary occupation" as an "author-journalist" and the inventor of prize stories, "something that is an entirely new departure" (*U* 15.804). Still later, having heard Stephen recite a version of his "Pisgah Sight of Palestine," he determines to gather it together with other of Stephen's stories and model schoolboy themes and submit them "following the precedent of Philip Beaufoy...to a publication of certified circulation and solvency" (*U* 17.651). Clearly, for Bloom, Beaufoy and Stephen Dedalus are similar paradigms of the literary life, and equally suitable for emulation. In "Eumaeus," he considers authoring and submitting a sketch he might entitle something like *My Experiences in a Cabman's Shelter* (U 16.11231). Thus with the aid of a genre of magazine that brings into question such distinctions, Bloom has personally confounded the figures of journalist and literary artist, artist and critic, reader and writer.

Tit-Bits

George Newnes, following a suggestion of his wife, founded *Tit-Bits from All the Interesting Books, Periodicals, and Newspapers of the World* as a sort of hobby in 1881. In fact, two years previously, a paper called *Replies*, "A Journal of Question and Answer," had been founded but met with no success (Pound and Harmsworth, 72). By contrast, *Tit-Bits* was an immediate, surprising hit with the public. Its huge success—it soon reached a circulation of nearly a million—was owed to the generation immediately affected by the Education Act of 1870 (Pound and Harmsworth, 53). By the turn of the century, what was essentially a new reading public had been created—according to *Thom's Statistics* for 1901, the literacy rate in Ireland rose from 20 percent in 1841, to 71 percent in 1891, and, of course, was still higher in the metropolitan areas. The 1891 Irish Education Act mandated compulsory attendance at school between the ages of six and fourteen everywhere but in the countryside, and included partial or entire abolition of fees (*Thom's*, 651). The key to commercial success for the new breed of print entrepreneurs lay in intuiting the taste and preferences of the new public. *Tit-Bits* set the pattern for a host of magazines that followed, including 12 direct imitators in the succeeding six months and 22 that year (Reed, 89). Of these, only two survived. One of these was *Pearson's Weekly*, the other Alfred Harmsworth's *Answers*, which he founded in 1888—one of some 200 new periodicals launched that year (Pound and Harmsworth, 89l). While still quite young Harmsworth had written for *Tit-Bits*. He is supposed to have commented, "The Board schools are turning out hundreds of thousands of boys and girls who don't care for the ordinary newspaper. They'll read anything that is simple and sufficiently interesting. The man who has produced this *Tit-Bits* has got hold of something bigger than he imagines. I shall try to get in with him" (Pound and Harmsworth, 54). Instead, he grew up to rival, and even surpass, his model.

Not only did *Tit-Bits* specialize in short stories, anecdotes, odd facts, responses to inquiries, and *faits-divers*, but from the first it also attempted to become an integral part of its readership's lives, with contests, correspondence, and numerous contributions from readers. It was, as Kate Jackson explains, a "uniquely interactive and self-referential form of the periodical text" (Jackson 1997, 201). Jackson suggests that the readership of *Tit-Bits* would have been eager for self-improvement, and probably acutely felt their lack of formal education. Although many assumed the readership of such magazines was working-class, Reed asserts that it was predominantly "the clerks and artisans, shopgirls, dressmakers and milliners, who pour into London every morning by the early trains" (93). In subscribing to *Tit-Bits* they could feel that they were at least making an attempt to better themselves in a relatively effortless and palatable fashion, much as they might enroll in vocational evening courses. "*Tit-Bits* in particular promoted a new concept of information as entertainment" (Reed, 93). *Tit-Bits* also offered them "Literary Excerpts" drawn from well-known authors such as Dickens, Disraeli, and Arnold himself, and, in the field of practical knowledge, ran regular columns of medical advice from a doctor, legal advice from a lawyer, and for general inquiries responses from the benevolent, all-knowing Editor himself.

Indeed, one of the reasons for Newnes's success was that his magazine was far more than a collection of writings regularly offered to whatever public chose to buy. Instead, Newnes was interested in "developing, publicizing, and promoting the text of *Tit-Bits* as the site of a community of mutual responsibility," by directly addressing, and thus imaginatively creating, his readership through the generation of a specialized reciprocal discourse (Jackson 1997, 201–2). Newnes always stressed the sections of the journal that involved editorial answers to the questions of correspondents. In the Inquiry column, short questions were published each week, with answers published two weeks later; even this interchange might involve the readers, who were challenged to themselves turn in the greatest number of correct answers in order to win a prize. Clearly, as Hugh Kenner recognized (145), the question-and-answer format here is one of Joyce's models for the format of "Ithaca," based as it was on a familiar pattern from the reader's school textbooks, including *Mangnall's Questions*. Further involving the magazines in its consumers' private lives, the 190th issue introduced an "agony" column, which included urgent messages from readers to loved ones, lost friends, or the world at large. Walter Benjamin, unlike many commentators who felt their own status as intellectuals threatened by the new literacy, saw a utopian potential in it. In "The Work of Art in the Age of Mechanical Reproduction," he observed,

> With the increasing extension of the press, which kept placing new political, religious, scientific, professional, and local organs before the readers, an increasing number of readers became writers—at first,

occasional ones. It began with the daily press opening to its readers spaces for "letters to the editor." And today there is hardly a gainfully employed European who could not, in principle, find an opportunity to publish somewhere or other comments on his work, grievances, documentary reports, or that sort of thing. (Benjamin 1969, 232)

Contests, which directly involved the readership in frenetic community activity, loomed large in the *Tit-Bits* universe. In one special promotion there was a bag of gold sovereigns buried and awaiting the first reader to successfully follow the clues in a series of stories (Cranfield, 217). Any reader might feel he had a good chance to win, and John Stanislaus Joyce was so regular an entrant that Joyce once called this his father's occupation (Scholes and Kain, 175). By the late 1800s, in a rather grotesque gesture, *Tit-Bits* was offering 100 pounds of automatic insurance to anyone killed in a railway accident with a copy of the magazine in his or her possession—an idea whose popularity depended upon the magazine's readership being largely an urban, commuting population. This ploy served as both promotion and as advertisement for the magazine; it also furnished narratives for it, since *Tit-Bits* regularly reported the stories of the deaths of readers whose family received the insurance payoff. *Answers* offered a similar policy, although it added a proviso that led to considerable merriment: "Suicides will not under any circumstances share in the benefits of the above insurance" (Pound and Harmsworth, 91).

Among the most popular contests ever was the "Tit-Bits Villa Competition," which offered a seven-room freehold house as the prize for the best short story. The competition was open to all "Loyal Tit-Bitites," as Newnes called his readers, and only required that the eventual owner should name his house "Tit-Bits Villa." Newnes received some 22,000 letters in response to his offer, some of them including as many as twenty entries. He stressed that the competition was open to "every member of every family in the kingdom, from the highest to the lowest," and justified this claim with the extraordinary condition that entries could be selected from published works rather than being original, so that even minimal literacy need not be a bar to success (Jackson 2000, 22). The Villa, described and constructed by Newnes as the ideal home, became a popular tourist spot. At a huge public ceremony, the villa was eventually awarded to a lucky entrant, and some 100,000 photos of the house were sold (Jackson 1997, 218-l19).

Obviously, Newnes had succeeded in creating a utopian space to which his readership responded on a deep emotional level; the sale of photographs suggests that each felt himself in some way connected with Tit-Bits Villa, whether or not he had actually won the prize. This villa, I would argue, is the immediate imaginative ancestor of Bloomville (aka Bloom Cottage, Saint Leopold's, Flowerville), the suburban retirement house of which Bloom fantasizes before going to sleep:

> ...a thatched bungalowshaped 2 story dwellinghouse of southerly aspect, surmounted by vane and lightning conductor, connected with the earth, with porch covered with parasitic plants (ivy or Virginia creeper), halldoor, olive green, with smart carriage finish and neat doorbrasses, stucco front with gilt tracery at eaves and gable, rising, if possible, upon a gentle eminence...situate at a given point not less than 1 statute mile from the periphery of the metropolis...(U 17.1505)

and so on *ad infinitum*, in an orgasmic flux of lovingly-imagined commodities. Joyce and Newnes obviously shared the perception that a freestanding home was situated near the center of the middle class's utopian aspirations, and Joyce's development of the idea suggests, as well, that visualizing such a space allows the bourgeois subject to imagine himself transformed by it into something closer to his unstated desires.

For obvious reasons, *Tit-Bits* stressed, in various ways, the idea that its readers had a good chance of winning prizes, discovering buried treasure, coming unexpectedly into money. Over the years the periodical ran features on unpatented inventions, clever devices society clearly needed but which had not yet been produced, life stories of men and women who were unexpectedly successful, "Fortunes Picked out of Dust Heaps," the discovery of Old Masters forgotten in attics, rare stamps languishing in abandoned collections, and heirs to fortunes who were unaware of their status. There were even contests incorporating clues found in the serial stories, such as "The Spoils of Asia": contestants were asked to send in their solutions marked on *The Strand's* War Map (a sister publication also edited by Newnes) in order to win 20 pounds *(Tit-Bits*, April 7, 1904). The emphasis was frequently upon a single discovery, realization, or act that transformed the protagonist's life, as winning a lottery might be expected to do. The title that Joyce assigns the Beaufoy story in *Ulysses*, Matcham's Masterstroke," suggests just this philosophy of life—that we are free to devise a single clever ploy that will win the girl, ensure business success, or confound our enemies. And perhaps *Tit-Bits* is the very place where we can learn how to do that. Advertised in *Tit-Bits* were repositories of general knowledge that might stand one in good stead in this effort, such as *Pears' Shilling Cyclopedia*, an 800-page tome that included a dictionary, a "compendium of general knowledge," "a mass of curious and useful; information about things that everyone ought to know," and a "ready reckoner" such as Bloom possesses (*Tit-Bits*, April 2, 1904).

The June 11, 1904, issue of *Tit-Bits* seems to be typical of the magazines during this period. The front page (a guinea per column is paid for contributions to it) consists entirely of short jokes, often satirizing various kinds of pretentiousness:

> *Doctor*: "I found the patient to be suffering from abrasion of the cuti-
> cle, tumefaction, ecchymosis, and extravasion in the integument
> and cellular tissue about the left orbit."
> *Judge*: "You mean that he had a black eye?"
> *Doctor*: "Yes."

The next page prints a calendar along the top, followed by "Some Remarkable Games of Single-Wicket Cricket" and "Crimes Which Have Been Prevented by Animals." The following page features "Interesting Stories of Artists and their Models" as well as an extended joke involving a Jewish salesman who speaks in broad Yiddish dialect (which is clearly meant to have comic effect), but who is not really the butt of the humor. As if to emphasize the idea that its frequent recourse to ethnic dialect is all in good fun, the following page is dominated by "Aliens Who Have Done England a Good Turn," including naturalized Dutch (such as Alma-Tadema), Americans (such as the academician E. A. Abbey), Italians (Marie Corelli, who claimed to be half Italian, although *Tit-Bits* was unwise to believe her) and Jews, notably Disraeli, the Rothschilds, and the Zangwill brothers.

Several pages on, after the serial "The Spoils of Asia," comes the announcement of prize winners for various contests, including those who sent in the solutions to the clues in the serial on their War Maps, and the man who won a fortnight's holiday in Wales by submitting a list of 100 place names that contained 2,104 letters, the greatest total. The opposite page, labeled "Our Premium Page," announces that it pays two guineas per column for material used on it. One of the articles there that might have drawn Bloom's attention gave the history of the "Royal Ascot" race: "Ascot well deserves its proud prefix 'Royal,' for it may claim to be the child of a Queen, and certainly it has been a prime favorite with nearly all her successors on the throne." Following this, the "Prize Tit-Bit Story," "The Strategy of Mr. Pilkins," was submitted by Mrs. S. M. Baines of Lancaster. Featured toward the magazine's end are "Personal Tit-Bits" (mostly odd facts about celebrities (e.g., Marconi has a fine tenor voice) and "Tit-Bits of General Information" (in some parts of Berlin there are special public houses for women). The feature "Answers to Correspondents" that inspired Newnes's rival seems especially canted toward the mathematical. Bloom would probably not be surprised that "the stupendous sum of fifty million pounds is lost every year on the race courses of the world." The editor is happy to answer rather arcane queries, such as which village in England is furthest from a railway station, or how much distance is traveled by the trains of England—they travel around the world in the time it takes the average Briton to have dinner. A reader who signed himself "Eclipse" and asked about odd names for racehorses is answered with a number of examples, including Safety Pin, Chatterbox, Piety, Double Sorrow, and There I Go with my Eye Out. Throwaway is not mentioned, but then his moment of glory was five days in the future.

David Reed claims that, in founding *Tit-Bits*, Newnes followed the tradition of the professional thief, since "he and his staff were paste and scissor plagiarists" (87). But holding a genius of the mass publishing market to the standard of romantic originality is inappropriate: Newnes gathered his material from the swirling morass of text available to him, recast, trimmed, and edited it, and presented it in a far more palatable fashion than he had found it. Joyce himself was well aware of the newly public nature of textuality in his time, and wrote to George Antheil, "I am quite content to go down to posterity as a scissors and paste man for that seems to me a harsh but not unjust description" (*Letters*, I 297). As to the effect of Newnes's recasting, Reed writes,

> By presenting information as discontinuous corpuscular fragments, its ironic contradictions, its diversionary qualities were emphasized. By eliminating the context, connections were ignored and undermined. 'Facts' were seen as random events, and such a presentation of data merges well with the way that those without the advantages of a sustained education converse and discuss. Whether by design or by chance, Newnes found a formula that reflected the informality and discontinuity, the peripatetic interest span of the everyday conversation of his readers. (88)

Attacks on the light weeklies for their ostensible lack of journalistic gravitas were common in the late Victorian and Edwardian periods, but the papers also had eloquent defenders. Philip Beaufoy himself wrote to the *Academy* in 1900, in response to an attacking letter entitled "A Revolution in Journalism," entering "a mild protest against the existing tendency in all serious journals to deprecate the class of papers represented by *Tit Bits*." Analyzing a recent issue, he finds "(1) A detailed explanation of military journalism; (2) an account of the workings of the Meteorological Office; (3) A biographical account of Sir George White; (4) nearly 200 scientific facts; (5) a story which although of minor literary merit is possessed of a certain interest. The above features alone should in my opinion redeem the paper from the charge of being made up of snappy paragraphs," he asserts (Beaufoy, 238).

In any case, dismissals of the papers because of the fragmentary, disjointed nature of their composition may be beside the point. Readers who are suspicious of meta-narratives and the great explanatory systems of the humanities that are available to those with sustained educations might feel that *Tit-Bits* uniquely offered its readers a world they recognized. His description of this discontinuous, fragmentary world, devoid of an encompassing explanatory matrix, also sounds a great deal like the world ineluctably encountered by readers of *Ulysses*, whatever their educational background. Especially to new readers, *Ulysses* seems to present a baffling flux of unrelated details, thoughts, and activities, a world wholly alien to that of the Victorian novel's unified narrative, but one that carries the conviction of modernity.

Answers

Most of the important characteristics of *Tit-Bits* were shared by *Answers*, with the difference that, in the place of the fatherly Newnes with his Nonconformist background, the guiding spirit of *Answers* was Harmsworth, a man the historian Anthony Sampson said "invented modern journalism, founded *Answers*, bought the *Times* and the *Observer*, and died of megalomania" (Sampson, 141). As he wrote in the Feb. 16, 1889, issue, "We are a sort of Universal Information provider. Anybody who reads our paper for a year will be able to converse on many subjects on which he was entirely ignorant. He will have a good stock of anecdotes and jokes and will indeed be a pleasant companion." Among the first items in the magazines (cited in Pound and Harmsworth, 82) were "What the Queen Eats," "Narrow Escapes from Burial Alive" (perhaps a source of Bloom's thoughts in "Hades"), "What has Become of Tichborne" (whom Bloom wonders about; *U* 16.1343), and "Why Jews Don't Ride Bicycles"—an idea with which Bloom would beg to differ, as a correspondent of *The Irish Cyclist* (U 15.233). Eugen Sandow (or someone writing in his name) regularly contributed articles on physical fitness (see chapter seven). This approach to information, after all, is not all that different from the traditional one Stephen Dedalus finds himself compelled to offer to his students—an apparently random collection of historical facts and literary tags. Harmsworth's popular touch worked on two magazines he founded with more limited ambitions than *Answers*, and by 1892, *Answers'* circulation of 375,000 was supplemented by the humorous journals *Comic Cuts* ("Amusing without being Vulgar") with 420,000 and *Chips* with 212,000. *Forget-Me-Not*, aimed at the female readership, had a circulation of 83,000, for total sales of Harmsworth publications of more than a million. Where *Tit-Bits* peaked in circulation around 1900, with 600,000, *Answers* went on to top its rival with a circulation of 717,000 weekly by 1910 (Reed, 129). This was the foundation of what was to become the largest press empire in the world, the Amalgamated Press (Pound and Harmsworth, 140). It would include the most successful daily exemplar of the new journalism, *The Daily Mail*, as well as the most popular illustrated paper, the *Daily Mirror.*

Like *Tit-Bits, Answers* strove for and claimed a nonpolitical stance, although this aspiration, of course, did not guarantee any such thing. Insofar as it projected an overall attitude, it was practical, unromantic, progressive, rationalistic, and at times surprisingly anti-jingoistic: the May 21, 1904, issue included "When Britain Goes a-Bungling," an article on ideas the British have "borrowed and improved upon," such as the (French) submarine, the (German) post system, and the (Italian) newspaper. The same issue includes "Revelations of a Society Solicitor," "How Animals Wage War," a series of "storyettes" supposedly contributed by readers (short anecdotes), a serial entitled "In Name Only," and an article entitled "How I Wrote My Plays" by C. Haddon Chambers.

There is the announcement of a new contest for rearranging the letters PASKEGOJUBIWF to form the greatest number of words (and since only ten spaces for words are provided in a single issue, an ambitious contestant would be forced to buy a great many copies of the same issue). The magazine on the whole is enthusiastic about the use of statistics and measurements, some of which are worked into contests, such as the one to predict the number of deaths registered in the United Kingdom for the first six months of 1904. An article entitled "Why I Hate England" gives complaints and criticisms of aliens in a sympathetic/humorous tone. A great many short items and verses are lumped together under "Gossip": how horses dream, how to smoke a cigar, the route to success. There are even tips for small investors. In an amusing article entitled "Mr Answers Writes a Serial Story," the figure known as "Mr Answers—a sort of managing editor whose identity changed over time—pretends that he is setting out to write a novel

> which should combine the subtle humour and delicate pathos of Dickens with the breezy dialogue of Richard Marsh, the nautical pen-pictures of Clark Russell and Cutliffe Hyne, the wealth of plot of the authors of "Judge Not," the bluff military touches of Kipling, and the detective instincts of Conan Doyle.

The editor suggests that while he is at it, the aspiring writer should "throw in a dash of H. G. Wells's Martian mysteries, a few of Marie Corelli's observations, and a touch of Arthur Morrison's East End life" (32). The result, which is critiqued point by point by the editor, is a kind of literary monstrosity, testifying to the limits of the cook-book approach to composition. But as a reader would realize, we have meanwhile been given a short list of the literary models the publication finds most worthy of emulation—and some of them, like Wells and Doyle, did indeed publish in the pages of *Answers*. Like all issues of the magazine, this one includes, interspersed or printed as running heads, ads for other Harmsworth publications. Indeed at the end of "Mr Answers Writes," the editor suggests that if he takes out all the sections where he was trying for humor, then Mr Answers should submit the remainder to the editor of *Comic Cuts*.

The edition of *Answers* that would have been available on Bloomsday (June 11, 1904) is a fairly typical specimen. The section headed "Editorial Chat" is composed of replies to readers, whose letters are excerpted, on a great variety of issues. While some turn on matters of fact or recount anecdotes, a good many offer advice about their personal lives for readers who ask. Often the reader is treated as among "those in the know," as in a paragraph explaining that shopkeepers sometimes post a misspelled sign in their windows to bring in customers eager to correct it. A section of the paper entitled "What Happened This Week," instead of a news summary such as we might expect, is made up of "passing glimpses of interesting people and events" taken from other publications dated June 4–11, 1904, but also from that week in 1838, 1852, and so on (107). The contrast to the fetishizing of the previous day's (or week's) events in an ordinary newspaper is striking. By removing the context of the immediate past as their rationale for the inclusion of items, such periodicals instead offered as a guiding principle the arbitrary or the stochastic.

Reading a page of *Answers* (or *Tit-Bits*, for that matter) thus resembles following the ramblings of Bloom's mind as one thought leads to a different one or as he comes upon sights that suggest ideas or memories to him. A section entitled "Answer's Who's Who" provides small facts or stories about famous people: George Watts is the only member of the R.A. who has exhibited there over 67 years; Mrs Langtry feels reviewers should be prohibited from taking their wives or sweethearts with them on opening night, since they adversely affect the reviews (101). A section entitled "Indeed?" includes odd or surprising facts, such as "The game of chess is still included in the curriculum of Russian schools," or "During the month of April 183 persons in London were bitten by dogs. This includes one policeman." An item that might have caught Bloom's eye reads, "There is a slump in auks' eggs. One has just fetched a mere 200 guineas under the hammer—speaking figuratively. The last one sold fetched 300 guineas" (120). From time to time we encounter the sort of items we find in *Ulysses*—riddles (like Stephen's "The cock crew …") or joking definitions (a bridge: a disappointed pier) or, especially, humorous anecdotes (like the story of Reuben Dodd's son, which is "capped" by Simon, its auditor, with his "one and eight pence too much"; *U* 6.291). The more we read the humorous weeklies, the more we realize that what we had taken for Joyce's portrait of the public oral culture of Dublin can equally well be seen as an oral rendition of the light weeklies.

What might the light weeklies offer to readers, aside from the obvious attraction of jokes, oddities, and clever anecdotes? One thing the newly literate population had in common was its schooling. There can be no doubt that these people found basic literacy and numeracy useful in their jobs. But a great deal of their education was, in fact, designed to lay foundations for the postprimary education that members of a higher class were far more likely to have attained. It must have remained, for the most part, an untapped resource during the rest of their lives. Bloom's mind is aswarm with bits of education, like his refrain of "thirty-two feet per second per second," the rate at which falling bodies accelerate. When would this fact come in handy for Bloom? Despite the assurances of his science teachers, it would probably only come in handy in solving the puzzles of the light weeklies. In *Answers* and *Tit-Bits* and their ilk, readers like Bloom could exercise their arithmetical skills, manipulate the letters of the alphabet, write and submit short anecdotes and jokes, or even full-fledged stories, just as they did in school, with some hope of the reward that their instructors rather vaguely promised. In at least a symbolic way, such magazines reify the fantasies of self-improvement and achievement that the middle class holds on behalf of the lower. With its quiz, recitation, or catechistic format, "Ithaca" is Joyce's tribute to the light weeklies and their audience. It is a potpourri of the sort of information Bloom might have, or wish to have, or at least could find, in the public sources (such as *Thom's*) where in fact Joyce found it. Pitched at a parodically elevated level of syntax and diction, it is the equivalent of the "Answers to Correspondents" section of the conundrum magazines, and to this day it engages us in responding to it.

Beaufoy and the New Literacy

Although *Tit-Bits* was relatively anodyne in content, it immediately became a lightning rod for critics decrying the new semi-literacy, and especially for Irish observers lamenting the spread of British mass culture in Dublin, which for ideological reasons they cast in an entirely negative light. For many Dublin commentators, defenders of an earlier model of cultural value founded in Matthew Arnold's confused invocation of "sweetness and light" or "the best that has been thought and said," British mass culture was equivalent to modernism in its attack upon or evasion of traditional literary and artistic values. In a *United Irishman* column in June, 1904, Arthur Griffith commented,

> The so-called education introduced by England has stamped out the native culture; it has half-taught the people English, and instead of "Seaghan Clárach" and "Tadhg Gaedhealach" it has given them at best Answers, Tit-Bits and the Freeman's Journal. It has turned them from a lively, intellectual people into the most mentally apathetic people in the world. (Griffith, 3 col. 3)

Griffith's invective here is curiously reminiscent of contemporary Irish attacks on Joyce, from a similar moral standpoint, a further reason to suggest that there are significant parallels between Newnes's and Harmsworth's enterprises and Joyce's.

As I have argued above, some modernist writers create a new relationship to the reader not only by inviting the reader's participation in the literary act but also by soliciting the reader's engagement in actively *creating* the text in a virtual, invisible, collaborative act. *Ulysses* is full of moments where readers are invited, in some ways required, to take an active hand in the book's composition—to write parts of the book that have been left blank by the original author, although they are necessary for an adequate reading. I have already cited Mulligan's unfinished "Mary Ann" rhyme (*U* 1.382) and several other examples. As the book progresses, there are many such instances where the reader must invent or resurrect passages that a conventionally realistic novel, or even the novel implied in the book's "initial style," would have made explicit. As Joyce begins to introduce a set of narrative and stylistic "filters," it becomes increasingly difficult for the reader to do this. The problem becomes most acute in "Oxen of the Sun," where Joyce overlays the minimal action with heavy stylistic filters reprising the canon of literary styles in English, producing passages which usually require considerable leaps in translation. When a passage in the style of Mallory states that Bloom was smitten by a dragon, we must consult other passages in the book to realize that, in conventional novelistic terms, he was stung by a bee.

Here, as throughout "Oxen," we are actually asked to rewrite these passages of brilliant pastiche into the relatively plain version allowed by *Ulysses*'s initial style, merely in order to understand the realistic action disguised by the voices of the many presumptive authors. In fact, the existence of a "Joyce Industry" that engages in continuing dialogue, meets regularly face-to-face, and generally regards itself as having something significant in common is the best testimony that Joyce did indeed form a community of readers. In a sense, he still engages in dialogue with us, and the many problems and difficulties of his works are not all that far removed from those that *Tit-Bits* offered to a different audience at a different time. "Ithaca," of course, is seeded with small puzzles and mock-puzzles, some of them arithmetical, some logical, some left as an exercise for the reader, others complete with answers:

> Was the clown Bloom's son?
> No.
> Had Bloom's coin returned?
> Never. (*U* 17.985)

The only wonder here is that we have been so slow to associate this procedure with that of Newnes and his imitators during the prime of Bloom.

Tit-Bits's inaugural issue offered a thousand-pound prize for its first serial story, won by Joyce's old nemesis Grant Allen, the notorious author of *The Woman Who Did*; aspiring authors submitted over 20,000 manuscripts. Perhaps the magazine's best-known feature was its shorter "Prize Tit-Bits Story," in which readers competed for publication at the rate of a guinea per column. Kenner has pointed out that, whereas Joyce failed to win with his story, which Stanislaus recalls as concerning Russian nihilists, Philip Beaufoy (whose address is generally given as the Playgoers Club, Strand, W.C.) on May 1, 1897, published a romance involving Russian nihilists entitled "For Vera's Sake"—thus raising the question, unlikely on the face of it, whether the young Joyce was attempting to imitate Beaufoy in a feat of actual literary impersonation that would anticipate Bloom's doubly fictive one (Kenner 1986, 11). In fact "Beaufoy" was probably a member of a *Tit-Bits* stable of writers and no doubt was somewhat less distinguished socially than his name and address might lead other readers to believe. He has recently been identified as the pseudonym of Philip Bergson (ca. 1872–1947). His use of a pseudonym adds irony to Bloom's trial in "Circe" during which he is accused of stealing the writer's identity. Given his real name, it is quite possible that "Beaufoy" was Jewish, a fact of which Joyce may or may not have been ignorant.[2] He published many Prize Tit-Bit stories—by my count, some thirty of them between 1896 and 1904—in a number of modes, from the romantic exoticism of "For Vera's Sake" to the comically disillusioned but devil-may-care irony of a story like "A Stratagem that Failed" (November 1, 1902): in this brief episode, the narrator, a gentlemanly thief of the tribe of Raffles, tells how he impersonates a man of wealth and has a jeweler bring a set of gems to his hotel room. When they are produced for his inspection, his lower-class confederate chloroforms the clerk, and both flee to Amsterdam, where they discover the gems are paste. As it turns out, the jeweler had brought two sets of gems with him that evening, one of which was intended for a client who needed paste replicas, and by accident he showed the wrong set to the story's narrator, whose clever plan was thus accidentally foiled.

This is perhaps a sort of masterstroke in reverse, but no story entitled "Matcham's Masterstroke" seems to have been published in *Tit-Bits* during Beaufoy's years of activity. The genre of the title accurately reflects many genuine Beaufoy titles, though: other stories include "The Man and the Mesmerist," "The Split Button," "Wilfred Manson's Engagement," "Dandy Dick's Device," "Dick Armstrong's Sacrifice," "The Tell-Tale Semi-Colon," and "The Jeweler's Mummy." There are also a series of "mysteries": "The Mablethorpe Mystery," "A Cheque Mystery," and, on November 7, 1903, a story that merits further discussion, "The Mysterious Postcard." There is, of course, no telling how long Bloom allowed his *Tit-Bits* magazines to age in the jakes before putting them to use, but it is probably no coincidence that this is the Beaufoy story closest in date to Bloomsday; if we look in *Tit-Bits* for "Matcham's Masterstroke," we inevitably stumble over "The Mysterious Postcard."

The story features the upper-middle-class couple Will Leicester and his wife Hetty. Opening his mail one morning, Leicester has a shock, and his wife asks him what is wrong.

> "Finish your breakfast," I said, trying to speak in a calm, jaunty manner. "Finish your breakfast, and you shall know all."
>
> When the meal had worn to its end I handed the postcard to my wife. She read it hurriedly. "Oh, Will, what can it mean? What can it mean?"
>
> The card, which bore no name or address, ran thus: "Prepare to Die before the End of the Year."
>
> "Mean?" I echoed. "Probably, dearest, it is a foolish hoax, but whoever is responsible for it ought to be ashamed of himself. I shall call in at the police station on my way in to town and hand the thing to the inspector."
>
> "Yes, do," she assented; "and when the wretch who wrote the card is caught, I do hope they'll send him to prison for life."
>
> Hetty's views of criminal procedure were somewhat vague.

Leicester consults the police, who ask him if he has any enemies. Suspicions turn to a man he once fired for embezzling funds, but soon Leicester receives a letter from the man, who is now in Australia, removing him from suspicion. "I went my way in fear and trembling," comments Leicester. "Frequently I would awake in the still watches of the night, believing that I should find an assassin bending over my pillow with dagger or revolver in hand. Hetty, who had always loathed dogs, and who had been subjected to several attentions in the shape of more or less painful bites, was actually heroic enough to suggest procuring one of the enemy to guard the house." Then a neighbor of his receives the same card and cries with a shudder, "I verily believe that this is the work of some homicidal maniac."

After three months, the authorities have discovered nothing about either card, and Leicester has taken to carrying a revolver around town. Then,

> One morning when I was perusing my daily paper, the following paragraph of a sudden burned into my brain. It ran thus: —"Intense mystery is being caused throughout the metropolis and the county at large by the circulation of some extraordinary anonymous postcards. The communications warn the recipients to prepare for death before the close of the present year. We understand that all efforts to trace the

writer or writers of the mysterious cards have thus far been doomed to failure. Various theories have been put forward by the police to explain the extraordinary occurrences, but the most feasible would seem that the cards emanated from the hand of a homicidal lunatic. Further developments will be awaited with eager interest."

Although Leicester is somewhat reassured, deciding the writer of the cards cannot easily "commit wholesale murder throughout Great Britain and Ireland," the public furor mounts. Angry letters are written to editors, clairvoyants offer their services, and the millionaire pill manufacturer Mr. William Cureall offers a 500-pound reward for the capture of the writer of the cards. "In a word, the whole kingdom talked of little save the mysterious communications, and even the continental journals referred to the business in a sarcastic manner." Finally, on the last day of the year, Leicester returns home to find his wife laughing uproariously:

"Oh, Will, Will," she exclaimed, "it is too funny—too funny!"
"What on earth is the matter?" I inquired, wondering whether she was on the borderland of hysteria. "Really, my dear girl, if you don't stop this nonsense I shall send for the doctor."
Again her laugh rang out long and loud.
"Oh dear, oh dear, I think I shall die," she exclaimed, whilst the tears ran down her cheeks. "It is the funniest thing that ever happened."
...She went to the mantlepiece and handed me a postcard.
"What! Another card!" I yelled. "Great Jupiter! This is no laughing matter."
"Read it, read it," she gasped.
Seizing the card with trembling fingers, I read the following words: —"Hold former card up to the light."
A sudden illumination began to break upon my misty brain.
"The other card," I shouted, "where is it?"
"Here, here," she laughed. "Oh, Will, Will, I shall remember this as long as I live."
I bounded toward the gas bracket,...then I too burst into a long, wild, uncontrollable peal of mirth. For when the card was held thus there appeared beneath the words "Prepare to Die before the End of the Year," the following sequel: —
"Which you most probably will do unless you purchase Cureall's Liver Pills, 1/9 per box at all Chemists, or post-free, 1/10, from the manufacturers, W. Cureall and Co., Ltd., St. Thomas' St., London, S.E."
"Well, what do you think of it?" asked my wife with a merry smile, when at length the real meaning of the extraordinary postcard had filtered into my brain.

"What do I think?" I echoed, slowly. "Well, I rather think that I shall instruct my brokers to buy me another hundred shares in Cureall and Co.

And I did.

A number of questions immediately come to mind in the light of this story. Obviously Joyce was acquainted with *Tit-Bits* magazine and specifically with the stories of Beaufoy, but did he check magazines of late 1903 and early 1904, as he did newspapers, in an effort at verisimilitude, and if so, was he so struck by Beaufoy's mysterious postcard that he devised the episode of Denis Breen's mysterious card as a sort of reply? And if it is a comic, fictive rejoinder, what does this add to our understanding of the "U.P.: up" episode? After all, the most likely reading of Breen's postcard is indeed that it is a veiled threat, along the lines of, "It's all u.p. UP with you"—or at least following his dream of the ace of spades climbing the stairs to his room, this is the interpretation that the disturbed Breen is most likely to be giving the postcard. Two books by Joyce's Irish contemporary Freeman Wills Crofts, *Inspector French's Greatest Case* (1922) and *The Pit-Prop Syndicate* (1922), use the phrase in this sense. In the first book, when he discovers he and his assistant have been outsmarted by a couple of villains, he remarks, "It's all U.P. Carter, as far as this trip is concerned" (16). In the second, fearing he has missed a vital clue, he exclaims, "If so...it was all u.p. with his career in the yard" (161).

The comparisons between the Breen and the Leicester anecdotes are instructive. Where Leicester acts like a Victorian gentleman, hiding his fear from his wife and treating her with lordly if affectionate condescension, in the Irish couple Breen is clearly the hysteric, especially compared with his stoic wife Josie. Rather than a Victorian gentleman, Breen reacts like a contemporary American, immediately deciding to sue, although it is not apparent whom he would sue for exactly what. Surely at least part of the point of the Breen anecdote is its pointlessness: I suspect that we are not meant to understand just what has so exercised Breen about the postcard, and the central mystery—who sent it, for what reason—remains unsolved in *Ulysses*. In this regard, it bears the same relationship to Beaufoy's story that Stephen's "Pisgah Sight of Palestine" bears to the newspaper story "with a bite in it" (*U* 7.616) that Crawford has urged him to write. Stephen's tale of the Dublin virgins is a kind of anti-newspaper story, precisely what Crawford would *not* print, for reasons too numerous to mention but including the lack of plot and resolution. The u.p.: up postcard is a very similar anecdote in the masculine register, an anti-anecdote to Beaufoy's winning specimen.

Yet, on reflection there are ambiguities to Beaufoy's story as well, points of tension and strain where "something quick and neat" (*U* 4.511) threaten to disseminate and ramify. The major such point of tension involves the characters' reactions to the solution of the mystery. Both Hetty's excessive laughter and Leicester's quick moves to join her in appreciation of the comedy—and then immediately to join Cureall in profiting from the hoax—simply don't ring true: how can the woman who has spent months in constant fear for her husband's life immediately decide it is the best joke she has ever heard, and why should Leicester join her in feeling that a wonderful prank has been played on the terrorized British public? Clearly what is at issue here is advertisement's uncanny aptitude for interpellation, a kind of powerful, immediate address that appears to be intimate and personal but ultimately reveals itself as universal and undiscriminating. Derrida captures some of the mysteriousness inherent in the postcard, asking, "What does a post card want to say to you? On what conditions is it possible? Its destination traverses you, you no longer know who you are. At the very instant when from its address it interpellates you, uniquely you, instead of reaching you it divides you or sets you aside, occasionally overlooks you" (Derrida, rear cover). At their most effective, advertisements, in ways we do not fully understand, manage to bridge the gap between the personal and the commercial spheres, with potentially dangerous consequences for the consumer. After all, the continued effect of the Cureall hoax is dependent upon the fact that Leicester inhabits a community that only discovers its shared experiences through the newspaper, rather than in direct personal contact.

Cureall's postcard is the perfect example of Bloom's desire to exploit "the infinite possibilities hitherto unexploited of the modern art of advertisement," which can be "of magnetising efficacy to arrest involuntary attention" (*U* 17.580). It effectively fulfills his fantasy "of some one sole unique advertisement to cause passers to stop in wonder, a . . . novelty, with all extraneous accretions excluded, reduced to its simplest and most efficient terms not exceeding the span of casual vision and congruous with the velocity of modern life" (*U* 17.1770). One must wonder whether the thrust of the intertextual interaction between Beaufoy's and Joyce's creations is not to suggest that in some way Bloom is responsible for Breen's postcard. One might also wonder at the question posed by John Gordon on hearing my discussion of this story: What would Breen's postcard say if he held it up to the light?

The fact that it is patent medicine that is being advertised is certainly not irrelevant here: patent medicines such as the Bile Beans for Biliousness of which Stanislaus was ironically fond or the Widow Welch's Female Pills that Gerty believes in—both of them frequently advertised in *Tit-Bits*—were an obvious arena for licensed corporate abuse of a credulous public, and were so recognized in 1904, since in that year the *Ladies Home Journal* in the United States launched a major muckraking investigation of the trade in patent medicines (Trager, 658). Magazines like *Tit-Bits* were important in blurring the boundaries between fact, claim, and fiction in such advertisements. The *Tit-Bits* Advertising Supplement for April 11, 1903, features an uninterrupted series of advertisements for Bile Beans, but all of them are laid out so as to resemble precisely the anecdotes that were *Tit-Bits*'s main features, with titles like "An Inhuman Monster: The Story of a Texas Desperado" or "The Highest Death Rate in England." Bloom may plan to emulate Beaufoy by contributing a story entitled "My Experiences in a Cabman's Shelter" (*U* 16.1231); but in this supplement the story entitled "A Cabman's Story," like the Desperado's story or the story behind the highest death rates in England, merely testifies to the miraculous restorative powers of Bile Beans.

Garry Leonard claims broadly that Joyce "presents the *overall dynamic* of advertising, as well as the broader social phenomenon of…'commodity culture,' in order to demonstrate the extent to which social relations, nationalist aspirations, power structures, economic disparities, gender constructions, and even consciousness itself, all depend upon, and interact with, the simulated universe of consumerism, cultural imperialism, and commodity culture" (Leonard, 128–29). As Leonard is aware, this rich complex of relationships is a unique, indeed a defining attribute of modernity. Only in a mass culture can an anonymous postcard, processed by the administrative anonymity of the postal service, arrive untraceably with a disturbing message whose context—intimate or generic, personal or public—cannot be determined by the recipient. As Derrida asks, "Who is writing? To whom? And to send, to destine, to dispatch what? To what address?…I owe it to whatever remains of my honesty to say finally that I do not know" (Derrida, 5). Breen's postcard is exemplary here, but so is what I am tempted to call "Cureall's Masterstroke." In "Matcham's Masterstroke," we may deduce, the protagonist fondly reminisces about the single clever coup through which he won his bride—an adolescent fantasy about the way love works that is closely related to Stephen Dedalus's conviction in *Portrait* that when he finds his Mercedes he will be "transfigured" in a magical moment in which "weakness and timidity and inexperience would fall from him" (*P* 65). But in modern life, as the mature Joyce realizes, the brilliant gestures are no longer those of romantic heroes, but of amoral entrepreneurs, and the payoff of their manipulations is not affection but cash and commodities. Bloom believes he would love to be among their company, but I suspect that he does not have the stomach for it; he has too much sympathy for the Josie Breens of the world to pull off Cureall's Masterstroke.

Chapter Seven

The World's Strongest Man: Joyce or Sandow?

Noble art of selfpretence. (*U* 15.4413)

With my chapter title here I mean to play a bit with the comparison of two apparently incommensurable figures: James Joyce, the modernist author, and Eugen Sandow, the now-forgotten strongman-performer who flourished in Britain in the early twentieth century. Here begins a gradual shift in my focus from texts to institutions, in that Sandow, who displayed a modernist mastery of advertising dispersed over the cultural spectrum, presented himself not only through language but preeminently through images—everything from postcards to staged spectacles. The present chapter deals both with Sandow as a broadly disseminated image that effectively interpellated consumers of the British Isles (and to a lesser extent those of Europe and American as well) and with the discourse of advertising upon which he depended and which effectively shaped him into a significant cultural nexus as well. As Vike Plock observes,

> Physical culture, which had its heyday in the years between 1850 and 1918, became, at the turn of the century, practically synonymous with the name Eugen Sandow, whose publication *Strength and How to Obtain It* marked the zenith of a fitness craze relying on new media such as advertising and photography; growing degeneration paranoia, and resurfacing concepts of Hellenistic body aesthetics as a means for aesthetic dissemination. (Plock, 115)

In examining the figure of Sandow at some length here, I mean to suggest that an understanding of his role in the British Isles around the turn of the century can illuminate much about Bloom, the citizen who "consumes" him. Bloom could have learned about Sandow from his first performance in Dublin, at the Empire Palace Theatre on May 6, 1898. An enthusiastic review in the *Irish Times* describes several of Sandow's impressive feats of strength, including tearing three packs of cards stacked together in two and lifting great weights onto horse-back. As a climax, "he carried away from a raised dais, a piano, and the pianist by whom it was being played" (*Irish Times*, 7). Sandow was recalled to the stage numerous times by enthusiastic applause. But whether or not his performance brought him to Bloom's attention, Sandow had already permeated the various entertainment and advertising media. Sandow managed to disseminate himself throughout a commercial empire that always reflected back upon himself, or at least his public persona; and thus, I want to argue that there is, indeed, a parallel between James Joyce, the disembodied center of the twentieth-century intellectual industry we might call *Joyce Inc.*, and Eugen Sandow, whose role and significance, which at first glance would seem to be as a primitive icon of brute strength, on the contrary generated a highly sophisticated social dissemination of meaning only possible under modernity.

Jennifer Wicke argues that advertising "arises as a radically new discursive practice over the course of the nineteenth century," during which it becomes "a center of knowledge production, a determining economic site, as well as a representational system" that develops concurrently—even symbiotically—with the establishment of the novel (Wicke, 1). *Ulysses*, she argues, is a preeminent example of the heteroglossic interdependency of novel and advertising: in Joyce's book, "advertising and mass cultural forms become the matrix of its textual practices"; advertising is "the premier language of the book," and typifies "the modern condition of writing" (Wicke, 121, 123). From a Bakhtinian perspective, the parallel between advertising and the novel is clear; for him, the novel is defined by heteroglossia, and to that extent is a genre that transcends genre. Its strength lies in its ability to incorporate within itself all other literary genres and—through parody, pastiche, assimilation, or even mere quotation—to absorb them in its heteroglossic matrix (Bakhtin 1981, 259–422). If we set aside the implication of authorial intentionality with which Bakhtin sometimes flirts, it is apparent that modern advertising functions similarly, but within an even broader range, as it is able to subsume image and gesture—and even, in cases of "self-advertisement," like Sandow or the dancing-master Maginni (*U* 8.98), the human being as well.

Sandow's image was woven into the fabric of Edwardian society, although today he is not always recognizable when he appears. In H. G. Wells's *Tono-Bungay*, the first and certainly one of the very few novels ever written about the creation and decline of a patent-medicine empire, a manic and fitfully ironic artist named Ewart explains to the protagonist and his uncle the "Poetry of commerce":

> You are artists. You and I, sir, can talk, if you will permit me, as one artist to another. It's advertisement has—done it....The old merchant used to tote about commodities; the new one creates values....He takes mustard that is just like anybody else's mustard, and he goes about saying, shouting, singing, chalking on walls, writing inside people's books, putting it everywhere, 'Smith's Mustard is the Best.' And behold it *is* the best....It's just like an artist; he takes a lump of white marble on the verge of a lime-kiln, he chips it about, he makes—he makes a monument to himself—and others—a monument the world will not willingly let die.

Encouraged by portly Uncle Ponderevo, the creator of Tono-Bungay, Ewart produces a poster portraying the protagonist and Ponderevo as two beavers busily bottling rows of the medicine. This isn't judged suitable, and his next creation is even less so: Ewart paints, according to the protagonist's narration, "a quite shocking study of my uncle, excessively and needlessly nude,...engaged in feats of strength of a Gargantuan type before an audience of deboshed and shattered ladies. The legend, 'Health, Beauty, Strength,' gave a needed point to his parody" (Wells, 131–32).

But despite the narrator's evaluation, Ewart is not being entirely parodic here. The sort of "creation" in which advertisers engage indeed parallels that in which serious artists engage, at least in contrast to functional production, which neither resembles. Both artists and advertisers are engaged in the creation of a consensual value that is, by its very nature, economically marginal—and no less powerful or important for being so. Furthermore, Ewart's caricature of fat, Napoleonic Uncle Ponderevo as Strong Man points to some of the ways his patent elixir creates that value: the tonic is advertised as an aid to health, but in such a way as to strongly suggest that it will revive sexual potency as well as muscular vigor. Health is thus strength; and strength, as the nude, mock-classical pose of Ponderevo suggests, is beauty, and thus beyond prudish reproach. These equations draw upon a number of Edwardian social formations, but especially upon the enthusiasm for "physical culture" and fitness, the popularity of "Strong Man" shows, and the circulation of reproductions of the nearly nude male and female form in modes that aimed at titillation but drew about themselves the mantle of classical art or didactic purpose. Bloom's *Photo-Bits* nymph is a familiar example of a "purity nude" who, like the mock-Ponderevo, can pretend to be compromised by context, as when she complains to Bloom, "I was surrounded by the stale smut of clubmen, stories to disturb callow youth," and such degrading items (*U* 15.3248).

The Career of Eugen Sandow

But the more specific referent for the poster is Sandow, easily the best-known male physique of his age. Sandow, now recognized as the first "body-builder" in the modern sense of the term (Dutton and Laura, 142) was both a physical and a social phenomenon. In order to appreciate the cultural figure he embodied during the late Victorian and Edwardian periods, it is necessary to have some idea of the outlines of his remarkable and varied public life. Born Friedrich Muller in Konigsberg, Prussia, in 1867, Sandow early showed interest in anatomy and in the circus; apparently he began his own program of strength training in adolescence, partly inspired by the sight of classical statues in Rome, during a holiday with his father. In his book *Strength and How to Obtain It*, he recalls,

> I remember asking my father if people were as well developed in modern times. He pointed out that they were not, and explained that these were the figures of men who lived when might was right, when men's own arms were their weapons, and often their lives depended upon their physical strength. Moreover, they knew nothing of the modern luxuries of civilization, and besides their training and exercise, their muscles, in the ordinary course of life, were always being brought prominently into play. (Sandow 1911, 96)

He may have followed a course in "physical culture" at Göttingen University, and he may have studied anatomy during a brief attendance at medical school in Brussels, but for most of his youth, much against his father's wishes, he worked as a circus acrobat.[1] He began to wander Europe in search of a means of self-support, and also in order to avoid the draft for the German army. At some point, he took the name Sandow, a version of his mother's name—she was either Russian or of Russian descent. After quarreling with his father, he attempted to support himself as a strongman but was refused by various theaters in Amsterdam. In a brilliant exercise in self-promotion he wandered the city at night, wrecking all the available strength-testing machines. After rewards were offered for apprehension of the gang of thugs thought to be responsible, Sandow came forward and successfully defended himself by demonstrating that he had simply put a coin in the slot and gripped the handle strongly enough to send the indicator around the dial and to leave the handle dangling from the machine. He was immediately engaged by a theater.

Sandow appeared with one "Professor Atilla," at the Crystal Palace and in France, in a pantomime where he threw another actor dressed as a large doll about the stage. Atilla apparently mentored him, introducing Sandow to the intricacies of life as a performer, and also served as an interpreter while Sandow learned English. In San Remo he met the German Emperor, who proudly tore a pack of cards in two; Sandow reciprocated by tearing two packs simultaneously, and was rewarded with a diamond ring from the Kaiser's hand. The painter Aubrey Hunt, seeing the young Sandow emerge from the Adriatic at the Lido, hired him to pose as a model for a painting of a Roman gladiator. Back in London, in 1889, he challenged "Samson," who was appearing at the Aquarium as the "Strongest Man on Earth," along with his pupil, "Cyclops." When Sandow emerged from the audience he was greeted with laughter because in ordinary dress he looked ordinary next to the theatrical giants: he stood five feet, eight and a half inches, and weighed 180 pounds. But stripped down, he inspired awe.

John Kasson observes that Sandow thus came to embody a fantasy of transfiguration, with his "virtually instant metamorphosis from man of the crowd to marvel of muscle. This simultaneously placed Sandow in a class by himself and appealed to fantasies of transformation in boys and men, much as Clark Kent was to inspire later generations" (38). Sandow further played to this fantasy by emphasizing that he had started out as an especially weak boy who improved his physique through determination and hard work (Sandow 1911, 95). The fantasy of transformation to which he appealed is simply the physical version of the fantasy in which Stephen indulges when he imagines miraculously casting off the awkwardness and shyness of youth when he is with a girl: "in a moment, he would be transfigured. Weakness and timidity and inexperience would fall from him in that magic moment" (*P* 65).

Sandow readily duplicated or surpassed all the stunts of both Samson and Cyclops—bending iron bars, snapping wire ropes, lifting above his head a 279-pound dumbbell one-handed, and so forth, although subsequent research has suggested that some of the stunts, such as breaking chains by flexing the arm muscles, may have involved specially prepared equipment. A formal challenge match, judged by

the Marquess of Queensbury and Lord De Clifford, was arranged
for the next week, and a contemporary newspaper remarked, "If the
fate of the Empire had depended on the outcome, no greater interest
could have been shown"; the best seats went for roughly the equivalent of $250. Here again, Sandow triumphed (Willoughby, 62). For
several years, he toured the British Isles and Europe with his own
troupe. In 1893, he appeared in New York, where with one arm he
slowly raised above his head a huge dumbbell containing two men,
supported on his chest a platform and three horses, and carried off
the stage a man playing a piano. During this period he also posed for
a series of "club" photographs by the well-known portrait photographer Napoleon Sarony, in which he appeared nude except for a small
artificial fig leaf (Willoughby, 62).

In New York, a then-unknown promoter named Florenz Ziegfeld
discovered him and took him to the Trocadero in Chicago and per-
manently altered his act and public image. Ziegfeld took Sandow out
of the traditional leopard skin and dressed him in nothing but tight
silk shorts, with a set of bay leaves on his brow. Billed as *Sandow,
the Perfect Man*, he first appeared on the darkened stage in a single
spotlight wearing bronze makeup and striking a series of classical
poses—the runner, the discus thrower, Rodin's *The Thinker*. Ziegfeld
arranged for Sandow to take a walk in the woods with theater critic
Amy Leslie, during which it became clear that the gentle strongman
really adored spring flowers. At the close of performances, Ziegfeld
announced that ladies willing to donate $300 to charity would be
allowed to come backstage and feel Sandow's muscles—an offer
accepted with alacrity by such social luminaries as Mrs. Potter Palmer
and Mrs. George Pullman (Higham, 12–14).

During his American tour, Ziegfeld encouraged Sandow's flair for
theatrics; at the climax of his show Sandow supported, on a stage
resting on his shoulders, his entire troupe of 32 persons. In San
Francisco, enlarging upon his gladiatorial image, in a rather anticli-
mactic battle he fought and defeated a lion wearing a muzzle; according to Sandow's account the lion had been cowed during an earlier,
private encounter, while a modern historian has suggested that the
animal was also drugged (Chapman, 87). In the interests of science,
a New York newspaper asked Harvard physiologist Dr. D. A. Sargent
to examine Sandow. Sargent was impressed with the bulk of Sandow's
muscles compared to his bones, and with his remarkably quick reaction time and gymnastic abilities, but was still more impressed when
Sandow demonstrated his ability to move various muscles, including ones normally undeveloped, in time to music—a standard part of

his act. At the end of the examination, Sandow raised his examiner, standing in Sandow's palm, to shoulder height without bending his elbow (Lane, 142). During the 1890s, Sandow toured incessantly as a featured performer in both America and Europe, including Dublin; as Thornton notes, the *Freeman's Journal* for May 7, 1898, features an advertisement for his performance at the Empire Palace, scheduled for May 2–14 (Thornton, 72). In 1894, he married the daughter of a photographer and—despite gathering marital tensions, perhaps linked to his womanizing and a series of close male friends—the couple produced two daughters.

Sandow, Inc.

As Dutton and Laura point out, Sandow successfully fused at least three separate traditions in his performances: the studio portrayal of aesthetic muscularity, with all of its classical resonance; the public platform tradition of circus and vaudeville performance, which emphasized the awe-inspiring, the unusual, and even the grotesque; and a more scientifically oriented gymnastic tradition dating from the mid-nineteenth century and coinciding with a public interest in physical fitness (Dutton and Laura,144–45, 163). In Sandow's career, starting from about 1896 and continuing for some thirty years, he embodied a fusion of social discourses that may have been unprecedented: he became an institution of his own creation, a walking self-advertisement of the sort Bloom recognizes and admires in Maginni the dancing-master (*U* 8.98), but one whose appeal covered an entire cultural spectrum. Like Charles Atlas several decades later, his name was synonymous with physical strength and fitness; but, in the aesthetic nineties, it was also synonymous with male beauty. His stage and photographed appearances as a variety of classical figures built upon the mid-nineteenth-century tradition of the *pose plastique* or *tableau vivant*, and lent artistic cachet to what had originally been a crude strongman act.[2] To a degree, because of his public personality (especially as Ziegfeld had shaped it through his public relations efforts), Sandow was also associated with moral virtue and optimism. The catch phrase "as jolly as a Sandow" came into use; several songs were written about him. Edison made a film of his routine (*Strongman Poses*, 1896), and a plaster mold of his nude body, meant to model the ideal Caucasian racial type, was made for the British Museum in 1901.

Sandow established a number of Institutes of physical culture in Britain—some twenty in the British Isles, including six in London alone—where even physicians regularly took the courses, and he encouraged the founding of hundreds of Sandow physical culture clubs in which he had no ownership (Chapman, 103). One of his Institutes was for the use of women only, and was run along remarkably progressive lines, using exercises similar to those he recommended for men and dressing women patrons modestly but sensibly. He was called upon by the pianist Paderewski to develop a series of finger-strengthening exercises, perhaps because Sandow was able to chin himself one-armed, gripping the bar with any one of his fingers. Well-known actors consulted him for training in stage stunts. In 1914, he was issued an annually renewed Royal Warrant as instructor in physical culture, and was frequently consulted by the British military services. Starting in 1898, he was listed as editor and director of a monthly magazine, *Physical Culture*, later known as *Sandow's Magazine of Physical Culture*, while he frequently wrote for or was featured in other magazines, such as *Tit-Bits*. His book, *Strength and How to Obtain It*, in various editions after 1897, was hugely popular. The most unlikely people felt compelled to follow his exercise routine in the interest of self-betterment; Bloom, of course, is one who went so far as to complete the before-and-after measurement of muscles on the chart included in Sandow's book (*U* 17.1815).[3] Perhaps an even more unlikely enthusiast was W. B. Yeats, who in a 1905 letter laid out his daily schedule, commenting, "to this I have added Sandow exercises twice daily."[4]

The key to Sandow's emergence as a cultural icon was advertisement; and Sandow exemplified better than any other figure of the day the omnivorous and protean nature of advertising as a discourse. Each of his enterprises encouraged and legitimated the others: his performances advertised his book, his book advertised his magazine and his Institutes, while his Institutes, magazines, and book advertised his patented devices, such as dumbbells with spring centers or the Sandow-Whiteley Exerciser that Bloom owns. At the end of his book—which is itself an extended advertisement—are ads for his book *Body-Building or Man in the Making* ("with 7 Cabinet Photographs of the Author posing; printed on art paper") claiming that Sandow's exercises can cure indigestion and prevent appendicitis, constipation, and liver trouble; physicians, it is asserted, send to his schools patients suffering from lung troubles, spinal curvature, insomnia, sluggish liver, and general neurosis. Obviously, a Sandow Man had no need of Bile Beans, and a Sandow Woman, aided by exercise with Sandow's Symmetrion, could bid farewell to the Widow Welch's Female Pills.

Sandow held regular contests and awarded prizes among his pupils for physical development, and encouraged physical culture for children and women, as well as men. Images of his wife and children are formally deployed in his book, and the frontispiece shows Sandow, formally dressed, seated in a meditative, perhaps visionary, pose. By the third edition of his book (1905), there are numerous plates, showing Sandow consulting with Teddy Roosevelt or training the Welsh Artillery, as well as assuming a variety of classical poses. There are also several plates showing Sandow with lines drawn upon his torso highlighting his musculature with anatomical clarity, demonstrating that Sandow means not only Art, but also Science. Sandow's cultural achievements are stressed: he informs the reader that he has composed a number of musical pieces, which have been praised by professionals. Equal emphasis is laid upon the scientific principles underlying his program of exercise. The result of all this self-cultivation, of course, is social respectability. One of the first plates in the book shows, formally dressed, a healthy-looking and unmistakably upper-middle-class "Sandow family." Perhaps unexpectedly, the photographs of women students show them fully clothed in dark dresses and tights, while Sandow himself typically wears only a leopard-skin loincloth. Women might admire Sandow's partially nude body, but they need not fear being themselves compromised in any way if they undertake Sandow's training. And even the male image here is somewhat desexualized: none of the racy images of Sandow nude except for a figleaf—which were widely circulated as "art photographs"—are included. Clearly, the keynote is Victorian respectability, the family, and social ascent. Sandow, once an immigrant circus strongman, is now portrayed as the friend of kings and presidents, a philanthropic benefactor of the national health. The explicit message of the book is emulation: what I did, you can do.

Sandow and the Modern

But for all the Victorian impedimenta displayed in his personal publicity photos, Sandow represented something quintessentially modern, the worship of speed and power that were to find aesthetic expression in Italian futurism and in vorticism. At the beginning of an age that was to highlight the role of superhuman machinery, Sandow came to represent not so much a nostalgic return to the pretense that bodily strength is still of major functional value, but a symbolic conjoining with the power and omnipresence of machines that helped define modernity. Sandow tells us "how modernity was understood in terms of the body and how the white male body became a powerful symbol of modernity's impact and how to resist it" (Kasson, 19). David Chapman points out that

> It was no accident that Sandow appeared in Chicago at the same time that philosopher and historian Henry Adams was wandering amazedly among the pounding dynamos of the fair. The young scholar would soon see in the gleaming and powerful machinery a new symbol of the modern world, just as Sandow would come to represent a new Adam to populate it. The force of steel and steam were joined for the first time to the force of sinew and will in a bold symbolic union there on the shores of Lake Michigan. (69)

Sandow's ascent coincides with both the commercialization of sports and the rise of modern advertisement, and the proliferation of his image into a myriad of cultural arenas mirrors the omnivorous proliferation of advertisement itself, its ability to co-opt any sort of cultural formation. If, as many have argued, Joyce in *Ulysses* brought to the novel a new level of discursive power by virtue of the work's sheer heteroglossic inclusiveness, Sandow brought to advertisement an unprecedented "chaffering allincluding most farraginous" (*U* 14.1412) heteroglossic mastery whose explicit theme was power. At moments of self-doubt throughout his day, or when faced with visions of horrifying desolation, Bloom reminds himself, "Must begin again those Sandow's exercises" (*U* 4.234; *U* 17.512). And ironically, when Bello threatens Bloom with "heel discipline to be inflicted in gym costume," she does it with the command Bloom associates with Sandow's exercises: "On the hands down" (*U* 15.2848).[5] If Sandow is Bloom's last, best hope of "rejuvenation" (*U* 17.509), he is also a key to the complete commercial success that has always eluded the flabby canvasser. He well knows what Edward Mott Woolley points out in a book Joyce owned, *The Art of Selling Goods*: "A weak physique is quite as objectionable in salesmanship as a weak mentality. Physical strength carries with it conviction …" (9–10).[6] Certainly Sandow, as an individual, was only one beneficiary of an overdetermined cultural complex in Edwardian Britain that associated physical fitness and strength with beauty, health, heroism, intelligence, progressivism, moral force, and even domestic virtue. He further benefitted from *fin-de-siècle* British malaise, and especially from the fear that the British race was in the process of physical degeneration that would leave them helpless before the Germans.[7] Given the British racial fear and repressed envy of the

German people during the prewar period, perhaps it was logical that they should look to an Prussian immigrant to save them. Sandow's cultural intervention was significant in itself; as masculine exemplar, he also helped shape the very codes that gave him definition.

Thomas Richards, following Debord and Baudrillard, has investigated the way in which Victorian advertisers "undertook the spectacularization of advertising" in the formative years of our contemporary "society of spectacle" (6). From this perspective, Eugen Sandow is an exemplary figure, and his appearance in *Ulysses* takes on paradigmatic significance. For the key to his social positioning was precisely the *spectacle*; and in the dispersal of his advertised image through countless commodities and numerous abstract attributes—beauty, health, science, art, masculinity, respectability—he perfectly embodies the "blurring of genres" characteristic of cultural representations in postmodern society—or, I would argue, in modern society. "The oldest social specialization, the specialization of power, is at the root of the spectacle," observes Debord. "The spectacle is thus a specialized activity which speaks for all the others." Furthermore, the spectacle is inevitably "the existing order's uninterrupted discourse about itself, its laudatory monologue. It is the self-portrait of power in the epoch of its totalitarian management of the conditions of existence" (#23, #24)[8]

Even Sandow as an erotic image can be seen to anticipate more modern advertising images of the body in its curiously ambiguous eroticism. Writing of what he terms "fetish-beauty," Baudrillard comments,

> What we are talking about is a kind of anti-nature incarnate, bound up in a general stereotype of *models of beauty*, in a perfectionist vertigo and controlled narcissism....It is the final disqualification of the body, its subjection to a discipline, the total circulation of signs....However, this anti-nature does not exclude desire; we know that this kind of beauty is fascinating precisely because it is trapped in models, because it is closed, ritualized in the ephemeral. (74)

Sandow portrayed as Greek youth or as gladiator is a strangely abstracted figure of male beauty, both erotic and anti-erotic; the very fact that such photographs can coexist in his book with others portraying him as visionary, as businessman, and as paterfamilias sufficiently demonstrates that the incessant circulation of signs has begun to turn advertising discourse back upon itself (as spectacle, we might say) and away from traditional modes of semiotic significance.

Advertising and the Novel

The signifiers of advertisement are notoriously protean and unan-
chored. Thomas Richards has traced the way in which, by the 1890s,
"advertisers were regularly superimposing their slogans over stan-
dardized images drawn from every sphere of public and private life"
(108). When Sandow, in 1890, decided he would lift a horse during an
anticipated tour and had the printers Allen and Son produce illustra-
tive posters, he delayed too long in taking delivery; when he finally
inquired after the posters, he was told that they had been sold to
Messers. Murphy of Dublin as an illustration of the strength of their
stout (Hindley, 84)[9] This sort of semiotic "drift" or "decentering" continually threatened to remove Sandow from the center of the network
of advertising forces in which he positioned himself. Sandow's *Physical
Strength and How to Obtain It* embodied the perfect countermove:
the novel, or better, the *advertisement as novel*. His book is divided
into two parts: Part I, "My System of Physical Culture," is devoted
to generalizations about physical culture, Sandow's recommendations
about exercise, breathing, bathing, and diet, along with chapters on
his special dumbbell and his schools, with particular attention to
"Physical Culture for the Middle-Aged"; Part II, "Incidents of My
Professional Career," is a highly novelized autobiography, somewhat
on the model of Samuel Smiles's popular success stories in *Self-Help*
or *Lives of the Engineers*.[10] But unlike Smiles's dutiful protagonists,
Sandow adds picaresque and melodramatic elements, as if Alger's
Ragged Dick were crossbred with *Ruby, Pride of the Ring*. Typical
episodes show Sandow meeting and defeating increasingly imposing
opponents: "How I Came to London and Defeated Samson," "I Meet
Goliath," "My Lion Fight in San Francisco," and so forth.

The incidents from Sandow's "private" life are perhaps even more
heavily stylized. In one, a Frenchman bent on picking a fight accosts
Sandow, who was anonymously playing cards with friends in a French
tavern. Sandow refuses to retaliate even after he has been struck in
the face three times and insulted, but when finally the man calls him
a coward Sandow rises and breaks a table with his tormentor, then
calmly reseats himself and lights a cigar.[11] He later attempts to visit
the man in the hospital, but is turned away. Only several weeks later,
in London, does the man appear to introduce himself, shamefacedly,
as an amateur strongman. Sandow has not even recognized him:

> Of course, why had I been so blind? This was my assailant of the French
> billiard room. All, however, was now forgiven and forgotten, and as a

token of our good understanding, he presented me with a handsome
gold watch. To-day we are the greatest friends, and, whenever I go to
Paris, I stay with him. He is a French Count, but for obvious reasons,
not the least being that he is my friend, despite the hard knocks which
came of our first meeting, it would not be fair to disclose his name.
(Sandow 1905, 110)

The pattern is familiar from numerous *romans-feuilletons*, especially
Sue's *Les Mystères de Paris*, and from countless Westerns since: the
hero, soft-spoken, gentlemanly, and slow to anger, finally is forced to
defeat an enemy who later becomes one of his closest friends.

Throughout the narrative, Sandow emphasizes the most familiar motifs: his obscure childhood as a weakling, his development
of strength by means of a half-secret, half-public system of his own
devising, his gradual rise to social prominence and economic success,
and his shouldering of increased responsibility for the health and wel-
fare of the British people as repayment for their recognition. In a final
chapter Sandow describes his wonder-dog, Sultan, who was presented
to him by Prince Bismarck, and who, though never specially trained,
is "the holder of seventeen first prizes" and is easily able to carry
Sandow about (Sandow 1905, 129). On several occasions Sandow
must himself apprehend thieves or see justice done, although he is
generally reluctant to take the law into his own hands. Especially after
noting the changes through several editions of the book, it is clear
that Sandow is in the process of creating himself as folk hero—one
who, paradoxically, is both awesomely superior to ordinary humanity
and yet wholly suitable for emulation.

Throughout, there is room for no one but Sandow; other figures,
like Ziegfeld, who were crucial to his success simply do not appear,
and rivals appear only to be totally vanquished. By the book's third
edition, even the Sandow-Whiteley Exerciser has silently become the
Sandow Developer. Sandow's physical accomplishments were indeed
impressive, but, in fact, it is quite likely that several of his rivals, such
as "Apollon" (Louis Uni, 1862–1928) and Louis Cyr (1863–1912),
were stronger than he; Sandow never accepted the challenges of either
man. His only formal weight-lifting record was for the "bent press," a
one-armed lift that he popularized, and this was soon bettered by Cyr
(Willoughby, 53, 57, 61, 75). Yet even the success of Lionel Strongfort,
who modeled himself physically and commercially on Sandow, did
nothing to diminish his predecessor's fame. So successful was his
campaign to identify physical strength and fitness with himself that
in England a "strong thread" on a spool is branded "Sandow," while

in French a sandow is a chest-expander of the sort he marketed or indeed any strong cord that can be lengthened by pulling its ends.

Theorists of the novel, from Georg Lukács through Ian Watt and Lucien Goldmann, have all stressed the major role of the assertion of the bourgeois self in the genre's formation. Although Bakhtin somewhat qualifies this formulation, he does so primarily with reference to the marginal "counter-tradition" of the comic, Menippean novel he privileges; less dialogical forms, such as the "mainstream" social novel, still rely upon a central self. Sandow's self-novelization in *Physical Strength and How to Obtain It*, like that in the popular adventure-romance novels that are its models, is an even more emphatic and violent assertion of the self in all its plenitude and autonomy. This has two simultaneous effects: on the one hand, it reinscribes the individual, novelized subject "Sandow" as the center of the shifting field of advertising forces surrounding him, and as the sole author of strength and health; on the other, it clearly positions the reader as potential Sandow. "Hundreds of letters reach me daily, asking 'Can I become strong?'" writes Sandow. "Yes, you can become strong if you have the will and use it in the right direction" (Sandow 1897, 1). The interpellation is crudely obvious. In "Circe," Wicke observes, "Bloom's internal gaze comes to rest on the promises of Sandow's ads as if they were a potential cure for the abuses of history" (134). In fact, Bloom probably regards Sandow's program with the same labile alternation of credence and cynicism with which he regards most public institutions. As an advertising professional, he understands the mechanisms of publicity; but as a nineteenth-century progressive given to self-reproach and utopian schemes, he clings to the hope that he, too, can be changed utterly by force of will and a good, scientific program of self-development.

Although he views advertisements with a critical eye—the placement of the Plumtree's Potted Meat ad under the obituaries rates his particular scorn—Bloom is no more proof against advertising's power than the hypercritical Stephen is immune to the "grace of language" (*U* 7.776) of the speeches in "Aeolus." It should, of course, be borne in mind that, by London standards, Bloom is hardly a professional—ad agencies had been flourishing there since the 1840s (Hindley, 20). Furthermore, he is an Irish provincial, and Thomas Smith in his London *Press Directory* during the 1890s recommended Ireland as a virgin field for clients because the "Irish gentry still retain their simpleness of heart and a consequent belief in the goodness of mankind; hence they answer advertisements very easily" (Hindley, 108). But more important than these considerations is the fact that neither the artist Stephen nor the advertiser Bloom—neither Joyce nor Sandow—is wholly master of the powerful discourses he attempts to command. Advertisement and the novel are like twin powerful serpents, each swallowing the tail of the other. Just as Sandow appropriates the novel for advertising purposes, so Joyce's novel is permeated with representations of advertising; not only the language of characters like Gerty MacDowell, but the very language of the parodic narrator of "Cyclops" is likely to mutate without warning into ad language in the midst of heroic narration. Joyce stretches the boundaries of literature by including in *Ulysses* all the allotropes of the subliterary, the nonliterary, and even the antiliterary, thereby "novelizing" them all; and Sandow, in his gargantuan program of self-advertisement, appropriates art, the classics, science, sexuality, the bourgeois cult of self-improvement, and the novel as well.

Joyce, Inc.

But even apart from the parallel discourses of advertisement and the novel, there is a social and political context in which Joyce and Sandow may both be seen as icons of modernity. Joyce, as a major figure in the "heroic" phase of high modernism, occupied a space that partook both of centrality and marginality; indeed, to some extent, this was true of Pound, Eliot, Yeats, and Stein as well. Each was a largely self-fashioned "culture hero" in ways that both recalled and decisively differed from nineteenth-century literary figures such as Dickens or Carlyle. While they shared with their predecessors the fundamentally romantic status of the acknowledged (or disputed) literary "genius," they differed from them in how and to what degree they personally initiated, shaped, and manipulated their own cultural reception. The best-known example of this was Pound, who freely expended his considerable cultural capital in an effort to promote the works of artists of whom he approved; but Eliot, who developed a reputation as modernist critic that equalled or surpassed his stature as poet, may have been more effective in the long run. Lawrence Rainey has explored at length the changed relationship between modernist artists and their public, and my argument here in some respects builds on his. Nineteenth-century literary figures, however vigorously they might try to shape their own reputations, did not have the opportunity offered by the fragmented, cliquish universe of twentieth-century literary journals, where a few energetic, talented and committed writer/critic/publicists like Pound could have an influence highly disproportionate to the extent of their acceptance (or even recognition) by the reading public. From the start, Joyce was aware of his commercial potential. Oliver Gogarty claims that Joyce

> had, at first, thought of forming himself into a company, the shareholders in which were to receive all the proceeds from his future writings. The idea was novel. The shareholders would have to keep and humour him. Already, I said, I could see them issuing an unbalanced sheet. It was left to the British government to invest the royal bounty of $500 a year in him, and to a Mrs. Weaver [sic], later, to put $100,000 into that stock. There were worse investments than in James Joyce, Inc. (Gogarty, 46)

A number of recent books, such as Kevin Dettmar and Stephen Watt's *Marketing Modernism* (1996) and Lawrence Rainey's *Institutions of Modernism* (1998), have investigated some of the practical maneuvers involved in establishing a group of artists who had to compete within the modern market economy but could not do so on the basis of immediate sales. Both Rainey and John Xiros Cooper, in *Modernism and the Culture of Market Society*, stress, in Cooper's words, "the artisanal sub-culture that was...deployed to get Joyce into print and to inscribe a work's value as a function of its singularity, newness, and rarity" (Cooper, 3). Joyce, like many of the modernists, published major works through subscription, a method dependent on the author's reputation and the implied guarantee that his or her work will increase in value, thus attracting the attention of collector/investors rather than mere readers. This changes the cultural positioning of the writer in question, and it is important to note this curiously anachronistic aspect of the rise of modernist art. In fact, one could argue that such writers took on some of the craftsman's "aura" to which Benjamin refers as a characteristic of art of the past, despite the fact that their art form was mechanically reproduced; a copy of an early edition of *Ulysses* that was produced through a small Parisian bookstore in very limited quantities (such as the fourth printing of the first edition in my bookcase, overbound in leather by a previous collector) even today occupies a somewhat ambiguous space between a mass-produced item and a handmade artifact. The fact that *Ulysses* was published by Shakespeare and Company on an amateur basis, or that *The Waste Land* appeared courtesy of a press run part-time out of their basement by Leonard and Virginia Woolf, certainly affected the cultural reception of these modernist landmarks, although it is equally important that, since the 1960s, each has been a set text in many Anglophone universities. The crucial question is how these works moved from the former to the latter condition, and what the first situation had to do with the second.

Here we cannot overstress the importance of the publicity campaigns waged by figures like Joyce, whose attempt to manage his own reception and literary career was unprecedented. He is surely the first literary figure who cowrote and supervised not only his own biography (by Herbert Gorman), but also the first important book of analytic criticism on his own novel (Stuart Gilbert's *James Joyce's "Ulysses"*). If some of his efforts at self-support, such as his letter asking the King of England to intervene in order to have *Dubliners* published, seem naive and comic, we should remember that many of his letters, requests, and petitions to fellow artists in fact bore fruit. If his readership during his lifetime was limited, Joyce as a figure was universally known; he appeared twice on the cover of *Time* magazine, and the trial and vindication of *Ulysses* gained him far more publicity than any amount of commercial success would have done. Kevin Dettmar, who has made this case most emphatically, has investigated "Joyce's own, usually surreptitious, attempts to market his 'usylessly unreadable Blue Book of Eccles,'" (*FW* 179.26–27), and concludes, "When all is said and done, I think he did a pretty damn good job" (Dettmar 1993, 795).

Paradoxically, at the same time that his production of *Finnegans Wake* alienated him from any sort of "common reader," (not to mention people like Pound who had vigorously supported his earlier work), his fame grew greatest, the value of his manuscripts increased significantly, and the first serious critical work on Joyce's career, by academic figures as eminent as Harry Levin, portended his embrace by the academy. To put it another way, the value of Joyce's signature increased while his readership decreased, even when the signature was attached to somewhat parasitic work, such as his daughter Lucia's *lettrines*. Joyce, as lone modernist literary genius, appeared to a wide audience as self-created and self-perpetuating, the author of his own literary *agon*; and his own romantic style of self-fashioning managed, for years, to obscure the extremely important role played by the group of women, from Nora Barnacle and Sylvia Beach to Harriet Shaw Weaver, who made Joyce's literary productions possible. In a different register, this is a close parallel to the tale of Sandow's life authorized—and to some extent authored—by himself, culminating in his universal recognition as guarantor of a network of physical fitness spas, magazines, devices, and spectacles.

Fredric Jameson has pointed to the new sort of "careerism," represented by the major modernists, which is susceptible to an analysis that is indebted to Pierre Bourdieu. He suggests we try

> grasping the once-famous names no longer as characters larger than life or great souls of one kind or another, but rather...as *careers*, that is to say as objective situations in which an ambitious young artist around the turn of the century could see the objective possibility of turning himself into the "greatest painter" (or poet or novelist or composer) "of the age." That objective possibility is now given, not in subjective talent as such or some inner richness or inspiration, but rather in strategies of a well-nigh military character, based on superiority of technique and terrain, assessment of the counterforces, a shrew[d] maximization of one's own specific and idiosyncratic resources. (Jameson, 306)

Put this way, the parallel to Sandow, and indeed to other examples of major "commercial personalities" of the early twentieth century, is clear. Ford and Edison, for example, were figures of "genius" who validated their own empires of production across a wide cultural spectrum, directing their careers like aggressive generals within the licensed, bracketed, and technologically complex warfare of monopoly capitalism. The similarity to, say, Joyce and Stein, each receiving acolytes and issuing emissaries from their Parisian *ateliers*, in constant communication with the larger world of letters and with key figures within it, is plain. In all these cases there is, no doubt, an element of nostalgia for the artisanal "maker" in the public adulation showered on such figures. Meanwhile, the deployment of capital during the century ensures that even powerful individuals will be as much at the mercy of mysterious economic forces as they are in control of them. And the public figure of Henry Ford is an especially ironic example, a "craftsman" whose signature on each car conferred on it a peculiarly modernist aura from the very heart of the realm of mechanical reproduction. Jameson suggests that this situation can be seen as an example of uneven social development: "the coexistence of realities from radically different moments of history—handicrafts alongside the great cartels, peasant fields with the Krupp factories or the Ford plant in the distance" (307).

Among the literary, perhaps the fates of "geniuses," such as Stephen Phillips, William Gerhardie, or even Wyndham Lewis, can remind us that there is nothing automatic about the process of self-canonization. A critic of the period has noted the lament of an unknown artist of the 1920s who lived in Paris along with Hemingway, and points out the unfairness of the fact that of all the ambitious and talented American writers of that time, Hemingway is nearly the only one who emerged with a great reputation. But this is probably not a matter of chance: completely apart from the degree of Hemingway's talent, there was something about the age of high modernism that virtually demanded a limited number of lone geniuses to represent the world of art—geniuses whose main public characteristic was their rebellion, and who therefore almost by definition were, like their writings, singular, rare, unique. Seen from this perspective, the narrowing and tightening of the canon, promoted by figures like F. R. Leavis, may be less a matter of personal ethical or moral standards and more an unacknowledged aspect of modernist ideology.

Artist and Ad-Man

The mediating principle between the worlds of Sandow, Ford, and Joyce, who are otherwise such contrasting examples of cultural production, is advertisement.[12] In "Ithaca," Joyce pictures an ironic and finally paradoxical confrontation between the literary art and what Professor MacHugh calls "the gentle art of advertisement" (U 7.608). There Bloom tells Stephen of his plan, which he rehearsed in "Lestrygonians," for "a transparent showcart with two smart girls inside writing letters, copybooks, envelopes, blottingpaper"—a sort of moving *tableau vivant* with a dramatic motif that must arrest attention, with "everyone dying to know what she's writing" (U 8.131). Thinking that Bloom is all too accurate about the interest of the public in a young lady's mysterious letter, Stephen responds with an imagined scene in a hotel:

> Twilight. Fire lit. In dark corner young man seated. Young woman enters. Restless. Solitary. She sits. She goes to window. She stands. She sits.... On solitary hotel paper she writes. She thinks. She writes. She sighs. Wheels and hoofs. She hurries out. He comes from his dark corner. He seizes solitary paper. He holds it toward fire. Twilight. He reads...
> What?
> In sloping, upright and backhands: Queen's Hotel, Queen's Hotel, Queen's Hotel. Queen's Ho...(U 17.612)

But just what has Stephen written, or rather spoken, here? A literary work, no doubt, an ironic epiphany even briefer than the "Pisgah Sight of Palestine" with which he immediately follows it; earlier, in the newspaper office, he had cast that story before the newsroom swine in response to a request to write something "with a bite in it" for the *Freeman's Journal* (*U* 7.616), perhaps in an attempt to demonstrate that his stories have entirely the wrong sort of bite. The "Queen's Hotel" story certainly demystifies a familiar Victorian *topos*, the young girl writing a letter in romantic circumstances. But is Stephen the master of this modernist discourse? MacHugh responded to the "Pisgah Sight" with a symbolic interpretation, like a good modernist reader; but Bloom responds to "Queen's Hotel" with a sudden vivid recollection of his father's suicide in the Queen's Hotel, Ennis. Like the circus clown who insists Bloom is his father (*U* 17.979), Stephen has unwittingly stumbled from slapstick into tragedy. And then, in the teeth of his own reaction, Bloom considers publishing a group of Stephen's stories either as model essays or as entertainment— something marketable, along the lines of the collected works of Philip Beaufoy. Clearly Stephen's mode of discourse has escaped his control here, eliciting reactions by which he would be appalled and of which he remains unaware. Perhaps the final irony is the fact that Stephen's story might in fact make an effective advertisement for the Queen's Hotel, though an ad whose self-reflexive, ironic mode had not yet arrived in 1904.

Whatever Bloom offers in the line of advertisement, Stephen can transmute into art; but whatever Stephen offers, Bloom can divert toward advertisement. *Ulysses* records the movement of advertising discourse into virtually every other discourse offered in the book, and, in that act of recording, once again transmutes it. Who is stronger, Joyce or Sandow? Joyce died at 58, near blind and worried that the *Wake* was a failure; Sandow died at 58, impoverished by bad investments, of a stroke suffered after he lifted a car out of a ditch—or at least so the story went. If we are to see Sandow and Joyce as two figures that resonate with one another, each embodying an aspect of the reaction to modernity and each creating a persona to stand at the center of a network of signification, then we must look for this parallel throughout their works and lives. Both supported entourages of considerable size, Sandow financially and physically, as in the various photographs in which he is shown holding a troupe of performers on his shoulders; Joyce through the distribution of cultural capital among his followers and friends and the decentered and dispersed, but nevertheless palpable, aura of the master craftsman. Although an investment in Joyce might take much longer to pay off than would be the case with Sandow, Joyce, Inc. is, in fact, still supporting those of us involved in the Joycean "industry."

I have argued that one of the ways of mediating between these two cultural icons is through the discourse of advertisement as Joyce explored it in *Ulysses*, especially with respect to the discourse of the novel genre itself. Another is simply through an appreciation of their efforts at self-promotion; although we are accustomed to seeing Joyce as the scrupulous devotee to his art, indifferent to commercial considerations, the testimony of the letters and biography is that that is far from the entire story. But Joyce's intentions are really not the issue here; whatever his desires, he became (and remains), to a large extent, the face of modernist art, just as Sandow, among all the performing strongmen, became known as the single "perfect man." Both are located at the center of a rich and complex cultural nexus. Sandow haunts *Ulysses*, contributing in indirect ways to Bloom's fantasy life, his sense of personal worth and the possibility of personal betterment, and his professional musings about the effects of advertisement. Self-exiled like Joyce, Sandow parlayed his physical gifts into a commercial empire, thanks to his advent on the British scene at the height of the physical culture movement and the widespread national insecurity over the British public's strength and health. Joyce, refusing to take a part in the Celtic revival, managed to become the most famous exemplar of it. Both figures elude easy definition, partly because each is politically and culturally decentered—no longer simply Irish or Prussian, but international figures whose significance is scattered over an enormously wide cultural field.

Chapter Eight

Ulysses *and the Orient*

Bakhtin's dialogics form a sophisticated system—though that is probably too strong a word for his generally unsystematic sort of analysis—allowing us to counterpoise writing by figures such as Phillips and Corelli against Joyce's Ulyssean web of words. Of course, these are a somewhat arbitrary selection of writers. Many others, from huge and obvious precursors, like Homer and Dante, to less obviously significant ones, like M. Elizabeth Braddon, Rhoda Broughton, or Paul de Kock, could be investigated to determine the kind of intertextual play allowed by their explicit or implicit presence in *Ulysses*. Although historically critics have tended to approach the works of individual authors as ostensible verbal unities emanating from a single unique source, in part as a legacy of romanticism, it is, of course, equally possible in most cases to look at literary works first as at least potential members of a genre. What were once regarded as "subliterary" popular works have often been approached in this way, and although he is not frequently invoked in such studies, Bakhtin is in many ways as dependent on the concept of genre as he is on the "voice" of the author. As Michael Holquist observes, "Dialogism assumes that the bases of genre formation are to be found...in the rules that govern speech activity in our ordinary conversations....Dialogism's assumption here is that in most conversations, one-to-one correspondence between discourses and institutions are not strictly observed" (71). What Bakhtin later comes to call "speech genres," which govern everyday intercourse, have priority over the linguistic conventions generated by the participation of individual speakers in social institutions.

But Bakhtin did not really pursue an interest in either the linguistic codes of institutions or even the ideological structures of genres such as the newspaper or magazine, reserving his most intense analysis for literary authors, such as Rabelais and Dostoevsky, writers famous for their distinctive stylistic "voices," but in whose works a multiplicity of voices could also be found in dialogical play. The partial analysis I have offered in the preceding chapters is for the most part generic, and constitutes an attempt to show ways in which *Ulysses*, the most unconventional example of the novel genre, has important correspondences with the emerging genres of the light weeklies the daily newspaper, under the new journalism. For all the importance the editors of these publications may have had in establishing their new print forms, none of them proved irreplaceable. Newspapers and magazines were, from the beginning, consciously collaborative, a farrago of different voices; in a primitive way, they were always already "novelized."

In this chapter I want to take a further step away from the pure interchange of what appear to be individual voices in order to deal with the presence in *Ulysses* of what Edward Said terms Orientalism. Certainly not the product of any single dominant speaker, Orientalism is still a way of speaking, although not in the generic sense. As what Foucault terms a "discourse," it is a way of deploying language that is both dependent upon and participates in the dominant structures of power of the culture. A way of speaking, a particular vocabulary of both word and image, a set of assumptions, and a political stance, Orientalism in Said's description has an uncountable number of progenitors; and yet, in a novel like Joyce's, its presence is as easily identifiable as a quotation from Milton. To invoke Orientalism is to bring into play a system of differences and similarities that for richness and complexity is difficult to match. Yet it is clear that by invoking Orientalism the critic to some degree becomes complicit in it, just as the citizen of the British empire whose relationship with the East is, on the surface, economic might find, to his surprise, that his involvement is libidinal as well. Perhaps HCE can be seen as emblematic of this: "He married his markets, cheap by foul, I know, like any Etrurian Catholic Heathen, in their…turkiss indienne mauves" (*FW* 215.19).

As critics, we must acknowledge that the same gesture that enables an observer to critique the Orientalist's confounding of so many wildly differing cultures and historical moments also enables a critique of that observer. Indeed, over the past 25 years or so, several arguments have been leveled against Said's own work. A significant critique is that of James Clifford in *The Predicament of Culture* (Clifford, 258–63), who argues that Said's use of Foucault's radical anti-humanism clashes with Said's own invocation of liberal humanist values in protest of the victimization of the Orient. From a different perspective, Aijaz Ahmad in *In Theory: Classes, Nations, Literatures* (166–68), argues that Said ignores differences in the precapitalist and postcapitalist discourse of Orientalism, and also unduly restricts his discussion to canonical writers. While such caveats have a good deal of force, it is probably also true that the cultural phenomenon of Orientalism would not have elicited the interest it has in British and American academia, and would not still retain much of its currency, if it were not to some degree assimilable within a liberal-humanist framework.[1]

Certainly the most thoroughgoing treatment of Orientalism to spring from Said's work, but specifically addressing the Irish context, is Joseph Lennon's *Irish Orientalism* (2004). Lennon points to the long-established belief in affinities between Irish and various Oriental cultures:

> The pervasive nature of the Celtic-Oriental affinity has long been seen as an underlying tissue of Irish culture, based on legends of successive migrations to Ireland from the Orient recorded as Ireland's origin legends in the medieval chronicle *Lebor Gabála Érenn*. Evidence of such affinities has subsequently been claimed in race, language, and culture—and more particularly in music (Arabian-Moroccan-Celtic), knot work (Ethiopian-Arabic-Celtic), mysticism (Indian-Persian-Irish), travel and trade (Scythian-Phoenician-Celtic) architecture (Egyptian-Indian-Eskimo-Celtic), physiognomy (Mongol-African-Gael), ancient dress (Chinese-Scythian-Celtic), ancient law (Brahmin-Brehon), warfare (Egyptian-Scythian-Celtic), politics (Irish-Indian-Persian-Egyptian-Chinese) and, generally, sensibility (Oriental-Celtic). (Lennon, xviii)

There is no telling how many of these affinities Joyce believed in; certainly he asserted, in "Ireland, Island of Saints and Sages," that the Irish language was "oriental in origin, and has been identified by many philologists with the ancient language of the Phoenicians, originators of trade and navigation (*CW* 156). Lennon concentrates on eighteenth- and nineteenth-century Irish poets and upon Yeats's mystical circle. He spends very little time on Joyce, mostly discussing the well-known parallel MacHugh asserts in "Aeolus" between Jews and Egyptians, Greeks and Romans, and Irish and English, in which the first, subordinate group is claimed to be essentially spiritual, and the second, imperial force to be materialistic (*U* 7.485). Elizabeth Butler Cullingford devotes a chapter to "Phoenician Genealogies and Oriental Geographies: Language and Race in Joyce and his Successors" in her work *Ireland's Others: Gender and Ethnicity in Irish Literature and Popular Culture*, but her focus is quite different from mine here. Most critics would agree that *Ulysses* is permeated with the traces of Orientalism, some of them textual, others structural or imagistic; the question is whether Joyce merely reflects this totalizing discourse, or in some way subverts it.

The Dream of the Orient

In *Ulysses*, Stephen and Bloom have shared a dream of the East, a fact which, in the eyes of earlier critics, served to establish a mysterious deep psychological linkage between them. Bloom has dreamed "of his dame Mrs Moll with red slippers on in a pair of Turkey trunks" (*U* 14.509); in the opening of "Circe" she appears with the further embellishments of a white yashmak, "toerings," and a "fetterchain," and is accompanied by a camel that obligingly picks her a mango (*U* 15.313). Stephen, on the other hand, vaguely recalls,

> Open hallway. Street of harlots. Remember. Haroun al Raschid. I am almosting it. That man led me, spoke. I was not afraid. The melon he had he held against my face. Smiled: creamfruit smell. That was the rule, said. In. Come. Red carpet spread. You will see who. (*U* 3.365)

Acquainted as we are with Bloom's persistent associations of Molly with melons, we are in little doubt as to who awaits Stephen, especially when Molly, musing on the possibility of Stephen moving in with the Blooms, thinks, "I'd have to get a nice pair of red slippers like those the Turks with the fez used to sell ..." (*U* 18.1494).

The first thing to note about these strangely interlocked fantasies, whose variations play throughout *Ulysses*, is that they are in fact *public* fantasies; the slippers, camel, slave-girl, red carpet, and melon are the standard furniture of a popular vision of the Orient that descended most directly from *Arabian Nights*, but that was elaborated, directly or indirectly, through a multitude of pseudo-Oriental European works from the narratives of Byron, Moore, Southey, Goethe, Nerval, and Chateaubriand, through the travel writings of Flaubert and Burton, up through Fitzgerald's *Rubaiyat*, and vaguely echoed in Robert Louis Stevenson's *New Arabian Nights*. Simultaneously, the Western myth of the Orient in its British avatar was displayed in stage adaptations, such as the pantomime versions of "Turko the Terrible," and popular expositions, such as the bazaar in "Araby." All these exemplars of high and popular culture contributed to and were constrained by the ongoing discourse of Orientalism. As Edward Said argued, even in its scholarly, ostensibly objective version, European Orientalism was "a western style for dominating, restructuring, and having authority over the Orient." While the fantasy vision of the Orient was governed by "a battery of desires, repressions, investments, and projections" (8), the key determinant of the Oriental was *difference*; "for Orientalism was ultimately a political vision of reality whose structure promoted the difference between the familiar (Europe, the West, 'us') and the strange (the Orient, the East, 'them')" (Said 3).

Just where this Orient was to be found was moot. *Arabian Nights* itself covered a great deal of ill-defined territory, including China; Lane thought the collection of tales was Egyptian in origin, Burton thought it Persian. The Near East, including the Biblical lands, were seen as Oriental, although, depending upon the writer's preference, either a Biblical or an Oriental intonation might be given to this geography. Byron's tales, reflecting his travels, steered the European imagination toward Turkey, Albania, and Greece under Turkish occupation.[2] And since the Muslem element in most literary evocations of the Orient predominated, the entirety of the Ottoman Empire, including Moorish Spain, came to be seen as Eastern. This, of course, validates Molly's claim to be considered the Oriental prize of Dublin, at least by her husband: "That's where Molly can knock the spots off them. It's the blood of the south. Moorish" (*U* 13.968). At its furthest expansion, Colette Le Yaouanc points out, the Oriental was thought to include the continents of Africa and Australia, and even the culture of African Americans; in this broadest perspective, the Oriental and the Exotic became virtually synonymous (16).

Like all cultural formations coded as Other, the Orient embraced extremes of signification. Rudolf Wittkower, who has studied the earliest representations of the "marvels of the East," argues that the pictorial iconography of Eastern "monsters"—giants, pygmies, unicorns, people with heads of dogs or with tails, cannibals, and amazons—was widely disseminated in popular as well as scholarly forms, and might alternately carry the burden of good or of evil: "the monster has been credited everywhere with the powers of a god or the diabolical forces of evil" (197). By the Renaissance, the cultural implications of exploration and colonization encouraged a more elaborate mythic status for the Orient. It became both an Eden, an Old World to which one might return, and a fresh, virginal territory for exploration, colonization, and missionary activity. By the time of the Romantics, the Orient had become the *locus classicus* of the dream state, both as a place of pilgrimage and endless wandering and as a wholly static spectacle or *tableau vivant* (Said 158). In the wake of Byron and Hugo, the East also came to represent possibility, a form of personal release where the enterprise of selfhood was untrammeled by the artificial restrictions of "civilization." Thus Bloom imagines himself a fearless pilgrim amid pasteboard scenery that is both banally exotic and strangely familiar:

> Walk along a strand, strange land, come to a city gate, sentry
> there...leaning on a long kind of a spear. Wander through awned
> streets. Turbaned faces going by. Dark caves of carpet shops, big man,
> Turko the terrible, seated crosslegged, smoking a coiled pipe. Cries of
> sellers in the streets. Drink water scented with fennel, sherbet. Dander
> along all day. Might meet a robber or two. Well, meet him....A shiver
> of the trees, signal, the evening wind. I pass on. (*U* 4.86)

This is the East of adventure and freedom which we see embodied in
popular poems like "The Arab's Farewell to His Steed," drunkenly
recited by the boy's uncle in "Araby," in an unconscious parody of the
boy's aspirations.[3]

Of course, Bloom is aware that he is romanticizing. "Probably not
a bit like it really," he comments, "Kind of stuff you read: in the track
of the sun" (*U* 4.99). Frederick Diodati Thompson's *In the Track of the
Sun: Diary of a Globe Trotter* (1893), which is probably the book in
Bloom's library, is certainly in the tradition of European Orientalism,
although its tone is far removed from that of Bloom's inner monologue.
As Weldon Thornton points out, the title page of a common edition
of this book features an Oriental woman playing a stringed instrument, perhaps Bloom's "what do you call them: dulcimers" (*U* 4.98;
Thornton, 70). Bloom, in fact, has little idea of the source of any of
his ideas about the East, a fact that testifies to the general unremarked
diffusion of Orientalist texts and myths in his society.

Furthermore, his ability to demythify the East—his "realistic"
perception that it is not actually a land of milk and honey—has curiously little impact upon his imagination, which returns again and
again to a vision of sensual richness and luxury. Minutes after he has
observed, "Not a bit like it really," the Agendath Netaim circular
sets him off on a vision of eucalyptus trees, orange groves, melons,
and Molly, after which again he pulls himself up short: "No, not like
that. A barren land, bare waste. Vulcanic lake, the dead sea: no fish,
weedless, sunk deep in the earth. No wind could lift those waves,
grey metal, poisonous foggy waters...the grey sunken cunt of the
world" (*U* 4.219). Bloom's sources for his countervision, like those
for his vision, are of course literary. In this case one such source is
probably the Reverend J. L. Porter's book *The Giant Cities of Bashan
and Syria's Holy Places* (1865), a copy of which was ready to hand in
Joyce's library, if not Bloom's.[4] "The Orient," Said observes, "is less
a place than a *topos*, a set of references, a congeries of characteristics,

that seems to have its origin in a quotation, or a fragment of a text, or a citation from somebody else's work on the Orient, or some bit of previous imagining, or an amalgam of all these" (177).

Joyce's *Arabian Nights*

In establishing the East as the site of endless wandering, no book was as influential as the *Thousand and One Nights* or, as it was otherwise known, *The Arabian Nights' Entertainments*, which was introduced to Europeans in Galland's French version in the early eighteenth century and, in various abridgements, was widely circulated thereafter. The best-known English versions were Edward William Lane's, published in 1840, and Sir Richard Burton's unexpurgated edition, which appeared 1885–88. Phrases and allusions such as "Barmecide Feast," "Open Sesame," "Solomon's Seal," "Old Man of the Sea," "The Slave of the Lamp," "The Valley of Diamonds," "The Roc's Egg," and Haroun al-Raschid with his "Garden of Delights" became staple references of popular culture and of popular literature during the nineteenth century. Even the simple mention of *Arabian Nights* took on rich and manifold connotations; it had become something like a brand name in the eyes of nineteenth-century Europeans, and spawned a group of Irish adaptations.

When, in the National Library, Stephen has completed his Shakespeare disquisition and is invited out for a drink by Mulligan, who has just been invited to an Irish literary soiree, he thinks, "Swill till eleven. Irish nights entertainment" (*U* 9.1105). At this point in the text, it is unclear whether he is imagining his own evening (in which, indeed, he swills till well past eleven) or the anticipated soiree in which Mulligan, Moore, Eglinton, A.E. and others will seriously discuss Irish literary swill. On the one hand, he is contrasting the bathetic evening ahead of them all with the enchantment of *Arabian Nights*; on the other, as Thornton points out, Stephen (or Joyce) may be alluding to the minor Irish writer Patrick J. MacCall's 1897 volume *The Fenian Night's Entertainment* (Thornton, 216). MacCall's work, putatively twelve evenings of storytelling at a Wexford fireside, is a collection of Ossianic tales from various sources, rendered popular by simplifying and rationalizing their narratives and by recounting the tales in a paddyesque version of peasant dialect:

> Wance upon a time, when things was a great 'le betther in Ireland than they are at present, when a rale king ruled over the counthry wid four

others undher him to look afther the craps an' other industhries, there
lived a young chief called Fan MaCool. Now, this was long afore we
gev up bowin' an scrapin' to the sun an' moon an' sich like *raumash*;
an' signs an it, there was a powerful lot ov witches an' Druids, an'
enchanted min an' wimin goin' about, that med things quare enough
betimes for ivery wan. (McCall, 2117)

McCall's version implicitly suggests certain continuities between the
Irish and Oriental tales: both are "marvelous," full of adventures and
strange sights, and both are emphatically oral renditions—in the case
of *Arabian Nights* because of the frame-tale situation, in the *Fenian
Nights' Entertainments* because of the strenuous use of dialect and
frequent appeals to the values of the audience. But in fact, although
Thornton does not note this, MacCall's volume itself alludes to an
earlier Irish adaptation of the *Tales*, Sir Samuel Ferguson's *Hibernian
Nights Entertainments* (1887), which Stephen J. Brown, S.J., describes
as "supposed to be told in 1592 by Turlough O'Hagan, O'Neill's
bard, to Hugh Roe O'Donnell and his companions imprisoned in
Dublin Castle (Brown, 103). Clearly, in Ferguson's version, there is
at least a gesture at establishing a dramatic parallel to Scheherezade
in the frame of the tales; in MacCall's version, only the oral element
remains. In still other works, such as Robert Louis Stevenson's *New
Arabian Nights* (1882), even the idea of oral delivery, or of framing, has vanished, and the tales, collected from Stevenson's periodical
publications, have only the barest hint of the supernatural or marvelous; they belong more to the genre of Sherlock Holmes than to that
of Sinbad. The point here is that Stephen is alluding not to a specific
popular work, but to an entire tradition of mock-Oriental tales stem-
ming from Galland's and Lane's original versions and proliferating
in more or less adulterated forms in the various national literatures
of Europe. Between the modern, Europeanized (or Hibernicized)
versions and the original there exists much the same sort of tension
as exists between the *Odyssey* and Joyce's *Ulysses*. Indeed, *Arabian
Nights* provides a counter-text for *Ulysses* in much the same way
the *Odyssey* does. Matthew Josephson intuitively recognized this in
his 1922 article entitled "1001 Nights in a Bar-Room, or the Irish
Odysseus."[5]

There are certainly more direct allusions to *Arabian Nights* than to
the *Odyssey* in *Ulysses*. Furthermore, it is easily arguable that whatever Homeric intertextuality Joyce may have established for his novel,
the characters of the novel would be far more likely to view their
own experience in terms of the more famous Eastern tales, especially

the universally known "Ali Baba and the Forty Thieves" and "The Voyages of Sinbad." The sailor Murphy, who appears to have translated himself into a walking representative of popular literature ("a bit of a literary cove in his own small way"; *U* 16.1677), is immediately identified as "friend Sinbad" by Bloom (*U* 16.858). Later, Murphy himself admits that *The Arabian Nights Entertainment* is his favorite book, along with *Red as a Rose is She* (*U* 16.1680). Murphy, however, is a false adventurer, an *Odysseus pseudangelos* who may have genuinely traveled, but who manages to destroy his own credibility by too blatantly telling his listeners what he thinks they want to hear. Bloom, according to the Ithacan narrator, is the true voyager who has traveled with Sinbad the Sailor and has marvelously squared the circle of his own experience: "Going to dark bed there was a square round Sinbad the Sailor roc's auk's egg in the night of the bed of all the auks of the rocs of Darkinbad the Brightdayler" (*U* 17.2328).

The motifs that pervade the seven voyages of Sinbad echo in *Ulysses* as well: voyaging and disaster, unanticipated rewards after suffering, doubling, abandonment and exile, sexual temptation, unwitting violation of taboos, and scapegoating are obvious in each. More specifically, several episodes of Sinbad's adventures themselves double episodes of the *Odyssey,* and thus of Joyce's book as well. During the third voyage, Sinbad and his companions are captured by an anthropophagous giant, blind him with a red-hot spit and escape on rafts that the giant and his wife destroy by hurling giant boulders, so that only Sinbad and two of his companions are left alive. The fourth voyage includes events that echo both "Lotus-Eaters" and "Laestrygonians," in that Sinbad alone abstains from eating an apparently narcotic food that his companions are given by unknown islanders, and then watches in horror as they are devoured. During the fifth voyage, Sinbad warns his companions against breaking open the roc's egg and eating its contents but, in a rough parallel to "Oxen of the Sun," they do so and all but Sinbad are destroyed by the parent rocs. In the same voyage, the "Old Man of the Sea" episode has clear parallels to "Proteus."

Such correspondences could be traced at much greater length; but the most striking parallel is in the character and actions of Sinbad, a perfect Odyssean hero who escapes by stratagems, rather than heroism, and often survives by being overlooked, ignored, or abandoned by his own companions as well as by his antagonists.[6] In his quest for survival, he is often forced to attempt embarrassing or morally dubious ploys. Like Bloom, Sinbad is engaged in commerce; he is more merchant than warrior, and is often reduced to taking rather menial jobs. His rewards are in the substantial wealth he accumulates, often accidentally, rather than in fame or glory. In many ways, despite the Oriental absolute monarchy under which he functions, he would be an even better exemplar of the roots of the capitalist bourgeoisie than Odysseus was for Adorno and Horkheimer. His greatest triumphs are inevitably those of self-control and self-denial, and during his final voyages he is a reluctant adventurer indeed. Only the express orders of Haroun al-Raschid can stir him from his hearth.[7] No doubt it is the unheroic premise and tone of Sinbad's adventures that allowed them to be endlessly adapted to the pantomime stage for purposes of farce, topicality, and mass entertainment.[8] After all, even in Arabic, the *Alf laila wa-laila* was long regarded by Muslim scholars as popular entertainment, fit only for coffeehouse storytellers—a fact that recalls the way in which some Dubliners would dismiss *Ulysses* as nothing more than the record of Dublin bar talk.

But while Sinbad, in one of his aspects, represents to the Western imagination an everyman thrust unwillingly into the realm of the marvelous, during the nineteenth century the Sinbad figure also took on a certain darkly romantic coloration. This occurred because, especially in Britain, the average reader's confrontation with the Orient was most likely to take place through the mediation of Romantic poetry, especially that of Byron; the Orient grew increasingly Byronic in the Western imagination as Byron's myth expanded following his death and as his verse romances became popular literature. It is this Byronized Orient that provides the setting for popular poetry, like "The Arab's Farewell to His Steed," while the Oriental heroes of narratives like Thomas Moore's *Lalla Rookh* came increasingly to resemble the popular notion of the Byronic hero—and, indistinguishably, of Byron himself. This transformation in the quality of Orientalist discourse took place during the nineteenth century, but its cultural consequences still echoed during the early twentieth century.

The most vivid testament to this effect is to be found in *The Count of Monte Cristo* (1844–45) of Dumas *père*. Edmond Dantes, following his escape from the Chateau d'If and his transfiguration through suffering, is the consummate Byronic hero. He has a dark secret in his past and is misanthropically embittered by the betrayal of his friends and of his fiancée Mercedes; he is cold and aloof but scrupulously polite and retains a somewhat chivalric attitude toward women despite (or perhaps as a consequence of) his misogyny. Part of his career is spent as chief of a band of pirates—like Byron's Corsair—and even during his career in Paris, when he presents himself as a foreign nobleman with limitless resources, his type is easily recognized by the Parisian public. On several occasions, characters refer to him as "Lord Ruthven," an allusion to the satiric and sinister portrait of Byron in Lady Caroline Lamb's *Glenarvon*.[9]

Meanwhile, he escorts about Paris his Greek slave/princess named Haidée, who shares her name and physical description with the Greek princess whom Don Juan encounters in the Cyclades. But the first pseudonym Dantes actually claims for himself, even before he becomes the Count of Monte Cristo, is Sinbad the Sailor. Having found the treasure to which the Abbé Faria directed him, and having adventured in the East, Dantes for a period establishes himself in a richly appointed cave on the island of Monte Cristo, accompanied by Haidée and by an Arabic servant. There he entertains a young Parisian socialite with hashish and the finest wines, foods, and perfumes. Like the Byronic hero, he is a pirate king with a mysterious past; like the Sinbad of the *Tales*, who narrates his adventures to his unfortunate double "Sinbad of the Land," this Sinbad mesmerizes his young guest with conversation and a feast of the senses. Quite self-consciously, he has established an "Aladdin's Cave" to play upon the sensibilities of his visitors; like an author of popular romances, he manipulates his audience by invoking the cumulative significations of the Orient.

The suggestion that Dantes intends to evoke is that he has acquired not only boundless wealth but also mysterious other powers during his sojourn in the Orient; by associating himself with it, he has become both more and less than human. He claims to embody the omnipotent indifference imputed to Oriental potentates, and at the beginning of his course of vengeance, exclaims, "Farewell kindness, humanity, and gratitude!" (Dumas, 329). It is, in part, this admixture of the utterly alien, the "inhuman," that establishes the Count of Monte Cristo as the ultimate figure of the dark avenger for the nineteenth-century bourgeoisie. He has become Other, with all the alienation that suggests, but with some unsuspected powers as well. Certainly he haunts the young Stephen Dedalus's imagination, and his figure comes immediately to Bloom's mind, as well, when he contemplates revenge for his cuckolding. In "Ithaca," Bloom imagines that he will become a comet, hurtling into temporary exile:

Whence, disappearing from the constellation of the Northern Crown he would somehow reappear reborn above delta in the constellation of Cassiopeia and after incalculable eons of peregrination return an estranged avenger, a wreaker of justice on malefactors, a dark crusader, a sleeper awakened, with financial resources (by supposition) surpassing those of Rothschild or the silver king. (*U* 17.2018)

For Dantès—and, by extension, for Bloom—the East provides a sort of inhuman empowerment, a space in which one can strip away sentimental values; and perhaps for European bourgeois culture in general the Orient offered a means by which the inhuman, devastating power of extreme wealth could be imaged in a suitably distanced frame. The narrative strategy of *The Count of Monte Cristo* vividly demonstrates this effect. Immediately following his escape, the Dantès whose thoughts and feelings we know vanishes from the narrative; when he reappears as Sinbad the Sailor, who may be capable of anything, we have no access to his consciousness, no direct narrative guarantee that this is the same man. The East is what stands in that transformative lacuna.

Oriental Erotics

But, for the Victorians, there is no doubt that the most important role of the East in the popular imagination was as a locale of sexual license and perversion within a context of sensual wealth—the original arena of *luxe et volupté*. Even Ernest Renan, the renowned Orientalist whose *Life of Jesus* Joyce admired (*Letters*, II 82), was quick to emphasize that in the vicinity of Nazareth "the beauty of the women...—that beauty which was remarked even in the sixth century—...is still most strikingly preserved. It is the Syrian type in all its languid grace" (Renan, 64). But beneath that beauty lurked a dangerous sensuality that brought out the censor in the Orientalist Edward Lane. Said comments, "everything about the Orient—or at least Lane's Orient-in-Egypt—exuded dangerous sex, threatened hygiene and domestic seemliness with an excessive 'freedom of intercourse,' as Lane put it" (167). But not even Lane's bowdlerizing of *Arabian Nights*, only corrected by Burton at the end of the century, could disguise the Orient's dark appeal.

So thoroughly has Bloom been mastered by Orientalist ideology that, for him, as for many imaginative writers of Europe, the East is one vast recumbent woman. As we have seen, the Holy Lands are equivalent to his wife when he is elated, the "dry sunken cunt of the world" when he is depressed. And the insistent, ambiguous sexuality of the brothel immediately triggers an Eastern motif in "Circe." As soon as he hands his potato to Zoe and feels her linking his arm in hers, he hears "oriental music" and gazes into her eyes, which, in the traditional imagery, are "ringed with kohol" (*U* 15.1319). "*Gazelles are leaping, feeding on the mountains. Near are lakes. Round their shores file shadows black of cedargroves....It burns, the orient, a sky*

of sapphire, cleft by the bronze flight of eagles. Under it lies the wom-
ancity, nude, white, cool, in luxury" (U 15.1324). Gazelles, cedars,
the burning sky, the imagery of precious metals and gems are all conventional emblems of the Orient, and all contributory to the rich fund
of female sexuality. Furthermore, as Dermot Kelly points out, each of
these scenic details reflects a detail of Zoe's dress, such as the "s*lim*
black velvet fillet" and the "*sapphire slip, closed with three bronze*
buckles" (U 15.1279) (Kelly, 59). Either Bloom, a literalist of the imagination, or the Arranger of "Circe" has followed the lead of Western
culture by showing in graphic fashion the way in which an available
woman and an Eastern scene are interchangeable. That Bloom experiences this in a brothel is unsurprising; as Said observes, "in time,
'Oriental sex' was as standard a commodity as any other available in
the mass culture, with the result that writers and readers could have it,
if they wished, without necessarily going to the Orient" (190).

What Said fails to note, however, is the curious way in which the
cultural complex associating the Orient with female passivity—or
indeed bondage and slavery, as in the harem women who were a staple of the bourgeois imagination[10]—was capable of abruptly revers-
ing itself. Just as Zoe, the "odalisque," immediately mocks Bloom's
advances, Molly, who earlier appeared to him in the trappings of
slavery, curses him in Moorish, calls him an "old stick in the mud,"
and advises him to "see the wide world" (U 15.330). As most of the
major modernist writers realized, any master-slave formation implies
a dangerous cultural ambivalence; the master is inevitably a slave to
the relationship's ideological structure. So Bloom is aware that even
Molly's harem costume is ambiguous with respect to power: "She
had red slippers on. Turkish. Wore the breeches. Suppose she does?"
(U 13.1240). No sooner has Bloom imagined Molly as odalisque than
he himself is transmuted into female-as-property, auctioned off to a
representative of Haroun al-Raschid to pander to the Oriental poten-
tate's "Gomorrahan vices" (U 15.3122).[11]

This sort of reversal is less a testament to any real ambiguity in
the situation of the Oriental woman in the Western mind, than to the
extreme Western ambivalence with respect to the Orient and power.
For Europeans, the East is the land of absolute despotism, of power so
unlimited that, like that of Aladdin with his lamp, it is unconstrained
even by the laws of the physical world. Simultaneously, it is the imaginative locale of the most abject slavery, where women, generally, but
many men as well, are chattel, mere fodder for the unimaginable per-
versions the West attributed to their owners. Indeed, like Aladdin
himself, or Sinbad, or most of the protagonists of the tales, a person

can immediately move from omnipotence to utter powerlessness at the whim of a sovereign or twist of fate. This pattern, of course, struck a familiar chord with a readership trying to acclimate itself to the painful vicissitudes of late bourgeois capitalism. Citing both Said and Perry Anderson in *Lineages of the Absolutist State*, Peter Wollen comments, "the Orient is the site of scientific and political fantasy, displaced from the body politic of the West, a field of free play for shamelessly paranoid constructions, dreamlike elaborations of a succession of Western traumas" (5). And even apart from the issue of power, the logic that constructs the Other in the European mind characteristically endows it with qualities that are opposing extremes. Stephen Owen speaks of an "ultimate Orientalism, in which all condescension is simultaneously a desperate longing for the Other. In that Other all contradictory extremes exist: youth and old age, sophistication and naivete, sensuality and decent restriction" (Owen, 141).[12]

There is an Oriental coloration to both Bloom's rise and his fall in "Circe": at his elevation "the beaters approach with imperial eagles hoisted, trailing banners and waving oriental palms" (*U* 15.1408), and during his trial Molloy defends him by reference to "his extensive property at Agendath Netaim in faraway Asia Minor" (*U* 15.981). Yet immediately following this assertion, Molloy explains that Bloom is of "Mongolian extraction and irresponsible for his actions," while Bloom as lascar makes a "shrug of oriental obeisance" (*U* 15.960). He is, as a voice in "Oxen" explains, "at his best an exotic tree which, when rooted in its native orient, throve and flourished...but, transplanted to a clime more temperate, its roots have lost their quondam vigor" (*U* 14.937). Still Bloom, the original rubber-man, has not traveled with Sinbad the Sailor for nothing; no matter how far he falls, he will rise again, and indeed escapes Nighttown wearing "caliph's hood and poncho," in the double guise of an incognito Haroun al-Raschid (*U* 15.4324).

So Bloom, who Orientalizes Molly in order to invest her with more exotic appeal, is himself intermittently Orientalized. His own Orientalization is in part due to his "Jewishness," which in his case is an especially arbitrary category of social marginalization, but which nonetheless looms nearly as large in his own mind as it does in the minds of other Dubliners.[13] Joyce underlines the notion of Bloom's racial marginality by scattering throughout *Ulysses* references to the common racial myth of the time in which Jew, Greek, and Irish are seen as "spiritual" races under the oppression of the "pragmatic" Egyptians, Romans, and English. As Renan makes clear, when the ineffectuality of the subject races is viewed in a different light, it translates into spirituality. Among the Semitic peoples, he asserts, there is "a total indifference to exterior life and the vain apanage of the 'comfortable,' a contempt for comfort and luxury which, when it is not caused by idleness, contributes greatly to the elevation of soul" (Renan, 140)—or at least so it might seem to a Western observer, who would thus be relieved of any guilt regarding his own relatively comfortable circumstances.

The Oriental Irish and Moore's *Lalla Rookh*

But there is a final irony in the Orientalization of Bloom, this one extratextual. It lies in the Romantic *fiat* through which, as I argued at the beginning of this chapter, the Irish themselves were cast as Orientals in the eyes of the British and often in their own eyes as well. The strength of this conviction varied, because (among other factors) to identify a cultural artifact as Oriental had varying commercial implications. Even in the mid-eighteenth century, before the genuine British vogue for "Oriental" poetry, the East had enough evocative power so that Collins entitled a collection of his poems, published in 1742, *Persian Eclogues*. On their republication in 1757, perhaps made nervous by the increasing number of prose narratives treating specific cultures of the East, he changed the title to a more vague *Oriental Eclogues*. But even this was too much; according to Dr. Johnson, on his deathbed Collins expressed some dissatisfaction with the poems, in that they did not deal clearly enough with Asiatic culture, and began to call them his "Irish Eclogues," suggesting that Persian, Oriental, and Irish for him were interchangeable terms, at least in a poetic context.[14] Indeed, Byron, the premier Orientalist in an epoch in which, as Edgar Quinet observed, "every writer made his debut with an Oriental poem," echoed the point in his dedication of *The Corsair* to Thomas Moore.[15] In a flattering reference to *Lalla Rookh* he writes,

> It is said . . , I trust truly, that you are engaged in the composition of a poem whose scene will be laid in the East; none can do those scenes so much justice. The wrongs of your own country, the magnificent and fiery spirit of her sons, the beauty and feeling of her daughters, may there be found; and Collins, when he denominated his Oriental his Irish Eclogues, was not aware of how true, at least, was a part of his parallel. Your imagination will create a warmer sun, and less clouded

sky; but wildness, tenderness, and originality, are part of your national claim of oriental descent, to which you have thus far proved your title more clearly than the most zealous of your country's antiquarians. (Marchand, 506–7)

This identification of Irish and Oriental is invoked by Yeats when he attempts to turn Dublin into a center for the study of Eastern mysticism, or speaks through a sixteenth-century Moorish anti-self. It is even echoed by the wandering Irishman Richard Burton in his essay on *The Book of a Thousand and One Nights*, when he speaks of the imaginative pleasures to be drawn from fairy tales and books of exploration alike: "The pleasure must be greatest where faith is strongest; for instance, amongst imaginative races like the Kelts, and especially Orientals, who imbibe supernaturalism with their mother's milk" (406).

Clearly, Byron was referring to a tradition of some antiquity in his address to Moore; but, in fact, it was probably Moore's *Lalla Rookh* that, because of the book's popularity, was responsible for the identification of the Irish with the Oriental in the nineteenth-century imagination. In some ways, *Lalla Rookh* was one of the first planned "best sellers." *Irish Melodies*, which began to appear in 1807, established the reputation of the Irish Catholic Moore, and his publisher, Longman's, had considerable faith in him. As he explains in the preface to the twentieth edition of *Lalla Rookh*, "it was about the year 1812 that, impelled far more by the encouraging suggestions of friends than impelled by any promptings of my own ambition, I was induced to attempt a poem upon some oriental subject, and of those quarto dimensions which Scott's late triumphs in that form had then rendered the regular poetic standard" (Symington, 37). Moore concluded an unprecedented arrangement with Longman's, whereby the publisher would pay him 3000 pounds upon delivery of "a poem of yours of the length of Rokeby." He then immersed himself in Oriental reading for some three years, meanwhile painfully turning out the poem's long narrative stanzas and pseudo-scholarly footnotes from a cottage in Derbyshire. There was nothing "natural" about the process, and Moore claimed that he went through a number of "disheartening experiments" before finding a theme he could transplant to an Oriental setting: "The cause of tolerance was again my inspiring theme; and the spirit that had spoken in the melodies of Ireland soon found itself at home in the East" (Symington, 10). Indeed, during the writing of *Lalla Rookh* he issued two or three further numbers of the *Irish Melodies*.

Like *Arabian Nights*, the book has a frame-tale, but Moore's is lighter in tone. A marriage is arranged between Lalla Rookh, the daughter of Emperor Aurungzebe at Delhi and the son of King Abdalla of Bucharia; the marriage is to be celebrated at Cashmere, where she will meet her groom. During the bridal journey Lalla Rookh is accompanied by Fadladeen (the Chamberlain of the Haram) and by a retinue that includes a poet known as Feramorz who had come to Delhi with King Abdalla. As the group travels, he recites "Stories of the East" accompanied by his kitar. Feramorz recites four major "songs" as they travel—"The Veiled Prophet of Khorassan," "Paradise and the Peri," "The Fire-Worshippers," and "The Light of the Haram"—much to the annoyance of the Chamberlain, who finds the lighter pieces frivolous and the more substantial ones offensive to a good Muslim. Lalla Rookh, however, is enchanted, falls in love with the young poet, and is overjoyed to discover on her arrival at Cashmere that he is, in fact, the prince she is to marry.

On its publication, in 1817, *Lalla Rookh* was much heralded for its authenticity. One Colonel Wilks, a historian of British India, was so impressed by the descriptive passages that he insisted Moore must have traveled in the East. Moore delightedly cites his friend Luttrell, who informed him that parts of the poem had been translated into Persian and were sung "along the streets of Ispahan" (Moore, 18). The work does carry a considerable freight of allusions to Oriental literature—and even more to the literature of Orientalists—but, as most commentators have noted, the allusions are virtually all casual and decorative rather than structural or organic to the poem. Furthermore, the grand theme of personal freedom and religious tolerance that so inspired Moore appears rather oddly transplanted within the reigning theocracy of the poem's setting. It seems at the least unlikely that the Muslim prince who narrates the stories should identify so wholeheartedly with the Ghebers, the Iranian rebels and fanatics of an older religion who are the heroes of "The Fire-Worshippers."

At times, Moore shows signs that he recognizes how closely tied to the Western humanist tradition his central values are, as when he arranges for young Azim, hero of "The Veiled Prophet," to have been a captive of the Greeks. Azim returns unwilling to accept the Veiled Prophet's yoke, because

> Oh, who could, even in bondage, tread the plains
> Of glorious Greece, nor feel his spirit rise
> Kindling within him? who, with heart and eyes,

> Could walk where Liberty had been, nor see
> The shining footprints of her Deity.... (Moore, 33)

But Azim, as it turns out, has contracted something worse than a disease of the Enlightenment; he has also fallen prey to the ideology of chivalry. Tempted by the Prophet's seductive harem girls, some of whom "mix the Kohol's jetty dye, / To give that long, dark languish to the eye," he holds himself as steadfast as any Victorian gentleman and apostrophizes his true love, Zelica:

> It is for thee, for thee alone I seek
> The paths of glory; to light up thy cheek
> With warm approval—in that gentle look
> To read my praise, as in an angel's book,
> And think all toils rewarded, when from thee
> I gain a smile worth immortality! (Moore, 69)

After he has defeated the false prophet and received the caliph's thanks, Azim remains as heroically unmoved as if he had understudied Byron's Conrad or Lara:

> He turns away—coldly, as if some gloom
> Hung o'er his heart no triumphs can illume;—
> Some sightless grief, upon whose blasted gaze
> Though Glory's light may play, in vain it plays! (Moore, 88)

Zelica, who simultaneously embodies the pure, absolute love of Azim's youth and the inevitably sinister attraction of the sensual woman, completes the farrago of Romantic themes. Driven to near madness when she believes Azim killed in Greece, Zelica has sworn fealty to the Veiled Prophet, a figure of ultimate corruption who revels in evil for its own sake. Once she confesses this to Azim, hinting darkly at her spoilation, Moore comments, " 'Tis done—to Heaven and him she's lost forever!" (Moore, 80) At the story's end, when Azim and his army breach the walls of the city where the Prophet has taken refuge, Zelica emerges in the Prophet's veil and dress and throws herself upon Azim's spear, gasping that

> ... death, with thee thus tasted, is a bliss
> Thou wouldst not rob me of, didst thou but know
> How oft I've prayed to God I might die so! (Moore, 113)

Certainly "The Veiled Prophet of Khorassan" seethes with barely-suppressed misogynist and more generally masochistic themes of the sort Mario Praz treated; it also has links with Anglo-Irish poetry of the "Dark Rosaleen" tradition. But from a political viewpoint it is most striking in its double embrace of the theme of doomed rebellion: the Prophet himself, ostensibly a figure of evil, attains an almost cosmic grandeur in his final *non serviam*, while the putative hero, Azim, who fights on the side of the caliph and against the usurper, does so as an outsider, fully realizing that what he is fighting for is already lost to him. The same theme is played out even more explicitly in the other substantial narrative, "The Fire-Worshippers." There the hero Hafed, lover of the Emir's daughter, leads his fellow Ghebers in a hopeless rebellion against the tyrant. At the poem's climax Hafed—who like the Veiled Prophet has led his retreating followers to a final fortress—throws himself upon the burning altar rather than be captured, while the Emir's daughter, seeing this, throws herself into the sea below.

For all his ringing affirmations of freedom, his sympathy with the exile unhappy in a foreign land, "Yet happier so than if he trod / His own belov'd, but blighted sod, / Beneath a despot stranger's rod" (Moore, 159), Moore is uneasy with the idea of rebellion.

> Rebellion! foul, dishonoring word,
> Whose wrongful blight so oft has stain'd
> The holiest cause that tongue or sword
> Of mortal ever lost or gain'd.
> How many a spirit, born to bless,
> Hath sunk beneath that withering name,
> Whom but a day's, an hour's success
> Had wafted to eternal fame! (Moore, 166)

Half apologia, half accusation, Moore's tone here wavers characteristically, and is further complicated by the premise that these words are supposedly spoken by the heir to the "tyrant" against whom the Ghebers rebelled. But then Moore's own position as the toast of literary Britain rested both on his "romantic" appeal as spokesman for the oppressed Irish and on an underlying conviction that he was not dangerous to British hegemony. The solution he found, one thoroughly acceptable to his bourgeois readership, was to affirm national and religious freedom—and even rebellion—but always within a context and a tone that clearly imply that the rebellion is foredoomed and its celebration nostalgic. The same recipe served Scott admirably in his celebration of Catholic rebels loyal to their Church and Queen in novels like *The Abbot*.

Thus Moore reshaped the East, however slightly, as a space of omnipotence and of abject powerlessness; with *Lalla Rookh* he established it as another arena for doomed, romantic rebellion as well—in short, as another Ireland, where "They went forth to battle / But they always fell."[16] The fact that the poem is mostly forgotten today should not obscure its remarkable success during the early nineteenth century, when it was greeted with virtually universal acclaim in England—although some, such as Byron, expressed private doubts as to the poem's value.

Moore's contribution to the image of the Oriental woman was far less original; she is still alternately the sensual temptress and the romantic ideal, or, like Zelica, both at once. In the poem's final section, "The Light of the Haram," Nourmahal wins back her lover with the help of her friend Namouna the Enchantress, who wreathes her with magic flowers and enchants her music so that when she sings her lover cannot resist her. The darker notes of the "Veiled Prophet" are completely absent, and instead Nourmahal, the other harem women, music, flowers, fine foods, and tempting scents are all interwoven in a massive sensory barrage that the male is powerless to resist. Moore's effect upon the peculiar cultural nexus of conflicting codes that constituted the Orient was primarily to reinscribe the East as feminine, to vest it with a pervasive nostalgia, to reinforce the association between the East and sensuality, and to transform its political terrain in an allegory of the romantic vision of Irish history. Bloom, like all the characters of *Ulysses*, is heir to this peculiar Hibernian Night's Entertainment.

Othering the Self and Others

This is why, during his initial encounter with Zoe, Bloom begins to recite (in fact, to misquote) perhaps the best known of the interpolated lyrics from *Lalla Rookh*:

> Oh! ever thus, from childhood's hour,
> I've seen my fondest hopes decay;
> I never nurs'd a dear gazelle,
> To glad me with its soft black eye,
> But when it came to know me well,
> And love me, it was sure to die! (Moore, 156)

In the poem, Hinda, who has begun to realize from her lover Hafed's expression that he will leave her, speaks the lines although she does not yet know that he is the leader of the Ghebers. For the Victorians who treasured it, the lyric lent a suitably exotic coloration to sentimental self-pity, and perhaps—through its Eastern associations—brought in an unconscious element of sexuality that could not be directly articulated, or that was confusedly mingled with sentimental romantic yearnings. Bloom, in particular, has invoked the lyric earlier in "Circe"; on meeting Josie Breen, he has first suggested "a square party, a mixed marriage mingling of our different little conjugials," and then defended himself against the possible charge of unromantic crassness by pointing out, " 'Twas I sent you that valentine of the dear gazelle" (*U* 15.433), as if the beloved verse's intense sentimentality were a guarantee of his nobler intentions.

When he invokes the same verse on meeting Zoe, he is merely using one among a remarkable repertoire of dialogical ploys with which he attempts to distance himself from a basically economic interchange: sentiment, man-of-the-world aplomb, sly sexual insinuation, grandiosity, abnegation, and so on. But the intertextual effect of the Moore citation in *Ulysses*, especially as it is embedded in the network of Victorian Orientalism, is richer and more complex. Certainly there is ironic humor in the unromantic situations in which the dear gazelle pops up, and a more bitter humor in the way in which Moore's exotic and decorative landscape is interchangeable with the body of a Dublin prostitute. But the intensity of Bloom's Eastern imaginings, mediated as they are by a popular literary tradition, suggests that he is far from master of this discourse of mastery. As the obvious representative of patriarchy in the brothel, he is easily unmanned by his own language; and as a subject in good standing of the British Empire, he is alarmingly easily colonized by the alien imagination he takes to be his own.

Thus like all the Irish, but to a greater degree, Bloom is the site of conflicting ideologies which are given shape by contrasting myths of selfhood and otherness. He is a citizen of the British Empire, yet outside it; an Irishman but a Jew; a European but an Oriental. His fantasies of omnipotence and abjection no doubt have a personal psychological component, but to a great extent they are simply emblems of the ambivalent structures of identity provided for him. That his sexual fantasies are Oriental is less a characterizing detail than it may appear; after all, a century of Romantic narratives has helped to persuade him that Molly is Moorish. That he and Stephen have shared a dream of Oriental luxury with a "melon-smellonous" woman is certainly significant; but the real dreamer behind these two is the bourgeois culture of Britain, which has set them to fantasizing over an anonymous woman of the East who is none other than themselves, in bondage drag.

Who is implicated in these multiple ironies? To whom are they obvious and upon whom are they lost? Too often they are lost upon us as readers, heirs as we are to a continuing tradition of Orientalism that is sufficiently deeply embedded in our ideology to remain transparent to us. Perhaps we are far more aware of the objectification of women portrayed in Joyce's work (with more or less complicity on Joyce's part) than we were forty years ago; but that the portrayal of woman as Other in *Ulysses* is in constant dialogical relationship with the portrayal of the Orient as Other is a phenomenon far less obvious to us. In an essay on "Imperialism and Sexual Difference" Gayatri Chakravorty Spivak warns that the tendency of academic feminism "to take the privileged male of the white race as a norm for universal humanity is no more than a politically interested figuration." It is, she claims, too easy to perform "certain imperialist ideological structures even as we deconstruct the tropological error of masculism" (Spivak, 319, 320).

But it is equally important to avoid an essentialist interpretation of the phenomenon I am describing as "Orientalism." Orientals are perfectly capable of performing this sophisticated sort of categorical condescension upon one another. Discussing Goethe's "East-West Divan," Stephen Owen points out that the Western poet's vision of the poet Hafiz's world is echoed by Hafiz himself: "Goethe's version of the East ironically and unwittingly assimilates Islamic poetry's version of 'orientalism': a poetic Bedouin world of caravans and oases that was to the supremely sophisticated Hafiz, the urbane and urban Persian, what the Islamic world as a whole was to Goethe" (Owen, 213n9). Was Joyce, the colonized, Orientalized Irishman, merely recuperating the imperialist gesture of the British empire in his use of Oriental themes, just as Moore proved himself unwittingly complicit in the nostalgic-romantic portrayal of the Irish that helped remove them to a sphere that was seen as transcending—and thus insulated from—the political? But perhaps the question is not one of Joyce's awareness, but rather of the function of the text of *Ulysses*.

From one perspective, the answer must be that, yes, *Ulysses* is virtually a compendium of Orientalist cliches, and to that extent it is complicit with the tradition. There is no attempt made in the book to imagine the Eastern Other as anything other than one extreme of those binary oppositions inscribed by Western culture; nowhere is the Orient ceded its own terms. But having allowed this, we must also recognize that it is the very exaggerated and schematic nature of the representation of Orientalism in the book that so highlights the phenomenon for us. Stephen's Eastern dream may seem darkly romantic when we first learn of it, but once we have set it in the context of Bloom's cut-rate version—complete with Tweedy's moustache and Poldy heroically shrugging off highwaymen—the comic, pasteboard elements of both are apparent. Furthermore, *Ulysses* unarguably presents Orientalism as an intertextual event. While Said has argued that this is the case, it is also apparent that Orientalist writers take pains to deny the fact, because they are purportedly writing about a "truth of nature," the essential nature of the mysterious East. Moore would never have taken the trouble to proudly publicize testaments to the accuracy of his portrayals if he had not been secretly uneasy about the wholly literary nature of his undertaking. In *Ulysses*, as I have suggested here, the Orientalism is explicitly intertextual. No one in the book has the faintest claim to experience of the East, but everyone has *read* it. Words lead endlessly to words, and everyone is ready to *speak* and to *write* the East as well, like A.E. and his apprentice pseudo-Eastern mystics, who will talk "swill till eleven" (*U* 9.1105). This is the purport of Joyce's *Irish Night's Entertainment*.

Chapter Nine

The Appearance of Rudy: Children's Clothing and the History of Photography

Mrs Marion Bloom has left off clothes of all descriptions. (*U* 11.497)

Well, almost any photoist worth his chemicots will tip anyone asking him the teaser that if a negative of a horse happens to melt enough while drying, well, what you get is, well, a positively distorted macromass of all sorts of horsehappy values and masses of meltwhile horse. (*FW* 111)

The Orient is a discourse, broadly dispersed through the culture of turn-of-the-century Great Britain and Ireland, whose signifiers permeate the text of *Ulysses* as well. Sometimes, as with *Lalla Rookh*, the locus of signification is a suggestive intertextual event. But just as there is no single dominant source for Orientalist discourse, there is no single textual location for it in *Ulysses* (or, for that matter, in Joyce's other books). If the preceding chapter can be said to take a "macroscopic" approach to its subject, pursuing Orientalism throughout the text, I now would like to take a "microscopic" perspective, examining a single textual moment in terms of several kinds of cultural discourse. Rather than analyze an intertext, here I am examining the appearance of a single image in the light of several unfamiliar cultural contexts. The moment is among the most significant in *Ulysses*, and is considered by some readers to be the book's climax: the fantastic appearance of Rudy to Bloom after he and Stephen have left Bella Cohen's house, while Stephen is lying semiconscious in the street. Rudy's appearance is so rich in potential symbolism as almost to constitute a parody of literary symbols, and the meaning of his helmet, waistcoat, lambkin, cane, and so forth have been energetically debated by generations of critics.[1] Rather than intervene in this argument over symbolism, I would like to consider Rudy's apparition in terms of his clothing, especially as compared to the childhood attire of Stephen and other characters in *Ulysses;* following that, I will analyze the mode and circumstances of his appearance, which I will argue evokes several genres of nineteenth-century photography.

Clothing as Social Semiotics in Joyce

Throughout *Ulysses*, male and female clothing seem to define characters in a paradoxically essential way. Bloom sees great potential for Stephen in society "if his clothes were attended to so as to the better worm his way into their good graces as he, a youthful tyro in society's sartorial niceties, hardly understood how a little thing like that could militate against you" (*U* 16.1830). Blazes Boylan, as Garry Leonard has pointed out, is little more than a walking fashion illustration, the latest in "smart" and sporty male apparel: "Boylan is nearly always described as something flashing past—a hat, skyblue clocks. He is the modern fashion machine incarnate" (Leonard, 8). Bloom's outfit during June 16 is of course the dark, classically functional funeral suit he wears throughout the day, echoing Stephen's shabbier dark suit of mourning for his mother. Nonetheless, both in memory and in the book's fantasy register Bloom participates in a fashion parade of his own. Here he appears in a variety of outfits, and is judged accordingly—or, to put it another way, the judgment of various figures causes him to appear to us in corresponding outfits. Molly remembers fondly "the day we were lying among the rhododendrons on Howth head in the grey tweed suit and his straw hat the day I got him to propose to me" (*U* 18.1572); here the straw boater recalls Boylan's hat, and takes on a suggestion of sexuality, just as Molly's black straw hat, perched on the chamber pot near the end of the novel, takes on significance from the two occasions in the book on which black straw hats have been worn by prostitutes.

As in the Howth Head example, Bloom in earlier (and presumably better) times generally dresses more flashily. When in "Circe" his father recalls the night the young Bloom ran with a group of "swells," he appears "in youth's smart blue Oxford suit with white vestslips, narrowshouldered, in brown Alpine hat, wearing gent's sterling silver Waterbury keyless watch and double curb Albert with seal attached"—quite impressive regalia even if "one side of him [is] coated with stiffening mud" (*U* 15.269). As he remembers keeping company with Josie Breen, he appears "in an oatmeal sporting suit, a sprig of woodbine in the lapel, tony buff shirt, shepherd's plaid Saint Andrew's cross scarftie, white spats," and so on (*U* 15.536).

On the other hand, recalling the embarrassments of his youth, Bloom is "pigeonbreasted, bottleshouldered, padded, in nondescript juvenile grey and black striped suit, too small for him, white tennis shoes, bordered stockings with turnover tops and a red school cap with badge" (*U* 15.3316). Meanwhile, the other boys from the High School are wearing blue and white football jerseys and shorts. They stand in a clearing shouting at Bloom, who is "warmgloved, mamamufflered, starred with spent snowballs" (*U* 15.3333). Although at this distance in time it is difficult to read with any precision the signifying details of his embarrassing appearance, it is clear that the elaborateness of his mother's care here counts against him, while a decent suit is canceled by its lack of fit and by the inappropriate tennis shoes. Judging simply from his clothing it is apparent that the young Bloom, exactly like the 1904 version, fails to be "one of the boys"; it is no real surprise that the current Bloom, even if no longer pelted with snowballs, has a biscuit tin hurled after him by an athlete.

Children's Clothing in *Ulysses*

The nineteenth century was in some respects a golden age of children's clothing. For most of history, children had been regarded as miniature and rather unsatisfactory adults, and dressed as such: "infants were swaddled and as soon as they were able to walk both sexes were dressed as females. Boys were 'breeched' at an age—between three and twelve—according to the mores of the society in which they lived. All children were considered young adults and dressed accordingly even to the details of powdered periwigs, silk stockings, garters and stays" (Dunleavy, 169). Rousseau's influence, with its recasting of the entire role of childhood as a privileged phase, led both to the development of special children's clothing and to a relaxation of the tyranny of adult dress restrictions. For boys, this relative freedom was first embodied in the informal "skeleton suit" ("pantaloons" buttoning over a simple jacket, with a frilled shirt), and then, by the 1880s, in a series of more formalized outfits. In Ireland, the first suits for children

in the early nineteenth century developed into the Eton suit—dark wool jacket and shirt with turned-down collar. The Eton retained its popularity and remained as a uniform of at least one Irish school into the 1940s. Shops specializing in ready-mades for boys and youths had emerged by the early 1880s, selling suits of named styles, which were internationally known, such as 'sailor,' 'midshipman,' 'Jack Tar' and 'military parade'. The 'Little Lord Fauntleroy' in velvet, and the 'Leinster' in Irish tweed, developed subsequently. (Dunleavy, 170–71)

The "knickerbocker suit," a suit with short jacket and pants reaching just below the knee, was spurred by the popularity of Washington Irving's fictional history of New York, ostensibly told by Diedrich Knickerbocker. The book appeared in an English edition with Cruickshank's illustrations in 1859, and by 1863 the suit "reigned supreme" among middle- and upper-class boys (Buck, 120).

As Garry Leonard, among others, has argued, the rise of a commodity culture in Victorian Britain allowed for the growth of elaborate fantasies of identity, in which commodified objects were deployed in an effort to repair the lack of any sufficient "natural" sense of identity.[2] Children's clothing was the broadest possible field of play for fantasies of identity, since the semiotics of adult garb required that the claims made by a particular outfit should not be too insistent or too outlandish. As Daniel Roche points out, in the dialectic of standardization and differentiation any item of clothing embodies both "the standardization necessary to all socialization and the difference favourable to distinction and imitation" (506). But outfits such as the Highland suit and the sailor suit, Anne Buck explains, "were not modifications of existing dress for practical purposes, nor a move toward adult dress, but clothes which gave the wearer a particular identity unrelated to his immediate everyday life; dresses of make-believe. Parents were expressing, by proxy in their children's dresses, their tastes and preoccupations" (251).

One of the elements which they were expressing, of course, was social class, or the aspiration to it; and it is no coincidence that these two early outfits were each modeled on the Royal family—the Highland suit on the dress of the Royal Family at Balmoral and the sailor suit on a favorite outfit of the young Prince of Wales (Byrde, 89).[3] It should be noted that the bourgeois queen and her family really offered the first practical opportunity for middle-class emulation; during the reign of eighteenth-century monarchs, for citizens outside the small group of courtiers to imitate the dress of the sovereign would have been seen as highly inappropriate. This is a startling contrast with the reign of Edward VII, who positively enjoyed the way gentlemen mimicked him. Penelope Byrde explains:

Edward VII was undoubtedly a revered and influential figure; he was passionately interested in clothes and was to a certain extent something of an innovator. His father considered that as a young man 'he took no interest in anything but clothes, and that even out shooting he was more concerned with his trousers than with the game.'...His clothes and appearance were closely watched and copied by the men of his generation and a contemporary remarked that 'there are in society several gentlemen who bear an extraordinary resemblance to him, and who take some pride in dressing and moving exactly like him so that it is often very difficult to identify him as he passes in the street on foot or in a hansom cab.' " (Byrde, 89)[4]

Children's clothing was allowed far more leeway than adult clothing during this period; it was treated with some of the indulgence that was shown toward the children themselves. As early as the mid-nineteenth century, it was permissible for bourgeois children to ape the styles of the courtiers of the seventeenth century, in the "cavalier" suit, later rechristened the "Little Lord Fauntleroy" outfit (to be discussed further below). Here, nostalgia and historical distance serve to blur the class presumptuousness of the bourgeoisie. Besides that, dressing a child as a courtier is clearly a metaphorical act of fantasy and is not strongly felt as social statement.

That Joyce appreciated the complexity of children's clothing as a set of social signifiers is most evident in the apparition of Rudy to Bloom at the end of "Circe." Rudy here appears garbed in a spectrum of signs, from the basic Eton suit—which suggests educational aspiration, although not necessarily aspiration after Eton specifically—through unlikely accessories such as the glass slippers, bronze helmet, and ivory cane, on to the wholly surreal lambkin peeping out of his waistcoat pocket. That Rudy takes on the appearance of a comically overdetermined farrago of signs reflects the essentially fantastic nature of much children's clothing of the period, its inevitable element of masquerade (or, in "Circe," of pantomime). Joyce here has merely extended slightly the element of the fantastic already present when Mrs. Dedalus dressed the young Stephen in the outfit of a Cavalier, creating a theatrical appearance that Molly fondly remembers: "he was an innocent boy then and a darling little fellow in his lord Fauntleroy suit and curly hair like a prince on a stage when I saw him at Matt Dillons ..." (*U* 18.1311). From the beginning, Joyce's writing makes it clear that tiny increments of difference in dress may have huge social consequences, even among children. Here, perhaps, is the true universal language of gesture of which Stephen speaks in "Circe" (*U* 15.105). For example, in "An Encounter," Mahony and the narrator are mistaken for Protestants and stoned by poor Catholic children because "Mahony, who was dark-complexioned, wore the silver badge of a cricket club in his cap" (*D* 22). A complexion that mimics a sporting tan and a cap that suggests cricket instead of hurley are sufficient to ensure that the boys are reviled as "Swaddlers" (a term of opprobrium used by Catholics of Protestants that is rather mysteriously based on infant's clothing).

Children's Outfits

No doubt it could be useful to analyze both adult's and child's clothing, real and imaginary, throughout *Ulysses*, but at this point I would like to look more closely at three of the generic types of children's outfits in particular: the sailor suit, the Eton suit, and the Fauntleroy suit. The sailor suit first makes its appearance in "Nausicaa," with the four-year-old "Tommy and Jacky Caffrey, two little curleyheaded boys, dressed in sailor suits with caps to match and the name H.M.S. Belleisle printed on both" (*U* 13.13–15).[5] These suits are clearly the source of some pride for the Caffreys; not only does the narrator lovingly detail them, but also Cissy, the boys's sister, carefully brushes the sand off Tommy after Jacky has thrown him into the sand castle. And the history of the sailor suit is indeed aristocratic. The young Prince of Wales had often appeared in sailor dress in the 1840s. "By 1887 *The Lady's World* was saying that sailor suits 'are now selling into thousands', and that boys were put into sailor suits 'as early as possible. A frock is now rarely seen upon a boy of four'" (Buck, 153). A late survival of the "breeching party" celebrating the child's graduation from infancy to full boyhood was recounted by a Mrs. Reynolds, who, in the 1890s, at a tea party, saw little Willy brought in with fair curls down to his shoulders; they were ceremoniously clipped off, the boy was brought behind a screen, and reappeared dressed in a sailor suit and introduced as a "real little boy." All the visitors were given a lock of Willy's newly shorn hair; although on returning home, Mrs. Reynolds's father, apparently feeling that too much had been made of the whole occasion, immediately threw his into the fire (Ginsburg, 182).

The cultural significance of the sailor suit for the British Empire in the late nineteenth and early twentieth centuries is complex. Obviously the Empire was primarily built upon sea power, so few outfits could have had such a patriotic connotation as the sailor, Jack Tar, midshipman, and other variants of the maritime outfit. On the other hand, the class connotations of the Navy varied: while career officers were looked upon as respectable mates for daughters of the upper bourgeoisie as early as Austen's time—often, like the clergy,

the profession was a resort for younger sons of wealthy gentlemen—
the ordinary seaman was generally seen as a ruffian beyond the pale.
All these connotations, however, were probably trumped by Prince of
Wales's adopting the outfit as his own; here, as in so many other arenas of cultural play, Edward's function was to build a bridge between
the realms of royalty and the bourgeoisie.

Joyce fairly clearly wishes to associate the suits with incipient militarism: Jacky and Tommy play Cain and Abel, and the first action of
the "darling twins" is violent aggression. In "Circe," Cissy Caffrey,
who had tended the twins and comforted Tommy without disciplin-
ing Jacky for his boyish aggressiveness, is accompanying Privates Carr
and Compton; in fact, she vacillates between trying to keep them from
attacking Stephen and urging them to fight him, in a series of scenes
ironically presided over by Edward VII carrying a plasterer's bucket.
The soldiers, in muddled though gallant fashion, believe that in attacking Stephen they are acting in defense of their lady (Cissy) and of their
King: "I'll wring the neck of any fucking bastard says a word against
my bleeding fucking king" *(U* 15.4643). Both with the children and
the adults, Cissy's dangerous ambivalence encourages the vicious psychological traits which, according to Guglielmo Ferrero, were inbred
in males by the European cult of militarism.[6] In "Nausicaa," Joyce
is taking advantage of the popularity of sailor suits to show how a
militaristic uniformity is imposed on the colonized subject from early
childhood. At the same time, I believe the rather elegant sailor suits,
which were beyond the means of the lower classes, indicate that the
Caffreys are solidly middle-class, even if from the lower ranges. If this
is so, we should realize that Cissy appears in "Circe" as a paradigmatic figure, not a naturalistic one; she is no more "really" present
than is Major Tweedy or King Edward, despite the preponderance of
criticism that has assumed she is.

Rudy's Eton suit, the naturalistic frame on which the rest of his
increasingly surreal appurtenances hang, is perhaps less restrictive
in its social class associations than might be assumed: as Madeleine
Ginsburg comments, "Eton and Harrow suits were worn in many less
élitist establishments" (182). Nonetheless, the suit's background and
connotations are suggestive. The suit originated when the boys at the
prestigious public school were put into black jackets and trousers during the public mourning for George III, and that outfit subsequently
became the school uniform. The characteristic short "bum freezer"
jacket and, especially, the stiff, wide, turned-down detachable shirt
collar were widely recognizable and widely imitated. Buck suggests
that the popularity of the Eton suit had a conservative influence on

boys' dress, especially as contrasted with the rise of school "sports" dress near the turn of the century, notably the flannel blazer with school crest on the pocket worn for cricket and rowing. Rudy's Eton suit thus might suggest two things: in the first place, it has a historical connotation of mourning dress, like what both Stephen and Bloom are wearing, and entirely appropriately so, since Rudy the "changeling" might well appear in order to mourn himself. Secondly, as a conservative outfit, the Eton suit associates Rudy with his father, rather than with the "sporty" boys of Bloom's High School who mocked him. Clearly the boy is imagined to be a scholar—a student of the Torah, as his reading from right to left and kissing the page suggest. The Eton suit finally helps proclaim that Rudy has achieved the magical synthesis that Bloom has never managed: he is entirely Jewish and also entirely assimilated. Unlike the real characters of the book, he has had to sacrifice nothing—except, of course, his humanity.

The Little Lord Fauntleroy outfit in which Molly remembers Stephen is perhaps the most symbolically resonant of the children's outfits in *Ulysses*, because it is largely based on a character of fantasy. The "cavalier" outfit with knickerbocker trousers, in velvet with lace trimming, first became popular in the 1870s and reached new heights of popularity with the publication of Frances Hodgson Burnett's novel, with the illustrations by Reginald Birch, in 1886. As Madeleine Ginsburg comments, "despite consistent juvenile resistance," the Fauntleroy suit "remained in children's wardrobes until at least the turn of the century" (Ginsburg, 182). Buck suggests that the suit was primarily admired by "artistic and romantic mothers" (Buck, 144), although certainly the growing late-nineteenth-century cult of the child epitomized in plays such as *Peter Pan* (1904) and books like *The Wind in the Willows* (1908) contributed to the outfit's popularity. And it is entirely possible that in Ireland a style of dress reminiscent of Charles I would have a special, rather subversive appeal among Catholics.

By the time Stephen was wearing the suit, Burnett's book, with its remarkable popularity, was very much involved in the outfit's connotations. To evoke the outfit in 1904, or in 1922 for that matter, means to evoke the novel, so that *Little Lord Fauntleroy* has a strong intertextual resonance in *Ulysses*. The novel's plot is extremely simple: a wealthy British earl has three sons, the eldest two of whom are vulgar cads and layabouts, so that the earl cannot help being ashamed of them. These two brothers are named Bevis and Maurice. The youngest boy, unlike them, is both handsome and well-mannered, except that he is rebellious against his overbearing father. He marries a beautiful

American woman and has a child by her, Cedric Errol Junior. The old earl rejects his youngest son entirely and assumes that the son's wife is a vulgar American fortune hunter. But both his older sons die, as does the younger, Cedric's father; the earl realizes that Cedric is in line to inherit the title, and is now Lord Fauntleroy. He sends for the boy, reluctantly allowing his mother to accompany him. The boy has been raised without any expectations or knowledge of his own aristocratic claims; he is thoroughly democratic in his instincts, and has befriended a local grocer and shoeshine boy, who are taken with Cedric's "quaint" ways and devotion to his mother, whom he always calls "Dearest." The Irish maid is only one of the many of his acquaintances who feel Cedric is a natural aristocrat, despite his relative poverty:

> "Ristycratic, is it?' she would say. 'Faith and I'd loike to see the choild on Fifth Avey-noo as looks loike him an' shteps out as handsome as himself. An' ivery man, woman, and choild lookin' afther him in his bit of a black velvet skirt made out of the misthress's owld gownd; an' his little head up an' his curly hair flyin' and shinin'. It's loike a young lord he looks.' (Burnett, 10)

Young Cedric has the gift of pleasing and charming everyone he meets with his careful, rather old-fashioned manners, his lack of pretense, and especially his precociousness, which leads to much of the book's humor. He learns to read at a very young age and frequently reads aloud to his mother. As the maid says, "Nobody cud help laughin' at the quare little ways of him—and his ould-fashioned sayin's!" (9). Cedric is especially precocious in his use of language: "He was fond of using long words, and he was always pleased when they made her laugh, though he could not understand why they were laughable; they were quite serious matters with him" (27). In his extreme closeness to his mother, as well as in his fascination with language, Fauntleroy anticipates Stephen Dedalus; he also does so in his eagerness to discuss politics, although in *Fauntleroy* the effect of this is primarily cuteness.

In their outlines, *A Portrait of the Artist* and *Ulysses* on the one hand, and *Fauntleroy* on the other, are, of course, wildly different books. Although Stephen hopes to come into his kingdom in time, in neither book does he do so, and both of Joyce's works end in open ambiguity. Fauntleroy, on the other hand, emerges triumphant, accepted as the earl's true heir by everyone. Once he is brought to his grandfather's estate, Cedric charms the old man and effortlessly wins over the retainers. Merely because Cedric expects nothing but good from the old earl, the wicked old cynic finds himself embarrassed to do any less. As the narrator puts it near the book's end,

> It was really a very simple thing after all—it was only that he had lived near a kind and gentle heart, and had been taught to think kind thoughts and to always care for others...He knew nothing of earls and castles; he was quite ignorant of all grand and splendid things; but he was always lovable because he was simple and loving. To be so is like being born a king. (Burnett, 264)

The book actually follows the outline of the genre of domestic Victorian romance in which the immensely pure young wife reclaims her reprobate husband through the power of her virtue and Christianity. The main difference between this genre and *Fauntleroy* is that the protagonist is a rather ambiguously gendered boy and that he is not required to sacrifice himself in order to redeem the old man. The main resemblance that cheery Fauntleroy bears to sullen Stephen Dedalus is in his putative salvatory role; but where Fauntleroy saves through goodness and innocence, Stephen, who fails at these qualities, hopes to save his race through artistic and spiritual intervention, the desire to "cast his shadow over the imagination of their daughters, before their squires begat upon them, that they might breed a race less ignoble than their own" (*P* 238), in a sort of spiritual prophylaxis. Although both are immensely romantic enterprises, Stephen's is marginally more convincing because Joyce makes it clear that there will be a large price attached, perhaps martyrdom, while in Burnett, all ends happily with a minimum of suffering and an affirmation of traditional authority structures.

A muted theme of the books involving both Dedalus and Fauntleroy is the relationship between virtue and aristocracy. The old earl, who believes that nobility is bred in certain families living in certain situations, is forced to recognize that it is something more essential and less contingent: "he began to see why the little fellow who had lived in a New York side street, and known grocery-men and made friends with boot-blacks, was still so well-bred and manly a little fellow that he made no one ashamed of him, even when fortune changed him into the heir to an English earldom, living in an English castle" (264). Indeed, it is the villagers and local retainers of the earl who first celebrate Fauntleroy's arrival, because they can see in him the moral and physical qualities of his beloved father. In this respect, the book seems curiously muddled in its ideology: the young lord is himself a strong democrat, being influenced by the Homais-like grocer, a sworn enemy of the aristocracy, but he himself is also the best possible argument for an aristocracy of blood which survives any displacement in place or social class. Of course, there are also Fauntleroy's two loutish uncles as a counter-argument, but they seem clearly the product of the old earl's misplaced pride and arrogance, something to which his younger son was mysteriously immune. They are the fault of nurture rather than aristocratic nature.

The question of Stephen Dedalus's kind of aristocracy—what Margaret Harper has termed "the aristocracy of art"—is too complex to treat here.[7] But clearly the issue is signaled by Molly's memory of him in his Fauntleroy outfit, which for her has connotations of artistic aspiration, wealth, nobility, and even sensuality. Stephen is a natural leader in his childhood, playing with his friends in Blackrock and emulating Napoleon's simple dress, or leading one of the academic groups in his school. He seems to be recognized immediately as different, and even as superior, by those around him in the way Fauntleroy is, but in Stephen's case that recognition always carries with it an aura of suspicion and the suggestion that his supporters are ready to turn against him at any moment. Fauntleroy has none of these problems, and has a great deal more natural tact than Stephen. For instance, when he wins a foot race against one of his friends, who is at first inclined to resent losing, he immediately explains that he only won because he is several days older. Fauntleroy's friends, whether they realize it or not, move on easily to playing the role of his retainers and acolytes, while Stephen, who virtually demands acolytes, has friends who are more likely to play Judas. But then, wearing the outfit of a Fauntleroy is not enough to draw Stephen into that child's imaginative universe.

Framing the Photograph

If clothing is a discursive practice allowing us some access to the popular consciousness of 1904, photography is obviously a representational practice that becomes discursive as we come to consider its cultural status. For the practice of photography in 1904 was radically different from its practice today, so that photographs then bore a substantially different symbolic weight. The passage in which the image of Rudy appears mysteriously against a tenement wall evokes some of the fear and wonderment that photographs were still capable of stirring in an audience at the turn of the century, along with a certain absurd humor and a measure of melodrama. As Bloom meditatively stands guard over the recumbent Stephen, "against the dark wall a figure appears slowly" (*U* 15.4956). In a chapter of apparitions, hallu-cinations, materializations, epiphanies, transformations, and whole-sale arrivals from nowhere, this appearance is unique. Rudy stands as a coda to the remainder of the episode, a sort of *clou* to "Circe," much as "Penelope" is a *clou* to the book as a whole; but where Molly, when she finally speaks, speaks endlessly, Rudy never breaks his charmed silence. What might he say, as a returned spirit from "that other world," a "changeling" captured by fairies, eleven years resident under the hill? Surely his message would be more enlightening than Paddy Dignam's news about all the "modern home comforts" avail-able to those who have "passed over" (*U* 12.353). But unfortunately Rudy, like us, is engaged in his reading, evidently of the *Torah*, and seems not even to see Bloom. Perhaps, like Stephen, he has in any case outgrown his father, and is now effectively of a higher social class, as the Eton suit might suggest. Such things must be possible in Tir na n'Og, even for the son of a Jew.

What sort of apparition is this? Bloom is so "wonderstruck" at it that he loses his voice and cannot call his son's name aloud, whereas he has earlier taken the appearance of the End of the World, not to mention his own dead father and grandfather, pretty much in stride. We are accustomed to reading "Circe" as an episode in which men are turned subhuman by a sorceress or, alternately, as one in which the buried desires and fears of Bloom and Stephen take on substantial form. Instead, I want to suggest that insofar as Bloom, consciously or not, participates in the appearance of Rudy, he does so out of a context of practices and conventions that surrounded the popular art form of photography and its attendant iconography. After all, he is identified by a stranger as "Photo's papli, by all that's gorgeous" (*U* 14.1535), a tag that surely implies more than his relationship to Milly.

From its beginnings, photography as a social construct has been framed in two divergent ways. On the one hand, the photograph has been received as an objective guarantor of appearances, the undeni-able testimony to factuality that makes a momentary visual appear-ance eternal. It gives us the superhuman ability to examine a broad visual field at our leisure. Emile Zola, the leading ideologue of liter-ary realism and an enthusiastic photographer, asserted in 1901 that "you cannot claim to have really seen something until you have pho-tographed it."[8] In this perspective, the photographer is presumed to be unimportant and the camera is assumed simply to replicate the human act of seeing, but unconstrained by the limited degree and span of attention available to humans.

On the other hand, photography, from the first, was also clearly something *more* or *other* than a replica of seeing. At the most obvious level, its unique mechanics and processes were reflected in the photographic image. Eugène Atget's portraits of Parisian streets, because of the long exposures his plates required, captured a deserted early-morning urban vista few Parisians had seen before. The simple fact of long exposure times also meant that, for a long while, it was difficult to photograph children and even more difficult to give the impression of action in a photograph. Photographic portraiture thus first became an exercise in static iconography long before the advent of the snapshot altered the dynamic possibilities of photographic portraiture. In place of the possibilities for meaning implicit in action and movement, the Victorian photograph tended to fill up the available semiotic space with a wealth of symbols. Rudy's elaborately detailed appearance in his materialization at the end of "Circe," as he takes on definition like a photographic plate within the developing solution, is in part a testament to the load of significance that the personal photograph in all its richness and rarity was expected to bear:

> *a fairy boy of eleven, a changeling, kidnapped, dressed in an Eton suit with glass shoes and a little bronze helmet, holding a book in his hand.... He has a delicate mauve face. On his suit he has diamond and ruby buttons. In his free left hand he holds a slim ivory cane with a violet bowknot. A white lambkin peeps out of his waistcoat pocket.* (U 15.4957, 4965)

Bloom, of course, is a connoisseur and something of a collector of photography, most notably the "Bath of the Nymph" from *Photo-Bits* magazine that is nearly as powerful an erotic icon for him as the photo of Molly herself with which he tries to tempt Stephen. His father's first cousin owned one of the first daguerreotype ateliers in Hungary, and Bloom has a daguerreotype portrait of his father and grandfather made there (U 17.1875) in his dresser drawers, where he also keeps his pornographic photo collection. He feels that he and Milly, who is "getting on swimming in the photo business now" and has just had her portrait made (U 4.401), may share a "hereditary taste" for the new craft (U 8.174).[9] Contemplating the Bloom of Flowerville, retired with utopian wealth, the first avocation he imagines for himself is "snapshot photography" (U 17.1589). But because we share Bloom's immersion in photographs, we forget that the late

nineteenth and early twentieth centuries had a very different relationship to this visual mediator than our own. Today, Americans alone
take some 550 snapshots each second; but for the nineteenth century,
a photograph was, at the least, an *occasion* (Batchen, 8).

So entrenched is today's popular assumption that photography is
simply an objective means of preserving visual appearances, so embedded in contemporary culture is the ideology of the snapshot, that it
is difficult for us to appreciate how photographs in the nineteenth
century were charged with mystery and with mortality, with *otherness*. Michael Lesey reminds us that "their deepest purpose was more
religious than secular, and that commercial photography, as practiced
in the 1890s, was not so much a form of applied technology as it
was a semimagical act that symbolically dealt with time and mortality" (Lesey, introduction). Recall, for instance, the Mormon Church
practice of warehousing vast collections of photographic negatives of
the images of church members. It is Church doctrine that members
should trace their families back as far as possible, and obtain photographs of any of them never baptized into the faith; these can then be
saved by performing a baptism for the dead.

Indeed, at some level, many feel that photography is always involved
with death; Susan Sontag writes that "all photographs are memento
mori. To take a photograph is to participate in another person's (or
thing's) mortality, vulnerability, mutability. Precisely by slicing out
this moment and freezing it, all photographs testify to time's relentless melt" (Sontag, 15). John Berger notes that "photography, because
it stops the flow of life, is always flirting with death" (Berger, 122).
Roland Barthes, whose meditation *Camera Lucida* is impelled by a
photograph of his dead mother, observes that sometimes "the photographer must exert himself to the utmost to keep the Photograph
from becoming Death." Photography is not even representation for
Barthes, it is "an image without code" (Barthes, 14), as he does not
"take the photograph for a 'copy' of reality, but for an emanation of
past reality: a *magic*, not an art" (Barthes, 88).

It is this sense of photography as magic—or, more precisely, the
sense that the possibilities of photography lay within a space within
which the domains of science and of magic were intermingled—
that underlies Bloom's vision of his dead son. Cathy N. Davidson
observes,

> Just as Alexander Graham Bell believed the telephone would allow
> him to communicate with his deaf parents (and his assistant, Thomas
> H. Watson, believed it would serve to commune with the dead), many

thought that one of the daguerreotype's most important uses would be to document paranormal phenomena such as ghosts or other visitants and forces formerly beyond human ken. (Davidson, 681)[10]

I want to point in particular to three genres of photography, now almost forgotten, that bear upon Rudy: *memorial* photography, *spirit* photography, and *fairy* photography. All of these, in different ways, evoke the uncanny, just as Rudy's materialization does for Bloom. Of the three genres, memorial photography—a family arranging to formally photograph a recently deceased member—was the only one that at least ostensibly relied upon the merely documentary capabilities of the craft. Yet there is something unsettlingly *other* about even relatively straightforward postmortem photographs. Historically, early photography was directly linked with mortality and the attempt to hold on to the dead by a means that must have long seemed supernatural. Corey Creekmur reminds us that "for much of its early history, commercial photography depended upon the now surreptitious (because 'tasteless') genre of 'postmortem' or 'memorial' photography in which the stillness of its corpse-subjects allowed for unusually clear exposures; . . . it is jarring to realize how many people were photographed for the first time 'in their lives' in their coffins" (Creekmur, 74). Creekmur's invocation of the "tastelessness" of popular memorial photography may remind us that, once the image of Rudy has materialized against the wall, we are at a loss what to make of it, how to react to it—what "tone" to assign it, balanced as it is between pathos and hilarity, a touching sentimentality (the Eton suit, the lambkin) and a bizarre element of the grotesque (the bronze helmet, the glass shoes). We cannot help but feel that here, as in the description of Bloomville, we have Bloom's aspirations laid bare, and the result is both moving and deeply comic. Above all, we feel Bloom's distance from us, both socially and historically. Our aspirations for our own children, comic or heartrending as they may be, do not look like this.

Memorial Photography

Similarly, our reaction to memorial photographs, which once were an accepted adjunct to grieving, has altered irrevocably. What was then constructed as a sentimental gesture is as likely to appear to us today as grotesque, disturbing, or otherwise dubious. Michael Lesey introduced the subject to most Americans in his unexpectedly successful book *Wisconsin Death Trip* (1973). More recently, Stanley

Burns has collected a number of postmortem photographs in his book
Sleeping Beauty, among them one of a dead girl preserved on ice for
nine days, then propped stiffly in a chair with staring eyes and pho-
tographed with a book propped between her hands. A note on the
photograph reads, "Mother could not part with only daughter" (caption #56). Other photographs of the dead show the disfigurement of
infectious diseases, blood from hemorrhages, or the effects of wasting
diseases. John Updike comments, "The piety of the previous century
clung to the Christian tenet, unemphasized in today's churches, that
the body *is* the person, with a holy value even when animation ceases.
This faith, embodied in these memorial images, tells us more than we
want to know about corporeality, and challenges our modern mysticism, the worship of disembodied energy" (Updike, 105). Early postmortem photographs could be quite frank about death, although by
the turn of the century there was a concerted effort, led by funeral
directors, to beautify the process.

It was common to dress children in favorite or ceremonial clothing and to surround them with their cherished toys. One photograph
(ca. 1850) in *Sleeping Beauty* shows Charlie with his wagon, hat, and
dress shoes. Lying on the bench, he might be imagined to be asleep,
like the deceased gentleman in a second image, who is upright in a
chair and appears to hold reading matter, like Rudy. Sometimes the
iconography of the occasion called for more elaborate treatment. In
a photograph of Rube Burrows, the "Lone Wolf train robber and
murderer" is stood upright in his coffin, which is apparently lean-
ing against a freight car, with all the tools of his trade. Burns has
noted that some folk artists became popular photographers, and
imported the sensibility of the folk arts into the new medium (caption
#9). However, a photograph of a mother holding her dead daughter
mimics a convention of "high art"—the painterly convention of the
"sick child" (as well as, more distantly, the Pietà), with the mourning
father visible in the background. In a later photograph collected by
Burns, the allegory is spelled out completely—the father and mother
hold their dead daughter, while on the table sit the useless medicine
bottles. Photography has become complicit in the performance of
loss, its theatricalization. And as photography was combined with
lithography, the memorial photograph could be inserted into the classical iconography of death, idealized by the commercial artist.

Each of the preceding series of postmortem images shares something with the image of Rudy at the end of "Circe." Dan Meinwald
has pointed out that "the making of a postmortem photograph is, like
embalming, a preservation of the body for the gaze of the observer"

(Meinwald, 8). The appearance of Rudy, of course, is not exactly this: it is not a memento, linked to someone now dead in that unmediated way Barthes insists upon, as a guarantor of their existence (Barthes, 87). Bloom, in fact, failed to arrange for a postmortem photograph of Rudy as he actually was in the (fictive) phenomenal world. Instead, Rudy's wondrous materialization affords Bloom a kind of magical access to his dead son as (somehow, somewhere) living. The question of how and where Rudy continues to exist raises the issues of death and the afterlife, as well as the related issues of fairies and changelings—or, at the least, it raises the issue of Bloom's belief in these things. The clearest point of entry into these issues is through what was perhaps the dominant social trend of the second half of the nineteenth century, the rise and the subsequent commodification of spiritualism.

Spirit Photography

In the preface to *Heartbreak House*, Shaw wrote testily that English society before the First World War was

> addicted to table-rapping, materialization séances, clairvoyance, palmistry, crystal-gazing and the like to such an extent that it may be doubted whether ever before in the history of the world did soothsayers, astrologers, and unregistered therapeutic specialists of all sorts flourish as they did during this half century of the drift toward the abyss. (Shaw, vol 1, 456)

Beginning in the 1860s, with the work of William H. Mumler, and continuing into the 1920s, the rage for spiritualism was as much a mainstream as a fringe phenomenon (Chéroux 12). It attracted writers such as Hugo, Tolstoy, Andrew Lang, and John Addington Symonds, as well as the more famous cases of Yeats and of Arthur Conan Doyle. A surprising number of scientists and intellectuals also embraced the phenomenon. The Society for Psychical Research, founded in 1882, included the philosophers Henry Sedgwick and Henri Bergson, professors of physics such as Balfour Stewart and William Barrett, several Members of Parliament, and Anglican bishops, as well as the psychologist William James. The scientists Russell Wallace and Lombroso were both advocates and—through their reputations—guarantors of spiritual phenomena. In 1908, an Anglican rector organized a "domestic Photo-Circle" to encourage the well-known supernatural photographer William Hope; and indeed Hope soon provided the rector with two rather murky images in which he was overjoyed to recognize his dead parents (Oppenheim, 70–71). Similarly, the distinguished scientist William Crookes, in 1916, became convinced that Hope had captured his dead wife's image on film (Oppenheim, 351).

It was by no means taken for granted that spiritualistic phenomena were inaccessible to scientific investigation and objective verification, such as the photograph might offer. Spiritualism, after all, "was itself the child of scientific naturalism and rational explanation," and was "steeped in the scientism of the period" (Owen, introduction). Many spiritualist believers with a technical background were indifferent, or even hostile, to pseudo-religions such as Theosophy, which offered a cosmology that tried to annex spiritualist phenomena. After all, X-ray photography, developed in the 1890s, offered ghostly images of the inside of human bodies, while infrared photography, which developed around 1880, could give evidence of the phantasms of things no longer present, such as the trace of a body no longer in a bed.

Clearly, photographic emulsion was not limited to registering what struck any unprivileged human eye; why might it not render evidence of what "sensitives" could see, or indeed what nobody had yet witnessed of "that other world"?[11] Edward L. Gardner, president of the Blavatsky Lodge of the Theosophical Society in London, argued this point persuasively:

> First, it must be understood that all that *can* be photographed must of necessity be physical. Nothing of a subtler order could in the nature of things affect the sensitive plate. So-called spirit photographs, for instance, imply necessarily a certain degree of materialization before the "form" could come within the range of even the most sensitive of films. But well within our physical octave there are degrees of density that elude ordinary vision. Just as there are many stars in the heavens recorded by the camera that no human eye has ever seen directly, so there is a vast array of living creatures whose bodies are of that rare tenuity and subtlety from our point of view that they lie beyond the range of our normal senses. Many children and sensitives see them, and hence our fairylore—all founded on actual and now demonstrable fact! (Doyle 1922, 172–73)

From early in the spiritualist movement, women appeared as privileged mediums, natural observers and useful conductors to the world of spirit. Whatever else Bloom and Stephen have attended in the course of "Circe"—an evening at a brothel, an interlude in Circe's cave, a harrowing of hell, a *Walpurgisnacht* gathering of witches, a pantomime complete with transformation scene, a Bakhtinian carnival—they have certainly attended a séance, the evocation of and communing with the dead through the agency of one or more women. Successful mediums were predominantly female, as "spiritualists assumed that it was innate femininity, in particular female passivity, which facilitated [the] renunciation of self and cultivation of mediumistic powers" (Owen, 19).[12] Stephen has spoken with his dead mother, Bloom with his dead father and grandfather, not to mention the recently departed, in the person of Paddy Dignam, and Shakespeare—the sort of historical luminary who was frequently evoked in upper-middle-class séances.

The raising of Rudy is, from one perspective, merely the culmination of this process. It was the possibility of communicating with one's dead spouse, child, or parent that gave the emotional impetus to the nineteenth-century séance, and several of the highly reputable figures who imperiled their reputations by embracing spiritualism were first driven to do so by a desperate desire to make contact with a loved one. Though Bloom certainly feels this, he is equally attentive to Stephen, with whom he also wishes to make contact. It is worth noting that if we regard the final tableau of "Circe" as a photograph, showing Rudy materializing above Stephen, prone on the street, while Bloom watches, then surely one conclusion we might draw is that Rudy is in some way the spirit of Stephen, perhaps his "astral projection," freed from its bodily cage by the poet's concussed and drunken semiconsciousness. Perhaps in a spiritual light, Rudy and Stephen are one in their sonship, if only in Bloom's yearning vision.

Spirit photographs surface quite early in the history of photography—nearly as early as pornographic photos, as if these were among the first applications of the new technology to occur to its practitioners. They seem to fall into two broad categories: on the one hand, generalized figures in costume—either contemporary or vaguely classical—who may hold or be adorned with symbolic accessories, such as the rather two-dimensional spirit being attempting to place an ectoplasmic wreath on the brow of the journalist W. T. Stead.[13] On the other hand, the spirits may resemble specific dead persons in their own contemporary dress, either famous ones, such as Walt Whitman, or friends and family of the sitter. In a photograph by Mrs. Deane, taken at Crewe in October 1915, Stead's daughter is visited by her father's image after his death on the Titanic in 1912. It might be noted that two aspects of the photographic process work especially well in conveying the notion of spiritual copresence on the earthly plane: the image of the spirit may overlap the image of the sitting client, suggesting ectoplasmic transparency (as in a double exposure), or else the image of the spirit—often only a head or bust—fades gently into the background, just as in the process termed "vignetting" (in which, during printing, the head of the subject is projected onto the paper through an oval cut-out that is gently moved).

While most spirit photographers were specialists operating in their own studios, spirit photographs were also taken at séances. In a photograph taken by Bisson in Paris in 1913, the medium Eva C., in intense trance, evokes what is termed an "extra." A quite different "extra" was evoked during séances arranged by Dr. Imoda with the medium Linda Gazzera in Turin during 1909—there was little uniformity in the forms in which the departed chose to materialize at séances. But a far more personal experience was that of parents like Mr. and Mrs. Gibson in a photograph taken by the Crewe Circle in 1919, in which their deceased child materializes just over their heads, although at the time of sitting they are unaware of the fact.

Bloom has the same need to make contact with and to memorialize his dead son as do the parents in these photographs—both those who pose with the bodies of their children and those who, to their astonished delight, find afterwards that they have posed with their late child's earthly spirit. But we should remember that if both spirit and memorial photographs frame and display the intensity of the parent's mourning, that extended mourning is itself to some degree a historical product of the plummeting rates of child mortality experienced by the European middle classes during the last half of the nineteenth century as a result of asepsis and improved nutrition. In contrast, Stephen Dedalus's family displays the more traditional stoicism about the death of children that was almost universal before about 1880; neither Simon nor May seems traumatized by the high mortality rate of their family. Bloom, a more reliably middle-class Dubliner, is far less able to accept the death of a single child; but then, in his family the mortality rate has been fifty percent.

In this regard, as in so many others, he looks forward toward the twentieth century. He is obviously an enthusiastic and a sentimental participant in the turn-of-the-century cult of childhood whose literary traces included *Peter Pan, Alice in Wonderland, The Wind in the Willows*, and the outpouring of fairy tales by George MacDonald, Andrew Lang, Oscar Wilde, and many others.[14] For complex reasons, the Victorians chose to make of childhood a utopian site, the conceptual repository of innocence, virtue, and clear-sightedness; one consequence of this was that Victorian children were also almost uniquely privileged in their access to the spirit world and to the world of fairies. As Carol

Mavor observes, "The child and the photograph were commodified, fetishized, developed alongside each other: they were laminated and framed as one" (Mavor, 3). In Bloom's photographic vision, Rudy is quite literally fetishized, as well as commodified, with his Eton suit a mass-marketed talisman of social success. That he is also identified by the narrator as "*a fairy boy, a changeling*" testifies to the uniqueness of Bloom's experience as an alienated Irishman poised on the cusp of modernity, dealing with death by using the tools available to him.

Fairies and Changelings

Bloom considers himself a man of science, but always remains aware of the wealth of folk beliefs that survived even in urban, twentieth-century Ireland. Thinking of Rudy's early death, he realizes, "Meant nothing. Mistake of nature," but then immediately thinks of the popular "wisdom" he has heard about such cases: "If it's healthy it's from the mother. If not from the man" (*U* 6.328). He is certainly not immune to the lure of traditional knowledge, and finds himself thrown back upon it when, in the magical environs of "Circe," his popular scientism proves ineffective. The idea that Rudy was a changeling—that the fairies have taken his son and left in its place a sickly thing of their own—is based firmly on Irish folk belief. Indeed, during Bloom's youth several cases were reported of Irishmen and Irishwomen attempting to force the fairies to take back their child by torturing the "changeling." In 1884,

> two women were reported in the "Daily Telegraph" as having been arrested at Clonmel on the 17th of the month, charged with cruelly ill-treating a child three years old. The evidence given was to the effect that the neighbors fancied that the child, who did not have the use of its limbs, was a changeling. During the mother's absence the prisoners accordingly entered her house and placed the child naked on a hot shovel, "under the impression that this would break the charm." As might have been expected the poor little thing was severely burnt, and, when the women were apprehended, it was in a precarious condition.[15]

Several folklorists have explored the motif of the fairy changeling as a reaction to the syndrome (or collection of illnesses) globally known as "failure to thrive" in infants and children.[16] Rudy is fairly typical in appearance: after being "changed" by fairies, the child in various stories "becomes uglier, becomes ill-favored and deformed, becomes diseased, is shrivelled up with withered face and wasted body, begins to look like an imbecile, and is wrinkled like an old man.... It is one of the hallmarks of the changeling that it does not grow" (Narvaez, 258). Changelings are frequently described as "wizened, with dark, wrinkled skin" (Eberly, 234), while Rudy has "a dwarf's face, mauve and wrinkled." (*U* 6.326). Often the parents consult a wise woman as to what to do about the child (Narvaez, 260), and it is the Blooms' midwife, a "jolly old woman," who "knew at once poor little Rudy wouldn't live" (*U* 4.417). Even Molly's worry that Rudy's death was a judgment on them for conceiving him while watching a pair of dogs mating in the street (*U* 18.1445) reflects the folk belief—one shared by many nineteenth-century scientists—that "maternal impressions and responses [could] produce certain clearly identifiable, 'psycho-genic' effects upon the unborn child" (Eberly, 229).

Rudy's apparent accomplishment and sophistication in the vision (the *Torah* and suit), as well as his magical appurtenances (the helmet and glass shoes), reflect the aura of the supernatural which has been associated with doomed, diseased, or different infants since Assyrian times. Some changelings are held to be highly skilled at dancing, sing-ing, or poetry, and to be far older than their infant appearance would suggest. In these cases, the changeling at first remains stubbornly silent and will not respond to its parents; only if it is tricked into revealing its abilities will the spell be broken (Eberly, 234). Perhaps this is another reason why Rudy will not break his charmed silence for Bloom. Such speculations, though, blur the distinction between the changeling as the child who is left behind by fairies and the change-ling as the original human child, raised by fairies and now inacces-sible to its parents. The former child is, however briefly, living, but is not "natural"; the latter, though dead, is not beyond reclamation, at least in folk belief, because its theft was an interference with nature. The eminent folklorist K. M. Briggs points out that there are many interconnections between the realm of the fairies and the realms of the dead, and concludes that "one might say that those of the Dead who inhabit Fairyland are people who have no right to be dead at all" (81, 96). In light of the interpenetration of the lands of Faerie and the realms of the dead, it becomes clearer that Bloom's vision of Rudy in "Circe" replays his earlier meditation on Rudy in "Hades," in which the sight of the child's coffin sets him to imagining that the dead child resembles Rudy.

More immediately, though, it is Bloom's situation standing guard over the recumbent Stephen that triggers Rudy's appearance; once more, Bloom finds himself the paternal guardian of a "son." Oddly enough, Stephen, too, is a "changeling," at least metaphorically; from early in *Portrait* he has made it clear that he feels radically disconnected from his natural family. There, he uses a different but related metaphor, fosterage, to explain his disconnection: "He felt that he was hardly of the one blood with them but stood to them rather in the mystical kinship of fosterage, fosterchild and fosterbrother" (*P* 98). In *Ulysses*, Stephen imagines a Dublin scene during the time of the Viking invasions:

> A school of turlehide whales stranded in hot noon, spouting, hobbling in the shallows. Then from the starving cagework city a horde of jerkined dwarfs, my people, with flayers' knives, running, scaling, hacking in green blubbery whalemeat. Famine, plague and slaughters. Their blood is in me, their lusts my waves. I moved among them on the frozen Liffey, that I, a changeling, among the spluttering resin fires. I spoke to no-one: none to me. (*U* 3.303)

Here he is adapting Irish racial myths to imagine himself in a previous incarnation, or perhaps a dream vision, an *Aisling*. He sees himself as a tall Milesian among dwarfish Firbolgs, with one foot in dear, dirty, conquered Dublin, up to its guts in blubber, and the other in Fairyland—a changeling who is only halfway changed.[17] Like Rudy, in this earlier incarnation he is silent. He is not quite silent as Bloom stands guard over him in "Circe," though. Instead, he is drunkenly muttering Yeats's "Who Goes with Fergus?", a lyrical invitation to join the hosts of Faerie, so as to become immune to human "hopes and fear," as well as "love's bitter mystery"—precisely, it seems, what Rudy has done, willingly or not. Certainly Yeats's vision of the purity of flight and exile, which he associated with the pure devotion to poetry, strikes a responsive chord in Stephen. Is Stephen not only a changeling, but a fairy boy as well? Is Bloom's vision of a Rudy who has been magically transformed simply a Bloomian version of Stephen's aspiration for himself? Unfortunately, Stephen's closest approximation to Fairyland is alcohol, and instead of finding himself under the hill in the morning, he is likely to be found under the weather.

Fairy Photography

Fairies are liminal creatures, defining by their very existence the boundaries between the clearly human and the clearly inhuman, straddling the line that separates the living from the dead. Time does not work on them as it does on us, and this difference makes them both purer and more dangerous. They are remarkably ambivalent in their dealings with humans, inclined alternately to playing cruel tricks and to granting unexpected boons. In many ways they are like children, in that they look something like small human adults but owe no allegiance to adult human social conventions. The nineteenth century, sensing this, came to a consensus that fairies must be small in stature. They have an ambiguous relationship to "that other world" that was the object of the Society for Psychical Research's investigations. Indeed, many devoted spiritualists had no patience with the idea of fairies. Even Sir Arthur Conan Doyle, who wrote a book about a famous sighting of fairies, tried to make a clear distinction between that and the larger question of a spirit world:

> ...this whole subject of the objective existence of a subhuman form of life has nothing to do with the larger and far more vital question of spiritualism. I should be sorry if my arguments in favour of the latter should be in any way weakened by my exposition of this very strange episode, which really has no bearing upon the continued existence of the individual. (Doyle, vi)

Clearly, Conan Doyle realizes that there is something compromising about a belief in fairies—or at least something different in quality from a belief in the spirit world. Part of what he is reacting to here is the fact that, by the turn of the century, fairies—like photography and like childhood itself—had been commodified, meaning that a person who endorsed their existence might be suspected of hoping to profit thereby. Popular magazines were jammed with illustrations of fairies, and the writing of contemporary fairy tales had emerged as a distinct and popular genre. The peak of this vogue was, in fact, in 1904, when Sir James M. Barrie's play *Peter Pan* had audiences declaring fervently that they *did* believe in fairies, not to mention boys who never grow up. This is the immediate context in which Bloom, "wonderstruck," declares softly that he believes in Rudy, his own boy who never grew up.

What does it mean to call Rudy "a fairy boy" and to consider his appearance a sort of photograph? As Joyce was completing *Ulysses*, a notorious drama was being played out in the popular press of the British Isles: the affair of the "Cottingley Fairies." The affair turned on just five photographs taken by two girls purporting to show fairies—two of them taken in 1917, three more in 1920. Elsie Wright, who lived with her parents in Cottingley, near Bradford, had left school at thirteen and, after a short spell at the Bradford College of Art, found a job spotting black and white prints at a local photographer's studio. In 1917, her cousin Frances Griffiths came to join the family from South Africa; she was ten, Elsie sixteen. The two girls liked to play in a wooded glen with a stream at the bottom of the garden, and Frances was berated for spending so much time there and for falling into the water. She blurted out in self-defense, "I go to see the fairies! That's why—to see the *fairies*."[18] When her parents expressed disbelief in this secret the girls had shared, Frances argued her father into lending her his simple quarter-plate box camera. The girls returned with an exposed plate which, when Mr. Wright developed it, showed Frances just behind a group of fairies.

Her parents were baffled, but did not find this demonstration entirely convincing, and were still not convinced when the girls somewhat later produced a photograph of Elsie looking at a gnome. The photos might have remained a family curiosity if Mrs. Wright and Frances's mother had not attended a meeting of the Theosophical Society in 1919; they mentioned the photos there, and they were eventually brought to the attention of the spiritualist Edward Gardner. Gardner had the negatives examined and determined to his satisfaction that they had not been photographically faked. He visited the family, and at his encouragement Frances and Elsie took three more photographs of fairies, including a "leaping fairy." Gardner had all five photographs made into slides to use in his lectures. Eventually the case came to the attention of Conan Doyle, who was writing an article for *The Strand* on "fairy-lore." The Christmas 1920 issue included his article and several of the photographs, although the Wrights were reluctant to give permission and agreed only when assured they would not be identified by name. The girls' identity soon became public knowledge, however, and they sometimes accompanied Gardner on his lectures. In 1922, Conan Doyle published an expanded version of his article, filled out with testimony from various spiritualists, including Gardner, under the title *The Coming of the Fairies*.

The article and book created great controversy, and conflicting opinions were vehemently expressed as to the authenticity of the photographs. Sporadically over the next sixty years, various interviews with the two women and technical investigations of the photographs were undertaken, most of them casting some doubt on the fairies. The most telling event in the story did not occur until 1983, when a writer named Joe Cooper, who was a committed believer in fairies and sympathetic to Elsie and Frances, reported that in an interview both women had admitted that the photographs were faked. Elsie had drawn the fairies, using a magazine illustration as model, and mounted the drawings on cardboard, supported by invisibly thin hat-pins. As Cooper commented, "partly to take [Frances's] mind off her troubles, and partly to play a prank on grown-ups who sneered at the idea that fairies could be seen, but who cheerfully perpetuated the myth of Santa Claus, they conspired to produce fairy figures that they could photograph convincingly."[19]

Paradoxically, the girls' photographs elicited such strong reactions of belief and of disbelief in their audience for the same reason— because they looked like everyone's idea of fairies. Arthur Rackham, the illustrator, was inclined, on the whole, to believe fairies existed, but he was a cynic about the Cottingley fairies because, as he pointed out, they looked so much like the fairies *he* drew. As young girls, Elsie and Frances were thought by many to be privileged observers; Gardner, in fact, worried whether Elsie might not soon become sexually mature and grow unable to see the fairies. But as young girls, they were also thought to live in a world in which pragmatic reality and the imagination are not easily distinguishable. In dealing with fairies, it would seem, the only possible observer is, almost by definition, an undependable one. In one of her interviews, held before their confession of fakery, Elsie put the point delicately: "As for the photographs, let's say they are pictures of figments of our imagination, Frances and mine, and leave it at that."[20] Even after their confession, the testimony of Elsie and Frances was intriguing. While Elsie maintained she had never believed in fairies, and that all five photographs were fakes, Frances insisted that she did believe in fairies, and the very last photograph was an authentic picture of them. Like Stephen and Bloom, the older and younger cousin have shared an experience, now almost lost in the mists of the past, and yet all along they seem to have inhabited different orders of reality.

Conan Doyle, in any case, was a believer, and a particular enthusiast of the photography of spirit phenomena; he commonly illustrated his lectures with slides of these. His embrace of the fairy photographs lost him much credibility, though, and perhaps a peerage, despite the popular sympathy aroused for him by his son's death in the war. Still, he was certainly not alone in his beliefs, and when, in a London lecture in 1920, he testified to having had personal experience speaking with and seeing the dead, and asked how many of his audience had had a similar experience, 250 out of 290 in the audience rose. There can be no doubt that he and his wife derived great comfort from their séances, and on several occasions, as he said, "I had the joy of a few last words with my arisen son, who blessed me on my mission" (Doyle

1988, 23). Bloom is denied this joy, but, when the silent Rudy fades, he does find a son of a sort, who eventually arises and stumbles home with him.

Like a man with a photograph of a dear departed one, Bloom both possesses and lacks a son; whatever his virtues, Stephen can be no more than a distorted and inadequate image of the young man Rudy might have become. Like Rudy's, his childhood costume spoke to the hopes of his parents. Curiously enough, after hearing Bloom speak about his encounter, Molly blends her memory of Rudy with her memory of Stephen in much the way her husband has:

> ...I saw him driving down to the Kingsbridge station with his father and mother I was in mourning thats 11 years ago now yes hed be 11 though what was the good of going into mourning for what was neither one thing nor the other...I suppose hes a man now by this time he was an innocent boy then and a darling little fellow in his lord Fauntleroy suit and curly hair like a prince on a stage...he liked me too they all do wait by God...he was on the cards this morning...(*U* 18.1305)

The Cottingley fairy episode as a whole demonstrates how late in the century a faith in the scientific validity of the spirit world and its inhabitants persisted. Bloom, obviously, could have known nothing of Conan Doyle's writing on fairies, but it is entirely possible that Joyce did. In any case, photography as a discourse at the turn of the century was certainly open to a variety of subjects other than the mundane.

The whole point of photography in its primary social use is to stop time from its incessant attrition or to give the momentary illusion that it has stopped: that Molly is still a young woman in her prime, that Stephen is still a "darling little fellow" instead of a drunken post-adolescent. And the forgotten genres of memorial photography and spirit photography are both, in their ways, exaggerations of this photographic function, while photography of the fairy world reminds us that the dimensions of the quotidian and the marvelous, at certain privileged times, can be made to intersect. As he watches Rudy materialize, Bloom's mind, saturated with the social practice of photography, cannot help seeing the hallucinatory event as mute, yet scientific, testimony that somewhere, somehow, his son has fulfilled a father's aspirations.

Notes

One   Introduction: Dialogics and Popular Culture in Joyce's Novel

1. Approaching Dublin as a failing port lends some pathos to the boys' expedition in "An Encounter," in which the protagonist looks in vain for an adventurous-looking sailor. Instead he finds a crowd of the unemployed watching a single ship being unloaded while an idle seaman shouts, "all right!" (*D* 23).

2. This lends some point to the episode in *Stephen Hero* in which the character named Wells asks Stephen if he has read *Trilby*, confusing Stephen's reputation for "advanced" taste with a taste for the mildly prurient. "The style would suit you, I think. Of course it's a bit…blue" (*SH* 71).

3. For the classic characterizations of the popular literature of the time, see Claude Cockburn, *Bestseller: The Books Everybody Read, 1900–1939* (London: Sidgwick & Jackson, 1972); Amy Cruse, *After the Victorians* (London: Allen & Unwin, 1938); and Margaret Dalziel, *Popular Fiction 100 Years Ago* (London: Cohen & West, 1957).

4. Raymond Queneau, a French admirer of Joyce, used his discovery of *Ulysses*, with its Homeric structure, to overcome a writer's block he had experienced after parting company with Breton's Surrealist group. His first important novel, *Le Chiendent*, uses a structure based on the seven letters of his first and last names, as well as a group of different "modes de récit" for the different chapters and subsections. See Kershner, 1972.

5. "What no eye has seen, nor ear heard, nor the heart of man conceived, what God has prepared for those who love him." (I Cor. 2–9) in Fr. Boyle's citation (viii).

6. The field of popular culture study has attracted many other Joyceans, including notably Mary Power, Stephen Watt, Mark Wollaeger, Katherine Mullin, Joseph Heininger, Joseph Voelker, Joseph Valente, Mark Osteen, Aida Yared, and Coilín Owens. In addition, contributors to the essay collections I edited, entitled *Joyce and Popular Culture* and *Cultural Studies of James Joyce*, show some of the ambition, variety, and interest of the field. Some of these critics simply attempt to accrue information about the forgotten furniture of everyday material culture; others attempt analyses based on the information gathered in this way. A treasury of popular culture is John Wyse Jackson and Bernard McGinley's *Dubliners: An Annotated Edition* (1993), which is full of period newspaper stories, advertisements, and period illustrations.

7. These include Ken Hirschkop and David Shepherd, eds. *Bakhtin and Cultural Theory* (Manchester: Manchester University Press, 1989); Michael M. Bell and Michael Gardiner, eds. *Bakhtin and the Human Sciences: No Last Words* (London: Sage, 1998); Craig Brandist and Gavin Tihanov, eds. *Materializing Bakhtin: the Bakhtin Circle and Social Theory* (New York: Palgrave, 2000); Greg Marc Nielsen, *The Norms of Answerability: Social Theory between Bakhtin and Habermas* (Albany: SUNY Press, 2002).

Two   Odyssean Culture and Its Discontents

1. Theodor Adorno points out that Lukács "groups together completely disparate figures under the concepts of decadence and avantgardism (for him they are the same thing)," and identifies them as Proust, Kafka, Joyce, Beckett, and as theoreticians Benjamin and himself (Adorno 221). For both sides of the Lukács-Adorno debate (and additional leftist perspectives) see Bloch et al., *Aesthetics and Politics.* There is some irony in Lukács's attack on Adorno late in his own career, since the "Critical Theory" of which Horkheimer and Adorno considered themselves to be exponents began as "a form of Lukácsian Marxism (meaning the Lukács of *History and Class Consciousness*)." See D'Amico, 39. My thanks to Robert D'Amico for help with parts of this essay.
2. Ellmann discusses this influence in *JJII*, 369.
3. The argument about the effect of this narrative presence is put forth by French, chapter six.
4. Denis Donoghue in "Is there a case against *Ulysses*?" discusses Kenner's and Jameson's readings from a related perspective, but I believe he seriously misreads Jameson's essay.
5. Letter, Oct. 22, 1942, quoted in Jay, 214. Incidentally, both the critique of modern society as being essentially asexual, despite its apparent flaunting of sexuality, and the attack on popular culture as a tool of the ruling classes can be found in Lewis, 81–82, 120.

Three   Authorial Interchanges

1. Her books can sometimes still be found in occult and new age bookstores, and she still has her partisans, including some unlikely ones: Henry Miller identified her as one of the world's ten greatest authors. See David Wallechinsky et al., *The Book of Lists*, vol. 1 (New York: Bantam Books, 1978), 227.

2. The original letter can be found in Gustave Flaubert, *Correspondence*, ed. Jean Bruneau (Paris: Gallimard, 1980), 2:354. This translation appears in Julian Barnes, *Flaubert's Parrot* (New York: Knopf, 1986), 173.

Four   Riddling the Reader to Write Back

1. A "conundrum," as in Cissy Caffrey's usage in this chapter's epigraph, was originally a nonsense term, used for a "thingummy," or some sort of complex and unknown mechanism. The OED suggests the term had associations with Oxford and pedagogues, especially farcical ones. Bloom's watch is in fact a kind of conundrum, as it has stopped at four-thirty for mysterious reasons, Bloom being a regular watch-winding sort of person, although he suspects that four-thirty is the hour at which Molly and Boylan consummated his cuckoldry. For us, this conundrum is ultimately insoluble, but it will certainly lead us to speculate about whether the universe of *Ulysses* is one in which watches mysteriously stop at melodramatic moments.
2. Attributing agency in "Oxen" is a vexed question. Hazard Adams uses David Hayman's term "the arranger" for the agency that controls the sequence of narrators, arguing that "there may be an additional story to be inferred about the narrators and even about the arranger, once we see the arranger as a performer" (600–601; see Kenner 1987, 65; and David Hayman, *"Ulysses": The Mechanics of Meaning*, rev. ed. [Madison: University of Wisconsin Press, 1982], 84, 88–104.) Once agencies like narrators and the arranger take on a diegetic dimension, he implies, they may be seen as character-like. For simplicity's sake (and in order to follow Bakhtin's usage) I attribute many textual interventions and interpolations to the author. "Authority" is always relative, and in *Ulysses* we could say that "authorship" is the same. However, I agree with Gérard Genette that Wayne Booth's term "implied author" needlessly multiplies entities. I am comfortable referring to "Joyce" as an implied textual construct whose relationship to the historical Joyce is ambiguous but not strictly relevant here. See Genette, *Narrative Discourse Revisited*, trans. Jane E. Lewin (Ithaca: Cornell University Press, 1988), 139–45.

Five   Newspapers and Periodicals: Endless Dialogue

1. Ironically, Gordon Bennett was himself a newspaperman.
2. *Bits of Fun*, *Photo Bits*, and *Illustrated Tidbits* all seem to have been related papers between the turn of the century and the 1920s. In 1923,

Bits of Fun was merged with *Photo Bits*, according to the *Waterloo Directory*.

3. Having come across this independently in 1973, I have since learned that Fritz Senn found the same article, according to Hugh Kenner in *A Colder Eye: The Modern Irish Writers* (New York: Knopf, 1983), 228–29.

4. Interestingly, the *Dublin Evening Mail* for October 3, 1903, has a story of the prosecution of an *Evening Telegraph* newsboy for "crying out false news," having sold a paper to H. Corley under the pretense that it announced the "death of King Edward" (p. 7, col.2).

5. The first issue of *Paddy Kelly's Budget* (November 14, 1832), which called itself "a penny-worth of fun," introduces in rhyme one-eyed Paddy, and addresses itself to the ladies:

> Fair maidens, now, to you I speak,
> Remember Paddy, once a week!
> And sport your penny! Never grudge it,
> To buy his entertaining "Budget".
> In it you'll every Wednesday find
> Matter adapted to your mind;
> 'Twill treat of heroes and romancing,
> Love sonnets, billets doux, and dancing.

Men were simply threatened, "Ye bricks of the town…come and buy it…or you'll figure in *print* (1). A typical issue of *Pue's Occurrences*, vol. 11 (July 24-July 27, 1714) features a declaration by the Lord Protector announcing that "no Perfon or Perfons, whatfoever in England or Wales, whofe eftates have been fequefdter'd for Delinquency, or who were actually in Arms for the late King against the Parliament" will be permitted to keep their weapons. The paper at this date is clearly an organ of government. An advertisement on the second page for "The moft incomparable eye-water Prepared by Sir Tho.Wetherly, Prefident of the College of Phyficians London" has "cured many thoufands of Perfons of Quality," and sometimes lets the blind see again.

6. For the historical source of this, see Timothy Weiss, "The 'Black Beast' Headline: The Key to an Allusion in *Ulysses.*" *James Joyce Quarterly* vol. 19 no. 2 (Winter 1982), 183–86.

7. See, for instance, Charles Dawson, *Greater Dublin: Extension of Municipal Boundaries* (Dublin: Sealy, Bryers, and Walker, 1899). I found some eighteen articles by Charles Dawson published between 1876 and 1913 in the *Statistical and Social Inquiry Society of Ireland Journal* on subjects such as housing, education, the Poor Law, and unemployment, none of them remotely like the example in *Ulysses*. He also published with some frequency in the *Irish Ecclesiastical Record*.

8. Prof. Cullen has made a study of the stationer/bookseller's Eason's and has copies of monthly invoices for the Belfast store from slightly after the turn of the century; unfortunately, he informs me, invoices from the Dublin stores have not survived.

9. Between Dec. 11, 1902, and Nov. 19, 1903, Joyce published some 21 book reviews in the *Daily Express*, and, as a Belvedere student, wrote practice reviews of the plays he had seen in order to compare his views with those of the professional reviewers.

10. Titles in the first category include the All Ireland Review, Church of Ireland Gazette, Constabulary Gazette, Daily Express, Dublin Gazette, Dublin Journal of Medical Science, Dublin Medical Press, Dublin Morning and Evening Mail, Evening Herald, Evening Telegraph, Farmer's Gazette, Figaro and Gentlewoman, Freeman's Journal and National Press, General Advertiser, Ireland Saturday Night, Ireland's Gazette, Irish Catholic, Irish Cyclist, Irish Independent, Irish Emerald, Irish Farming World, Irish Field, Irish Football and Athletic World, Irish Golfer, Irish Homestead, Irish Law Times, Irish Packet, Irish People, Irish Protestant, Irish School, Irish Society and Social Review, Irish Truth, Irish Weekly Independent, Leader, Leinster Express, Nationalist, National Teacher, New Jurist, Shamrock, Social Siftings, Sport, Sporting Echo, Sporting Record, Sunday Independent, Irish Times, Warder, United Irishman, Weekly Freeman and National Press.
The second category includes the Annals of St. Anthony, Bee-Keeper, Bill of Entry, Catholic, Catholic Young Man , Celtia, Christian Irishman, Church of Ireland Parish Magazine, Gaelic Journal, Ireland, Irish Builder, Irish Draper, Irish Ecclesiastical Record, Irish Engineering Review, Irish Hardware Review, Irish Investor's Guardian, Irish Leather Trades Journal, Irish Military Guide, Irish Monthly, Irish Naturalist, Irish Rosary, Irish School, Irish Technical Journal, Irish Teetotaler, Irish Tobacco Trade Journal, Irish Tourist, "£.s.d.," Lady of the House, Lady's Herald, Legal Diary, Leprecaun, Motor News, New Ireland Review, T.C.D., Visitor, and the J. G. Wilson and Co.'s Pocket Railway Guide.

11. In fact, the National Library's collection of the *Enniscorthy Guardian* does not start until December 1904, and by 1984 it had no holdings of the *Kilkenny People* or records showing that it had formerly carried the paper. It did, however, have long runs of the *Northern Whig* and the *Cork Examiner.*

12. Note Ignatius Gallaher's "We'll paralyze Europe" (*U* 7.628).

13. Gallaher's historical model was an acquaintance of John Joyce's named Frederick Gallaher who died of cardiac failure in 1899. By the time Crawford eulogizes him, he has been dead five years.

14. In its glory days, the owner, Sir John Gray, did this for *Freeman's Journal* reporters. See Oram 1983, 70.

15. A search of the *New York World* files for the relevant period in 1882 failed to show such a map, and the Bransome's coffee advertisement has been equally hard to trace down, although Crawford makes it clear that he is only giving an example of a possible location for the ad—as usual, the actual details have escaped him. Although Ignatius Gallaher is supposedly modeled on a real journalist named Fred Gallaher who actually

carried off this stunt (*JJII* 46n, 219n), I have been unable to find any
record verifying the story. Fred Gallaher himself appears in a more positive light than Joyce allows him in M. J. MacManus's *Adventures of an
Irish Bookman* (Dublin: Talbot Press, 1952). Francis MacManus recalls
meeting figures such as Liam O'Flaherty, Austin Clarke, and Seumas
O'Sullivan for weekly discussions, and mentions that he saw "Frank
Gallaher every Wednesday for tea, politics, the stories behind the news,
and just good comradeship" (preface). Gallaher died in 1899 of cardiac
failure, and so by the time of Crawford's encomium had been dead for
five years.

16. The following material was mailed to me in 1985 by Louis Cullen, and
combines his transcriptions with photocopies of the original records.

17. In both his books, *James Joyce's Techno-Poetics* and *Beyond the Word*,
Donald Theall, following arguments initiated by Marshall McLuhan,
presents Joyce as a kind of engineer, and *Ulysses* as a "techno-poetic"
epic. Throughout his writing, Theall highlights Joyce's awareness of the
technological "extensions of man" that emerged in the twentieth century.

18. See, for example, the news coverage of a day in the Parnell trial in
Kershner, ed. *Portrait*.

19. On Foucauldian surveillance in *Portrait*, see Kershner 2006.

20. Although the fictional Keogh-Bennett fight is in part based on a fight
between an M. L. Keogh and a man named Garry in late April of 1904
(Gifford, 283), a classic fight between English and Irish boxers Spring
and Langan is recounted in the *Licensed Victualler's Gazette* for June
17, 1904, on p. 402. A sample of the narrative style: "At the beginning
of the fourth round Langan rushes up with desperate impetuosity. The
blow which he aims seems meant to knock his opponent's head clean
off his shoulders. But Spring waits quietly for it, dodges it, and receives
Langan's nose on his fist in such a way as very nearly to demolish it alto-
gether. Then follows the finest tussle of the whole fight. Wrestling and
hitting, hitting and wrestling, the combatants spin round and round,
till at last, having for a time literally held Langan up in the iron clasp of
his right arm while he pounds and pounds him with the steam-engine-
like action of his left, Spring lets him fall, and a good deal of doctoring
has to be done to the ferocious Irishman before he can again come up
to the scratch—as ferocious as ever.... "I'll foight yer, me bhoy, till Sin
Pathrick's, if yah like," Jack Langan exclaims, after one fall. ..." (col. 2).
Throughout, the Irishman is pictured as strong but brutish and his followers frequently cheat by coming into the ring and holding him up. The
Englishman, on the other hand, is shown as a gentleman who practices
"science" in his fighting.

21. Although Adams states that the accused was not remanded until the
17th (Adams, 229) and Gifford follows him, the *Telegraph* for June 16
plainly states that fact (p. 3 col. 2).

22. On binarism in "Cyclops," see Vincent J. Cheng, *Joyce, Race, and
Empire* (Cambridge: Cambridge University Press, 1995), 191–218.

Six *Tit-Bits, Answers,* and Beaufoy's Mysterious Postcard

1. Bloom seems bitingly satirical about the lack of difficulty of these contests, but some, in fact, were trivially easy. Arthur Pearson, in starting his undercapitalized *Pearson's Weekly,* demanded a small entry fee of all contestants and then redistributed the money among the great number who answered correctly. David Reed remarks, "before the courts declared that he was running a lottery and had to stop, his fifty third competition had drawn 473,574 entries" (93).
2. This discovery was made by John Simpson according to Harald Beck. "Philip Beaufoy's cover blown at last?" E-mail to the author. June 19, 2010.

Seven The World's Strongest Man: Joyce or Sandow?

1. Details of Sandow's life, of which relatively little is known, come from David L. Chapman, *Sandow the Magnificent,* the *Oxford Dictionary of National Biography*; and Frank W. Lane, "Sandow: The Strong Man."
2. In this, he enlarged upon the fame of his only major predecessor, the equestrian Andrew Ducrow. See Richard D. Altick, *The Shows of London* (Cambridge, MA: Harvard University Press, 1978), 343; on the tableau vivant, see this entire chapter.
3. An interesting footnote on the problem of Bloom's impossible chest measurement in "Ithaca" is accidentally provided by the sports historian David Willoughby, who notes that Sandow claimed a "normal" chest measurement of 48 inches and an "expanded" measurement of 62 inches. Willoughby claims that this is impossible and estimates that the true dimensions were probably 45 inches and 48 inches (Willoughby, 317). Following an observation by Robert M. Adams, Hugh Kenner pointed out that Bloom's chest dimensions on the chart from Sandow's book are 28 and 29 ½ inches, which would be impossibly small for a person five foot nine and a half inches tall weighing 158 pounds. He notes that one of the "sample" student measurements in Sandow's book lists a chest of 29 inches before beginning the exercises; Kenner suggests that Joyce saw this and failed to note that the student was 19 years old and only five feet in height (Hugh Kenner, *Ulysses,* rev. ed. [Baltimore: Johns Hopkins University Press, 1987], 164–65). A further note was added by Jennifer Savino, who found an article in the *New York Times* of June 6, 1904, on the physical characteristics of European Jews in which a Dr. Fishberg argues that Jews are by nature narrow-chested, since they are inclined to develop their intellect before their body (*Times Literary Supplement,* 27 June 2003, no. 5230, p. 16).

4. Quoted in John Stallworthy, *Between the Lines: Yeats's Poetry in the Making* (New York: Oxford University Press, 1963), 14. It is not known whether Yeats actually followed this routine for any length of time; his son Michael tells me it seems to him "the unlikeliest thing in the world."

5. "On the hands down" appears nowhere in *Strength and How to Obtain It*; perhaps Bloom means to refer to Sandow's Germanic speech, which he could have heard during one of Sandow's Dublin performances. It, of course, is nowhere apparent in his (probably ghostwritten) book, which is a model of Edwardian hack eloquence.

6. See Michael Patrick Gillespie, *James Joyce's Trieste Library* (Austin: University of Texas Press, 1986), 263 (#554).

7. See R. B. Kershner, "Degeneration: The Explanatory Nightmare," *Georgia Review* 40 (Summer 1986), 416–44.

8. Cf. Baudrillard: "Power, too, for some time now produces nothing but signs of its resemblance. And at the same time, another figure of power comes into play: that of a collective demand for signs of power—a holy union which forms around the disappearance of power." (*Simulations*, trans. Paul Foss et al. [New York: Sémiotext(e), 1983], 45). Here Baudrillard's notion that the actuality of power has disappeared in a world of simulacra might be related to the controversy over Sandow's actual abilities, and the irrelevance of that controversy to Sandow as social fact.

9. The Hindleys refer to Sandow as "Eugene Shadow."

10. On this Victorian genre see Ira Bruce Nadel, *Biography: Fiction, Fact, and Form* (New York: St, Martin's Press, 1984), 21–30.

11. Sandow once observed, "You can't engage in a prize-fight and be a gentleman" (Chapman, 17) and his gentlemanly status, which had been so hard-earned for a former circus performer, was at least as important to him as his reputation for strength.

12. The basic reference on Joyce and advertisement is Garry Leonard's *Advertising and Commodity Culture in Joyce* (Gainesville: University Press of Florida, 1998); cf. also the special issue of the *James Joyce Quarterly* on Joyce and Advertising, edited by Wicke and Leonard: *JJQ* 30 (Summer/Fall 1993), in which an early and partial version of this chapter appeared.

Eight   *Ulysses* and the Orient

1. A brief list of other significant work on Orientalism might include Ali Bedad, *Belated Travellers: Orientalism in the Age of Colonial Dissolution* (Durham, NC: Duke University Press, 1994); Joseph A. Boone, "Vacation Cruises; or, The Homoerotics of Orientalism," *PMLA* 110 (1995), 89–107; Emily A. Haddad, *Orientalist Poetics: The Islamic Middle East in*

Nineteenth Century English and French Poetry (Burlington, VT: Ashgate, 2002); Rani Kabbani, *Europe's Myths of the Orient* (Bloomington: Indiana University Press, 1986); Vasant Kaiwar and Sucheta Mazumdar, eds. *Antinomies of Modernity: Essays on Race, Orient, Nation* (Durham, NC: Duke University Press, 2003); Joep Leerson, "Irish Studies and Orientalism: Ireland and the Orient," in *Oriental Prospects: Western Literature and the Lure of the East*, ed. C. C. Barfoot and Theo D'haen (Atlanta: Rodopi, 1998), 161–73; Lisa Lowe, *Critical Terrains: French and British Orientalisms* (Ithaca: Cornell University Press, 1991); A. L. Macfid, ed. *Orientalism: A Reader* (New York: New York University Press, 2000); B. J. Moore-Gilbert, *Orientalism, Postmodernism, and Globalism* (London: St. Martin's Press, 1986). On gender and race or nation as categories of the Other in Joyce the basic reference is Vincent J. Cheng, *Joyce, Race, and Empire* (Cambridge: Cambridge University Press, 1995). See also Emer Nolan, *James Joyce and Nationalism* (London: Routledge, 1995).

2. Two useful works discussing some of the Orientalist implications of Byron's writing—a subject beyond the scope of this essay—are Daniel P. Watkins, *Social Relations in Byron's Eastern Tales* (London and Toronto: Associated University Presses, 1987) and Anakid Melikian, *Byron and the East* (Beirut: American University of Beirut, 1977).

3. See R. B. Kershner, *Joyce, Bakhtin, and Popular Literature: Chronicles of Disorder* (Chapel Hill: University of North Carolina Press, 1989), 59–60.

4. See R. B. Kershner, "The Reverend J. L. Porter: Bloom's Guide to the East," *James Joyce Quarterly* 24 (Spring 1987), 365–67.

5. Matthew Josephson, "1001 Nights in a Bar-Room, or the Irish Odysseus," *Broom* 3 (Sept. 1922), 146–50.

6. Robert G. Hampson, "The Genie out of the Bottle: Conrad, Wells, and Joyce," in *The Arabian Nights in English Literature: Studies in the Reception of "The Thousand and One Nights" into British Culture*, ed. Peter L. Caracciolo (New York: St. Martin's Press, 1988), 229–43, surveys some of the many parallels between Bloom and Sinbad, while Zack Bowen, "All in a Night's Entertainment: The Codology of Haroun al-Raschid, The Thousand and One Nights, Bloomusalem/Baghdad, the Uncreated Conscience of the Irish Race, and Joycean Self-Reflexivity," *James Joyce Quarterly* 35 (Winter/Spring 1998), 297–308, argues the parallel with Haroun al-Raschid.

7. Note that both Sinbad and Haroun al-Raschid recur frequently through the *Wake* as well, where, among other things, they may be seen as avatars of Bloom. If nothing else, this testifies to Joyce's enduring interest in *Arabian Nights*. The relative lack of serious critical attention to this communal masterwork of world literature is an example of Orientalism at its most pernicious.

8. The essential discussion of the allusive role of pantomimes in *Ulysses*, including Sinbad, is in chapter three of Cheryl Herr, *Joyce's Anatomy of Culture* (Urbana: University of Illinois Press, 1986).

9. See James Twitchell, *The Living Dead: A Study of the Vampire in Romantic Literature* (Durham, NC: Duke University Press, 1981), 108 on Ruthven.

10. On the harem, see Carol Shloss, " 'Behind the Veil': James Joyce and the Colonial Harem." *James Joyce Quarterly*, vol. 35 no. 2/3 (Winter/Spring 1998), 333–48.

11. See Herr, chapter four, on cross-dressing and transvestitism.

12. Cf. Peter Stallybrass and Allon White, *The Politics and Poetics of Transgression* (Ithaca: Cornell University Press, 1986), 191: "But disgust always bears the imprint of desire. These low domains, apparently expelled as 'Other,' return as the object of nostalgia, longing and fascination.... These contents, or domains, are subject to misrecognition and distortion precisely because idealization and phobic avoidance have *systematically* informed their discursive history."

13. On both the issues of Bloom's Jewishness and the Oriental typology of the Jew, see Ira B. Nadel, *Joyce and the Jews: Culture and Text* (Iowa City: University of Iowa Press, 1989) and Neil R. Davidson, *James Joyce, "Ulysses," and the Construction of Jewish Identity* (Cambridge: Cambridge University Press, 1996), 189.

14. *Life of Collins*, in Chalmers' *English Poets*, cited by Le Yaouanc, 8.

15. Quinet cited by Le Yaouanc, 12.

16. This is Matthew Arnold's famous characterization of the Celtic melancholy of James MacPherson's Ossianic poems. See Arnold, "On the Study of Celtic Literature," *The Complete Prose Works of Matthew Arnold*, ed. R. H. Super (Ann Arbor: University Of Michigan Press, 1962), 3:370.

Nine   The Appearance of Rudy: Children's Clothing and the History of Photography

1. Probably the fullest discussion of Rudy's symbolism is found in Tara Williams, "Polysymbolic Character: Irish and Jewish Folklore in the Apparition of Rudy," in Michael Gillespie, ed. *Joyce through the Ages: A Nonlinear View* (Gainesville: University Press of Florida, 1999), 117–32.

2. Cf. also Thomas Richards, *The Commodity Culture of Victorian England: Advertising and Spectacle, 1851–1914* (Stanford, CA: Stanford University Press, 1990).

3. Madeleine Ginsburg in *Victorian Dress in Photographs*, 182, mentions, as a picturesque alternative outfit for children, "the Highland suit popularised by the Royal Family who wore kilts and plaids during holidays at Balmoral." The uniqueness of the Irish colonial situation is illuminated by realizing how impossible it would have been for the Royal Family to have assumed some sort of traditional Irish garb on holidays.

4. First quotation is from F. Donaldson, *Edward VII* (London: Weidenfeld and Nicolson, 1974), ch. 12; second quotation from F. Cowles, *Edward VII and His Circle* (London: Hamish Hamilton, 1956), chapter 7.

5. Note that a well-known studio portrait of the Joyce family shows James, at the age of six, dressed in a sailor suit posing with his father and mother and his grandfather John Murray (*JJII* Plate I).

6. On Ferrero and militarism, see R. B. Kershner, *Joyce, Bakhtin and Popular Literature* (Chapel Hill: University of North Carolina Press, 1989), 80–82.

7. On the issue of heredity and aristocracy in *Portrait*, see Kershner, "Genius, Degeneration."

8. Zola, quoted by Susan Sontag, *On Photography* (New York: Delta, 1977), 87.

9. In Bloom's drawer is "an indistinct daguerrotype of Rudolf Virag and his father Leopolf Virag executed in the year 1852 in the portrait atelier of their (respectively) 1st and 2nd cousin, Stefan Virag of Szesfehervar, Hungary" (*U* 17.1875–77). Joyce clearly put a good deal of thought into Bloom's family background, and perhaps some research as well. Quite recently, an assistant of Endre Tóth, who is director of the Hungarian National Museum, was looking over a list of Hungarian photographers and ateliers and spotted one Sandor Virag who lived from 1881 until 1920 and worked in Székesfehévár. This actual Virag atelier was located in the Rakoczi Ferenc Street, in the heart of the city, in a building that has since been destroyed. Endre Tóth suggests that Joyce may have seen the name and location of the photographic atelier stamped on the back of a photograph he came across while living in Trieste, and took advantage of it to lend some historical credibility to his fictive Virag family.

10. Davidson is summarizing Avital Ronal, *The Telephone Book: Technology, Schizophrenia, Electric Speech* (Lincoln: University of Nebraska Press, 1989), 242–50.

11. "The Other World" was the accepted phrase describing the spiritual plane, which gives an interesting intonation to the apparent typo of Bloom's epistolary partner.

12. On the role of women in the spiritualist movement, and some political implications of this, see Alex Owen, *The Darkened Room* (Philadelphia: University of Pennsylvania Press, 1990) and Ann Braude, *Radical Spirits: Spiritualism and Women's Rights in Nineteenth-Century America* (Boston: Beacon Press, 1989).

13. All "spirit" images described here are from Fred Gettings, *Ghosts in Photographs: The Extraordinary Story of Spirit Photography* (New York: Harmony Books, 1978).

14. On the revolution in the social image of childhood during the nineteenth century, some basic texts are Philippe Ariès, *Centuries of Childhood: A Social History of Family Life* (New York: Knopf, 1962); Peter Coveney, *The Image of Childhood: The Individual and Society, a Study of the Theme in English Literature*, rev. ed. (Baltimore: Penguin, 1967); and

James R. Kincaid, *Child-Loving: The Erotic Child and Victorian Culture* (New York: Routledge, 1992).

15. Edwin Sidney Hartland, *The Science of Fairy Tales: An Inquiry into Fairy Mythology* (Detroit: Singing Tree Press, 1986), repr. 1891. Quoted in Joyce Underwood Munro, "The Invisible Made Visible: The Fairy Changeling as a Folk Articulation of Failure to Thrive in Infants and Children," in *The Good People: New Fairylore Essays*, ed. Peter Narvàez (New York: Garland, 1991), 264.

16. See Munro, 251–83 and Susan Schoon Eberly, "Fairies and the Folklore of Disability: Changelings, Hybrids, and the Solitary Fairy," also in Narvàez, ed. *The Good People*, 227–49.

17. Munro notes that the verb "change" can mean both "exchange" and "render different," and both senses are operative in the popular understanding of "changeling." As she puts it, "The ambiguity of the changeling legend is enacted on the very level of the language itself" (257).

18. Information on the Cottingley fairies is taken from Smith and from Nicola Brown, "'There are Fairies at the Bottom of our Garden': Fairies, Fantasy, and Photography," *Textual Practice* 10 (Spring 1996), 57–82.

19. Joe Cooper, "Cottingley: At Last the Truth," *The Unexplained* 117 (1983), 2338, quoted in Smith, 396–97.

20. Joe Cooper, *The Case of the Cottingley Fairies* (London: Robert Hale, 1990), 76, quoted in Smith, 393.

Works Cited

Adams, Hazard. "Critical Constitution of the Literary Text: The Example of *Ulysses*." *New Literary History* 17 (Spring 1986), 595–616.

Adams, Robert Martin. *Surface and Symbol: The Consistency of James Joyce's "Ulysses."* New York: Oxford University Press, 1962.

Adorno, Theodor (1975) "The Culture Industry Reconsidered." *New German Critique* 6 (Fall). Cited here as in Brantlinger (1983), 235.

———. *Notes to Literature.* Ed. Rolf Tiedemann. Vol. 1. New York: Columbia University Press, 1991.

A.E. [George Russell]. *Controversy in Ireland: An Appeal to Irish Journalists* [pamphlet]. Dublin: O'Donoghue and Co., n.d.

Ahmad, Aijaz. *In Theory: Classes, Nations, Literatures.* London: Verso Press, 1992.

Anderson, Benedict. *Imagined Communities: Reflections on the Origin and Spread of Nationality.* Rev. ed. New York: Verso, 2006.

Archer, William. *Poets of the Younger Generation.* London: J. Lane, 1902.

Arnold, Matthew. "Culture and Anarchy." In *English Prose of the Victorian Era.* Ed. Charles F. Harrold and William D. Templeman. New York: Oxford University Press, 1938. 1117–88.

Attridge, Derek and Marjorie Howes, ed. *Semicolonial Joyce.* Cambridge: Cambridge University Press, 2000.

Bakhtin, M.M. *The Dialogic Imagination: Four Essays.* Ed. Michael Holquist. Trans. Caryl Emerson and Michael Holquist. Austin: University of Texas Press, 1981.

———. *Problems of Dostoevsky's Poetics.* Trans. Caryl Emerson. Minneapolis: University of Minneapolis Press, 1984.

———. *Speech Genres and Other Late Essays.* Trans. Vern McGee. Ed. Caryl Emerson and Michael Holquist. Austin: University of Texas Press, 1986.

Barthes, Roland. *Camera Lucida: Reflections on Photography.* Trans. Richard Howard. New York: Hill and Wang, 1980.

Batchen, Geoffrey. *Forget Me Not: Photography and Remembrance.* New York: Princeton Architectural Press, 2004.

Baudrillard, Jean. *For a Critique of the Political Economy of the Sign.* St. Louis: Telos Press, 1981.

Beaufoy, Philip. "A Revolution in Journalism." *Academy and Literature* 58 (17 March 1900), 238.

Benjamin, Walter. *Illuminations.* Ed. Hannah Arendt. New York: Schocken Books, 1969.

———. *Understanding Brecht.* Trans. Anna Bostock. London: Verso, 1998.

Berger, Arthur Asa. *Bloom's Morning: Coffee, Comforters, and the Secret Meaning of Everyday Life.* Boulder, CO: Westview Press, 1997.

Berger, John. *The Sense of Sight.* New York: Pantheon, 1985.

Bigland, Eileen. *Marie Corelli: The Woman and the Legend.* London: Jerrolds, 1953.

Bloch, Ernst et al. *Aesthetics and Politics.* Trans. ed. Ronald Taylor. London: NLB, 1977.

Bloom, Clive. *Bestsellers: Popular Fiction Since 1900.* New York: Palgrave Macmillan, 2002.

Booker, M. Keith. *Joyce, Bakhtin, and the Literary Tradition: Toward a Comparative Cultural Poetics.* Ann Arbor: University of Michigan Press, 1995.

Boyle, Robert, S.J. *James Joyce's Pauline Vision: A Catholic Exposition.* Carbondale: Southern Illinois University Press, 1978.

Brantlinger, Patrick. *Bread and Circuses: Theories of Mass Culture as Social Decay.* Ithaca: Cornell University Press, 1983.

Briggs, K. M. "The Fairies and the Realms of the Dead." *Folklore* 81 (Summer 1970), 81–96.

Brown, Stephen J. M., S.J., *Ireland in Fiction: A Guide to Irish Novels, Tales, Romances, and Folk-Lore.* Rev. ed. Dublin and London: Maunsel and Co., 1919.

———. *The Press in Ireland.* New York: Lemma Publishing Corp., 1971; Reprint, Dublin: Brown and Nolan, 1937.

Buck, Anne. *Clothes and the Child.* New York: Holmes and Meier, 1996.

Burnett, Frances Hodgson. *Little Lord Fauntleroy.* London: Frederick Warne and Co., 1891.

Burns, Stanley. *Sleeping Beauty: Memorial Photography in America.* Altadena, CA: Twelvetrees Press, 1990.

Burton, Richard Francis. "The Preternatural in Fiction." In *Irish Literature.* Ed. Justin McCarthy et al. New York: Bigelow, Smith & Co., 1904. Vol. I, 404–7.

Byrde, Penelope. *The Male Image: Men's Fashion in Britain, 1300–1970.* London: B.T. Batsford, Ltd., 1979.

Chapman, David L. *Sandow the Magnificent: Eugen Sandow and the Beginnings of Bodybuilding.* Urbana: University of Illinois Press, 1994.

Chéroux, Clément et al. *The Perfect Medium: Photography and the Occult.* New Haven: Yale University Press, 2004.

Clark, Suzanne. *Sentimental Modernism: Women Writers and the Revolution of the Word.* Bloomington: Indiana University Press, 1991.

Clifford, James. *The Predicament of Culture.* Cambridge: Harvard University Press, 1988.

Collier, Patrick. *Modernism on Fleet Street.* Burlington, VT: Ashgate, 2006.

Collins, Jim. *Uncommon Cultures: Popular Culture and Post-Modernism.* New York: Routledge, 1989.

Colum, Padraic and Mary. *Our Friend James Joyce*. Garden City, NY: Doubleday, 1958.

Cooper, John Xiros. *Modernism and the Culture of Market Society*. Cambridge: Cambridge University Press, 2004.

Corelli, Marie. *Free Opinions Freely Expressed on Certain Phases of Modern Social Life and Conduct*. London: Archibald Constable, 1905.

———. *A Romance of Two Worlds*. "A New Edition." New York: Lovell, Corywell, & Co., 1887.

Cranfield, G. A. *The Press and Society: From Caxton to Northcliffe*. New York: Praeger, 1959.

Cruse, Amy. *After the Victorians*. London: Allen and Unwin, 1938.

Creekmur, Corey K. "Lost Objects: Photography, Fiction, and Mourning." In *Photo-Textualities: Reading Photographs and Literature*. Ed. Marsha Bryant. Newark: University of Delaware Press, 1996.

Crofts, Freeman Wills. *Inspector French's Greatest Case*. New York: Penguin Books, 1988 (1922).

———. *The Pit-Prop Syndicate*. New York: Penguin Books, 1978 (1922).

Cullen, Louis. 1984. Interview by author. Dublin, Ireland. April 9.

———. 1985. Unpublished ms. and notes. In author's possession.

Cullingford, Elizabeth Butler. *Ireland's Others: Gender and Ethnicity in Irish Literature and Popular Culture*. Cork: Cork University Press, 2001.

Curran, Constantine P. *James Joyce Remembered*. New York: Oxford University Press, 1958.

Daly, Mary E. *Dublin: The Deposed Capital: A Social and Economic History, 1860–1914*. Cork: Cork University Press, 1985.

D'Amico, Robert. "Karl Popper and the Frankfurt School." *Telos* 86 (Winter 1990–1991), 33–48.

Davidson, Cathy N. "Photographs of the Dead: Sherman, Daguerre, Hawthorne." *South Atlantic Quarterly* 89 (Fall 1990), 667–701.

Davison, Neil. *James Joyce, "Ulysses," and the Construction of Jewish Identity*. Cambridge: Cambridge University Press, 1996.

Debord, Guy. *Society of the Spectacle*. Detroit: Black & Red, 1983.

Delany, Frank. *James Joyce's Odyssey: A Guide to the Dublin of "Ulysses."* London: Granada, 1983.

Derrida, Jacques. *The Post Card: From Socrates to Freud and Beyond*. Trans. Allan Bass. Chicago: University of Chicago Press, 1987.

Dettmar, Kevin. "Selling *Ulysses*." *James Joyce Quarterly* 30 (Summer/Fall 1993), 795–812.

Dettmar, Kevin and Stephen Watt, eds. *Marketing Modernism: Self-Promotion, Canonization, and Rereading*. Ann Arbor: University of Michigan Press, 1996.

Donoghue, Denis. "Is there a case against *Ulysses*?" In *Joyce in Context*. Ed. Vincent J. Cheng and Timothy Martin. Cambridge: Cambridge University Press, 1992. 19–39.

Doyle, Arthur Conan. *The Coming of the Fairies.* New York: George H. Doran Co., 1922.

———. *The Wanderings of a Spiritualist* (1921). Reprint. Berkeley, CA: Ronin Publishing, 1988.

Duffy, Enda. *The Subaltern "Ulysses."* Minneapolis: University of Minnesota Press, 1994.

Dumas, Alexandre. *The Count of Monte Cristo.* New York: McGraw-Hill, 1946.

Dunleavy, Mairead. *Dress in Ireland.* London: B. T. Batsford, Ltd., 1989.

Dunlop, Andrew. *Fifty Years of Irish Journalism.* Dublin: Hanna and Neale, 1911.

Dutton, Ken R. and Ronald S. Laura, "The Birth of Bodybuilding," *Muscle and Fitness* 51 (January 1990), 142–45, 163–65.

Eberly, Susan Schoon. "Fairies and the Folklore of Disability: Changelings, Hybrids, and the Solitary Fairy." In *The Good People: New Fairylore Essays.* Ed. Peter Narvàez, New York: Garland, 1991. 227–49.

Eliot, T. S. "*Ulysses*, Order and Myth." [Orig. pub. *The Dial*, 1923.] In *Selected Prose of T. S. Eliot*, Ed. Frank Kermode, 175–78. New York: Harcourt Brace Jovanovich, 1975.

Ellmann, Richard. *The Consciousness of Joyce.* New York: Oxford University Press, 1977.

———. *Ulysses on the Liffey.* New York: Oxford University Press, 1972.

Escott, T. H. S. *Personal Forces of the Period.* London: Hurst and Blackett, 1898.

French, Marilyn. *The Book as World: James Joyce's "Ulysses."* Cambridge, MA: Harvard University Press, 1976.

Garvin, John. *James Joyce's Disunited Kingdom and the Irish Dimension.* New York: Harper and Row, 1977.

Gibbons, Luke. "'Have You No Homes to Go To?' James Joyce and the Politics of Paralysis." In *Semicolonial Joyce.* Ed. Derek Attridge and Marjorie Howes. Cambridge: Cambridge University Press, 2000. 150–71.

Gibson, Andrew. *Joyce's Revenge: History, Politics, and Aesthetics in "Ulysses."* Oxford: Oxford University Press, 2002.

Gifford, Don, with Robert J. Seidman. *"Ulysses" Annotated*, 2nd ed. Berkeley: University of California Press, 1988.

Gilbert, Pamela K. *Disease, Desire, and the Body in Victorian Women's Popular Novels.* Cambridge: Cambridge University Press, 1997.

Gilbert, Stuart. *James Joyce's "Ulysses": A Study* (1930). Reprint. New York: Vintage Books, 1952.

Ginsburg, Madeleine. *Victorian Dress in Photographs.* London: B. T. Batsford Ltd., 1982.

Gogarty, Oliver St. John. *Mourning Became Mrs. Spendlove and Other Portraits, Grave and Gay.* New York: Creative Age Press, 1948.

Gordon, John. *Joyce and Reality: The Empirical Strikes Back.* Syracuse, NY: Syracuse University Press, 2004.

Gorman, Herbert S. *James Joyce.* New York: Rinehart, 1940.

Griffith, Arthur [Domnall O Maoilmicil]. *United Irishman*, vol. 11, no. 276 (June 1904).

Groden, Michael. *"Ulysses" in Progress.* Princeton, NJ: Princeton University Press, 1977.

Gross, John. *The Rise and Fall of the Man of Letters: Aspects of English Literary Life since 1800.* London: Weidenfeld and Nicolson, 1969.

Gunn, Ian and Clive Hart. *James Joyce's Dublin: A Topographical Guide to the Dublin of "Ulysses."* London: Thames and Hudson, 2004.

Harper, Margaret Mills. *The Aristocracy of Art in Joyce and Woolf.* Baton Rouge: Louisiana State University Press, 1990.

Hart, Clive and David Hayman, eds. *James Joyce's "Ulysses": Critical Essays.* Berkeley: University of California Press, 1974.

Hayman, David. *"Ulysses": The Mechanics of Meaning.* Rev. ed. Madison: University of Wisconsin Press, 1982.

Henke, Suzette. "Gerty MacDowell: Joyce's Sentimental Heroine." In *Women in Joyce.* Ed. Suzette Henke and Elaine Unkeless.Urbana: University of Illinois Press, 1982. 132–49.

Herr, Cheryl. *Joyce's Anatomy of Culture.* Urbana: University of Illinois Press, 1986.

Higham, Charles. *Ziegfeld.* Chicago: Regnery, 1972.

Highet, Gilbert. *The Classical Tradition: Greek and Roman Influences on Western Literature.* New York: Oxford University Press, 1949.

Hindley, Diana and Geoffrey. *Advertising in Victorian England, 1837–1901.* London: Wayland Publishers, 1972.

Holquist, Michael. *Dialogism: Bakhtin and His World.* London and New York: Routledge, 1990.

Horkheimer, Max and Theodor W. Adorno. *Dialectic of Enlightenment.* Trans. John Cumming. New York: Continuum, 1986.

Huyssen, Andreas. *After the Great Divide: Modernism, Mass Culture, Postmodernism.* Bloomington: Indiana University Press, 1986.

Irish Times. [Review of Sandow performance]. 7 May 1898, 7.

Iser, Wolfgang. "Indeterminacy and the Reader's Response." In *Aspects of Narrative: Selected Papers from the English Institute.* Ed. J. Hillis Miller. New York: Columbia University Press, 1971. 1–45.

Jackson, John Wyse and Bernard McGinley. *James Joyce's Dubliners: An Annotated Edition.* London: Sinclair-Stevenson, 1993.

Jackson, John Wyse and Peter Costello. *John Stanislaus Joyce.* New York: St. Martin's, 1997.

Jackson, Kate. "The *Tit-Bits* Phenomenon: George Newnes, New Journalism, and the Periodical Texts." *Victorian Periodicals Review* 30:3 (Fall 1997), 201–26.

———. "George Newnes and the 'Loyal Tit-Bitites': Editorial Identity and Textual Interactions in *Tit-Bits.*" In *Nineteenth-Century Media and the Construction of Identities.* Ed. Laurel Brake, Bill Bell, and David Finkelstein. New York: Palgrave, 2000. 11–26.

James Joyce Quarterly 30:4 (Summer 1993). Special issue on "Joyce and Advertisement." Eds. Jennifer Wicke and Garry Leonard.

Jameson, Fredric. *Fables of Aggression: Wyndham Lewis, the Modernist as Fascist*. Berkeley: University of California Press, 1979.

———. *The Political Unconscious: Narrative as a Socially Symbolic Act*. Ithaca, NY: Cornell University Press, 1981.

———. *Postmodernism, or, the Cultural Logic of Late Capitalism*. Durham: Duke University Press, 1991.

———. "*Ulysses* in History." In *James Joyce and Modern Literature*. Eds. W. J. McCormack and Alistair Stead. London: Routledge and Kegan Paul, 1982. 126–41.

———. *Late Marxism: Adorno or the Persistence of the Dialectic*. London: Verso, 1990.

Jay, Martin. *The Dialectical Imagination: A History of the Frankfurt School and the Institute of Social Research, 1923–1950*. Boston: Little, Brown, 1973.

Kasson, John F. *Houdini, Tarzan, and The Perfect Man: The White Male Body and the Challenge of Modernity in America*. New York: Hill and Wang, 2001.

Kelly, Dermot. *Narrative Strategies in Joyce's "Ulysses."* Ann Arbor: UMI Research Press, 1988.

Kenner, Hugh. "Beaufoy's Masterplaster." *James Joyce Quarterly* 24, 1 (Fall 1986), 11–18.

———. *Dublin's Joyce*. Bloomington: Indiana University Press, 1956.

———. *Ulysses*. Rev. ed. Baltimore, MD: Johns Hopkins University Press, 1987.

Kershner, Richard Brandon, Jr. *Joyce and Queneau as Novelists: A Comparative Study*. Dissertation, Stanford University, 1972.

Kershner, R. Brandon. "The Culture of Dedalus: Urban Circulation, Degeneration, and the Panopticon." In *A Portrait of the Artist as a Young Man*. By James Joyce. Ed. R. Brandon Kershner. 2nd ed. Boston: Bedford Books of St. Martin's Press, 2006. 357–77.

———. "Dialogical and Intertextual Joyce." In *Palgrave Advances in James Joyce Studies*. Ed. Jean-Michel Rabaté. Basingstoke, New York: Palgrave, 2001. 183–202.

Kershner, R. B. *Joyce, Bakhtin, and Popular Literature: Chronicles of Disorder*. Chapel Hill: University of North Carolina Press, 1989.

———, ed. *Joyce and Popular Culture*. Gainesville: University Press of Florida, 1996.

———, ed. *Cultural Studies of James Joyce*. Amsterdam and New York: Rodopi, 2003.

Kiberd, Declan. *Irish Classics*. London: Granta, 2000.

———. "Irish Literature and Irish History." In *The Oxford History of Ireland*. Ed. R. F. Foster. Oxford and New York: Oxford University Press, 1992. 230–81.

Knapp, James F. *Literary Modernism and the Transformation of Work.* Evanston: Northwestern University Press, 1988.

Lane, Frank W. "Sandow: The Strong Man." *The Saturday Book* 24 (1964), 140–147.

Latham, Sean. *"Am I a Snob?" Modernism and the Novel.* Ithaca, NY: Cornell University Press, 2003.

Lawrence, Karen. *The Odyssey of Style in "Ulysses."* Princeton: Princeton University Press, 1981.

Le Yaouanc, Colette. *L'Orient dans la poésie anglaise de l'époque romantique, 1798–1824.* Paris: Librairie Honoré Champion, 1975.

Leavis, F. R. *The Great Tradition.* New York: New York University Press, 1948.

Leavis, Q. D. *Fiction and the Reading Public* (1932). Reprint. London: Chatto and Windus, 1968.

Lee, Joseph. *The Modernisation of Irish Society, 1848–1918.* Dublin: Gill and Macmillan, 1972.

Lefebvre, Henri. *Everyday Life in the Modern World.* New York: Harper, 1971.

Lennam, Trevor. "The Happy Hunting Ground," In *A James Joyce Miscellany.* Ed. Marvin Magalaner. 3d series. Carbondale: Southern Illinois University Press, 1962. 158–74.

Lennon, Joseph. *Irish Orientalism: A Literary and Intellectual History.* Syracuse: Syracuse University Press, 2004.

Leonard, Garry. *Advertising and Commodity Culture in Joyce.* Gainesville: University Press of Florida, 1998.

———. "Advertising and Religion in Joyce's Fiction." In *Joyce and Popular Culture.* Ed. R. B. Kershner, Gainesville: University Press of Florida, 1996. 125–38.

Lesey, Michael. *Wisconsin Death Trip.* New York: Random House, 1973.

Lewis, Pericles. *Modernism, Nationalism and the Novel.* Cambridge: Cambridge University Press, 2000.

Lewis, Wyndham. *Time and Western Man.* New York: Harcourt, Brace & Company, 1928.

Litz, A. Walton. *The Art of James Joyce: Method and Design in "Ulysses" and "Finnegans Wake."* London: Oxford University Press, 1961.

Lloyd, David. *Anomalous States: Irish Writing and the Post-colonial Moment.* Durham, NC: Duke University Press, 1993.

Loss, Archie K. "Joyce's Use of Collage in 'Aeolus.'" *Journal of Modern Literature,* 9:2 (May 1982), 175–82.

Lyons, F. S. L. *Culture and Anarchy in Ireland, 1890–1939.* Oxford: Oxford University Press, 1979.

MacLochlainn, Alfred. 1984. Interview by author. Galway, Ireland. March 30,

Magalaner, Marvin. "James Joyce and Marie Corelli." In *Modern Irish Literature.* Eds.Raymond J. Porter and James D. Brophy. New York: Twayne, 1972. 185–93.

Mao, Douglas. *Solid Objects: Modernism and the Test of Production.* Princeton: Princeton University Press, 1998.

Mao, Douglas and Rebecca L. Walkowitz. "The New Modernist Studies." *PMLA* 123.3 (May 2008), 737–48.

Marchand, Leslie A. Ed. *The Selected Poetry of Lord Byron.* New York: Modern Library, 1951.

Marsh, Tess. "Is there More to *Photo-Bits* than Meets the Eye?" *James Joyce Quarterly* 30/31 (Summer/Fall 1993), 877–93.

Masters, Brian. *Now Barabbas Was a Rotter: The Extraordinary Life of Marie Corelli.* London: Hamish Hamilton, 1978.

Matz, Jesse. *Literary Impressionism and Modernist Aesthetics.* Cambridge: Cambridge University Press, 2001.

Mavor, Carol. *Pleasures Taken: Performances of Sexuality and Loss in Victorian Photographs.* Durham, NC: Duke University Press, 1995.

Mays, J. C. C. "Some Comments on the Dublin of *Ulysses*." In *"Ulysses": Cinquante Ans apres.* Ed. Louis Bonnerot. Paris: M. Didier, 1974. 83–98.

Meinwald, Dan. *Memento Mori: Death in Nineteenth-Century Photography.* Exhibition catalogue for the California Museum of Photography. Riverside, CA: University of California Press, 1990.

McCall, Patrick J. "Fionn MacCumhail and the Princess." In *Irish Literature.* Ed. Justin McCarthy et al. New York: Bigelow, Smith & Co., 1904. Vol. 5. 2117–22.

Minh-ha, Trinh T. *Woman, Native, Other.* Bloomington: Indiana University Press, 1989.

Moore, Thomas. *Lalla Rookh: An Oriental Romance.* Chicago: M. A. Donahue, 1822.

Mullin, Katherine. *James Joyce, Sexuality and Social Purity.* Cambridge: Cambridge University Press, 2003.

Narvaez, Peter, Ed. *The Good People: New Fairylore Essays.* New York: Garland, 1991.

Nevett, Terence, "Advertising." In *Victorian Periodicals and Victorian Society.* Ed. J. Don Vann and Rosemary T. VanArsdel. Toronto: University of Toronto Press, 1994. 219–34.

Nohain, Jean and F. Caradec. *Le Petomane.* Los Angeles: Sherbourne Press, 1967.

Nolan, Emer. *James Joyce and Nationalism.* London: Routledge, 1995.

North, Michael. *Reading 1922: A Return to the Scene of the Modern.* Oxford: Oxford University Press, 1999.

O'Brien, Joseph V. *"Dear, Dirty Dublin": A City in Distress, 1899–1916.* Berkeley: University of California Press, 1982.

O'Brien, William. *When We Were Boys,* 2nd ed. London: Longmans, Green, and Co., 1890.

O'Connor, Ulick. *Oliver St. John Gogarty.* London: Granada, 1981.

Oppenheim, Janet. *That Other World: Spiritualism and Psychical Research in England, 1850–1914.* Cambridge: Cambridge University Press, 1985.

Oram, Hugh. *The Newspaper Book: A History of Newspapers in Ireland, 1649–1983.* Dublin: MO Books, 1983.

Oram, Hugh. 1984. Interview by author. Dublin, Ireland. March 15.

Orel, Harold. *Popular Fiction in England, 1914–1918.* Lexington: University of Kentucky Press, 1992.

Owen, Alex. *The Darkened Room: Women, Power, and Spiritualism in Late Victorian England.* Philadelphia: University of Pennsylvania Press, 1990.

Owen, Stephen. *Mi-Lou: Poetry and the Labyrinth of Desire.* Cambridge, MA: Harvard University Press, 1989.

Phillips, Stephen, *Ulysses.* London & New York: John Lane, The Bodley Head, 1902.

Plock, Vike. *Joyce, Medicine, and Modernity.* Gainesville: University Press of Florida, 2010.

Pound, Reginald and Geoffrey Harmsworth. *Northcliffe.* New York: Praeger, 1959.

Power, Mary. "The Discovery of Ruby." *JJQ* 18:2 (1981), 115–21.

Praz, Mario. *The Romantic Agony.* Rev. ed. London: Oxford University Press, 1970.

Rainey, Lawrence. *Institutions of Modernism: Literary Elites and Public Cultures.* New Haven: Yale University Press, 1999.

Reed, David. *The Popular Magazine in Britain and the United States, 1880–1960.* Toronto: University of Toronto Press, 1997.

Reizbaum, Marilyn. *James Joyce's Judaic Other.* Stanford: Stanford University Press, 1999.

Renan, Ernest. *The Life of Jesus.* New York: A. L. Burt, 1863.

Reppke, James A. "Journalist Joyce: A Portrait." *James Joyce Quarterly* 45 (Spring-Summer 2008), 459–68.

Rice, Thomas J. "His Master's Voice and Joyce." In *Cultural Studies of James Joyce.* Ed. R. Brandon Kershner. Amsterdam and New York: Rodopi, 2003. 149–66.

Richards, Thomas. *The Commodity Culture of Victorian England: Advertising and Spectacle, 1851–1914.* Stanford: Stanford University Press, 1990.

Roche, Daniel. *The Culture of Clothing.* Cambridge: Cambridge University Press, 1994.

Rose, Danis and John O'Hanlon. *James Joyce: The Lost Notebook.* Edinburgh: Split Pea Press, 1989.

Said, Edward. *Orientalism.* New York: Random House, 1978.

Sampson, Anthony. *Anatomy of Britain Today.* New York: Harper and Row, 1965.

Sandow, Eugen. *Strength and How to Obtain It. With Anatomical Chart, Illustrating the Exercises for Physical Development.* London: Gale and Polden, 1897.

———. *Strength: And How to Obtain It.* 3rd ed. London: Gale and Polden, 1905.

———. *Strength and How to Obtain It.* Rev. ed. London: Gale and Polden, 1911.

Scholes, Robert, and Richard M. Kain. *The Workshop of Daedalus*. Evanston, IL: Northwestern University Press, 1965.

Schutte, William. *Joyce and Shakespeare*. New Haven: Yale University Press, 1957.

Seldes, Gilbert. *The Seven Lively Arts*. New York: A.S. Barnes and Company, 1962.

Senn, Fritz. "Remodeling Homer." In *Light Rays: James Joyce and Modernism*. Ed. Heyward Ehrlich. New York: New Horizon, 1984. 70–92.

Shaw, George Bernard. *Complete Plays with Prefaces*. 6 vols. New York: Dodd, Mead, 1962.

Shloss, Carol. "Choice Newsyreels: James Joyce and the *Irish Times*." *James Joyce Quarterly* 15:4 (Summer 1978), 325–38.

Smith, Anthony. *The Newspaper: An International History*. London: Thames and Hudson, 1979.

Smith, Paul. "The Cottingley Fairies: The End of a Legend." In *The Good People: New Fairylore Essays*. Ed. Peter Narvàez. New York: Garland, 1991.

Sontag, Susan. *On Photography*. New York: Delta, 1977.

Stanford, W. B. "The Mysticism that Pleased Him: A Note on the Primary Source of Joyce's *Ulysses*." *Envoy*, 5 (1951), 62–69.

———. *The Ulysses Theme*. New York: Oxford University Press, 1954.

Stevenson, John. *The Pelican Social History of Britain: British Society, 1914–45*. New York: Penguin Books, 1984.

Stories from the Thousand and One Nights. Trans. Edward William Lane. Rev. Stanley Lane-Poole. New York: P. F. Collier & Son, 1937.

Symington, Andrew James. *Thomas Moore the Poet: His Life and Works*. New York: Harper and Brothers, 1879.

Theall, Donald F. *Beyond the Word: Reconstructing Sense in the Joyce Era of Technology, Culture, and Communication*. Toronto: University of Toronto Press, 1995.

———. *James Joyce's Techno-Poetics*. Toronto: University of Toronto Press, 1997.

Thompson, J. Lee. *Politicians, the Press, and Propaganda: Lord Northcliffe and the Great War, 1914–1919*. Kent, OH: Kent State University Press, 1999.

Thom's Statistics. Dublin: n.p., 1901.

Thornton, Weldon. *Allusions in "Ulysses."* New York: Simon and Schuster, 1972.

Todorov, Tzvetan. *Mikhail Bakhtin: The Dialogical Principle*. Trans. Wlad Godzich. Minneapolis: University of Minnesota Press, 1984.

Trager, James. *The People's Chronology*. Rev. ed. New York: Henry Holt, 1994.

Trotter, David. *The English Novel in History, 1895–1920*. New York: Routledge, 1993.

Tymoczko, Maria. *The Irish "Ulysses."* Berkeley and Los Angeles: University of California Press, 1994.

Untermeyer, Louis, ed. *A Critical Anthology: Modern American Poetry / Modern British Poetry*, combined edition. New York: Harcourt, Brace and World, 1930.

Updike, John. "Facing Death (American Memorial Photography, 1845–1925)." *American Heritage* 43 (May–June 1992), 98–105.

Valente, Joseph. *Dracula's Crypt: Bram Stoker, Irishness, and the Question of Blood.* Urbana: University of Illinois Press, 2002.

Watt, Stephen. " 'Nothing for a Woman in That': James Lovebirch and Masochistic Fantasy in *Ulysses.*" In *Joyce and Popular Culture.* Ed. R. B. Kershner. Gainesville: University Press of Florida, 1996. 74–88.

Wells, H. G. *The Literary Criticism of H. G. Wells.* Ed. Patrick Parrinder and Robert Philmus. Sussex: Harvester, 1980.

———. *Tono-Bungay.* Boston: Houghton Mifflin, 1966.

Wicke, Jennifer. *Advertising Fictions: Literature, Advertisement, and Social Reading.* New York: Columbia University Press, 1988.

Willison, Ian, Warwick Gould, and Warren Chernaik, eds. *Modernist Writers and the Marketplace.* New York: St. Martin's Press, 1996.

Willoughby, David. *The Super-Athletes.* New York: A.S. Barnes & Co., 1970.

Winston, Gregory. "Dublin Dreadfuls: Race, Imperialism, and the Harmsworth Story-Papers in 'An Encounter.' " Unpublished ms.

Wittkower, Rudolf. "Marvels of the East: A Study in the History of Monsters." *Journal of the Warburg and Courtald Institute* 5 (1942), 159–97.

Wolff, Michael, John S. North, and Dorothy Deering. *The Waterloo Directory of Victorian Periodicals, 1824–1899.* Phase 1. Waterloo, Ont.: Wilfrid Laurier University Press, 1977.

Wollen, Peter. *Raiding the Icebox: Reflections on Twentieth-Century Culture.* Bloomington: Indiana University Press, 1986.

Woolley, Edward Mott. *The Art of Selling Goods.* Chicago: American Business Man, 1907.

Yeats, William Butler. *Memoirs.* Ed. Denis Donoghue. New York: Macmillan, 1992.

Index